CHRISTOPHER EVAN... ... ...
Tredegar, South Wales ... ...
Chemistry and a Postgraduate Certificate in
Education from the University of Wales. After
moving to London in 1975 he worked in the pharm-
aceuticals industry before becoming a full-time
writer in 1979. He was a recipient of an Arts Coun-
cil grant in 1980 and is the author of three novels:
Capella's Golden Eyes (1980), *The Insider* (1981)
and *In Limbo* (1985). He has written a guidebook,
Writing Science Fiction, for A&C Black, and is now
at work on a new novel.

ROBERT HOLDSTOCK was born in Kent in 1948.
He has degrees in Zoology and Medical Zoology
and worked in medical research before becoming a
freelance writer in 1975. His novels include *Eye
Among the Blind* (1976), *Earthwind* (1977),
Necromancer (1978) and *Where Time Winds Blow*
(1981). More recently he has published a volume of
short stories, *In the Valley of the Statues*. He has
written historical fantasies, as Christopher Carlsen
(*The Berserker*) and a series of occult novels as
Robert Faulcon (*Night Hunter*) as well as the
novelisation of *The Emerald Forest*. His latest
book, *Mythago Wood*, won the World Fantasy
Award in 1985. Its companion volume, *Lavondyss:
Towards the Unknown Region*, will be published in
autumn 1988.

OTHER EDENS
Edited by Christopher Evans and Robert Holdstock

'every tale is a potential award-winner'
British Fantasy Newsletter

'the whole collection is excellent value'
New Statesman

'here at last is a book for the non-believer and en-
thusiast alike' *Eastern Evening News*

'It is a winner' *Edinburgh Evening News*

'a fine showcase for British science fiction'
Paperback Inferno

'demonstrates the contemporary vitality of the science
fiction short story in Britain' *Tribune*

OTHER EDENS
II

EDITED BY
CHRISTOPHER EVANS
AND
ROBERT HOLDSTOCK

UNWIN
PAPERBACKS

LONDON SYDNEY WELLINGTON

First published in Great Britain by Unwin ® Paperbacks, an imprint of
Unwin Hyman Limited, in 1988.
Copyright in the individual stories belongs to the writers or their heirs or
executors.

All rights reserved. No part of this publication may be reproduced, stored
in a retrieval system, or transmitted in any form or by any means,
electronic, mechanical, photocopying, recording or otherwise, without
the prior permission of Unwin Hyman Limited.

UNWIN HYMAN LIMITED
15–17 Broadwick Street
London W1V 1FP

Allen & Unwin Australia Pty Ltd
8 Napier Street, North Sydney, NSW 2060, Australia

Allen & Unwin New Zealand Pty Ltd with the Port Nicholson Press
60 Cambridge Terrace, Wellington, New Zealand

British Library Cataloguing in Publication Data

Other Edens 2.
1. Science fiction short stories in
English, 1945– —Anthologies
I. Evans, C.D. (Christopher D.) *1951–*
II. Holdstock, Robert *1948–*
823′.0876′08 [FS]
ISBN 0–04–440154–X

Set in 10 on 11 point Times by Grove Graphics, Tring, Herts
and printed in Great Britain by Cox & Wyman Ltd, Reading

Contents

Introduction

Since the publication of the first *Other Edens*, the 'original science fiction and fantasy anthology' has had a new lease of life in Britain, with at least five other collections either planned or forthcoming from various publishers. This is good news indeed, and we hope that it's a trend which will continue. Certainly the climate seems right, and *Other Edens II* appears as a result of the excellent response from both writers and readers to volume one.

As before, our aim has been to assemble as varied a collection of stories as possible. Despite its title, *Other Edens* is not intended as a theme anthology; far from it: we place no restrictions at all on subject matter. If anything, this second collection is even more eclectic than the first, demonstrating the extraordinary variety of style and subject matter which the science fiction and fantasy field now encompasses. The stories range in locale from Ancient Greece to Mars and far beyond; they deal with classic themes such as time travel, parallel universes, outcast kings and even battles with dragons; they vary in mood from the droll to the surreal or the elegiac. Yet in every case there's a strong sense of an individual writer at work, interpreting even the most familiar of themes in a distinctive fashion. These are stories which, though often they arise *out* of a tradition, are not content to be *constrained* by it; and as a result they offer proof of that tradition's continuing vitality.

Once again, we're very happy to have contributions from some of the best-known names in the field as well as two new writers. We are open to stories from any source, and our one regret is that we were unable to include work by writers from Continental Europe; we received only two submissions. Nevertheless we have sixteen stories by writers working (however temporarily) outside of the USA and therefore offering a different perspective on a field which is more than ever dominated by the requirements of the American market. And in that difference lies their strength.

Our thanks to Jane Johnson of Unwin Hyman for her continued support and encouragement. Thanks also to everyone who wrote to us after the first volume appeared. We'd love to hear from you again.

Chris Evans and Rob Holdstock
London, May 1988

OTHER EDENS
II

GARRY KILWORTH

On the Watchtower at Plataea

There was the chilling possibility, despite Miriam's assurance that she would dissuade the government from physical confrontation, that I might receive the order to go out and kill my adversary in the temple. They might use the argument that our future existence depended on answers to be dredged from further back in the past. I wondered if I could do such a thing: and if so, how? Would I sneak from the watchtower in the night, like an assassin, and murder him in his bed? Or challenge him to single combat, like a true noble warrior is supposed to? The whole idea of such a confrontation made me feel ill, and I prayed that if it should come to such a pass they would send someone else to do the bloody job. I have no stomach for such things.

It was a shock to find that the expedition could go no further back than BC429: though for some of us, it was not an unwelcome one. Miriam was perhaps the only one amongst us who was annoyed that we couldn't get to Pericles. He had died earlier, in the part of the year we couldn't reach. So near – but we had hit a barrier, as solid as a rockface on the path of linear time, in the year that the Peloponnesian War was gaining momentum. It was the night that Sparta and its allies were to take positive action against the Athenians by attacking a little walled city-state called Plataea. Plataea, with its present garrison of four hundred local hoplites and some eighty seconded Athenians, was virtually the only mainland supporter of Athens in the war amongst the Greeks. It was a tiny city-state, even by ancient world standards − perhaps a mile in circumference − and it was heavily outnumbered by the besieging troops led by the Spartan king, Archidamus. It didn't stand a chance, but my God it put up resistance which rivalled the Alamo for stubbornness, and surpassed it for inventiveness.

Miriam suggested we set up the recording equipment in an old abandoned watchtower on a hill outside the city. From there we could see the main gates, and could record both the Spartan attempts at breaching the walls, and the defenders as they battled to keep the invaders at bay. The stonework of the watchtower was unstable, the timber rotting, and it was probably only used to shelter goats. We did not, therefore, expect to be interrupted while we settled in. In any case, while we were 'travelling' we appeared as insubstantial beings and were seldom confronted. The tower was ideal. It gave us the height we needed to command a good view, and had aged enough to be a respectable establishment for spectral forms.

There were three of us in the team. Miriam was the expedition's leader; John was responsible for the recording equipment; and I was the official communicator, in contact with base camp, 2017 AD. By 429, we were not at our harmonious best, having been away from home for a very long time: long enough for all our habits and individual ways to get on each other's nerves. I suppose we were all missing home to a certain extent, though why we should want to go back to a world where four-fifths of the population was on the streets, starving, and kept precariously at bay by the private military armies of privileged groups, was never raised. We ourselves, of course, belonged to one of those groups, but we were aware of the instability of the situation and the depressingly obvious fact that we could do nothing to influence it. The 'haves' were no longer in a position to help the 'have nots', even given the desire to do so. One of the reasons for coming on the expedition was to escape my guilt — and the constant wars between the groups. It was, as always, a mess.

'What do base say?' asked Miriam.

I could see the watch-fires on the nearby city walls through her ghostly form, as she moved restlessly around the walkway of the tower. John was doing something below.

'They believe the vortex must have an outer limit,' I said. 'It would appear that we've reached it.'

This didn't satisfy her, and I didn't expect it to. Miriam did not operate on beliefs. She liked people to *know*.

'But why here? Why now? What's so special about the year 429? It doesn't make any sense.'

'You expect it to make sense?'

'I had hoped . . . oh, I don't know. An answer which wasn't still a question I suppose. Doesn't it worry you? That suddenly we come up against a wall, without any apparent reason?'

I shrugged. 'Surely natural limitations are a good enough reason. Human endeavour has often come up against such things — the sound-barrier for example. They believed that was impassable at the time, but they got through it in the end. Maybe this is a comparable problem?'

'It's a bitch, I know that much,' she replied in a bitter tone. 'I really wanted Pericles — and the earlier battles. Marathon. Thermopylae. Damn it, there's so much we'll have to leave. Mycenae and Agamemnon. We could have confirmed all that. If we can't go back any further, Troy will remain covered in mist . . .'

Which was not altogether a bad thing as far as I was concerned. Already too many illusions had been wiped away. Why destroy all myth and legend, simply for the sake of facts? It's a pretty boring world, once the magic has been stripped off.

'Well, perhaps we shouldn't do it all at once,' I

3

suggested. 'I feel as if I'm drowning as it is . . . let someone else destroy Homer.'

She said, 'We're not *destroying* anything. We're merely recording . . . '

'The *truth*,' I said, unable to keep the sarcasm out of my tone.

She glared at me, a silvery frown marring her handsome features. We had clashed in the same way several times recently and I think she was getting tired of my outbursts.

'You have an attitude problem, Stan − don't make it my problem too.'

'I won't,' I said, turning away.

In the distance, I could hear the jingle of brass: the Spartan army tromping through the night, their torches clearly visible. These sounds and sights were the cause of some consternation and excitement amongst the Plataeans on the walls of the city. The enemy had arrived. Little figures ran to and fro, between the watch-fires. They had known for a few hours that Archidamus was coming: Theban traitors, spies and double-agents had been busy during the day, earning a crust. The warnings had come too late for flight however and it was now a case of defying the vastly superior force, or surrendering the city. Some of the defenders were relying on the fact that Plataea was sacred ground − it had been consecrated after a successful battle with the Persians earlier in the century − but Archidamus was not a man to take much notice of that. There were ways of appealing to the gods for a suspension of holy rights, if the need was there.

I wondered how the Spartans would react if they knew they were being recorded, visually. They were already pretty good at strutting around in grand macho style, cuffing slaves and flaunting their long hair. We had been told that historical recordings such as this would be studied for possible answers to the problems of our own time. I couldn't help but feel cynical about this idea, though I did not have the whole picture. The future, beyond my own time, had been investigated by another team and the result

4

was a secret known only to that expedition and our illustrious government, but I suspected it was a very bleak picture.

Besides Spartans, the invading army consisted of slave-auxiliaries, a few mercenaries, and volunteer forces from the cities allied with Sparta: Corinth, Megara, Elis, Thebes, many others. These cities looked to their big cousin to lead them against the upstart Athens, a city-state of little significance until the early part of the century, when it had thrashed a hugely superior force of Persians at the Battle of Marathon, and had since become too big for its sandals. If there was one thing the Ancient Greeks could not stand, it was someone thinking they were better than everyone else.

Except for Plataea, Athens stood virtually alone in mainland Greece, though its maritime empire encompassed almost all the Aegean islands and the coast of Asia Minor. One of the reasons why the war would last so long was because a stalemate was inevitable. Athens was a strongly-walled city, which included its harbour, and could not be penetrated by a land force. Its formidable bronze-toothed fleet of ramming triremes discouraged any idea of a naval blockade. On the other hand, Sparta had no ships to speak of, was an inland unwalled city, but positively encouraged an invasion of their territory since they relished battles and their hoplites were considered almost invincible in battle. Certainly no Spartan would leave a field alive unless victory had been assured. Direct confrontations with such warriors, cool and unafraid of death, were not courted at all keenly, even by brave Athenians.

So, a military might and a naval power, and rarely the twain met. Stalemate. Little Plataea was in fact nothing more than a whipping-boy on which Sparta could vent some of its frustration and spleen.

Miriam was looking through night viewers at the advancing hordes. She said, 'This may be the last historical battle we're able to record.'

I was glad of that. Expeditions like ours tend to start out

5

fortified by enthusiasms and good nature, only to end in disillusionment and bitter emotions, as any geographical explorer will tell you. Discoveries exact a high price from the finders, who have to pay for them with pieces of their souls.

There was a terrible scream from down below, sending lizards racing up my back. I stared at Miriam. A few moments later, John came up the makeshift ladder, looking disgusted.

'Goatboy,' he explained. 'Wandered in looking for a place to hide from the troops, I suppose, now that they've closed the city gates. He saw me and ran. That earth floor already stinks to high heaven with goat droppings. They must have been using it for decades.'

Miriam said, 'Pull up the ladder, John. We may as well settle for the night. Nothing's going to happen until morning.'

Below us, the weary Allies began to arrive and put up tents, out of range of any archers who might be on the walls of the city. Trumpets were sounded, informing the Plataeans that a bloody business was about to begin, as if they didn't know that already. They were pretty noisy in unloading their gear, clattering pots and clanking bits of armour; bawling to one another as new groups arrived, in the hearty fashion of the soldier before the killing starts. We required rest, though we did not sleep while we were travelling, any more than we needed to eat or drink.

'Noisy bastards,' I grumbled. 'I wish they'd shut up.'

John, saying his prayers as he always did at that time of night, looked up sharply from his kneeling position and frowned. He did not like interruptions during such a time, and I found myself apologising.

Here we were, making sure these squabbles amongst humankind reached a pitch of historical accuracy nobody needed. What the hell was it all about? And were our recordings doing even that useless job? I doubted it. Going back into history, you tend to get caught in the confusion of one small corner of an issue, just as if you lived in the times. One needs God's eyes to see the whole, and weigh the reasons.

It might be that God dwells beyond some far ripple of the time vortex. If you think of the vortex as an old-fashioned long-playing record and the groove as linear time, you will have some idea how travellers are able to skip through the ages, as a too-light arm of a record deck skates over a disc. It is a mental process, requiring no vehicle. Somewhere beyond those grooves, dwells the Almighty. Who wants to meet God and see *absolute truth* in all its blinding whiteness? Not me. Not me, my friend. *Eyes I dare not meet in dreams*, as the poet Eliot said.

By the next morning the Spartans had surrounded the Plataea and were intent on encircling it with a palisade of sharpened stakes, leaning inwards. Archidamus wanted to be sure that no one could escape from the city. He wanted to teach the inhabitants a lesson: that siding with those nasty imperialists and free-thinkers, the Athenians, was a dangerous thing to do.

It was true that Athens had created a confederacy, mostly consisting of island states, which she subsequently milked of funds, using the money to build the Parthenon, generally beautify the city, and increase the number of ships in her fleet. It was true that anyone who requested to leave the confederacy found the equivalent of several British gunboats in their harbour within a few days. But it was equally true that the Spartans, with their two kings (one to stay at home, while the other was at war), really could not give a damn about anyone but themselves. Athens was full of woolly-minded intellectuals who not only indulged in progressive thinking and innovations, but were carefree and undisciplined with it. Sparta had long since fossilised. They had put a stop to progress some time ago. In Sparta it was forbidden to write new songs, poetry or plays, or introduce anything into society with a flavour of change about it, let alone the avant-garde stuff allowed in Athens. Why, the northern city was positively licentious in its attitudes towards art and science. Nothing which would disturb the perfection of the life style Spartans had achieved at an earlier time, was permitted in Lacedaemonia. Asceticism, the nobility of war, plain food and state-raised children destined for the army: these were the ideals to be upheld. Give a Spartan a coarse-hair shirt, a plate of salty porridge, a lusty three-hundred-year-old song to sing, and send him out onto the battlefield, and he'll die thanking you. To the Athenians, who loved good food, new mathematics, eccentric old men asking interminable questions, incomprehensible philosophies, weird inventions, plays making fun of the gods, love, life and the pursuit of happiness — to these people the Spartans were homicidal lunatics.

I suppose it was little wonder that these two Hellenic city-states disliked each other so much.

While the thousands of figures, the keen ones still sweating in their armour, scurried about below us, busy with siege-engines, we got on with our regular tasks. John had set up a hologram at the entrance to the tower. It was supposed to represent Apollo and appeared instantly on any human approach, to warn away hoplites who would otherwise have used the tower as a toilet. The hologram uttered its threats in what was probably an appalling accent, but it was the best we could do with the devices to hand. It seemed to do its job, because by noon on the first day, gifts had been placed at a respectable distance from the entrance to the watchtower. They could see us, of course, drifting around the top of the tower, but I suppose we were gods too, witnessing the heroic struggles of mortals. I did my best to assume a Zeus-like posture. We had some 'thunder and lightning' for emergencies, but hadn't needed them up to that point.

The heat of the day made us generally testy and irritable, for although many of our bodily functions were suspended, we still had our senses. I found some shade under the parapet and proceeded to contact base. This time they had a little news for us, which was still very vague. Something – they were not sure quite what, but told us to watch for the unusual – something was preventing a further spread of the vortex.

Watch for something unusual? Only those bloody desk-riders back at base would say something like that, to travellers in an antique world, where the unusual was all around, in almost every facet of daily life. Personally, I hoped they didn't solve the problem. I was weary and homesick and a solution would mean continuing the journey. I didn't say that, of course.

I told Miriam what base had said, and she nodded.

'Thanks. We'll have to wait and see.'

Boredom, that's what time-travel is mostly about. Like war, it's five per cent feverish action, and ninety-five per cent sitting around with nothing to do. I settled down wearily for a game of chess with John.

'You're the Athenians and I'm the Spartans, so I get to have two kings,' he joked.

I thought John uncomplicated and open, and we seemed to get on well together, though he was a good deal younger than me. I was reticent, but he didn't seem to mind that. He had not lost the bubbling enthusiasm of youth, took religion seriously (both of which got on my nerves sometimes, when I was feeling bloody) and had a love for his fellows which was difficult to resist.

Miriam was of a similar disposition to my own. Sometimes to while away the hours, I imagined a romantic connection between us, which was actually as far-fetched as any fairy-tale romance. Although she is a fine-looking woman, with a strong will and good mind, I was not in the least attracted to her. Interested in her, but not attracted. One of those chemical negatives I suppose. I'm sure the feeling was mutual, if she thought about it at all. She had a husband back home, and two kids, not that she ever talked about them. I expect they were none of our damn business.

9

'Your move.'

John shifted his head, to interfere with my line of vision.

'Oh, yes – sorry. Daydreaming.'

'Occupational hazard,' he said, with more seriousness than was warranted, but I didn't have time to question his tone. At that moment a bird, a bee-eater I think, flew into the parapet with a *smack*. I picked the beautiful creature up, whereupon it pecked me, struggled from my grasp and groggily took to the air. It seemed to be all right.

John gave me a significant stare. It is one of his theories that the vortex interferes with the orientation of natural creatures (time-travellers being *unnatural* I expect) and he intended to write something of the sort when we returned to civilisation. He could be right, but if he believed that anyone would care about such things, he was in for a disappointment. It is one of *my* theories that, back at base camp, they don't even care about the orientation of humans, let alone bee-eaters.

Over the next few weeks we watched the activity below with a little more interest. It became a battle of wits, not swords, the main combatants being the engineering corps of both sides. The Spartan army laboured long and hard to build an earth ramp against the city wall, up which they intended to march and take the city, at the same time catapulting fireballs through the air and making futile attempts at scaling the walls with ladders. Before the ramp was completed the wily Plataeans had raised the height of the wall at that point, cannibalising their houses for stone blocks. It became a race. The taller grew the ramp, the higher went the wall. In the end, Archidamus put every available man on earth-carrying duty and by this means he managed to gain on the Plataeans, threatening to reach the top of the wall.

Undaunted, the defenders then tunnelled underneath their own wall and through the earth ramp, removing the loose soil until the ramp collapsed. On seeing his beautiful mound fall in on itself, Archidamus stamped around threatening death and destruction. He sacrificed a dozen goats to us, and to another shrine − a small temple about half a mile from our position − hoping we would intervene divinely on his behalf in subduing these irksome Plataeans. He came to us in full armour, wearing the classic Corinthian helmet, with its decorated, elongated cheek-pieces and transverse crest of horsehair, his brass-faced shield and muscled greaves, and a heavy bell cuirass. For a Spartan he was pretty flashy, but then he was a king. It was obvious that he was hot and testy, and I think it took all his reserve to remain polite to the gods who were giving his troops such a hard time. The goats' entrails stank like hell when thrown into the copper bowl of flames and we retreated below for a while, leaving a hologram of Athena to receive promises of temples to be erected, and pilgrimages to be undertaken, once victory was within Spartan grasp. On reflection it was not the most tactful thing to have done, since Athena was the goddess protector of Athens, but we didn't think about that at the time. In any case, what was irritating Archidamus was the fact the enemy would not come out and fight like men. Spartans do not make the best besieging troops in the world. They hate messing around with mud, sticks and stones, when they could be looking their best, charging across a windy plain with their long black hair streaming and their mouths uttering terrible war-cries, ready to stick or be stuck by some sharp instrument. There were lots of jokes about the Spartans, even amongst their own allies. The one about the shrew's brain in a lion's skin was a particular favourite.

After delivering his dubious gifts, Archidamus then went to the small temple, inside the palisade, and repeated the exercise. Miriam became very curious about this rival for our affections and managed to find a spot around the tower wall where she could see the building through her viewers. Finally she asked John to take some footage, though it was not possible to see directly into the obliquely-positioned temple and our line of sight was hampered by the points of some tall stakes on the palisade. We ran this through, afterwards, and managed to catch a glimpse of a figure between the marble columns. He had some kind of tri-legged device with him, the head of which seemed to incorporate revolving flaps of stiff material, that flashed like mirrors when it was operated. More significant than this, however, was the fact that the white-robed figure working this machine seemed to have semi-transparent flesh. Certainly he was treated with distant, wary reverence by the Hellenes, in the same way that we were ourselves. There was very good reason to suppose that we and this elusive person, and possibly any companions hidden by the temple walls, had a great deal in common.

'Look at those beggars — you've got to hand it to them,' said John, with admiration in his voice. He was of course talking about the Plataeans. Archidamus's engineers had stopped the Plataeans' little game of removing earth from under the ramp by packing baskets with clay and placing them as foundation blocks for the ramp. These could not be drawn away like loose earth. The defenders met this device by digging a subterranean mine to beyond the ramp and allowing the whole effort to collapse again. By this time the earth was having to be carried from some considerable distance by the besiegers and they were becoming dispirited and thoroughly disgruntled by the whole affair. Deserters began to drift by our watchtower at night, and one or two minor kings packed their tents and took their citizen-soldiers home. Archidamus executed some malefactors, possibly to create an interesting diversion to the gruelling manual labour, but was unable to stem the increasing tide of dissatisfaction amongst his troops. He had sent for some Scythian archers of his own, but the Plataeans erected animal-hide screens on top of the walls to protect themselves, and the bowmen were less than effective. Added to this there was the smell of sickness in the air, which was part of the sordid business of a war in stalemate.

Some time after calling base regarding the possible presence of another group of travellers, we were asked to obtain further information. Miriam had already spent a great deal of time studying the mysterious occupants of the small temple through the viewer, but there were too many obstacles in the way to get anything concrete.

'We'll have to go over there,' she said, 'and get a closer look.'

John and I glanced at one another. Although the watchtower was far from secure against aggressive action, it provided protection for us in that it had become a sacred building to the Greeks and was unlikely to be violated. It ensured that we remained distant, aloof figures which could be avoided simply by giving the crumbling structure a wide berth. Once we started wandering amongst them, like ordinary mortals, we were in danger of becoming too familiar. It was not beyond the realms of possibility that some brave hoplite might decide to challenge the 'gods': after all, Odysseus had got away with it. It was a risky business. Of course, we could protect ourselves with our own weapons, but never having had to resort to such drastic action, we were unsure of the consequences.

'What do you suggest?' asked John.

Miriam said, 'I'll take the portable and go over there for some close-ups – Stan, you come with me.'

Not *too* close, I thought, but nodded in assent. I must admit, the anticipation of some excitement gave me a charge, despite my apprehension.

We set off just as the Hellenic dawn was coming up. Miriam carried the hand-recorder, while I self-consciously cradled a weapon in my arms. I knew how to use It, but it was more a question of whether It knew how to use me. I have never had to hurt anyone in my life – physically, that is. We walked between tents and lean-to shacks that had been razed by the invaders, without hindrance, though one or two wide-eyed early risers moved quickly out of our way. When we got to the gate in the palisade of stakes we had a problem. It was closed.

13

'What do we do?' I said. 'We can't walk through the damn thing. And gods don't fiddle with gates, wondering how they open.'

Before Miriam could answer, one of the sentries rushed forward and pulled at a leather thong. The gate swung open. He had not, of course, understood the language of the gods, but our intentions were obvious and the mere fact that I had voiced some strange words must have spurred him to action.

We made our way towards the temple. I prayed that the archers on the walls of Plataea would be too overawed by the sight of a pair of semi-transparent beings to fire any arrows.

We stood off about a hundred yards from the temple, where we had a clear view into the interior, and Miriam began recording. Half-hidden in the heavy shadows thrown by the columns we could see a translucent form operating the instrument with the metallic flaps, which was possibly some sort of heliogravic recording device, though it looked like something knocked-up in a Swiss toymaker's workshop for an Arabian prince. The stand was fashioned of polished wood covered in hieroglyphics and there were lead weights on plumblines which balanced wooden arms connected to cogged wheels. Behind the operator, hanging from the pillars, were two elongated scrolls of painted parchment. one with a picture of a dog's body with a monkey's head, the other depicting some sort of wading bird.

As we stood, both he and us, recording each other – a situation that struck me as rather ironic – another wraith-like figure appeared, wearing a long, flowing robe and decorated headcloth. He whispered to his companion, then went back into a side-room. I was sure that the directional mike would capture that whisper which, when amplified, would reveal their language.

Miriam gestured to me without speaking and we stopped recording, making our way back.

The gate had been left open for us and we passed

through without any problems, but on the other side of the palisade it was a different matter. Word had got around that the gods were abroad and a huge crowd had gathered, though there was a wide path through the middle of it leading to the tower. I could see John on the ramparts of the watchtower with a weapon in his hands.

'Okay,' said Miriam, 'let's go, Stan. Don't look back . . .'

I had no intention of doing anything of the sort. All I wanted to do was reach the tower, safely.

As we walked down the avenue a murmuring broke out amongst the troops, which grew in volume to uncoordinated chants. I hadn't any doubt we were being petitioned for various miracles, both collective and individual. Two-thirds of the way along there was a horrible incident. A young man broke from the crowd and threw himself at my feet, attempting to clutch my ankle. Before he could lay a hand on me, he was pinned to the mud by several spears, thrown by his comrades. I wanted to be sick on the spot as I watched him squirming in the dirt like some wounded porcupine. We made the tower without any further problems and shortly afterwards the crowd broke up as Spartan officers moved amongst them with whips. The young man's body was removed, and as he was carried away I wondered what had made him so desperate as to brave touching a god. Maybe his mother or father was terminally ill? Or a close friend had been killed whom he wished us to raise from the dead? Or perhaps he was just a helot, a slave, who thought we could free him from the oppression of his Spartan masters with a wave of our hands? Poor bastard.

Later, I went to Miriam and asked her about our friends in the temple. We had already mentioned the word 'Egyptian' to each other, though all we had as evidence for that were the hieroglyphics and the pictures. A group of future Ancient Egyptian revivalists? Just because they wore the costume and carried the artefacts didn't make them residents from the banks of the Nile. Though there

15

didn't seem any logical reason for a masquerade, cults are seldom founded on reason, or by rational thinkers.

'The bird picture was an ibis,' said Miriam, 'and the dog-monkey . . . well, the Ancient Egyptian god Zehuti was represented by both those symbolic characters.'

'Zehuti?' I knew a little of the culture in question, but this was a new one to me.

'Sorry, you probably know him as Thoth − Zehuti is his older name. The Greeks identified him with Hermes, which makes sense. Hermes the messenger − a *traveller*?'

'Anything else?'

'Yes − Thoth was also the patron of science and inventions, the spokesman of the gods and their keeper of the records. Thoth invented all the arts and sciences, including surveying, geometry, astronomy, soothsaying, magic . . . do I need to go on?'

'No. I get the picture. If you wanted a god of time-travel, Thoth fits the bill quite nicely. So what do we do now?'

She gave me a grim smile.

'Wait. What else? Once you've transmitted the recording back to base, we wait until they come up with definites.'

So we did what we were best, and worst, at: waiting.

One evening the three of us were sitting, more or less in a rough circle, engaged in frivolous tasks. I was actually doing nothing. The stars were out, above us, and I could hear the snuffling of livestock and the clank of pots from down below. The area around Plataea was becoming as unsavoury as the no-man's land of World War Two, with cess-pits filling the air with an appalling stink and churned mud giving the landscape an ugly, open-wound appearance. We had been discussing our situation. Something was preventing the outer ring of our vortex from going any further, and base believed that what was stopping it was another vortex, coming from the other direction, the distant past. The two whirlpools were touching each other, and neither could proceed before the other retreated. Our friends were, indeed, early Egyptians. It had taken a while for this idea to sink in, but when I thought deeply about it, it was not at all far-fetched.

On a simple level, time-travel involved a psychological state induced by the use of darkness and light, resulting in the fusion of infinites, of space and time. The dark and light became unified into a substance which formed a shape. That shape was common enough in the night sky: a spiral on a flat plane, moving outwards from the centre of the group, some of whom remained behind to form an anchor point for the vortex. The base-camp group. The room in which we had begun the vigil was no longer a room, but something else: a superphysical universe that possibly exists in all minds at some level of perception. There was no technological reason why an earlier civilization could not have made the same mental discovery. On the other hand, people of our rank were still not privy to the source of the discovery, and it could well be that the knowledge had *come* from the past. Egyptian documents, perhaps, only recently decoded? I remembered something about mirrors being used to flood the dark interior passages of the pyramids with light from the sun.

A horrible thought occurred to me.
'We're not going to stay here, until they go back?'
Miriam shrugged.
'I don't know. I'm awaiting instructions from base.'
'Now look, we're the ones that are here. Not them.'
'You know how it is, as well as I do, Stan.'
I stared at her.
'I know how it is,' I said, bitterly.
Her phantom features produced a faint smile.
I lay awake that night, thinking about the stalemate I had got myself into. Egyptians? If they had had time-travel for so long, why hadn't they visited future centuries? But then, of course, they probably had, and we had run screaming from them, just as the goatboy had fled from us. They probably had a similar policy to ourselves: no

17

interference, just record and return. So, on their ump-teenth journey into the future, they had come to a halt, suddenly, and had no doubt come to the same conclusion as we had: someone was blocking the path.

It wasn't difficult, either, to see how such a discovery might be lost to future civilisations. Hadn't certain surgical techniques been lost too? Time-travel would undoubtedly have been in the hands of an elite: probably a priesthood. Some pharaoh, his brain addled as the result of a long lineage of incestuous relationships, had destroyed the brotherhood in a fit of pique; or the priests had been put to death by invading barbarians, their secret locked in stone vaults.

On the current front, the Plataeans were still one jump ahead of the Spartans. They had abandoned their mining operations and instead had built another crescent-shaped wall inside their own, so that when the ramp was finally completed, the Spartans were faced with a second, higher obstacle. Peltasts tried lobbing spears over the higher wall, only to find the distance was too great. Archidamus had his men fill the gap between the two walls with faggots and set light to it, but a chance storm doused this attempt to burn down the city. We got a few indignant looks from the Spartans after that. As gods, we were responsible for the weather. The war-trumpets of the invaders filled the air with bleating notes which we felt sure were a criticism of us and our seeming partiality towards the defenders.

Finally, battering rams were employed, over the gap be-tween the walls, but the Plataeans had a device — a huge beam on chains — which they dropped onto the ram-headed war-machines and snapped off the ends.

Archidamus gave up. He ordered yet another wall to be built, outside the palisade of stakes, and left part of his army to guard it. Winter was beginning to set in and the king had had enough of the inglorious mudbath in which he had been wallowing. He went home, to his family in the south.

The majority of the Egyptians, too, withdrew at this point. One of them remained behind.

We received our orders from base.

'One of us must stay,' said Miriam, 'until a relief can be sent. If we all go back, the vortex will recede with us and the Egyptians will move forward, gain on us.'

'A Mexican stand-off,' I said, disgustedly.

'Right. We can't allow them the opportunity to invade the territory we already hold . . .'

'Shit,' I said, ignoring a black look from John, 'now we've got a cold war on our hands. Even *time* isn't safe from ownership. First it was things, then it was countries . . . now it's time itself. Why don't we build a bloody great wall across this year, like Archidamus, and send an army of guards to defend it?'

Miriam said, 'Sarcasm won't help at this stage, Stan.'

'No, I don't suppose it will, but it makes me feel good. So what happens now? We draw straws?'

'I suggest we do it democratically.' She produced three shards of pottery that she had gathered from the ground below, and distributed one to each of us.

'We each write the name of the person we think most competent to remain behind,' she explained, 'and then toss them in the middle.'

'Most competent − I like the diplomatic language,' I muttered. John, I knew, would put down his own name. He was one of those selfless types, who volunteered for everything. His minor household gods were Duty and Honour. He would actually *want* to stay.

I picked up my piece of pot. It was an unglazed shard depicting two wrestlers locked in an eternal, motionless struggle, each seemingly of equal strength and skill, and each determined not to give ground. I turned it over and wrote JOHN in clear letters, before placing it, picture-side up, in the middle of the ring.

Two other pieces clattered against mine. Miriam sorted through them, turning them over.

My name was on two of them.

I turned to John.

'Thanks,' I said.

19

'It had to be somebody. You're the best man for the job.'

'Bullshit,' I said. I turned to Miriam. 'What if I refuse to stay? I'll resign, terminate my contract.'

Miriam shook her head. 'You won't do that. You'd never get another trip and while you get restless in the field, you get even worse at home. I know your type, Stan. Once you've been back a couple of weeks you'll be yelling to go again.'

She was right, damn her. While I got bored in the field, I was twice as bad back home.

'I'm not a type,' I said, and got up to go below. Shortly afterwards, Miriam followed me.

'I'm sorry, Stan.' She touched my arm. 'You see it for what it is — another political attempt at putting up fences by possessive, parochial old farts, Unless I go back and convince them otherwise, they'll be sending death squads down the line to wipe out the Egyptians. You do understand?'

'So it had to be me.'

'John's too young to leave here alone. I'll get them to replace you as soon as I can — until then . . .'

She held out her slim hand and I placed my own slowly and gently into her grip. The touch of her skin was like warm silk.

'Goodbye,' I said.

She went up the ladder and John came down next.

I said coldly, 'What is this? Visiting day?'

'I came to say goodbye,' he said, stiffly.

I stared hard at him, hoping I was making it difficult, hoping the bastard was uncomfortable and squirming.

'Why me, John? You had a reason.'

He suddenly looked very prim, his spectral features assuming a sharp quality.

'I thought about volunteering myself, but that would have meant you two going back alone — together, that is . . .' He became flustered. 'She's a married woman, Stan. She'll go back to her husband and forget you.'

20

I rocked on my heels.

'*What?* What the hell are you talking about?'

'Miriam. I've seen the way you two look at each other.'

I stared at him, finding it difficult to believe he could be so stupid.

'You're a fool, John. The worst kind of fool. It's people like you, with twisted minds, that start things like that war out there. Go on — get out of my sight.'

He started to climb the ladder, then he looked down and gave me a Parthian shot. 'You put *my* name on your shard. Why should I feel guilty about putting yours?'

And he was right, but that didn't stop me from wanting to jerk the ladder from under him and breaking his bloody neck.

They were all gone, within the hour, leaving me to haunt the Greeks all on my own, a solitary ghost moving restlessly around the parapet of the tower. I saw my Egyptian counterpart once, in the small hours, as a shimmering figure came out into the open to stare at my prison. I thought for a moment he or she was going to wave, but nothing so interesting happened, and I was left to think about my predicament once more. I knew how slowly things moved back home. They had all the time in the world. I wondered whether Egyptians could learn to play chess. It was a pity Diogenes wasn't yet alive, or I might have been tempted to wander down to Corinth. He would certainly have enjoyed a game, providing I stayed out of his sun. Me and Diogenes, sitting on top of his barrel, playing chess a thousand years before the game was invented — that would have been something. Plato was a new-born babe in arms. Socrates was around, in his early forties, but who would want to play with that cunning man? Once he got the hang of it, you'd never win a game.

Flurries of snow began to drift in, over the mountains. The little Plataeans were in for a hard winter. I knew the result of the siege of course. Three hundred Plataeans and seconded Athenians would make a break for it in a year's time, killing the sentries left by Archidamus on the outer wall and getting away in the dark. All of them would make it to Athens, fooling their pursuers into following a false trail, their inventive minds never flagging when it came to survival. Those Plataeans whose hearts failed them when it came to risking the escape, almost two hundred, would be put to death by the irate Spartans. The city itself would be razed. Perhaps the Spartans would learn something from the incident, but I doubted it. There was certainly a lot of patience around, in the ancient world.

Patience. I wondered how much patience those people from the land of the pharaohs had, because it occurred to me that the natural movement of time was on their side. Provided we did nothing but maintain the status quo, standing nose to nose on the edges of our own vortices, they would gain, ever so gradually. Hour by hour, day by day, we were moving back to that place I call home.

We might replace our frontier guards, by one or by thousands, but the plain fact of the matter is we will eventually be pushed back to where we belong. Why, they've already gained several months as it is . . . only another twenty-five centuries and I'll be back in my own back yard.

Then, again, I might receive that terrible message I have been dreading, which would turn me from being the Athenian I believe I am into a Spartan. Which would have me laying down my scroll and taking up the spear and shield. A ghost-warrior from the future, running forth to meet a god-soldier from the past. I can only hope that the possible historical havoc such action might cause will govern any decision made back home. I can't help thinking, however, that the wish for sense to prevail must have been on the lips of a million million such as I, who killed or died on fields, in trenches, in deserts and jungles, on seas and in the air.

The odds are stacked against me.

GRAHAM CHARNOCK

She Shall Have Music

I first met Liane at the birthday party the Crosbys arranged for their eldest boy. The occasion was Jerry Crosby's twenty-first birthday and his parents − third generation merchant bankers − staged a suitably stylish affair. There was a buffet on the veranda, with caterers moving amongst the crowd, expertly balancing silver trays of segregated glasses, whites and reds, sherries and juices. Beyond the veranda lay the formal lawn, with its bandstand and the incumbent jazz band. They were a smartly-dressed and dicky-bowed crew, but they all seemed somehow strangely 'dusty', with an indefinable air of being time-worn, which was at least authentic to the music they were playing: phrases cribbed from the original shellac but rapidly wearing down through repetition and attrition. Needles in dead tracks. Even in close proximity the music seemed *thin*; and it cannot wholly have been a quality of the midsummer evening air.

I was literally a neighbour residing directly beyond the Crosbys' secluding box hedges, and they had invited me on that basis. I had visited them only once before, and that had been a brief courtesy call in the spirit of neighbourliness when I had first moved in. I remember thinking, on that occasion as on this, that once within the household I was efficiently kept at a distance by the conventions of politeness, so expertly wielded by my hosts. I remember the feeling of being tolerated but not accepted.

Artists of any description who are financially successful are usually considered, I find, by their more spectacularly successful artisan peers, to be no more than the benefactors of some obscure lottery, and thus ill-deserving of their fortune. Their achievements are accepted with superlative grace, but viewed as somehow alien. There I was, an outsider, maybe, but only in that I lacked that underlying backbone of basic cupidity that distinguishes the mainstream of *riche*.

There I was . . .

Notice how elliptically I approach the beginning; in life too, as well as in this specific practice of my art, *beginning* things has always been a problem. How else could I have reached, in my box-hedged haven of security, next door to the Crosbys, a comfortable middle-age without the bolster of one really firm, lasting relationship or true friendship. I have never felt sufficiently *in control*, I think, to approach *beginnings* with confidence. There has always been the fear that any endeavour or relationship, once embarked upon, would run away out of control. A recurring dream of mine, even before the accident that is so central to this story, was of trying to drive a car from an 'out of body' state; in this dream I would always be several hundred yards in arrears of the vehicle's headlong rush, always unable to prevent the invariably dire outcome of a collision. Then, one chill November evening, of painfully recent memory, the dream collided with reality. It was the result of wheels failing to grip on an icy road, a graphic demonstration of the consequences of loss of control. Although the accident was not my fault, I felt this irony keenly, together with an irrational but very real sense of guilt.

And what followed?

Why, the remorseless *control* of the admirable Dr Questillion and his crew of surgeons and nurses, all assisting in my recovery. The physical damage largely healed (except in one significant detail), but the blow to my self-esteem plunged me into a depression that was still a

24

daily battle for me even some nine months later at Jerry Crosby's coming-of-age party.

We first met, Liane and I (the start now, the quick intake of breath and into the gulf we step), in the Crosbys' garden on that very evening.

But my background immediately slaps me in the face again. For me, historically, the word 'garden' describes a modest suburban plot. For the Crosbys the term 'garden' will simply not suffice. Theirs was an 'estate', no less; here were many gardens in one: a lawn, smooth enough for croquet on a summer's evening; an ornamental garden, as symmetrical as a Rorschach test, with paved paths converging on an Italianate fountain; a water-garden, hidden away, idyllic, with rustic benches at every turn; an arboretum beside a classical lake (in such a lake you could imagine consumptive poets dying). And a herb garden, hedged with hibiscus, hatched with neatly-tailored plots of sage, rosemary and purple valerian, the utilitarian culinary specimens side by side with the more arcane medicinal varieties.

And, of course, rue.

Rue. Here it comes, lurching up from the cellar of memory, rattling its chains, the veritable ghost at this feast, the memory I thought safely interred along with the pitter-patter, the subtle drumming of my pulse.

For it was beside the *rue* (bitter prophetic herb) that Liane and I first met.

I had gone down to the herb garden that night, quite frankly, to be alone; a sense of detachment was one of the few clinical symptoms of my depression. That night I felt its spectral fingers sinking into my flesh. I didn't feel like drinking, and that was usually the only thing which could throw off this particular phantom.

Why did I go to the herb garden?

It was the anosmia, of course.

The accident of which I have spoken, that crumpling of my car against the abutment of a motorway bridge, had crumpled the tender folds of my brain as well, leaving

25

lesions which had rendered my sense of smell impotent. Questillion, the specialist who had taken me under his wing, had told me that the destruction was irreversible, there was no hope of regeneration. It was a prognosis I must admit I didn't care for, and my refusal to accept it had coloured the last few weeks before my final discharge from Questillion's care with an element of sullen anger and frustration. Questillion had maintained that this was surely the mildest of disabilities and one to be borne with good grace; I was stubborn in my disagreement. Maybe my stubbornness – which I confess was surely uneducated and irrational – *was* merely a ritual locking of horns, a confrontation between two accredited specialists in their respective fields, both sporting fully- and finely-honed egos. It may have been a spasmodic and largely autonomous attempt by my crippled self-esteem to re-assert itself, but it was truly felt, and its outward manifestation was a conviction that, as with any muscular injury or disability, exercise and stimulation could only be beneficial. As soon as I was discharged, therefore, I embarked upon my own programme of what can only be called olfactory 'physiotherapy'. The lengths to which I went are comical in retrospect, as comical indeed as the intrinsic notion itself. I haunted wharves where spices were unloaded and fish gutted; I lingered on refuse sites where gulls picked over rotting garbage; my recreational tours were not of stately homes but of sewage farms, the very tenements of filth and excrement; my kitchen was redolent of garlic and ripe Stilton. I was convinced that one day, subject to this sensory onslaught, the synapses would spark once more and make me whole.

And so it was natural, I suppose, that I should make my way down to the Crosbys' herb garden that evening, in solitary pursuit of aromatic healing.

I was not immediately aware of her presence; how should I be, on my knees there, supplicant before the rue, fixedly inhaling and exhaling, a man seemingly bent on hyper-ventilation? Her polite cough, however, as she approached, interrupted my endeavours.

26

My first impression was that I had encountered a ghost.

It was partly the shock of the sudden discovery, and partly the peculiar perspective I had of her. The dying light against which she stood delineated her body quite clearly through the thin white cotton dress she wore; she was a dark core of almost anorexic insubstantiality. Her face, long and thin, with high cheekbones, seemed starved too and was also in shadow, with only highlights glinting on her eyes and lips.

Then several things happened, whether consecutively or simultaneously I don't know. My feeling is that they were sequential and that the sequence may be significant, but I am at sea here, and my memory swamped by the sensations themselves. I can only present them as distinct and separate experiences.

Surprised, I gasped, and inhaled a flood of air.

My nose was full of the bitterness of rue. As stinging and as transient as an insect bite, as potent as wine to an abstainer, it lasted but a second and then was gone.

I felt a flood of almost overwhelming erotic desire that took as its object her supple, clearly revealed outline.

I heard the sound of a clarinet playing a familiar phrase with an expression and feeling that could have come from Benny Goodman himself, except that there was a hint of tremulous hesitancy to it. It was not as direct and assured as Goodman. It was as if a novice was searching out the melody from memory.

The other sensations were transitory, only the haunting sound of the clarinet remained as I clambered to my feet in self-conscious confusion. But why, and wherefore, a *solo* clarinet? Where the jaunty swing of the other band-members, weaving their counterpoint, where the rhythmic pulse? I immediately framed a mental scenario which featured members of the jazz-band (from where else could this fragmentary melody have come?) taking a boozy break half-way through the set, retiring to their own smoky, closed company, that musicianly clique where sly asides and secret lusts predominate. (They were outsiders

27

like me; I fancied I had some insight into their psyches, as a member of the same caste.) And up on the stand, perhaps, an outsider amongst outsiders, a musical caretaker, rapt in yet another solitary pursuit: getting to grips with Goodman.

When she spoke, this vision, it was so softly I could barely discern her words above the plaintive melody.

'Are you all right?' she said. 'I mean, are you ill?'

'I'm fine,' I said. 'Really, I am. I'm sorry if I startled you.'

She laughed. 'You did rather. I thought you might be having a heart-attack. I'd glad you're not. I don't think I'd be terribly good at coping with anything like that.'

'Come now,' I said. 'I'm sure you're a very capable woman.'

It was a throwaway remark, small talk, but it seemed to fluster her.

'No,' she said. 'No, that's not true. All my friends at school were always finding sick animals to care for — birds with broken wings, shell-shocked squirrels, bruised badgers, traumatized tabbies, that sort of thing. They used to make me cringe — the animals, that is. The casualties. It wasn't just that they were damaged. The horrible thing was that they might end up *dependent* on you. I'm too self-centred to play the ministering angel, I suppose. All that Florence Nightingale stuff has always left me cold.'

Why, she's only *young*, I found myself thinking, with surprise. This woman who had had such a strong erotic impact on me only seconds before seemed barely an adult.

Now she was studying me with a frank directness.

'You're Paul Grover,' she said, 'the writer who lives next door. You had that terrible accident. I read all about it. My name's Liane Greenwood. I'm a friend of Jerry Crosby. You could say I'm an old flame.' She laughed. 'A very *old* flame, practically *extinguished*.'

There was a sudden venom in her tone, a transitory but revealing anger. I had been thinking of her as a reed: thin, frail and tremulous; but I was reminded that reeds can whip and flail in the wind.

'I only came here tonight out of sentiment,' she continued, 'and that seems to have been misplaced; have you *seen* what he's got in tow now? Some creature called Zela, if you can believe that. She has a lovely body — she's a defector from an Eastern Bloc dance troupe on a cultural exchange — but she's got a brain like overcooked bortsch. Talk about a peasant mentality.'

'He hardly strikes me as very bright himself,' I said.

She looked at me, her face set in serious concentration.

'He thinks *you're* weird,' she said.

'But he hardly knows me . . .' I started to protest. Then I realised how neatly I'd been set up, how my own touch of jealous venom (what else?) had been turned around. She could have capitalised on my discomfort but she didn't. She laughed and stuck her tongue out at me, and suddenly we were co-conspirators. It was a gesture which I am sure was quite knowingly ambivalent, combining, as it did, elements of the ingenuous and the erotic. We became, in a sense, joined, at that moment.

'Let's walk back to the house,' she said, slipping her arm naturally through mine. 'And you can tell me what it's like being a famous writer living next to a famous financier.'

Beginnings. *Control.* She took control upon our first meeting, so expertly (perhaps because I surrendered it so abjectly) that I couldn't help thinking, as I walked beside her, as the sound of the distant clarinet seemed to reach a peak of emotional intensity with glissando tumbling after glissando, that her simple white shift was a nurse's starched white uniform, and I was back in the hands of Questillion.

'And when you returned to the house . . . ?' prompted Questillion. We were in his consulting room. So much fine Italian leather made me sniff the air, hopefully, but, alas, impotently.

'The jazz-band had gone. The stand was empty.'

'And still you heard the music, or imagined you did?'

'It was all around me. I couldn't escape it.'

'You didn't want to escape it,' said Questillion. He tilted his chair back and folded relaxed hands across his chest. His eyes, his dead eyes, tracked fractured frames of light from the fluorescent tubes glowing in the ceiling. 'You didn't want to escape from *her*. Just the opposite.'

Did I tell you that Questillion is blind? Or nearly so. His eyes are clouded by cataracts. In need of a guide himself in the physical domain, he remains a dependable porter in the realm of his own discipline, his particular branch of neuro-surgery, smoothing the passage for those of his acolytes less adept in its practice.

In consultation he is still aggressive and openly pugnacious. Blindness has come upon him late in life, and there is none of the slackness about his features that stigmatises the congenitally blind. He has the complete acquired arsenal of facial expressions all we sighted souls share — the day-to-day repertoire of smiles, frowns, grimaces, scowls — and he uses it to good effect. You could hardly believe it was merely shadow-play. Now those milky eyes regarded me with a disconcerting directness.

'This woman . . .'

'Liane. Her name is Liane.'

'This woman.' It was like a foot stamping out my interjection as if it were a troublesome insect. 'You desired her?'

'Isn't that obvious, from what I've told you?'

'*Nothing* is obvious. Not to me. So . . . you desired her?'

'Of course.'

'But you didn't dare admit this to yourself. Everything you have told me so far points to this. Every way you have framed the details of your first meeting. She struck you as *young*, remember? Perhaps you thought she was *too* young to be touched by this notion of desire that was forming in your mind? The corollary is that *you* felt old, too old to be entertaining such a notion. Old-fashioned guilt, you see. It was the first of all sorts of imaginary obstacles you put in your own way. You are paranoid about *lack of control*, but that is a deceit, like all your other petty deceits. All you are saying to me, all I am hearing, is that you desired this woman spontaneously and explosively. I have to tell you that is not an uncommon reaction amongst men.'

'Questillion, are you a psychiatrist or a specialist in nervous disorders?'

'I am a doctor. All doctors have a common approach to diagnosis, which is what I am involved with here. We try to find out what is usual and what is unusual in the way our patients present, in the stories they tell us. You say you felt an intense, spontaneous desire upon first meeting this woman.'

'Yes.'

'Is she beautiful?'

'Very.'

'Then that is only natural, surely? Most men would feel nothing unusual about feeling desire in such circumstances.'

'Its *strength* was what struck me as. unusual,' I said. 'And its *immediacy*. And the music, Questillion. The bloody Benny Goodman. The clarinet player that wasn't there, even though I could hear him, quite plainly. Was he a figment of my imagination? Am I mad, Questillion?'

'We will come to that.'

Questillion's eyes, blank, empty though they were, seemed to pierce through me, nail me like a butterfly dragged from the killing jar.

'Did you make love that first night? Tell me what happened. In detail, please.'

Questillion, you are a paradox embodied: the blind *voyeur*.

I will give you, then, what you want. In detail:

We went back to my lonely bachelor house, secluded and private. I wanted her desperately, but not enough to

31

risk losing her by some transgression upon propriety. It would have been easy for her to rebuff me, or me her, so hedged were all our sexual bets that evening. And yet we both knew that rebuttal was not in the air. Yes, it was chemistry, but *what* chemistry I was yet to realise. I was only grateful for the fact that this arcane magic of the flesh and senses seemed to make things so much easier.

She undressed for me. I was already naked, cold, a nocturnal lunar landscape of gooseflesh waiting for the benediction of her sunlight.

She undressed for me. Simply done: straps off the shoulders, a dip and bob in the convention of shyness, a smile almost hidden in darkness and yet discernible as a crescent moon of confident, unselfconscious joy. And then the sheer fabric slid from the sheer flesh. Naked, she seemed as enigmatic as when clothed, a core of darkness with no sexual context, quite unlike when I had first seen her. And then the *music* of her struck me. I recognised it instantly. It was the essence of Holst's 'Beni Mora'. A wind was blowing out of the desert, a hot dry wind, stirring the mingled scents and tawdry cosmetics, the odours of sweat and burnt meat, cinnamon and leather, the very perfume and stink of the *souk*. I smelt none of this, you understand, but I *heard* it.

The sound of an *oud*, its strings softly resonating in the darkness/her breath was hot upon my chest/the *oud* picked out a refrain, four notes, no more, inexorably repeated/ her mouth closed upon me, drawing, drawing/the rhythm picked up, sustained by violins/her body slid upon mine like a car on a slick road/thinness, ethereality.

There were melodies, direct transmissions, and they burnt in me like ghosts of suns, with all of space to burn in. We climaxed and music span out forever into the space between galaxies. We rode crescendo after crescendo (*sostenuto*) and then we ebbed and faded (*diminuendo*) as my fingers calmed her and her trembling stilled. Entropy. Energy running out. The tendency of love towards absolute stillness, infinite decay. Bodies at rest.

She slept, Questillion, a sleep of satisfaction and contentment, curled like a cat. The smile of her face bespoke the cream. I stirred several times, reaching to her quiet body whenever I awoke. Never have I felt the urge to *possess* so strongly, not even in my capricious adolescence. I lay awake, watching her sleep, like a guard watching a slumbering prisoner.

And throughout the night the desert of her body sang to me. I travelled towards the dawn with music in my ears.

There you are, Questillion.

Sufficient detail, dear *auditeur*? But are we any nearer a diagnosis? I apologise for being vague, nebulous, but I have no *nose* for this, you understand.

Without her there is not a scent of music, only silence.

The next morning she sat in one of my terry bath robes over my customary breakfast of freshly-squeezed orange juice, fried eggs and steak cooked rare. She worked in publishing, she told me, as a copywriter with an independent packaging company I had only vaguely heard of.

'Steak for breakfast seems terribly decadent,' she said, 'more Jerry's style than yours, I would have *thought*.'

'You must put all preconceptions about *me* aside,' I said, 'whether they're about what I have for breakfast, or how I feel about eating it. I'm not a person who can be tackled that way. When can I see you again?'

'Any time. Ring me. Fridays are bad. Jerry is still in the habit of calling me up every now and again whenever he wants a shoulder to cry on, and it's invariably on a Friday. I gather this Zela woman is giving the poor boy a hard time. She's holding out for some kind of commitment. I think she means financial as well as emotional.'

'My heart bleeds,' I said.

33

She stood up, came around the table and sat on my lap, I swear, and kissed me chastely, I swear, on the forehead, letting her body relax into mine for the briefest of moments whilst her eyes and her thoughts remained safe inside a grey inscrutability.

I heard:

A lazy piano, as lilting and lethargic as steak and eggs for breakfast, and cuddling a voluptuous woman on your lap. Satie's 'Gymnopédies'. I turned my head in surprise, with a sharp inhalation of breath. There was no music source in my kitchen. I knew that much. There was nothing in my house of modest miracles that was programmed to feed me music at breakfast-time, or any other time. I was looking, Questillion, for an open window, a louvre left an inch ajar, something that would harvest an ambient melody from the air. It was some indiscreet neighbour, perhaps, using Satie as a sound-track for their early morning exercises. But no. In my hermetic kitchen, there was only me, Liane and the metronomic drift of the piano, echoing the blood-sway of her body on my lap.

Well, Questillion? If I had been disconcerted before, now I was both suspicious and scared. Here I was, if not bright-eyed and bushy-tailed, at least sober and rational, the morning after, and hearing music. The food of love, indeed; not steak and eggs, but Erik Satie.

Zing, went the strings of my heart.

We talk about being crazy with love; suddenly I found myself propelled into this Broadway song-writer's world of love as musical cliché. What surer road to madness?

That was my fear: that I was mad.

Believe it.

Reassure me.

'There is a protein,' said Questillion, 'a complex chain of chemicals. It is not an odour, or a scent; it is something as powerfully volatile, but more primal, a *pheromone*. It identifies her and her alone.

'They are remarkably adaptive, pheromones. They are signatures, essentially, and yet they are so much more. They are *you*, perfectly, defining the internal core of your sexuality, and yet they can also be perceived as extending *you*, defining territory.

'We possess no single defined sensory organ with which to perceive them, as the eye sees light or as the tympanum resonates according to the differentials in air pressure, thus processing sound. And yet they are a staple of the animal kingdom. Many people perceive them as *magical*, *mysterious*, and yet it is certainly some area of the sensorium that perceives them, and transmits their meaning to the darker folds of the cortex. It is simply because we are unable to assign a specific sensory organ to them that we often cloak the perceived response in the magic of such loose definitions as *intuition* or simply *feeling*. There are people, for instance, you simply *know* upon first meeting you will never get on with: take heart, you are not cranky, opinionated or even prejudiced; you are simply heeding the still small voice of the pheromone.

'You are not mad, Grover, but you are damaged. It is not unknown, in cases such as yours, for what we can clumsily call a "short-circuit" to occur, for one area of the sensorium, the auditory centre, for example, to find a cuckoo in its nest, as it were, and to be triggered by stimuli occurring in another, quite separate centre, the olfactory, perhaps. What you hear is what you smell.

'This is patently not happening in your case: your stiltons do not bombard you with the "1812 Overture"; your waltz around a sewage farm is obviously not to the refrain of the "Blue Danube". Your short-circuit is far more targeted, I'm afraid, responding to the sexual content of her pheromone, and hers alone. *I* do not make music for you because, although my pheromones may be as ripe as hers, I do not represent a sexual object to you. At least I hope not.'

A dry chuckle escaped him, and then his face took on an altogether less convivial aspect.

'I am blind, Grover. I may have come lately to that state, but I am adjusting all the time, compensating, developing skills to make up for my short-comings. I can read the discomfort of your mannerisms in the rustle of your clothing. I am hypersensitive to the sound of your fingers stroking your brow in anguish. The creak of your chair tells me of the agonies of your posture. Your suffering speaks to me.'

His tone became scathing. 'And what a suffering is this? This curse that will live with you, even when your juices are dried, your gonads shrivelled, your *cojones* hung up to dry like dead moles on a fence. What a magnificent curse, this symphony of the flesh, this orgasm to a constant crescendo of cymbals, this ability to hold a young girl in your arms, in the night, and to plunder her softly, piercing her with barbs from a silver flute.'

Questillion rocked back in his chair, his blind eyes closed, seeing . . . *what?*

Ah, but Questillion, you do not know the half of it.

One of the indisputable privileges of *riche*, whether on the beaches of Southern France or Brazil, or in the secluded villas of the metropolitan hinterland, is *al fresco* nudity.

It was a simple but pure privilege to watch her lying there by the side of the pool, harvesting the intermittent sun on the golden fields of her body. My mind was untroubled. Questillion had exorcised the ghost of suspected madness. Now I knew my disability was no barrier to my enjoyment of her; on the contrary, as Questillion had hinted, it could be viewed as a gift, an additional door of perception.

The sky was sketchy with clouds, some darker than they should have been. It was midsummer but the air was heavy and humid, the pores of the body quick to start into a flush of perspiration at the slightest degree of physical exertion.

She had an untouched glass of Perrier, growing lukewarm. I fetched a jugful of ice-cubes from the freezer and topped it up for her, planting a kiss between her shoulder-blades. She was so still, I felt sure she must be asleep, but she rolled over, suddenly, spasmodically, and came into my arms, clutching at me with a sob. She was trembling. With that surge of her into my arms came the sound of a drum-beat, distant and yet tantalisingly familiar, a two-bar phrase repeating with an inexorable relentlessness.

'You're crying,' I said.

'I'm not crying.'

Her head was thrust deep into my shoulder and the words were muffled, any emotion masked by the physical press of her against me.

'There's a storm coming, that's all,' she said. 'An electrical storm. Can't you feel it? I'm allergic. I always stream before an electrical storm. It stirs up the dust particles, all those positively and negatively charged ions, all that stuff. You know?'

She pulled away from me suddenly and all the grey inscrutability was gone from her eyes. Large drops of rain began to fall from the sky, splashing on her closed eyelids, her cheeks, her belly.

'You're always watching me,' she said, and I really couldn't tell now whether she was crying or not. 'You watch me all the time, as if you couldn't bear for me not to be there, as if *I* can do something for you that no one else can. I can't stand that. Please don't make it so complicated. I don't want a dog with a broken back. I'm not that noble.'

I barely heard her now; I certainly didn't comprehend her. Ravel's 'Bolero' was a drowning tinnitus in my ears, quickening by the second and echoing the wild thrashing of our bodies. She seemed as charged as the air. At one moment she was clutching at me, the next pushing me away.

I was beyond direction or control, a focus of primal lust; when release came it was exquisitely selfish. *I* had reached a point of ecstasy beyond which *I* could not go. I fell to earth.

She lay in my arms, as the storm, and as Ravel, abated. She seemed as consumed as I, and when our eyes met, she smiled with a dazzlingly perfect, immaculate understanding that made me feel, by contrast, inadequate and dirty. The *rat-tat-tat* in my temples may have been the coursing of blood, or it may have been the decaying ring of the 'Bolero's' snare drum, but it also carried a stentorian cadence that spoke of guilt. It was like the drum-roll the fraction before the drop of the guillotine.

I couldn't shake myself free of the feeling that I had somehow *raped* her.

We didn't see each other for a week, maybe more. I tried telephoning her but she was never in her office, never in her flat in town.

Then she called me and we arranged to meet for dinner at a Russian restaurant near Garrick Street.

She was affectionate and out-going, her normal self in fact, but there was no music. She was the soul of silence.

'Jerry's ditched that Zela woman,' she said.

'Bortsch-brain?'

'That's the one. He's going to America, to run the office in New York. He's asked me to go with him. Do you think I should?'

'He certainly wouldn't make life complicated.'

'That's for sure.'

There was a crystal glass of fresh roses on the table between us. She took one and held it out for me to smell.

But it was her I smelt, of course, finally and bitterly.

A saxophone in hell. John Coltrane's 'Ascension'. Chords and dischords. Sheets of notes, torn from the belly of music, that were beyond any conception of time. It was music that was physically painful, that stabbed through the flesh, tearing and rending it, that took you to the brink of orgasm and held you there, trembling and teetering, unable to climax. It was pure Coltrane, a man driven by the burning in his gut that finally, finally, consumed him, spewing pain, torment and transfiguration over the world. Love is fine, said Coltrane, but this is what remains in that dark abyss following the retreat of love. Is this really what you want?

I smiled.

'You forget,' I said, folding the rose into her hand. 'I'm a broken man. Can't smell a thing.'

SCOTT BRADFIELD

Dazzle

Dazzle was a dog with bushy red hair, fleas, and an
extraordinarily good attention span – especially for a dog.
He was particularly fond of pastry, philosophies of
language, and Third World political theory. It was
Dazzle's express opinion that unless somebody started
paying the Third World a little concerted attention, serious
consequences faced all mankind. Philosophies of language, on the other hand, were just a hobby, and when
it came to pastry Dazzle preferred Sarah Lee Strawberry
Cheesecake. There was more dog than dogness about
Dazzle. Generally Dazzle knew how to keep his mouth
shut, and strenuously avoided calling any attention to
himself.

'The little doggy go woof,' said Jennifer Davenport, the
youngest member of Dazzle's patron family, the Davenports. Jennifer was six years old. Whenever anybody
visited, they said how beautiful Jennifer was. Dazzle
thought Jennifer was just okay. 'Woof, doggy. Be a good
goddy – oops, I said doog goddy, I mean –' Jennifer
looked theatrically around at her family, who had positioned themselves conscientiously around the living-room
television, but nobody looked back.

'Doggies don't go woof,' Dazzle thought, suffering
Jennifer's cold hand on his nose. 'The *canus domesticus*
utters a guttural diphthong, much like the Mandarin
Chinese diphthong, only less enunciated. Now why don't

41

you leave me alone and go watch a little TV.' Jennifer was already tempted. The television radiated warm noise and a flickering colourless haze that illuminated the faces of Father, Mother, Billy and Brad like nuclear isotopes. Mother was the Big One who fed Dazzle. Billy was the Little One who took him for the best walks.

Dogs don't like people, Dazzle thought. Dogs like dogs. Dazzle liked Homer, a resolute and well-groomed dalmatian who often roamed the park during Dazzle's afternoon walks, and Dingus, the hideous lapsu-apsu which snorted at Dazzle through the slatted pine fence of Dazzle's back yard.

'Life's a game, Dingus,' Dazzle would say, contentedly pawing his rawhide bone and gazing up at the blue, translucent sky. 'Life's a game, and you learn to play it by the rules, or else you learn to make everybody else play by your rules. You can either be the ruler or the ruled, and that's the crux, isn't it, old pal? That's the decision we've all got to make. Me, I'd rather live by the rules I'm dealt. I'm no high-achiever, Dingus. I like my life. I eat well and get plenty of exercise, and I've pretty much got this whole damn yard to myself most days. Of course I'm what you'd have to call an exceptional dog, but being exceptional's one of those things that takes a lot of effort, let me tell you. Being exceptional takes nothing but lots of hard work, work, work. Being exceptional just means lots of pain and suffering, pal, believe you me. Look at Kerouac. Look at Martin Luther King. They were exceptional, and where'd being exceptional get them? I'll tell you where it got them. It got them nowhere. It got them nowhere at all.'

Dingus snuffled against the pine fence. 'Dog smells,' he said. 'Food and water. Food and water and dog smells.' Dingus snorted and snuffled again, and eventually lay down in the warm dirt and fell asleep. In his dreams of quick rabbits, Dingus kicked. 'Rabbits,' he muttered in his sleep. 'Quick rabbits.'

42

Some days, though, Dazzle was so depressed he couldn't even get out of bed to go to the bathroom. He lay on his desultory, twisted blanket beside the water-heater in the basement and awaited the occasional click of the thermostat and the rush of the gas fire which indicated Mother was washing dishes or doing laundry. Dazzle never knew what it was exactly. He just felt a sort of vague and indefinable anxiety, a certain fundamental sadness at the inconclusiveness of things. It was the way he felt when he saw a dead cat in the road. Dazzle hated cats, but when he saw them squashed and senseless in the spattered street he didn't hate them at all any more. He sniffed at them; they didn't even smell like cat. They smelled like hot asphalt, transmission fluid, and gasoline. Sometimes Dazzle just lay on his blanket for hours, contemplating the meaninglessness of dead cats. When the postman pushed mail through the grate he might try to emit a half-hearted growl, but usually he didn't bother. Eventually he would hear Billy's bike clattering onto the dirt driveway, and force himself shaggily to his feet, shaking off his loose, dandruffy hairs. Dazzle simply didn't have any clear idea what was bothering him, but did his best to keep up a good false front. He didn't want people to think he was just feeling sorry for himself.

'It's a good life,' he told Homer in the park. Billy was sitting on the softball bleachers with his friends and absently handling Dazzle's disenfranchised leash. 'Of course it's a routine, we all know that. A dog's life, as they say. Dog-days in a dog's life, and all that. But you take away routine and what have you got? Have you read the papers lately? Do you know what the world population figures are going into the next century? Check it out, pal; check it out. And do you know what our President's official policy is on overpopulation? Well, hold still just a second and I'll tell you. Our President thinks any increase in population only creates a larger, wealthier consumer market. That's what our President thinks. The more overpopulated the world gets, the more Volvos we'll sell.

The more canned spinach. The more Levis. The world's going to hell in a handcart, Homer. Let me tell you. So routine, well, maybe it's a bit boring at times. But it's better than no routine at all — and you know what no routine at all means, don't you, Homer? It means chaos, entropy, deindividuation, madness and death. How's that sound to you, Homer? Does that sound better than one square meal a day, and a warm blanket to sleep on? Does it, Homer? You tell me. Because maybe, just maybe, *I've* had it wrong all these years.'

'Relax and eat a bone,' Homer said, imperiously panting, gazing off dreamily at a big black bird on a wire. 'Gnaw a bone and dig the yard.' Homer was a sage and sensible dog, Dazzle thought. But he was also, like every other dog Dazzle had ever met in his entire life, extraordinarily stupid. Even Dazzle's brave and obvious exercises in false bravado were lost on stupid dogs like Homer and Dingus. It was a very lonely world, Dazzle thought, this world of dogs.

Nights Dazzle suffered long knotty bouts of insomnia which arose in him as charged eccentric monologues filled with delusions of grandeur and then, just as impossibly, plunged him into the depths of irony, self-mockery and suicidal despair. 'The best lives are simple lives,' Dazzle tried firmly to convince himself, unable to sit still even for a minute. He heard the mice in the garbage, the beetles on the walls. He got up and turned and turned again on his frazzled blanket. Then, of course, the irrepressible antitheses arose too. 'Simple lives are filled with loneliness, vacancy, and self-deception.' For days he would go without eating, just gazing emptily at the liquefying Gravy Train in his big red bowl. Flies settled in it; then, at night, the mice came. It didn't really matter, he thought. Sometimes when he urinated on the newspaper a few tiny drops of blood dripped out. His stomach twitched and growled; he experienced long energetic periods of flatulence. Some

44

days he couldn't even bear the thought of facing the world's other dogs.

The family veterinarian, Hsiang the Merciless, prescribed antibiotics. This is life's real horror, Dazzle thought, prone on the ice-cold formica table, closing his eyes and abiding the flea spray's aerosol hiss. Streams of black fleas spilled across the thin tissue sanitary sheet. We live and we die by the hundreds and thousands, Dazzle thought. And in order to live we visit our doctor. Dr Hsiang's gloved hands prodded and violated Dazzle in every conceivable way, and in many inconceivable ones. Dazzle shivered with terror, surrounded by the cold antiseptic office, the menacing banks of glittering stainless-steel blades and instruments. This is the horror of life, he thought. This is life's trial, and then we die.

When Billy hid the antibiotic pills in tiny edible lumps of Dazzle's Alpo, Dazzle would carefully disengage and deposit them behind the hot water boiler where nobody, to his knowledge, ever cleaned. He had heard too much about the debilitating effect of antibiotics on the body's immune system, and, anyway, he knew his grief was not merely physiochemical. It was philosophical, ethical, and spiritual. It was a logical problem he would have to deal with. Intellectually, he knew he was on firm grounds. Maybe life wasn't filled with all the excitement and challenge he might have desired, but, he reflected, you can't always change life. You can't always change history, Kenneth Burke once said, but you can change your attitude towards history. Dazzle had a bad attitude, for which he could only hold himself responsible. Fundamentally, Dazzle considered himself an existential humanist. This meant he didn't believe in God, but he did believe in guilt.

'Good dog. Nice dog. Dazzle is a nice dog,' the psychiatrist said, cradling Dazzle's freshly laundered blanket in his arms as if it were a baby. The psychiatrist was balding and slightly pockmarked; he wore thick wire-rimmed glasses. 'He looked a little ludicrous, if you want to know the truth,' Dazzle told Dingus later. The

45

psychiatrist's name was Dr Bernstein, and Dr Bernstein told Mr. Davenport that Dazzle suffered from acute feelings of insecurity initiated by a birth trauma and castration. ('I think it was castration,' Dazzle said. 'You want to talk about trauma, let's forget birth altogether. Let's talk about getting your balls chopped off. Bastards.' Dingus snuffled miserably.) 'Nice dog. Good dog,' Dr Bernstein said, burying his silly face in the blanket and sniffing audibly at it as if he, and not Dazzle, were the dog. Then he smiled. 'Dazzle smells nice. Dazzle's blanket smells nice.' Once each week Dazzle lay on the tiny hearth rug beside the electric fire, peering up at the visibly disturbed and often unsettling Dr Bernstein. Dr Bernstein pranced about, made barking and growling noises, and offered Dazzle a red rubber chew toy which Dazzle merely contemplated lying there before him like a mantra or something by Wittgenstein. 'I think it's true what they say about psychiatrists,' Dazzle said later. 'They're all crazy. They're all fucking nutty as fruit bats.' As Dazzle said this, Dingus lay down in the dirt and began licking himself noisily.

Veterinarians, canine shrinks, other dogs, Big and Little Ones. Things seemed to be getting worse and worse rather than better and better, at least as far as Dazzle's state of mind was concerned. The Family even began to regard Dazzle with a sort of diffracted familiarity. 'Hi, Dazzle,' they said, without bending to pet him. 'How you doing, boy?' They looked genuinely concerned, but they also looked like they didn't really want to get too involved. Dazzle didn't know what to say. Every evening he watched them assemble around the glowing television and sometimes, out of the corner of their eye, they watched him watching them. He sat and listened unemotionally to the news. The entire world was rapidly being transformed into a gigantic petrochemical dump, Dazzle thought. We are all being steadily infiltrated by carcinogens, toxins, radiation, and some sort of irrepressible sadness which is probably the only underlying meaning anyway. Jennifer

46

never snuck Dazzle into her room any more so he could sleep on the big bed. By now, though, Dazzle had learned to prefer the garage.

Then one cold afternoon while Dazzle was sitting in the back yard talking to Dingus he noticed the gate was open. The latch had not engaged, and the wind was beating it gently against its creaking hinges. Dingus noticed it first, and began snuffling and darting back and forth against his own fence, insensibly sensing the sudden miracle of Dazzle's. 'Cats!' Dingus cried. 'Piss everywhere! Kill all the cats!' Dazzle watched his frenetic neighbour with a cool and cynical distemper. The bravest dogs in the world are the dogs who bark behind fences, Dazzle thought philosophically, and got up and went to the gate which, with a tiny pull from his paw, swung widely open and revealed the rolling hills of the Simon Hills tract estates covered with their uniform houses. With a sinking feeling in his chest, Dazzle stepped outside into the unfenced world.

For days and days he wandered aimlessly, urinating weakly on trees, lamp-posts and hydrants with a distracted, almost surreptitious expression, as if he were secretly determined to eliminate all the world's traces of other dogs. His legs carried him steadily and rhythmically in no direction at all, and for a while he preferred this sort of primal, nomadic state of disaffected consciousness. 'It's not the rhythm of the primitive we've lost,' Dazzle said out loud sadly, to nobody in particular. 'It's the rhythm of history itself.' Other dogs often appeared and sniffed at Dazzle and, with impatient formality, Dazzle sniffed back. 'Don't eat our food or piss on our posts,' the dogs said. 'Don't fuck our bitches.' Dazzle disregarded the blind caution of their first warning, contemplated the ironic sadness of their second. One night while he tried to sleep in an alley he was even approached by a bitch in heat. She was filthy and bone-hungry, and stank terribly. He looked up drowsily

47

as she sniffed at him. 'Sorry, dear,' he said, watching her lumber off in her manic, erotic daze. We just bang around the world like that, Dazzle thought. We travel around the world banging into things.

Out here in the unfenced world, Dazzle's dream life gathered strange energy and momentum. They were muted, vegetable dreams, filled with formless bodies and soundless words, and when Dazzle awoke he found himself inexplicably contemplating the migration of birds, the constellations of his youth. He remembered as a pup lying out on the back yard's green grass with his chew toys and identifying them: Orion, Taurus, Hydra, the Pleiades. His sharp canine eyes could discern the rings of Saturn, the moons of Jupiter. Space was filled with awesome distances and complications. It went on forever and ever. Quasars, pulsars, stars, galaxies, vast convoluted nebulae like memories, shattered planets and exploding stars. As Dazzle grew older and older all this universal wonder seemed to shrink and encapsulate him like a glove. He forgot his own wonderment, or at least considered it frivolous. 'I'm no adventurer,' he used to tell the equally youthful Dingus. 'I'm a housepet. I know how to keep my four paws planted right here on old *terra firma*.' Recalling now his own heartless and cynical affectations, Dazzle started to cry. He didn't understand this inexpressible sadness, and wished it would end and leave him in peace. He wanted to be happy in his yard again. He wanted his bland regular meals and his blanket. He wanted that hard musty world in which he knew the locations of things. He desired the simple dreams before language began, and regretted his own smug complicity in the world's systematic disavowal of imagination.

Needless to say, however, Dazzle didn't find much imagination out in the unfenced world either. Instead he found rampant street crime, bulleting cars and buses, underfunded public schools, political corruption, sad songs, homeless families, bad meat and tall office buildings. 'Sometimes there's just nothing you can say,' Dazzle told himself, chewing morosely at a slice of stale

48

bread he had pilfered from some addled pigeons. 'Sometimes there aren't any explanations. Or if there are explanations, they don't make you feel any better.' He slept in parks, alleyways, underneath parked automobiles, sensing his own true home diminishing in the world and reeling further and further away, like stars and nebulae and other planets in a universe of constant motion. All the stars in the world are hurtling further and further apart, Dazzle thought. Dissolution, heterogeneity and death. Even the Davenports were fading from the map of Dazzle's mind. Soon, Dazzle thought, the map will only contain direction and gravity and heat. It will lack a central landmark. There will just be the world, and me in it. It was hard for Dazzle to believe he could feel any more forlorn and helpless than he had when he was living with the Davenports, but now his sadness had become actually inarticulable. He couldn't even compose sentences about how he felt; he couldn't alleviate the weight of his misery with metaphors or figurative language of any sort. His monotonous legs carried him deeper into the world of noise and lights and cities. Sometimes he encountered stray coyotes, or even wild wolves who had gotten lost for years in the big cities and were now almost completely insane. They talked out loud to themselves and yelped pitifully at the least sudden sounds. They suffered from skin diseases, vitamin deficiencies and a wild, unexaggerated fear of all mankind. Howl at the moon, Dazzle told them. The moon's a bitch.

Dazzle was sleeping in an overturned trash can on a neglected and undeveloped Encino lot when he met Edwina. Edwina was a nicc dog, though a little lean, who suffered from chronic indigestion and a severe overdependency on father figures. 'Fuck me,' she said 'Feed me. Beat me. Hurt me. Love me.' She bowed her head as she approached Dazzle's trash can, sniffing suspiciously at Dazzle's unalpha-like yawn. 'Sit down and rest,' Dazzle said, shifting a little to one side. Edwina sniffed more intimately. 'Forget it,' Dazzle said. 'Go to sleep,' and Edwina did. This was the closest Dazzle had ever come in his life to a real relationship, and as such he blithely accepted much which, intellectually, he often considered impossible or irrational. For while most of the time Edwina was disturbingly submissive, at other times, entirely without warning or apparent provocation, she would take vicious and sudden bites out of Dazzle's rump or tail. 'Jesus Christ,' Dazzle would say. Edwina was like a beheaded or defaced street sign. There was very little understanding Edwina, which actually reassured Dazzle in a strange way, for Dazzle was a dog who for many years had felt he could understand just about anything, particularly dumb dogs.

Edwina didn't know anything, and relied on Dazzle to find food, evade dog-catchers and traffic, and some nights even to get to sleep. 'Everything's going to be okay,' Dazzle comforted her, gazing out at the starless, smoggy sky. 'You just relax and go to sleep.' Edwina was a hopeless case and even more screwed-up than Dazzle, and that was why Dazzle suspected, at times, that he just might love her. He paid her close attentions. 'You're not going to eat that, are you?' he might ask, or 'Try taking a little bath in the pond in the park. You'll feel better.' Whenever Edwina was in heat, she would bring home the mangiest, most smelly and disreputable dogs she could find and fuck them in the bushes behind Dazzle's trash can. Afterwards the spent and irritable dogs would often try to pick fights with Dazzle, or bully him into giving away some of the food he kept wrapped up in newspapers inside his trash can. 'One of these days, Edwina, you're going to get fucked by the wrong sort of character,' Dazzle warned her after another very long night. 'You know what that means, don't you? Rabies. Yeah, you heard me. Frothing at the mouth. These enormous lesions develop all along your spine and inside your brain. You'll be one fucking crazy bitch, Edwina. I mean. I'm just thinking about your health; I think I'm old enough to say quite frankly I've outgrown pride and all those other silly provocations to marital conflict. But I do wonder sometimes, Edwina, I really do. Where do you find these guys, anyway? I mean, do you actually go *looking* for low-lifes, or is it just that low-lifes are irresistibly attracted to you?' Sometimes Edwina made Dazzle feel extraordinarily weary and discomposed, and despondently he would root through his remembered past trying to unearth some forgotten scrap of nostalgia. He tried to formulate romantic images of himself back then, the lone roamer seeking truth in the world, learning about himself and his fellow dogs. But the romantic images rarely held together for more than a few moments at a time. When push came to shove, Dazzle had to admit it was much warmer sleeping in the trash can when Edwina was there.

Even though Dazzle had tried to explain contraception to Edwina about a million times she never once paid him a moment's notice, and in May during her second month of term Dazzle decided they should head north, into the high and unpaved country where Edwina's litter could at least expect a few simple years of the reflective life before they were meaninglessly smashed beyond recognition by some errant and uncomprehending bus. 'Sometimes it's not the lived life that matters at all,' Dazzle told them. They were blind and sucking and crawling all over one another, still marked by bits of unlicked blood and placenta. Edwina lay deflated and insensible in the bole of a large tree which Dazzle had padded with leaves and a few scraps of charred blanket he had discovered near an abandoned campsite. They were living in Big Sur overlooking the rough Pacific, the gnarled and wind-shaped elms and shore. 'The lived life's just a big con, too,' Dazzle told them. 'Events, possessions, sights, sounds, travel, achievement, oh, and what's the famous one – oh, yeah, *experience*. It's all a big cultural snow job, if you ask me. It's primitive accumulation, the myth of the entrepreneur. There aren't any entrepreneurs any more, kids. There's just IT&T,

Mobil, and General Dynamics – and you know what they all thrive on, don't you? War, slaughtered and commodified animals like us, economic and political repression. Us unincorporated just have to do our best to carve out our own little alternative pockets of living. That's why the family's so important. I guess what I'm trying to say about all this nonsense is simply try and be happy with your life and don't worry too much about *experiencing* it. Let's all relax and enjoy ourselves a little. Let's all find a nice long pause together, okay, and not be in such a damn rush to get anywhere or do anything.' The squirming pups just squealed and sucked. Sometimes during those first few days Dazzle felt he was the one who had just been born.

If there was such a thing as happiness, Dazzle thought he had found it. The role of patriarch fitted him quite snugly, and he realised that even if he could not find any sort of subjective comfort himself he could at least meticulously envelop Edwina and her pups in comfort's illusion, that long slow dream of culture Dazzle had always examined but never successfully comprehended before. It was Edwina's last litter, and since she didn't desire to get fucked that much any more they were able to construct a relatively stable family environment. The pups grew with sudden and frightening alacrity, and there always seemed to be one or two of them pulling at Dazzle's tail or pawing at Dazzle's face. Dazzle hardly slept at all any more, and generally he preferred this dulled unquenched fuzziness of brain and perception. It's best to keep the old brain a little blurred, a little battered, Dazzle decided. He had cleared out a small cave underneath an outcrop of black, igneous rock on a mountainside. As the pups grew, he trained them to maintain a system of revolving security watches around their home, and drilled them in defensive techniques and manoeuvres.

'A man?' he asked them.

'Hide,' they said.

'Wolf?'
'Submit.'
'Bear?'
'Run.'
'Inexpressible sadness?'
'Run.'
'Restless, unhappy dreams?'
'Dream again.'

Often in the middle of Dazzle's patient drills, while the addled and hyper pups were growing distracted by buzzing flies and high birds, Edwina snuck up behind Dazzle and took a quick, nasty bite out of his ass.

'Jesus Christ,' Dazzle said.

There was a smooth diurnal rhythm to life now. Dazzle thought. You could feel the safe beat of the entire world in your blood, your heart, your dreams. Half-asleep at the mouth of their cave, he liked to listen to Edwina and the pups snoring and contemplate the stars outside again. Pisces, Cassiopeia, Ursa Major, and of course the craters and mountains of a vast and irreproachable moon. This is where the cycle ends, he thought, if a cycle it is. It's that convergence of the stars and the blood, the moon and the heart. It's not the world of men. It's not the Davenport's smelly garage. It's not Dingus urinating on everything. It's not clinical depression, or obsessive, convoluted thinking. It's not even barking at the mailman.

There were still days when Dazzle would slip off into the nearest town and check out the newspapers. Islamic fundamentalism, AIDs, the international debts crisis, yuppie liberals, adamant right-wing perjurers. It's not to disavow the world that I've left it, Dazzle thought, and made his mark on the *Examiner*'s Op Ed page. It's to live in the world I've always before disavowed. If he moved quickly, he could pull a nice steak from the grocery's refrigerated cabinet and sneak quietly out the back door like some innocuous delivery boy.

Periodically, though, Edwina grew ill and somewhat disaffected, lying in the cave alone for days at a time gazing insensibly at the blue sky beyond their tidy and self-sufficient cave. 'Melancholy,' Dazzle wondered. 'Sad reflections. Lost love. Dead friends.' But Edwina never told him what was on her mind; she just growled distantly at him. She never even bit him any more, and eventually Dazzle realised she was suffering from physical rather than merely philosophical distress. The whites of her eyes grew sallow and bloodshot. Her breath was bad, and she suffered frequent discharge of diarrhoea. Small rashes formed occasionally on her back and stomach, and eventually Dazzle diagnosed a low-grade infection, perhaps septicaemia, or a common form of acute gastroenteritis. Dazzle recalled the library of antibiotics he had so smugly discarded behind the water heater in the Davenports' garage. You can't go back and change some things, he thought. He liked that world better, the simple one of medicine.

Early on a Monday morning Dazzle descended to the town with Flaubert, the laconic and reserved pup who, like his brothers and sisters, was really a pup no longer. Flaubert was developing assurance and a quick stride. There was something wild about Flaubert which Dazzle didn't understand, something which Flaubert had either inherited from his mother or his uncivil upbringing. It wasn't just his eyes, for he carried a certain alertness in the very poise of his musculature. 'The world's crisis is a crisis of representation,' Dazzle explained as they descended the mountain. 'We're always representing our lives one way or another. We never live them. We never even live them *as* representations, which is an idea I've been giving a lot of thought to recently.'

Alpine was a minimal town which contained a small grocery, a pharmacist's, an abandoned movie theatre, a Woolworth's which had been recently converted into a Bill's Jumbo Discount House, and approximately six hundred people. 'There's a hidden continuity between signs and things, thoughts and world. Our fears of discontinuity are a fiction, actually, but one which we must be maintaining for some reason. Our anxieties about the world, things, other people, that world which doesn't conform to our dreams of it. We're letting those anxieties determine our world. Instead we should try to determine the world for ourselves.' Coolly, Flaubert loped along like a wolf; he didn't say anything. Dazzle thought Flaubert was starting to look a little bit like Warren Oates in *The Wild Bunch*. 'They're anxieties because we can't admit the validity of our own dreams,' Dazzle said aimlessly. 'That's what the world keeps telling us, you see, and that's what makes us so goddamn miserable. We believe what we're told, even when we're told to believe in everything but ourselves. I'm not trying to sound like some adolescent solipsist or anything, Flaubert. I'm not saying we should deny the world or anything. I'm just saying let's give our dreams half a chance too. Let's maintain some faith not only in the world, but in our dreams of it.'

They had come to a stop across the street from the Mercury Pharmacy where the pharmacist, a tall man named Bill who wore a white jacket and patent leather shoes, was outside on the front curb training his guard dog, a large mean-looking Doberman whom the pharmacist referred to as Dutch, but who referred to itself in its most secret thoughts as Jasmine. The pharmacist pulled sternly at the Doberman's gleaming stainless-steel choke-collar; at the same time he showed the captive dog a handful of chicken biscuits. 'Sit,' the pharmacist demanded impatiently, and gave the collar another sudden pull. 'Sit, Dutch.'

'Chicken biscuit,' the Doberman said. 'Chicken biscuit biscuit.'

'Sit. Sit *down*, Dutch. *Sit!*' the pharmacist said.

'Maybe he doesn't want to sit,' Dazzle said out loud, but nobody in the world was listening. 'Maybe he just wants his goddamn chicken biscuit. Maybe he just wants to eat his goddamn chicken biscuit and then take a nice long nap.'

When Dazzle was just a puppy his favourite television programme had been called *Lassie* and had starred an attractive Scottish collie of the same name who saved members of the human family she lived with each week from various life-threatening situations. Lassie dived into raging rivers and burning buildings. She stood up against wild bears and men with guns. Lassie was a brave dog, Dazzle had thought, but an exceptionally foolhardy dog as well. 'Save yourself,' Dazzle would cry weakly, whimpering a little under his breath at the terrible trials and misfortunes endured by brave dogs everywhere. 'Run like hell. Timmy can take care of his damn self.'

'Sit,' the pharmacist said. It was a warm day, with only a few high white clouds. 'Sit *down.*'

The less and less I understand, the simpler everything seems, Dazzle thought, and, at his signal, Flaubert took off and broke the pharmacist's grip of the Doberman's collar like a sprinter breathlessly striking the victory ribbon.

'Cats!' Flaubert cried, dashing off down the street. 'Cats!' The Doberman, with a brief flickering expression like the lens of a camera, poised and then, with a sudden start, took off after Flaubert. The pharmacist took off after him.

'Sit!' the pharmacist shouted, running and shaking his gleaming choke-collar at the bright sky. 'Heel! Stop! Sit!'

Without a moment's hesitation, Dazzle loped into the pharmacist's office, found the Prescription Out tray, and snapped up one hundred capsules of 250mg Tetracycline and fifty 100mg Aerethromycin. Then, with a flourish, he ascended again into the high mountains.

MICHAEL COBLEY

Waltz in Flexitime

Time, they say, waits for no man: I'll vouch for that. Time is too busy being drawn out and chopped up by humanity's tick-a-tock mentality to try staying in the one place. Time wouldn't really be a mild old greybeard, hauling a scythe around from dawn to dusk, serenely counting grains of sand. No, Time would be a screaming, gibbering maniac, bouncing off walls, propelled by chronochaotic dementia. Schizoid entropy.

Time is seriously maladjusted, which is why I wear a watch. Always. Never take it off. The origins of this singular habit go back nearly four years (or however long it was) to one winter morning in Glasgow. The specific location was the underground station at St Enoch's Square and the time, as seen on my battered old Rolex with the frayed hanging-by-a-thread-or-two leather strap, was just on 8.30 a.m.

Rush-hour on the Glasgow tube is always shoulder-to-shoulder bodyheat, but that morning it was especially packed. When the car doors opened I nearly floated out on clouds of humidity. Gasping for air, I glanced at my watch, then hurried up the stairs and through the barrier.

At just that moment, crowds from the other platform were surging up and out, all of them as eager for clear air as we were. So of course the crowd became a throng, then developed into a drove. And at some point between the rotary tripod barrier and the icy street air at the top of the escalators, the Rolex parted company with my wrist. You know, of course. You can sense the absence of familiar pressure on your wrist before you yank your jacket sleeve up to expose that band of pale flesh.

I was furious; I pushed my way back to the up-escalator but saw nothing on or at the top of the moving steps. I went back down to the barrier, cursing humanity and pickpockets all the way. Nothing. There was no point in further searching — what's more, the station clocks read 8.41 and I was already late — so I left my name and address with the uniformed woman behind the glass then hurried back up the escalator.

At street level I paused beneath the entrance canopy to readjust my scarf and overcoat. Across Argyle Street, above the corner jewellers, a clock said 8.43. Intending to approach the road and cross to the other side, I stepped out from under the canopy and began walking. Suddenly I was reeling from pain radiating from my nose and filling my head with lights. I staggered past the thing into which I'd barged. Tears blurred my sight, and it seemed uncommonly dark . . .

Fear grabbed at me and I rubbed my eyes, wiped away wetness and felt relief. I hadn't gone blind after all, it really was dark. When it had been bright morning moments before.

Fear of blindness transformed itself into dread looking for a reason. Had I blacked out? Just been dislocated from reality like a bulb, turned off for a while and switched on again at random? Maybe I'd been mugged, grabbed from behind and pushed into something hard?

And left unconscious *and* standing up? — countered reason. Okay, mugging was out.

I then remembered what it was I'd collided with, recalled clearly its rough wrinkled surface, even the moss under my fingers. It had been a tree.

I looked about me: closed-up darkened stores, a pair of phone-boxes neon-lit from within, and nothing between me and the locked gates of the underground station. Just a stretch of tiled pavement. Something weird had happened and I shivered as I crossed Argyle Street, with the idea of heading up Buchanan Street, maybe catching a late-night bus near George Square. The clock over the jewellers now read 1.22, the sky was a solid shroud of night cloud and the air was cold. I tell you this to show that I was taking notice of my surroundings, and that subsequent events were due to factors beyond my control and/or sanity.

I carried on up Buchanan Street, past the brick nooks and concrete bowls festooned with greenery. As I walked by the Argyle Arcade a wave of dizziness washed over me – well, *two* waves really, and rather than washing over me they collided nauseously through me.

For a moment I was disorientated, confused, then with slow amazement I became aware of the street that sloped steeply before me.

Those of you acquainted with Glasgow probably know that Buchanan Street slopes gently down to St Enoch's Square: not so the road I stood on at that moment. The pavement consisted of broad shallow steps rising up a steep incline. The pedestrian precinct had vanished, replaced by a cobbled roadway littered with curling brown leaves from the mossy trees lining the way.

The sky was a sullen boil of blue-black and violet, casting harsh shadows across baroque architecture. The light was grainy and the stone surfaces of column and pilaster, corbel and window casement had the same texture as if hewn from a single cliff. The buildings loomed all the way uphill and in the upper distance terraces of grotesque housing proliferated in courts, squares and avenues. Mingled shelves of bizarre roofs and towers fading into hazy detail. I turned to look behind me, *down* at the sluggish Clyde, saw dark ships at anchor, ribbon-like pennants rippling from masts and crosstrees. Warehouses stacked back from the opposite riverbank, giving way to offices, trading houses, taverns, residences, ascending in levels . . .

This vast concave cityscape was a staggering sight, and

not a little frightening. I mean, you hear such testimonies from the puerile and superstitious among us, but you don't expect to experience a phenomenon yourself. But there I was, doing an authentic bit of experiencing, when two brawny fellows emerged from an alley in hot pursuit of a man dressed in a flowing blue garment.

The fugitive saw me and started to head my way, until a large hand seized his collar and threw him to the ground. The hand's owner, the larger of the two bulky gentlemen, wore a shapeless black longcoat with an asymmetrical stovepipe hat attached by a chinstrap. He crouched and ground a knee into his quarry's back. His companion, dressed in a leather apron over working clothes, opened a clanking, grimy sack, tugged out a hammer and a chainless manacle bearing a glass-covered watch face. They were handed down to the first, who proceeded to hammer the manacle on to the captive's wrist.

'Please! help! . . .' came a wavering cry.

Stovepipe Hat looked up at me, seemed to glance at my hands, then gave a gleeful grin.

'Aha − another criminal!'

That was all I needed to hear. There was a confusion of shouts as I turned away uphill.

'Stop! − in the name of the City!'

'Run faster, you fool!'

'Swage! Stop him and I'll chase this one . . .'

'Help! . . .'

'And lag that one . . .'

'Help! − pleeeaaoouuhh . . .'

Dizziness.

Then relief, the trembling kind that makes you feel slightly weak. I was back in *my* Glasgow, further up Buchanan Street at the Gordon Street turn-off. I collapsed gratefully on to a bench beside a brick-walled bush trough, looking back down to Argyll Street. A bank clock to my right said 5.39, and a stoic-looking man at the corner of the building advertised the *Evening Times* with enigmatic syllables.

Then, in a flash of satori, I understood. Without my watch I was a rudderless vessel crossing a sea of time or — I fumbled for metaphors — between calm pools regulated by big . . . er, clocks. And the waters between belong to the currents of deeper — parallel? — planes of existence.

I stood up. I had to lay hands on another watch, but the closest place was the Argyll Arcade, back in that archaic phantom Glasgow. The nearest after that was the jewellers opposite St Enoch's station, so I'd have to go round. A big clock hung over Dixon's two blocks along Gordon Street, so I began walking, watching for the crossover, ready to run.

The transformation from prosaic late-eighties Glasgow to phantom whenever-Glasgow was smooth, flowing. As if a vast invisible hand poured violet, blue, black inks across the sky while buildings grew gaunt pillars and the streets narrowed. Shop windows shrank and lost their glass, flashy store signs sunk into the stonework that writhed slowly with friezes and fluted cornices.

The air swirled, became dark shapes, people crowding around a man standing gesticulating in a portico. A shout went up behind me and I glanced back to see Stovepipe Hat with his hammer, raging his way through the crowd which drew back from him. I lost no time in doing a bit of crowd-parting myself.

I reached the Dixon's clock-zone, surroundings re-arranged themselves, and I found Union Street busy with revellers. It was 1.29 and the night sky was generously providing a constant drizzle. The pubs were closing and members of the constabulary were in watchful attendance.

I walked down the right-hand side of Union Street, watching carefully for the metamorphosis. When it came it was milder, and the pavement altered between one step and the next. I was ready for that but not for the sight to my right.

The facade of offices and shops concealing the city's Central Station dropped several yards and went through slow undulations of re-ornamentation. Brick and stonework faded into arched windows filled with smoke-stained panes of glass. I paused for a moment to gaze in at the locomotives far below, engines broad as houses, monsters of iron belching smoke amid a metallic din that was muffled by the windows.

One thing I noticed as I hurried downhill, attracting imperious glares from the citizenry, was the similarity in street layout between the sunken Glasgow and my city. Even as I walked, the ostentatious mock turret flying flags at the next corner on the left changed into the Boots building, complete with jumbo-sized clock.

At last! I thought, turning left into Argyle Street again. *There* was a couple of jewellers; jewellers sell watches; with a new watch I would once more be able to journey to and fro across my own immutable city! Jubilant and undeterred by the shop and office workers swarming into restaurants (it was 1.07 – gorge-along-a-pizza time) I wove and bodyswerved my way along the busy pavement.

Imagine my horror when, instead of the welcome glitter of a well-stocked window, I found myself staring into a fluttering hazy mirage only faintly reminiscent of a shop. The logic of the situation was undeniable – jewellers have this strange habit of setting each of their display watches to a different time from the rest, thus that shop window was a chronological maelstrom. Even at its edge I could see my surroundings warp, discern embellished contours and reliefs beneath Arnotts department store front.

The sky darkened swiftly and fast-motion blurs of humanity flitted around me. I walked on a short way out of the zone of distortion into a night-time Argyle Street. Filled with misery I sat in an unlit doorway . . . just as a tall man in an overcoat appeared on the paved area before the dimmed St Enoch's underground entrance. He was clasping both hands to his face and swearing quite inventively as he staggered to a halt.

I watched *me* become aware of my surroundings, swear a bit more, then rub frantically at my eyes.

'Are *you* in for a surprise!' I muttered as my precursor

gawped about him like a prize fool, then crossed the road and up Buchanan Street out of sight.

I couldn't resist the temptation (how often do *you* get to see yourself in action?) so I skirted the influence of a second jewellers' and turned on to Buchanan Street in time to see me/him kind of twist and vanish.

Uh oh.

I ran towards that spot, felt the twin squeeze of queasiness and arrived just as Stovepipe Hat was shouting:

'Stop! – in the name of the City!'

Me/him was *really* taking his time . . .

'Run faster, you fool!' I yelled.

Stovepipe Hat was screaming commands at his leather-aproned associate, leaping to his feet and chasing me/him. Leather Apron fiddled with their captive's manacle watch and the pleas for help slowed to a deep rasp. As Stovepipe Hat ran off round a corner, Leather Apron lumbered in my direction.

I timed my blunder nicely; my foot managed to slip on a cobblestone as the pocket Frankenstein caught me on the shoulder with his clunking sack. Driven by sheer panic and fear I grabbed his wrist and slammed *his* manacle watch into the tree behind me. There was a crack, and as glass shards tinkled on stone Frankie pulled away and toppled stiffly to the ground.

The captive lay immobile on his back, mouth open and emitting a low buzzing sound. It was the work of moments to twist the dial on his manacle and bring him back to life.

'Thank you,' he said. 'You must be a Meanderer.' He gave me a cool look as he tested the width of the manacle against his wrist.

'You could say that,' and I told him my story as we moved away downhill. All across the city toneless bells were sounding their chimes, and people began to emerge on to the street.

'Ah, yes,' he said knowingly as I finished. 'And I take it you wish to return to your own Qlaas Gehr – Glas Go? – yes?'

'Ever so slightly.'

'I beg your pardon?'

'I mean, yes, I do — very much!'

He nodded, smiled. 'Not difficult.'

It took a bit of dodging here and there, finding places where zones crossed, where timeflows run counter to one another. At any rate, with the help of my fellow Meanderer ('Xavier Gillespie, secretary of the Honourable and Illegal Guild of City Meanderers — at least, I was at the last meeting. Whenever that was') I found the right place at the right time. On the edge of a clock-zone we said farewell and I watched him finger his manacle, walk away, accelerate and disappear against the baroque streetscape.

With minutes to spare I was down the steps, positioned at the foot of the escalator and ready for the crowds to come bustling up from below. And as the sucker with the overcoat, scarf and frayed watchstrap appeared, I must admit that a low chuckle passed my lips. After all, if you're going to make someone's life a misery, there's no time like the present.

IAN WATSON

The Resurrection Man

I still have the ear of the resurrection man. It hasn't fallen to pieces.

Oh, I don't mean the ear of Jesus. I'm referring to a different resurrection man. Namely, William Burke – of Burke and Hare fame, or infamy if you prefer. Maybe you don't prefer. Perhaps, though this strikes me as unlikely, you're a little rusty as to the activities of Mr B and Mr H, back in the 1820s?

If so, let me hold forth. (You can't really stop me, can you?) William Burke, an Irishman, grew up as a vagabond in County Cork. In 1818, when he was twenty-six years old, he moved to Scotland to work as a navvy on the Union Canal, then under construction. A certain William Hare from Londonderry was engaged in the same task. Hare moved on to become a huckster and presently the keeper of an Edinburgh doss-house, Log's lodging-house in Tanner's Close. Burke took up residence there in 1827. That November an old lonely pensioner died in the house. Instead of having the body decently buried, Messrs B & H hit on the bright idea of selling the corpse to Dr Robert Knox's school of anatomy, for dissection by students.

The windfall of seven pounds and ten shillings persuaded these two rough Williams that there was good money to be made. Soon they, and their commonlaw wives, were luring lonesome travellers into various houses, getting the wretches drunk, then suffocating them. They used suffocation so that the corpses should seem un-injured. The culpable, or gullible, Dr Knox provided a ready market until the October of 1828 when at last his suspicious neighbours tipped off the police. Raiding Knox's home in their chimney-pipe hats, the police discovered an old woman's body in a box in the cellar.

Hare turned king's evidence; consequently Burke was hanged for murder while a huge crowd howled, 'Burke him! Burke him!'

Because Hare had peached on his partner, an attempt to indict him for the killing of one Daft Jamie failed legally; and Hare was set free from the Edinburgh Tolbooth — to vanish over the border into anonymity.

Perhaps Burke wasn't, strictly speaking, a 'resurrection man'. That sobriquet properly attached to those grave rob-bers who dug up freshly-buried corpses to sell to the medical schools. Yet Burke took this grim process one stage further, short-cutting the brief sojourn in the graveyard. Thus in a sense he and Hare were the *kings* of the resurrection men. The panic-stricken public certainly regarded them as such, and anxiety lasted for years, especially with Hare on the loose.

So how did Burke's right ear come into my family, pickled in a jar of formalin? And a hundred miles south from the scene of the crimes! On Tyneside, in the North of England. That's quite a story; though it'll be over-shadowed by the story I have to tell you presently . . .

Back in the 1820s, my great-something grandfather and his family lived here in Grosvenor Place, North Shields, in what was then a rather elegant, newly-built Georgian ter-race house. My ancestor, Mr Park — and that's my name too, Jim Park, pleased to meet you, though we can't shake hands — he owned a thriving paint shop in Clive Street, supplying both domestic and marine customers. He was also a great fancier of our native bird-life. This house in Grosvenor Place was full of cages, confining twittering and trilling and cheeping bundles of feathers. He had song thrushes, nightingales, and the mottled skylark. The lively chiff-chaff warbled its 'chivy-chavy!' He owned yellow wag-tails, which look like golden-green canaries, though these only squeak sharply — and greenfinches, forever busy washing themselves, warbling their humble, mellow 'tway' — and there were twittering sand martins, prevented from burrow-ing into their favourite clay banks like little engineers; just as the larks were prevented from ascending, the wagtails from migrating, the chiff-chaffs from weaving their oven-nests. Still, who's to say that these birds were less fortunate than their wild kin? Even if frustrated; even if the insect-eaters amongst them probably had a diet of fish-bait?

'How,' I hear you ask, 'do you know so much about the aviary of your Granddad several times removed?'

'Ah,' I reply, 'that's because I've heard his birds. I'm an ear-witness to them.'

'You're a . . . what?'

'Wait . . . and be amazed.'

Mr Park obtained all his birds from the Papageno of North Shields, Joney Aird, who trapped them with nets and limed twigs and whatever — ranging over the whole locality from the ponds on the Town Moor to the woods of Jesmond Dene and Holywell Dene, from the cornfields to the sand-dunes. Joney Aird sold his feathery captives from a stall on the fish quay. Some skippers liked to take a bird to sea, to remind them of the softness of the land, to distract from the harsh screaming of the gulls. Joney, who was on something resembling friendly terms with Mr Park, frequently called at the paint shop in Clive Street.

The bird-catcher kept his things in a dilapidated attic above Brown's Flour Mill. He was a twittery creature of nature himself. Behold his patched-up raggy jacket, often torn by crawling through briars till it seemed like a sort of plumage worn by a man who was half-bird himself. And could he whis-tle! Not Mozart, not popular airs, not hymns — but a kind of dawn chorus all of his own, which seemed to bring woodland and pondside to the fish quay. Joney lured birds by this means, and was very knowledgeable about their habits. A fey, strange fellow.

'Do you mean he was soft in the head?'

'I do not. He was always canny with his coppers, though he never accumulated too many. I refer to the Irish in him, the leprechaun strain.'

'So why, in the winter of 1828,' you may well ask, 'should Mr Park have decided that this same Joney Aird was in actuality William Hare, murderer and resurrection man?'

'I may well ask,' you say.

'Ah,' I respond, 'you must understand the nature of public hysteria.'

It was on the night between 21st and 22nd February 1823, almost six years before the revelations about the dreadful duo, that Dr Greenhow of Dockwray Square, North Shields, was called to the bedside of a Mrs Gaunt. The Gaunts only lived in Tyne Street a hundred yards away. After examining the lady and returning home, Dr Greenhow made up a suitable prescription and roused his apprentice out of bed to deliver it. Half-asleep, and knowing that it was no distance at all he had to go, the apprentice – young John Margetts – merely dragged on trousers and coat, ignored hat or stockings, and ran out.

He never returned. Enquiries next day revealed that Margetts had delivered the medicine, only halting briefly at the Gaunts'. Had he then run away to sea, on impulse in the middle of the night? Unlikely! When John Margetts quit Dr Greenhow's house he might have looked slipshod, yet in other respects he was diligent. He was almost ending the term of his apprenticeship. He had never shown the slightest interest in a mariner's life.

A mason called Mr Profit, who lived at the end of Church Street, reported hearing a scuffle in adjacent Tyne Street at that hour of the night, and a voice crying out, 'What are you doing with me?' Furthermore, a watchman stationed at Chapman's Bank in Howard Street had witnessed two men leading another down Union Street. He supposed that the man they led was drunk, not an uncommon sight, so he took no more notice.

Had agents of the Honourable East India Company kidnapped Margetts for service abroad, the way that they had kidnapped other victims? Had they fastened him under hatches in a ship in the Tyne till the hue and cry could die away?

If so, it failed to die away. During the succeeding weeks and months and even years the whole of Shields remained in a feverish froth over the lad's disappearance. For years the offices of the Hon. East India Company in London's Leadenhall Street were bombarded with passionate letters and pleas and suggestions from the citizens of Shields. Deny as they might that anyone called Margetts was on their books, they weren't believed. When news came that Afghan rebels had captured an army surgeon with a name that resembled Margetts, hysteria broke out afresh on Tyneside. Then a soldier came forward to declare that he had known Margetts in India. Now an army surgeon, Margetts had described his kidnapping. A public meeting was held to hear the soldier's tale. But later the same soldier wrote to the newspapers confessing that the Gaunt family had bribed him with £100 and the offer of their prettiest daughter in marriage – to clear *them* of suspicion.

For yes, the Hon. East India Company were not the only targets of calumny. When the news of Burke and Hare finally broke, a fellow swore that he had seen John Margetts enter the Gaunts' house that night and *never come out again*. Rumours soon spread to the effect that the Gaunts' little son – who must have been rather young six years earlier – had blurted out in school that 'they had soon done for Margetts, and put him in a box'. Before long the distressed Gaunts were having to issue writs for defamation. They won damages, but no matter; in danger of their lives from a half-crazed public they had to flee the town. New tenants moved into their house in Tyne Street, and presently a sizeable skeleton was dug up from the back garden. This proved to be that of a Newfoundland dog, beloved pet of the previous occupants. But no matter; no one quite believed it. The house was branded as haunted.

Any stranger visiting the neighbourhood became an instant suspect. One fellow who moved in, accompanied by long boxes — which actually contained machinery for spinning worsted cloth — was nearly lynched: he did escape with his life after the boxes were jemmied open at his insistence; though he wasn't any too welcome to pursue further business in Shields. The boxes *might* have contained bodies; and might do so again.

Oh, I heard it all. The rumours, the whispers, the howls of the mob crying, 'Burke him! Burke him!' at the unlucky owner of those boxes.

As for the family of the missing lad, at first they enjoyed the warmest public sympathy, and derived much practical benefit from this. A local bard gave tongue:

> 'Good people, to my tale give ear,
> Sad, shocking news you soon shall hear,
> For I have lost my darling son.
> Alas! alas! I am undone,
>   I fear he is no more.
>
> Two ruffians stole my son away,
> 'Twas on the twenty-second day,
> At five o'clock on Thursday morn.
> My heart! my heart! my son is gone,
>   And now he is no more.
>
> He with some medicine was sent,
> To cure the sick was his intent,
> When these two ruffians seiz'd their prey,
> They bound my son — took him away —
>   And never yet was found.
>
> Now, with a mother share a part,
> And judge the feelings of my heart
> As I am left for to deplore
> My dearest son I'll see no more —
>   I hope he's happy now.'

I have omitted several verses.

However, the fickle populace of Shields began to take umbrage at the way the fortunes of the Margetts had improved thanks to that selfsame kindly populace. Could it be that the Margetts knew perfectly well what had become of their son? – but weren't saying, in case the stream of charity dried up? Thus suspicion fell upon the Margetts household too. As a result, John's mother went insane. Every day she would make her way to a nearby ash-heap, and poke it for hours trying to find her son's slippers. Mr Margetts sank into imbecile dotage. John's brother eventually became a lunatic pauper confined in the Tynemouth Workhouse. What mumblings, what ravings.

Let's call another witness. I summon Mrs Cornforth of the Whitby Arms in the Low Street near the New Quay. Mrs Cornforth declares that on the night in question she heard a cry of murder. Upon looking out, she saw two men dragging a third man along the Low Street. This trio never arrived at the New Quay, otherwise – 'Next witness, please!' – the watchman posted outside the Northumberland Arms would have seen them.

Thus the three men must have cut down the lane towards Brown's Flour Mill.

By now Dr Greenhow's son, Mr Conrad Haverkam Greenhow, was pursuing his own enquiries assisted by the Reverend Mr Neal from South Shields, an Anglican precursor of Chesterton's Father Brown. Procuring a warrant, the amateur detectives searched the mill and found evidence of a struggle in Joney Aird's attic in the shape of a torn leather neck collar. True, the collar could have been ripped during over-hasty exit from a briar-patch clutching a frantic song-thrush. But Joney Aird had also disappeared. The bird had flown the nest.

Aird. Hare.

Hare. Aird. Do you note a resemblance?

No? Well, Mr Greenhow and Mr Neal did. Struck by this, and by the puzzle of where Joney Aird had vanished to, the two gentlemen were electrified by the news from

Edinburgh about Hare's arrest, and Burke's, and their terrible crimes; as was the whole country. Burke and Hare hysteria reinforced the local Margetts hysteria. Ignoring the conundrum of how Joney Aird could simultaneously have been trapping linnets on Tyneside and stifling down-and-outs in Auld Reekie — unless he metamorphosed into a bird of passage himself, and a fast one at that — Mr Greenhow prevailed on the bird-loving Mr Park to set out post-haste for Edinburgh to identify Hare as Aird; and pressed guineas on him for his fare.

Alas, winter's storms and snow-drifts held up the coach, with the result that Mr Park arrived in Edinburgh only after Hare had been released (to vanish, like a bird on the wind) and Burke had been newly executed, though not yet buried in quicklime. Because Mr Park had travelled such a long way all for nothing, the warder in charge of Burke's corpse asked if the gentleman would care for a piece of the murderer as a memento.

'Wey aye, Aa'd thank ye!' said Mr Park, who must bring back something to Shields for his trouble, apart from a chill.

The warder promptly took out his clasp-knife and cut off Burke's right ear. He presented this to Mr Park, who hurried to an apothecary's shop to have the flap of flesh embalmed in a jar of formalin. Thus for many years on the mantelshelf in Grosvenor Place the last remaining earthly trace of Burke floated in its little preservative bath.

But maybe there exist situations beyond good and evil, when ordinary reality bends a little, into the shape of an ear, say?

During my childhood that ear was an accepted part of the furniture. Some visitors would glance at it askance and refrain from comment, perhaps imagining that it was a pickled cancer, souvenir of a successful operation, or even something gynaecological. Later in life I read how the poet Verlaine's mother — I think it was Verlaine — kept the preserved foetuses (assorted sizes) of all his miscarried would-be brothers and sisters in a line-up of jars on her mantelshelf.

But if someone asked my mother, she would explain matter-of-factly, 'That's the ear of William Burke the murderer, who sold his victims' bodies to be cut up by anatomy students in Edinburgh.' And she would add, 'It's been in the family for generations.'

This was what she said to Cousin Dick from Canada, when he visited England in 1947 or so. Though the war was over, rationing was still strict and our relations in Vancouver continued to send food parcels containing tins of red salmon, which my mother would serve up in a white sauce dabbled with vinegar poured over mashed potatoes.

Cousin Dick seemed to think we should show our gratitude by being healthier, cleaner in mind and body and household management than he found us. A pickled ear was hardly a wholesome antique.

'I guess the Red Indians used to take scalps,' he remarked, looking baffled at the warped uncleanliness of the old country as my mother agitated the jar, bumping the ear from side to side. The mantelpiece – and by extension the house – would have lacked a certain character without it.

I was only five at the time, and I remember asking, 'Did they punish the man by cutting him up? Was that the only way they could stop him?'

I imagined a story-book ogre whom the citizens of Edinburgh finally trapped in a pit they dug; they could only destroy his power by cutting him into little bits and sending the pieces all over the kingdom to be kept securely in separate locations, one of these being our front-room. I gained the idea that we were, from father to son to grandson, Custodians of the Ear. An important, secret duty.

'Why, of course they didn't cut him into pieces, Jim. They hanged him.'

'Did they hang him *by* his ear? Is that how it came off?'

One of the teachers at the school where I had just started used to twist the ears of older boys who annoyed him, till they howled. Did it kill you if you had your ear torn off? Fear flooded me.

73

My mother chuckled. 'Of course not. They cut it off afterwards, and gave it to us.'

To us, us especially.

'Scalps, yeah,' muttered Cousin Dick, knitting his brows. Here was some primitive dirty native ritual which his own modern, sanitised country had outgrown. After years of generosity, to save us from malnutrition, skin diseases, web eyes, or stunted growth, he had come all this way thousands of miles along the Canadian Pacific Railway and over the Atlantic Ocean to visit the old home country, and had discovered us roosting in this dingy room in a drab town with a pickled ear as our mascot, our totem.

'What's an Atomy?' I asked my mother. 'Is that like bombs?'

'Anatomy is the body,' she explained. 'The parts of the body. How they join together inside you.'

Cousin Dick looked increasingly offended, and in fact he made his excuses within a quarter of an hour and departed to tour Scotland's glens and heathery moors where maybe other branches of our family were neater and less sordid. Cousin Dick made his living in the salmon canning industry, but fish guts were one thing; a human ear in a jar was another. The ear had large lobes and little brown hairs sprouting from inside, with a blob of orange wax still attached. Ear-wax! It hadn't even been cleaned out. Yeah, that was the score — I imagine his mind ticking over — he had sent all those cans of good red fish flesh, and we showed him our own version, our own satire on his kindness: a preserved lug-hole. Food parcels ceased thereafter.

Before too long it was 1951, which was the year of the Festival of Britain. Down in London, in Battersea Park, the silver Skylon pointed up at the clouds just like a rocketship in the new comic, *The Eagle* — and the Dome of Discovery was a larger version of the flying saucers in which the green Treens from Venus landed during a village cricket match in the far-off South of England.

I compared the coloured pictures in *The Eagle* with the

photos of the Festival in the *News Chronicle* and dearly wished we could visit London. But my father hated the smoky smell of steam trains, which made him sick — he had chest trouble; and the bus journey down the Great North Road would be a ghastly, cramped twelve hours at least. Besides, the cost!

In a fit of frustrated hope, when no one was about, I sneaked into the front-room — our ceremonial room, which was otherwise unused. Maybe if I held the ear, maybe if I rubbed it genie-in-bottle style, my dream of visiting the Festival would come true?

After all those years the lid was tight. I almost skidded the jar off the mantelpiece to shatter on the tiles of the fireplace.

Sticking in two fingers, I removed the dripping ear and dried it on my hanky then dabbed up the drops I'd spilt here and there. An ear's quite like a soft sea-shell, isn't it? You can listen to the sea in sea-shells, the hiss of the surf.

So I held Burke's ear to my own ear.

'Chivy-chavy!' cried a birdy voice. 'Chivy-chavy!'

All at once a dozen birds were cheeping, twittering and trilling. I was harkening to this same front-room of ours a century and a quarter ago, when it had housed many of Mr Park's bird cages!

Of course, I didn't realise that immediately. I wasn't yet aware of my ancestor's hobby. Mainly I thought that the ear was kept under liquid to drown the noise it would otherwise make.

Yet when I jerked the ear to arm's length I couldn't hear a thing.

So maybe the jar and the liquid were a device to deter people from picking the ear up idly from the mantelpiece, and hearing *secret* things? (I wasn't too much *au fait* with the chemistry of preservation.) What could be secret about bird-song, so much like the warblings of morse code on the short-wave radio band?

We had a big walnut radio set through in the kitchen, the glass panel marked with strange stations with names like

Hilversum . . . Aha, maybe the ear could play other tunes as well? Holding it to my own ear again, I rotated it slowly, as I would turn the dial to tune our radio set when my father let me.

Voices!

'Good people, to my tale give ear!' recited a prim young lady.

With the literalness of childhood, I decided that the ear I was clutching must be the selfsame ear to which she referred. This was the ear which had been given to her tale, of − it began to unfold − a lad's mysterious disappearance . . .

Subsequently we took a holiday. Instead of going to London to see the Festival of Britain we travelled a shorter distance in the opposite direction, just over the border into Scotland. We stayed by the seaside at St Abb's in Berwickshire, in a sort of semi-religious hotel. Before tucking into meals, all the guests would sing in chorus:

> 'Let us with a gladsome mind
> Praise the Lord for he is kind!'

Since the weather was hot, a lot of salads were served; or maybe it was cheaper to serve salads. I assumed that we were all singing, '*Lettuce*, with a gladsome mind.' Children are a literal lot.

Again I twisted the ear.

'Burke him! Burke him!' a mob roared in the distance, voices burring with hatred, like many big pussy cats with sore throats.

Even as I put the ear back into its jar, I was thinking in a very practical way that, the next time I was able to extract it, I must empty every last lurking drop out of the coil of the ear into the container itself to keep the level of liquid from diminishing and thus betraying me. Already I had become cunning, and suspected that maybe my parents might be innocent of the secret.

Might be. I wasn't sure.

As I say, our front-room was a ceremonial room, seldom entered unless there were visitors. I kept my eyes and ears open for any hint that my father and mother might slink in there surreptitiously. Often I climbed out of bed and tiptoed to the stairhead to peep. Or I lay awake and strained to decode noises in the house until my parents also turned in for the night. Within a year or two I was sure that they hadn't the slightest notion of the ear's unusual properties.

Not that *I* had many opportunities – initially – to use the ear without risk of discovery. Back in those early years, before I grew older and supervision loosened, I had to ration myself strictly, which was good discipline for the future. Instead I would play with the radio set in the kitchen. Noting my apparent interest, my father reminisced about the first radio sets when *he* was a lad, the crystal sets, and the excitement of sticking a 'cat's whisker' inside a big china cooking bowl to amplify the tinny voice of '2LO'. It occurred to me that those first radio sets, with their 'cat's whiskers', no doubt plucked from the family cat, must have been semi-organic – something like *my* private radio set, of an ear in a jar of liquid. Perhaps science had missed out on a neat trick by going in for wires and electricity and glowing valves instead.

At school I learned that the name science gives to the external ear is the 'auricle' – which naturally echoed the 'oracles' of olden days who spoke about the future; though my oracle only voiced the past. I also learned the word 'penance'. Was William Burke's ghost inhabiting his last remaining earthly segment as an atonement for his misdeeds? If so, he never spoke to me directly.

Alternatively, was Margetts' ghost involved? Was I destined to solve the mystery of his disappearance and lay his spirit to rest, whether his bones lay mouldering in an Edinburgh charnel pit or at the bottom of the sea or up the Khyber Pass?

Was Joney Aird involved? Joney the fey bird-man, endowed perhaps with second sight (thus he fled from

Brown's Flour Mill) or, in this case, with second hearing. Oh no!

It was years before I realised that the magic wasn't inherent in the murderer's ear, but in myself. Many years before I *understood* my unique talent, so fortuitously – so accidentally – awakened by our possession of an amputated sense organ. But for Burke's ear, I might never have discovered my true self, the quality which sets me apart like saint or artist from the rest of the world. I might have grown up to be like Cousin Dick the Canadian.

So welcome, new friend, to my museum of resurrection in Grosvenor Place, North Shields! Definitely not open to the public – otherwise they would chorus, 'Burke him! Burke him! Burke him with a gladsome mind!'

Nowadays a couple of dozen jars sit on the mantelpiece. Old friends, new friends. Please join them.

Do you find it gloomy here, with the curtains closed? Has the house degenerated since my father died (that chest trouble! – early heart attack) and since I moved my mother into a nursing home? Has our home grown fusty and dirty and rickety?

We wouldn't want any cleaning woman to pop in, or any decorators, or workmen to repair things, would we?

Keep it all exactly the same. Keep the spirit of the place identical, just in case my talent breathes this air, and no other.

Same easy chairs, same drapery, same cracking plaster; same ancient radio set and cooker; same china sink, same cutlery, same family photos and large framed print of a sunset. Same pile of tattered old *Eagle* comics, which I still read and enjoy, featuring Harris Tweed the portly amateur detective, Sergeant Luck of the Foreign Legion, Dan Dare the pilot of the future, and cut-away centrefolds exposing the entrails of a luxury liner (creep, little finger, from cabin to cabin) or of an imaginary space-rocket, like anatomy drawings not of cut-open animals but of huge machines. Really, all life is here inside this house. For I am the pilot of the past – which I resurrect.

Keep uninvited visitors away, too. Let them have their Canada, their fitted kitchens and TV sets and all mod. cons.

But let economics intrude, by all means. You're curious as to how I earn my keep?

'Do you have a job, Jim?'

'I was wondering when you'd ever ask. Actually, I'm away from Grosvenor Place a fair bit. So obviously I had to move my mother, now that she's ailing. I have a fine job for my purpose.'

'Really?'

'Yes, I'm a publisher's representative for the north of England. Take proof copies and covers round the book-shops and library buyers; sing praises; solicit orders. I've an instinct for what'll appeal. Give me a cover, a quick flip through, the blurb in the catalogue − and I'll tell you the advance orders to within twenty-five. Don't need to study the books in depth; I've other more vivid things to "read". Don't make a fat income by any means − don't need one − but I get around in the old Cortina car. Lancs., Yorks., Cumbria, Borders. I get around.

'And I'm disciplined about collecting specimens for my jars. Discriminating, and disciplined. Never more than twice a year. Always at least fifty miles from where I've lately been doing business.

'Likelihood of being detected? Tracked down? Not high! The events don't make much sense, or form an obvious pattern, do they? Dead body in Liverpool lacking an eye. Corpse in Leeds, with the tongue cut out. Finger missing in Manchester. Miles, and ages, apart. What on earth for? BLACK MAGIC CULT OPERATING IN NORTH OF ENGLAND? Ha ha!

'Let me unscrew this jar and take out the tongue that floats within. Hold the tongue to my own tongue, turning it to tune through the waveband of the menu. Indian lady, Leeds. Spicy banquets.

'Now put it back.

'Next jar. Eye of former merchant sailor; years of

travelling the globe. Rotate his eye against my eye to see foreign parts. Hong Kong, Singapore, Sydney.

'Take out a nose and smell such fragrances. Lilies, patchouli, bonfires, sweat.

'Take out a finger, and feel all manner of things.

'And you, my friend — I believe — were once a bit of a Casanova, eh? You had a way with the girls, and you had your way with them, didn't you? Whereas I, living the life that I have, a life that guards a secret, needed to avoid girlfriends or fiancées. While away from home, I have never been to a prostitute. Leaving aside the danger of disease, I'm sure it would have been unsatisfying. Thus: no sexual experience on a mutual basis, for Jim.

'Now, at long last, you're here to remedy that, aren't you? When I hold your organ to my organ, we shall make up for lost time. We shall make the music of love.

'How sweet life has been since Burke's ear first twittered bird-song at me! If that Irish navvy was a king of resurrection men, I must be the king of kings, the emperor, the sultan. After a banquet, after a vision of Bangkok, after a dazing with musk, let me turn out the light. In the darkness let me discover my harem.'

Good people, to my tale give ear. And eye, and tongue, and nose, and you know what.

GWYNETH JONES

Laiken Langstrand

Nigel Pickering, are you still out there?
Remember the ram caught in the thicket?
This one's for you, from G & P.

Once upon a time there was a king who broke his fishing-line. It may seem that such an incident is scarcely worth recording: but it was the last fishing-line. And on the lost end of it was the last fish-hook. Now that it was gone there would be no dinner, nor supper or breakfast either for this king and his court.

'I said you should have cast it further down the beach – '

The king looked at his courtier with some disfavour.

'Don't talk to me like that!'

'Why shouldn't I?'

The king's court consisted of one impudent eight-year-old child, with a pale, pointed face and a flame of red hair. The king himself was a very young man. His hair was limp sugar-blond, and his chin indecisive. He had large, wistful, hazel eyes, and generally possessed the kind of accident-prone, helpless appeal that spells grief, disaster and financial embarrassment for strong women: but at present his charm was somewhat battered by circumstance. The two faced each other on the bleak, muddy shore, the only human creatures – in fact the only living things in sight.

'That was my dinner as well as yours, you stupid king. You're a born loser, that's what you are. You're always, always losing things! You're hopeless!'

Around them the barren mud-flats stretched forever: a waste of puddles and gravel between the mountains and the sea where once there had been a snug little country. Laiken, the young king, did not feel that he needed to be reminded of his unhappy talent.

'This is the last straw,' he moaned.

And so it was. The impudent, red-haired child took to her heels and ran, her skinny legs flashing as she legged it for the pale, distant streak of the highway. The last straw of comfort in Laiken's miserable existence departed with her. He shouted after her, 'Courtier! Courtier?' They had both forgotten her real name. But it was no use. The child had already vanished, leaving him alone in the ocean of mud.

Laiken turned back to the sea. 'I'm hopeless,' he told the evil-coloured scummy tide that was now creaming up to his feet. 'I'm hopeless.' He knew himself well enough to realise the futility of trying to force his cringing body into the water. That couldn't be the way out. He looked after his courtier again. Maybe he could follow her — hitchhike over the border, get a job in some foreign town. The trouble was, being a king he hadn't any proper qualifications. And from what he'd heard he didn't think working for a living would suit him anyway.

But what was this? A tiny figure had appeared far away, covering ground swiftly, drab as the mud from head to toe. He strained his eyes and saw that it was a full-grown man, as skinny and poorly dressed as Laiken himself.

Soon the messenger stood panting before the king, puddle-water slopping out of his shoes. The burrs and bits of dead grass clinging untidily to his clothes showed that he'd just come over the border. There was no vegetation left at all in Laiken's kingdom.

'Sire, I am a servant of the Oracle. In answer to your query —'

(It had been two years ago that they had sent off to ask the Oracle. Laiken remembered the tiny flutter of hope as the delegation set out — though even then there had been very little left worth saving.)

'A servant of the Oracle? Well, where's my delegation? — '

The man looked embarrassed. 'Er — they're not going to bother coming back, Sire.'

No one knew why the Great Sea Serpent had decided to wreck their country, but no one really cared any more. Most of the population had already departed before the delegation left. The last stragglers had grown tired of waiting months ago. Whatever advice the Oracle might provide, it came far too late to do any good.

The messenger stared around, shaking his head mournfully. He'd seen some wastelands in his time, owing to the nature of his work, but this beat them all.

'Come on, come on, man.'

'The answer of the Oracle is, that the power of the king in the hands of the people will restore Laiken's lands and destroy the Great Sea Serpent.'

'The power of the king?'

That was a poor joke. He turned to glare at the thick brown water that had just swallowed his fish-hook.

'In the hands of the people . . .'

'Courtier!' yelled the king, frantically.

'Well, that's it. Now usually we'd invoice you for the full amount, but owing to the circumstances . . . I've had a terrible job getting here. There's no transport. I've been sleeping rough — '

King Laiken ignored him. Away he sped across the mud, shouting furiously. Half the ransom of his kingdom had just slipped from his grasp, and he wasn't going to let the other half escape him.

The messenger wasn't really surprised. As a professional bringer of bad tidings he'd had worse receptions. Muttering gloomily to himself about out-of-pocket expenses he set off in pursuit at a tired jog trot, his ruined shoes squelching. The drab tide lapped on the greyish-brown shore, and the barren flats lay sad and silent and empty.

Laiken managed to evade the servant of the Oracle, and to reach a more comfortable country. But he didn't find it easy to hold down a job. He kept running after red-haired children in the street and grabbing at them, which earned him a rather unsavoury reputation. As the calculated age of his quarry increased he was in less danger from the law or local vigilantes, but his other problems grew on him. He drifted and slithered down the social scale. Laiken was tired. He was tired of trying to keep boring, dead-end jobs. He was tired of his future and tired of his past. He managed to get drunk quite often, despite his poverty, because he never did acquire a head for alcohol. What he liked to do best was to sit in a comfortable stupor in some dark corner of his current local, and forget he was alive.

He was busy getting himself into his disgusting state one evening, in a bar in a small, dirty port on the other side of the world from his lost kingdom, when he found himself listening half-resentfully to the talk of some seamen who had settled down nearby. It was good, drunken talk. Floating islands appeared in the discussion, and people whose heads grew out of their armpits, and fire-breathing dragons. Another Laiken would have enjoyed it all immensely, and might even have joined in. This Laiken sat recalling his former cheerful nature and almost weeping in self-pity — until suddenly a new subject arose, and jerked him out of his misery. The sailors were describing a place they called the Langstrand. There was a complex, fuddled explanation of how tides work all around the world, and the conclusion drawn that somewhere, sometime, everything that ever goes into the sea has to come out again. And far away (in fact, the speaker didn't know the exact location, but he knew a man who did), far away from anywhere, you must be able to find the wonderful stretch of shore where all the lost things came to be found. The Langstrand.

Laiken jumped up and banged down his glass. He was just drunk enough to see hope in the feeblest of plans. 'That's where I'm going!' he shouted. 'I see it all now. I just haven't been *tackling things from the right angle!* Hahaha!'

Everybody turned to stare. Laiken hurried out of the bar covered in embarrassment, but his heart was leaping. At last his life had purpose again. He would pursue the fish-hook. Laiken saw it very clearly in his mind's eye: lying all shiny and bright on a bed of clean silvery sand. The Langstrand.

So that was how Laiken found a use for his principal talent. There goes Laiken Langstrand, people would say, admiringly. He's a real loser – you must get him to tell you the story. From that day on he wasn't drifting any more: he was searching. He still spent a lot of time getting drunk in seedy bars. But now he usually didn't have to pay for the drinks. A man with a quest is someone to be respected.

In fact when he stood one day and heard a man say, 'Yes, just turn to your left where the fingerpost says "To the Beach" ', Laiken felt more than a little uneasy. He resented the careless way the Langstrand had turned up with no fanfares or fireworks, and he wasn't sure he was ready for the chores of success. His uneasiness certainly did not lessen as he cleared the final dunes and surveyed that ten-mile sweep of white sand still called, though hor-ribly mutilated, the most beautiful beach in the world. Laiken was not alone. He was looking down on a ten-mile shanty town. Thousands of strange people in bizarre and ragged garments were wandering about, and in front of some of the grubby little huts were smoky fires. With a deep, bitter sigh Laiken stepped down onto the sand.

He found an old abandoned hut to live in, made friends with his neighbours and was soon sponging off the tourists, drinking all night and sleeping half the day like a regular old strandie. After some months he was half-way through his first sweep of the ten miles, and had developed a serious crush on a girl called Mysotis, who lived in the hut next door. Her appearence was arresting. She wore her hair in thick, short, springy curls of brightest blue, and the eyes that looked out of her narrow, fine-boned face were yellow as mustard. However, it wasn't the bizarre colour-scheme that really intrigued him. No, it wasn't the colour of her eyes, but their direction. Mysotis was never seen beachcombing. She was clearly one of the beach's professional camp-followers: an amiable group of young men and women who preyed on any sex-starved questing beasts who still had money; and worked the tourist trade. But all the other camp-followers kept to beach etiquette in one respect at least. They cruised the Langstrand way, with their eyes hardly ever leaving the littered sand. Mysotis walked with her head up.

One day Laiken devised a cunning plot. He would go round to the strange girl's hut and ask to borrow a cup of sugar. They would strike up a conversation about food (always a fascinating topic on the beach) and he would invite her back to share his meal. He tidied the hut and arranged an artistic impression of interrupted cooking. Then it occurred to him that he'd better hide his own sugar. He poured his whole supply into a cup, took it out behind the huts and dug a sandy hole . . . As he was digging he started to muse on the lost treasures that must be buried in this sand. He had found some very strange things by the sea's edge himself; and he had left them all lying, wondering if their owners would ever come to collect them. Funny to think of all the ends of stories waiting here. But never, never a fish-hook . . .

Laiken woke up, to find the sand smooth again under his hands. He had buried the sugar, and absentmindedly buried the cup too.

'Oh no −' he wailed.

He only possessed one cup. Now they'd both have to drink out of jam-jars. He scrabbled about helplessly: and eventually noticed the girl with the yellow eyes. She was watching with open amusement.

'What's the matter, neighbour?'

'Oh, Mysotis. I was just coming round to borrow a cup of sugar from you. But — um, I seem to have lost my cup.'

There was a mocking twinkle in her yellow eyes. He realised that she had been standing there by the dune throughout his whole absurd little performance. He began to blush.

Mysotis laughed. 'Well, why don't you come round anyway. You can share my supper. There happens to be plenty for two.'

After they had eaten he asked her about the attitude of her eyes.

'It's simple,' she said. 'If your eyes should be turned down because you are a searcher, then my eyes should be turned upwards.'

Laiken looked bemused.

'So you didn't come to the beach to look for something?'

'No, I came here from the other direction.'

'Ah, I see. Someone is looking for you?'

She grinned, with a flash of small pointed teeth. 'The man who is going to kill my father. I don't know his name, I'm afraid.'

The romance blossomed swiftly. Mysotis's hut was much roomier and more weatherproof than Laiken's old lean-to. So Laiken moved in, and soon became convinced that he had found the end of his life's quest after all. But when he vowed eternal love Mysotis only laughed. He felt a little sorry for himself on this account, but he was brave about it.

Laiken went on searching and Mysotis went on waiting to be found. But in spite of this proper behaviour their relationship caused talk. It seemed to be going on for an indecent length of time by Langstrand standards and people were offended. The nasty gossip reached Laiken at last (it had reached Mysotis long before, of course) and there was a tearful scene. Laiken vowed love more eternal than ever; he swore that nothing could possibly come between them. And at last Mysotis, who had shed no tears, looked into those swimming, wistful, hazel eyes and decided it might be true.

'Laiken, there are things you don't know about me . . .'

'I don't care about your past,' he sobbed courageously. 'You don't have to tell me anything!'

'I will tell, I will tell you. If we are lovers, then you should know. Laiken, what am I?'

'You're the kindest, sweetest, loveliest woman (snivel) – '

She sighed. 'Am I really? Am I a woman, Laiken? Look at my hair. Did you ever see a woman with blue hair before?'

Laiken blinked through his tears. 'Erm, well, I don't mind. You can wear it green or pink if you like. It's your hair, after all.'

'Laiken, pass your hand along my arm.'

Her skin was always dry, always cool. It had a faint rasp to it, like a cat's tongue. He'd noticed this roughness often, but never thought anything of it.

'Look closer – ' she whispered.

And then he saw the tiny yellow scales.

'What *are* you?'

'I am the child of a king from under the sea.'

Laiken gasped. He gaped in sentimental wonder at the mythical beauty in his arms.

'You're a mermaid!'

Mysotis looked away. 'Sort of – ' she agreed.

'And you're a princess – why, isn't that strange. Because, you know, I used to be a king. Did I ever tell you the story?'

Beach people were always swapping their quest stories. It was art, it was entertainment; and everybody understood that you wouldn't get the same story from the same strandie twice. Laiken had told Mysotis several versions of his epic. But now, for some reason, he told her the truth.

And while he told her, the mermaid's hand stole up to her throat, to a little sharkskin pouch she always wore around her neck on a cord of woven seaweed.

'So the Great Serpent sucked away all our water . . . Why, no one knows. Anyway, the place is a wreck. But if ever I find my old fish-hook I'll be able to sort it out, I'm certain of that. Why, what's wrong, Mysotis? You look quite ill.'

'When I was young,' said the mermaid, 'my father found out by magic that, through me, a mortal man would destroy him. He tried to get rid of me by making me come and live on the land. I begged for mercy, and he said I could have the power to breathe dry air but it would cost half a king's ransom. I was at my wits' end, but then a sea witch gave me this amulet. She said she had found it on the sea-bed. My father laughed when he found out and said this thing couldn't be in better care; and he was satisfied. As long as I keep it, I live. If I lose it, I will die.'

The lovers stared at one another. Laiken had turned a little pale. Mysotis seemed to be waiting for him to speak, but he said nothing.

At last she said, abruptly, 'Of course, this all happened a very long time ago. Mermaids don't age like human beings, you know.'

'How long – ?'

'Oh, about five hundred years.'

Laiken looked thoughtful. The mermaid shivered, touched the little pouch again and quickly jerked her hand away.

A few days later, Laiken moved out of the shared hut. He said he needed some time to be alone.

Mysotis went walking very early one morning shortly after Laiken had left her. Perhaps it was the half-light that made her afraid she would stumble, but she never lifted her eyes from the sand. She'd almost knocked herself out on the post before she saw the noticeboard that had sprung up overnight. The paint was shiny and the lettering was clear.

GENERAL DEPARTMENT OF CLAIMS

A CLAIMANTS' DEPARTMENT WILL BE SET
UP ON THE BEACH FOR THE SPACE OF ONE
MONTH. A DOCTOR IN CLAIMS WILL DEAL
WITH DEMANDS CONCERNING LOST PRO-
PERTY LOVE OR FORTUNE CLAIMED TO BE
LYING ABOUT THIS BEACH. THEREAFTER
THE BEACH WILL BE CLEARED. THIS IS YOUR
LAST WARNING.
            BY ORDER.

It was also their first warning, but never mind about that.
'What are we going to do?'
'We'll fight!'
'Is it worth it?'
'After all, it's not the only beach on the pebble.'
The Doctor in Claims set up shop in a big white
hygienic-looking tent. A steady trickle of beachcombers
went in, and nearly all of them came out the other side and
kept on walking. Mysotis and Laiken met one night by the
sea's margin, below the swiftly fragmenting shanty town.
'You know what I have in my amulet pouch?'
'I think so.'
'It was no use lying, then.'
'Forget about it. I don't care,' Laiken muttered sulkily.
'I wasn't very good at being a king anyway.'
'Supposing it wasn't around my neck? If you had found
it the way you dreamed you might, lying on the sand looking up at you. Would you have thrown it back to the sea
and come home to our hut for supper? Suppose you didn't
have to kill me. Only to leave me, marry a suitable
princess, forget me?'
There was no need for him to speak.
'Take it, then,' she told him calmly, 'if the wasteland is
more important than what we have. I only want you to be
happy. And you never know, my father may have forgotten about me by now.'

90

Two figures on the shore, the sound of the sea, and not another living thing in sight. Laiken told himself he couldn't tell what she really wanted. Perhaps she was tired of passing for human.

'Mysotis, I — '

'Ah — '

'I need time. I don't know what to do. Give me another week.'

Mysotis's strange eyes had been warmly bright a moment before, like water with the sun on it. Now they turned cool and shadowed.

'Of course,' she agreed. 'Such a difficult choice, you need to think it over.'

And they parted again.

Laiken's week was just about up when he was summoned to the big white tent. The Doctor in Claims wanted to see him. Why Laiken, out of all the lost souls who still remained? He didn't know. He stood in the porch feeling rather frightened and obscurely guilty. Everyone knew by now that the Doctor in Claims was a woman. Maybe she's fallen in love with me, he thought. The porch of the tent was decorated like a waiting-room, with big potted plants arranged beside the furniture on the canvas floor and a mirror standing by one wall. He looked in the mirror, and his idea didn't seem too unlikely. He almost started thinking about his coming interview with Mysotis: but that was unpleasant.

'Laiken Langstrand? Doctor Kortia will see you now.'

He pushed back the flap nervously. The Doctor's secretary slipped by him, smirking. Laiken was left alone, facing a young woman whose hair was a cap of vivid rust red and whose face was still as bright and impudent as ever.

'Kortia?' he gasped.

'It stuck,' she explained, simply.

Laiken wished the floor would open up and swallow

him. For he suddenly saw the figure in the waiting-room mirror clearly: and all the years of his quest fell on him with a horrible crushing weight. 'I always knew we'd meet again,' Kortia told him. 'It was because of you, Laiken, that I took up a career in the lost property business, just in the hope that one day our paths would cross.'

They talked and talked. That little country between the mountains and the sea lived again: its landscapes, its people, its bad jokes. Kortia didn't know about any faithful mermaid. To her Laiken was still the silly but charming young king of her childhood. In all innocence, she invited him back to her living-quarters. She cooked up a celebration meal on her little camp kitchen. Laiken stayed to eat, and drink her wine: they eyes meeting often, and fingers touching over the food and drink.

Laiken, drunk on nostalgia and sentiment, had forgotten entirely that he was supposed to be meeting his lover down on the shore, to accept or refuse her extraordinary sacrifice. He was astonished when he woke up in the middle of the night to find Mysotis's yellow eyes staring at him. He sat up sharply, pulling the blankets around his chin. Kortia stirred and muttered, cuddling up close in the narrow camp bed.

'Ah, Mysotis. Ah, I can explain – an old friend. It doesn't mean anything – '

His feeble babble faded into a whimper. He had noticed that the mermaid was not wearing her human form.

Mysotis knew he was not deliberately insulting her. She knew that he had innocently forgotten their tryst. But she was, after all, a princess of sorts: and she was desperately in love with poor Laiken. A lightning, sinuous movement passed between the two alien, warm bodies. The human girl shuddered, gasped once without waking, and lay deathly still.

'You've killed her!' wailed Laiken.

'I hope so,' hissed the blue-and-yellow serpent. 'And why not? You would have killed me, tonight, wouldn't you?'

Then she was gone, and Laiken was left staring at the little sharkskin pouch lying on its broken cord beside Kortia's body.

'Keep it,' whispered Mysotis's voice in his ear. 'I don't want it any more.'

Laiken's fingers clutched his heart's desire, but he didn't know it. His eyes wild with horror, he ran sobbing from the tent, down over the deserted sands: and went on running and running until the salt water closed over his head . . . As he started to choke and drown he remembered another seashore with bitterness. He could have saved everyone a lot of trouble . . .

The next thing Laiken knew, someone was speaking to him: a rich, cold muscular broth of a voice which was somehow not entirely unfamiliar.

'Your eyes have a very odd look in them this morning, creature,' drawled this tremendous voice idly. 'Are you feeling unwell?'

'Where am I?' asked Laiken dazedly. 'Is this hell?'

'Oh, how boring. You've started going sane. Now who would have thought it, after all these years?'

'Years?' repeated Laiken.

He was sitting on something like a pile of enormous old tyres. But the thick, rubbery rings pulsed rhythmically, and seemed full of steely life.

'Dear me. Do I understand that the whole of our pleasant relationship has now slipped your mind? What's the last thing you remember, Laiken?'

He shuddered. 'The tent . . . Kortia dead. Drowning.'

The Great Serpent sighed. 'Ah well, I suppose all good things must come to an end. Unless − do you think if I were to tap you gently with the tip of my tail that would reverse this unwelcome development?'

Laiken observed the tail-tip in question. There was very little doubt as to the result of such a manoeuvre.

'By all means, tap away,' he sighed. 'But first, if you

93

don't mind. How is it I'm not dead already? How did I learn to breathe water?'

'Ah, that's very simple. You hold clutched in your hand a powerful amulet. It appears that a charm which can keep a sea-creature alive in the dry air also works in reverse. Isn't that interesting? You know, it is my own magic but I still find out something new about it every day.' After a pause, the great voice chuckled. 'Little man, I know more of your story than you guess. Do tell me: why have you not instantly dropped that silly fish-hook? You do want to die, don't you?'

Laiken stared at the thing in his hand. 'I don't know. I suppose I should.'

A deep sigh quivered through all the massive shining coils. 'Ah, Laiken, you don't remember now, but we have had some fine talks, you and I, about magic and prophecy, predestination and free will . . . A long time ago – a long time by your standards, that is – I learned that the king of a distant country would cause my death. Naturally, I laid that country to waste. It was a thoughtless reflex, the old, blind urge to hang on to power. For the truth is, I *want* to die. I'm old, I'm tired. It's time to let go . . . Sometimes, you know, I think occult knowledge is more trouble than it's worth . . . these foolish twists and turns that only lead you back to where you started. Laiken, if your death-wish is not so urgent at the moment you could do me a favour before you go.'

'What's that?'

'Just get up and start walking. The rest will follow.'

Laiken got up and started walking. His wits were feeling rather addled again. What was happening? Was this the cause and the circuitous end of all the tragic confusion of his life? Quite soon his head broke the surface and Laiken walked on, dripping and naked, out of the sea. He stood alone with the barren land behind him, and watched two figures coming slowly towards him along the shore, a woman and a boy. As they approached he saw that the woman was Mysotis. The boy seemed to be about fifteen years old. He had red hair.

94

'What are you doing here?' asked the king.

She was as beautiful as ever. He could not imagine how he could have contemplated exchanging her for any other love, at any price.

'I tried to save her for your sake, Laiken. But it was no good in the end. My own poison was too strong for me, and she died soon after the child was born. I brought him home, as you see. It seemed the least I could do. Besides, where else should I live? Between the water and the land I will stay forever, belonging to neither.'

'You are breathing dry air.'

'Because I have with me the other half of the ransom, don't you see?'

The red-haired boy was staring with calm disapproval at his father's nakedness. The two lovers stared at each other.

'You have the fish-hook? Then let the boy cast his line.'

'Mysotis − can you forgive me?'

'Oh, yes. You can't help your nature.'

'Then why are you looking so sad? This is the happy ending, isn't it? Everything's healed, we start again − '

King Laiken held the mermaid in his arms. Behind them the boy tossed his line out over the waves. The fish-hook disappeared, and it was done. There was a moment's doomladen silence, and then the whole ocean seemed to rear up into the sky. But it wasn't the ocean, it was the great Lord of the Sea himself. The tiny figure of the boy on the shore flicked its line casually over its shoulder to cast up the catch. The whole sky turned black as the great serpent passed over them, and then his enormous body fell onto the land.

Mysotis was in Laiken's arms but she was falling. He stumbled to his knees as she crumpled on the sand.

'Mysotis, what's happening to you?'

'Through me, a mortal has destroyed my father. Don't you understand? I said my father was a king under the sea but did I ever mention a mother? I never had one. I am a work of magic, and when the sorcerer dies, I too must die: die or change . . .'

She was changing, changing. There was a strange, loud, rushing sound in Laiken's ears: he thought it was his own blood pulsing.

'Mysotis, I love you. It's true, this time. Oh, I can't bear to lose you again, I'd give everything – '

'Don't cry Laiken, poor boy. You will never lose me now. Never lose me, never forget me . . .'

The mermaid was gone. Laiken found himself alone, standing up to his thighs in a great river, and his arms were full of flowers.

If you go to Laiken's country now you may still see him. It is not much talked about but everyone knows where you can find the President's old mad father. He'll be paddling by the bank of the river, mumbling to himself: 'I used to have a problem but not any more. I never lose things now. Never lose her, she's mine forever.' And his arms will be full of blue-petalled, yellow-eyed forget-me-nots.

ANNE GAY

Roman Games

Rome station seemed to rattle as the train began its farewells. A hand, freeze-frame black-and-white, banged silently on the outside of the pullman's double-glazing that slid away. Inside, a boy with his leg in plaster babbled in anguished Italian. In her corner, Sister Thomas read a detective book so that − for once − she could pierce the secrets of men's souls. It was typical, so it was, that she almost missed the Drama of the Ticket, as she hid in her book from her failure in Rome. And when she got back to Ireland − ?

'My ticket!' The boy pulled at her skirt. 'I no have the my ticket!'

Sister Tom looked: saw the boy with his crutches, whose ticket was outside the window. The poor bobbing uncle, distraught, tied to the train's motion by the ticket he could not pass in to the nephew, trotting along the platform walloping the panes. A frenzy of silent shouting like a fish outside its bowl.

Sister Thomas ran to the door, hurled it back in its track; the corridor; the carriage door; slammed down the window and snatched the ticket.

'*Grazie! Mille grazi* − '

The platform fell away to gravel: goodbye uncle. Outside the station it was dark. Sister Thomas pushed the window up, no longer leaning on the sign that said 'It is dangerous to lean out of the window'. Where her head might have been, a telegraph pole whizzed past. A miracle that passed her by.

Nephew, his leg horizontal in graffiti and gypsum, was very thankful in his heathen tongue. A pity our somewhat good sister didn't understand one word of the canticle. But she smiled.

The train headed north as Sister Tom tried to remember what faith was like. It was impossible. So she tried to sleep instead.

Stops and stations, then a long blank journey towards dawn. The boy and the graffiti on his leg were gone. The Rome–Ostend express was a world of light and life travelling through the outer darkness of Italy.

What of Thomasina's opponent? She's hungry, that's what. Dawn is brilliant up in the mountains, and on this particular dawn she blunders over the valleys, hunting. Her scales, like her teeth, need cleaning. As her wings crank her stiffly over the rosy Alps, she thinks of fresh marrow and picking her fangs afterwards with a nice, juicy rib.

The trouble is, people don't believe in her any more. There isn't room in this bright winter's sky for her and jumbo jets: their slip-streams dull her scales and bring on her bronchitis. Draco Vulgaris is mucky with other people's neglect.

She turns her head, trying to spot a victim. Hope – and memories – of feasts always make her nostalgic. Those Romans were nice and crunchy with brass and spiky iron. There'd been a virgin or two – knight-bait, they were, a morning's sport *molto bene*, very good. Thieves and murderers, fat millers with lungs *en croute*.

Draco spotted the train as a stream of colours, hugging the snowy side of the pass. She spiralled in lower. Sulphurated saliva dripped from her jaws. Her last meal was partisans with gunpowder sauce. Dinner was forty years ago and she was ready for breakfast.

Round One

In her compartment, only Sister Tom was awake. It was incredibly hot, redolent of garlic and bodily effluents. The double-glazing, of course, maintained its efficient seal. Five-feet-eight of Irish nun did not fit the seat; her short-cropped head was jammed at an uncomfortable angle, so that every time her unwilling eyes jolted open she could see the frightening mountains. Little faith and less hair did a poor job of cushioning her. Her curls had stopped growing by themselves thirty years ago. She sometimes thought her hair was more religious than she was.

'*Is this a dragon I see before me?*' Sister Tom rapidly checked her watch, set to this foreign time. Not yet six o'clock. Besides − when the frost-jewelled cliff shot by − Holy Mary! − the abyss held no dragons.

Back in her village in the Mountains of Mourne − proper mountains they were, nice and soft and gentle − it would be just past three o'clock, the witching hour. Many's the night Sister Tom had sat up with the dead in a candle-lit room. *She* knew that midnight was nothing. But three o'clock in the morning, when death squeezes the souls out of bodies, that was when horrors enter the mind of a nun. For doesn't a nun see only the underside of men, now? At three o'clock by God's time in would slide a banshee, maybe, in the soft mist around the corner of vision. Or a large, creaky dragon over the sudden, jagged Alps.

It was nothing, now. Just a bad dream. And it was gone.

Draco dimmed a little more, wounded by disbelief.

Dragon 0 − Sister Thomas 1.

Round Two

Draco singed a pine tree out of pique. Disbelief always put her in a flaming temper. No doubt she had once been a pure, innocent hatchling, but she'd soon grown out of a diet of sheep and chamois. We are what we eat, and she

99

had eaten liars, cheats, cowards and killers, man-unkind with all his little failings. In short, she had eaten people.

After the nightmare, Sister Tom needed air. Yawning and stretching, she staggered along the corridor as the train swayed round the cornice. At the carriage door, she lit a filthy, cheap, foreign cigarette, all the better to savour the cold air. She rested her forearms on the top of the window, trying not to see the river right down in the black depths of the gorge. Sure the Alps were pretty now, but better with a picture-frame safe around them.

More importantly, could a nun who apparently believed in dragons not have a little more faith in God?

There it was again! Dull bronze, dull green, dull soot – Mother of God, it was there before her eyes! All it needed to be believable was a tongue of –

Flame ripped out at the smart carriages, crafted by robots in Milan. The blue paint blistered, that was all.

No is like the old days, thought Draco nostalgically, going through her gizzard to find another belch. *Then I really make them blaze!*

Pride was just one of the sins she had consumed.

'Oh God, I wish I wasn't an atheist,' a humorist once said in danger. Sister Tom prayed, for real this time, as if it might do her some good. Too long had prayer been a comfy, cosy thing, like her night-time Guinness or warm slippers.

Hands together, eyes closed – but with one eye cheating, because the dragon was closer than God, Sister Thomas *prayed*. Harder still, when the dragon's talons raked along the roof, and in fear Sister Tom closed her other eye.

Draco backwinged, puzzled, and hauled herself higher in retreat. Why hadn't her claws ripped through the metal? The pink sun shone in her eyes and she shook her head in annoyance. She must be getting old.

Arrowing her tail, she dived like a cormorant, trying, trying, trying again. A downdraught from the snowfields gave her a helpful shove.

'Saints preserve us!' croaked our nun, recognising all the symptoms of fear from her thrillers.

It *was* dangerous to lean out, and she didn't need the notice to tell her. Head and shoulders crammed through the window, Sister Tom howled her prayers upwards, eye to eye with the dragon, only partly so she wouldn't see the chasm below.

English, Latin and Gaelic — Sister Tom tried everything. *What did the dragon speak? What would work?*

Draco was an omnivore. That is, she'd eaten men of all tongues, and so she spoke the lot. And she knew the power of prayer, whether the deity was called Mithras or God.

Nonchalantly she wheeled away over an arete.

'Saints be praised!' cried Sister Tom, falling to her knees in the corridor the minute the beast was gone. The sky was as blue as Mary's robe, the mountains white and majestic. Pale sunlight gilded all, even the battered old face with its thorny crown of Irish hair, even the bulbous nose her mother had passed on from the tinker who'd made her laugh — until she conceived Sister Tom. She'd not laughed then till the dates worked out, and it might have been her husband after all.

Sister Tom shook her head. What a terrible confession to hear from her own darlin' mother on her deathbed. Had that started her doubts?

What if it had? She'd done a Saint Patrick! Smiling, full of faith, she resolved to give up the weed for good and put the money in the poorbox. This would be her last cigarette. Faith! She could do it now.

Dragon 1 — Sister Thomas 2

Round Three

Draco was in a bad way. *Quindi* — she'd pretended she'd just changed her mind, but the prayers had made her sick *de vero*. Perched on a black rock in the corrie, her tail

101

draggled on the snow and her head drooping, she gave way to the pains that griped in her stomachs. She almost over-balanced when she put a claw down her throat, but the indigestible prayer gave her hell. It wouldn't come out but wouldn't stay down.

Sister Tom walked back along the bouncing corridor, bouncing herself with joy. The spring-door fought back when she slid it open, but what did it matter today?

The boy with the broken leg had got out at Turin; now two tubby men slept on his seat. One was a salesman, one an accountant; besuited but naïve in sleep, their scepticism dormant in their pockets with their spectacles. It was too early yet for businessmen.

What time was it? Sister Tom's watch on its old leather strap said still before six; she could tell by its single pointer.

'Must get a big hand,' said Sister Tom to herself, and opened her one bottle of Lambrusco. 'Never too early for a heroine to drink,' and she thanked God for screw-caps. She was in that rare, generous mood that ascribes to the Creator all the good things He – or She? – had dreamt up. Sister Tom would have thanked God for the velcro on her veil if she'd thought of it.

Imagine her surprise, then, as she swigged surreptitiously from her bottle – silently, out of consideration for her sleeping partners, watching the cars on the autostrada – and Draco appeared!

For Draco had eaten atheists, and their proteins swallowed prayers in the stomach of unbelief. It just took time.

Sister Tom gulped wine from the bottle. The beast was still there, though, hovering behind a big motorway sign, lurking until the sparse, early cars thinned out.

The cheek of it! thought Sister Tom, pushing the damned door sideways. Pound, pound, went her boots along the corridor, and her heart did the same. Back to the carriage door, where a dog-end lay before the open window.

What weapon could she use this time? If it was sweat,

she'd have won hands down. Sister Tom lit a cigarette with shaking matches.

Sure the beast was so vain, wasn't she creaking over the train now? Making sure Sister Tom had seen her. And on the stilted autostrada, no cars but one for miles. A mother – black hair, blue coat – was peering in its bonnet that was open to curses, if not to coercion. For the thing wouldn't start.

Lazily cocking her tail as a snoot at the nun, Draco strolled across the sky. What could the nun do, but nothing and rage?

On its corniche, the train had stopped for no reason, as trains do. On the flyover with delusions of grandeur, the woman was slamming shut the boot, putting up a *push-chair*, wheeling her *baby* to the emergency phone! Mother of God, the dragon was going to –

'You're no dragon at all! Just an overgrown lizard, so y'are!'

Draco balked in surprise, and had to flap twice to stay up.

'Dragons are noble, glittering beasts,' yelled the woman who'd kissed the Blarney Stone. 'Hordes of treasure they've got, and never eat less than a virgin princess. You don't want her – she'd not make a mouthful for ye.'

And she prayed again in desperation for a natural catastrophe, just a little one. Dragon-size, for preference.

Vanity, vanity, all is vanity. Our present imperfect Draco had eaten plenty of it. She leered at her puny foe – grubby grey serge and skin, waving a fist through the window of the train – and Draco showed off her vanity.

And for all Sister Tom's prayer, there wasn't a cloud in the sky, not a ghost of an avalanche.

Flaming, screaming, terrible, Draco dive-bombed the mother.

Madonna of the motorway! Yes, she ran – but she snatched her baby to her breast and fled – towards the phone.

Draco's breath hurled the pushchair *through* the parapet. Sister Tom watched the pushchair's parachute progression. Held on its web of metal, it tumbled into the gorge, a gorgeous red flare on fire on its charred black frame.

Sister Tom almost collapsed – vertigo was catching. Two all.

Round Four

Then Draco, seeing no other cars about, nor anyone else astir on the sleepy train, craftily burnt up the phone. Vain, yes, about her ability to destroy, to scare, to terrify. But smart enough to know that armies in the eighties have tracker-planes and bombs. And all for the price of a phone-call.

She settled, wings spanning the concrete carriageway, teasing tufts of fire towards the mother. The woman stopped. Stood still, while a wind from nowhere picked up her skirts. The baby wailed – wouldn't you? But the woman didn't. Pale face, pale legs – only the blue of her clothes was colour against the white of the concrete and the black of the cliffs. Mouth slack, she didn't scream. She could see the monster's eyes.

With an insolent wink at the nun, on the train on the hillside helpless across the yards and yards of air, Draco advanced. A step at a time.

'My prayers are useless!' Thomasina – she'd be Sister Tom no longer! – slammed her forehead on the window.

Prayer was no good! The trip to Rome had done no good. A lifetime's savings gone to *prove* faith had no virtue. The Vatican was just a museum. All those monuments of marble and gold, canvas and flesh, to glorify God. And what had God got to show for it? People.

And Thomasina had heard enough confessions to know what people were.

Draco strutted another step. Her wings rattled in a sudden gale while she concentrated on grandstanding to the arena. Even her cockscomb crest was playing to the crowd.

Even the mother's tear-ducts were frozen with fear.

Like a gladiator, Draco minced forward. Step by step. Closed in for the kill. Belched like hell.

Will the Madonna die? Will her infant?

Thomasina couldn't watch faith's final death.

Out sprang the fire –

Two things happened. All over Europe on the farmers' news, weathermen moved symbols to show wind over the Alps. A small, natural catastrophe, just dragon-sized: the mini-hurricane blew the dragon's flames in again. In short, Draco backfired.

And while Draco skittered in surprise and the child cried and the woman's shaky legs tottered her away as far as the parapet, and while the weathermen pushed stick-on isobars around their maps, and the full-cheeked wind roared off down the valley, carooming off the train – while all that was going on, our doubting-again Thomasina from back of Ballymartin groaned a prayer for the effectiveness of prayer. Despairing, self-loathing, eyes shut, she missed the lot.

Around another cigarette she wailed, 'Oh Lord, help Thou mine unbelief!'

Slowly, slowly, slowly, lace appeared on Draco's skin. The woman saw cliffs through Draco's wings. She saw the veins, the viscera, the ichor.

Draco glanced wildly at herself, the inner dragon. *Ecco qua!* She hadn't known her guts were *that* colour.

And Sister Tom opened one eye just a crack, peeking to see where the thunderbolt had got to. She couldn't believe her eye.

The train started up again with a jolt. Away on the autostrada hung a surprised outline of a dragon, made entirely of soot. The tail end of the wind pulled it along to play. Like a newspaper kite, it fell to bits.

As the train rounded a bend, all Sister Tom could see was the woman in blue with a baby, the Madonna of the Flaming Phone-Booth. Sister Tom hoped her car would start.

Dragon 3 — Sister Thomas 4.

Oh — and Sister Tom took out a cigarette to savour with her heroism's wine. And sent the rest of the packet spinning into the abyss.

JOHN CLUTE

Eden Sounding

After arranging safe passage for their toboggans, the mice came in chiming cohorts from all the nooks and crannies of their snow-choked subterranean demesne to the grotto of the enormous body of the Lord, travelling only at night, or within trees. The six garlanded and beribboned mimes who had commanded their presence awaited them at the carved mouth of the cave, and paraded at their head into the incubation chamber and the life-support tank at its heart, where the flesh of the Lord lay steaming from its recent birth. Niches popped open in the sides of the enormous ancient vehicle, revealing stacks of body gloves to protect both mouse and mime against radiation, for the servants of the Lord were nocturnal, easily damaged by the light of the sun.

'Hurry hurry,' carolled the mimes, ceremonial spangles dancing time to the hoarse urgent sprechstimme of the song, and obediently, inch by inch, disregarding the basso complaints of the onboard incubation monitor, the seventy valiant and deeply loyal mice shifted the great armoured coffer into the ferocity of the open air, where giant dray snowshoes awaited to speed the task. The rays of the sun lanced through the body gloves. After several days of unremitting labour, the surviving mice — none less than middle-aged after so long in the open air — finally reached the huge gaping excavation that housed genuine Bath, far below the surface of the world. Groaning with rote trepidation, the snowshoes edged the blackened and complaining tank slowly downwards, hour after hour, until they had descended to the level stones of the ancient city. The six mimes continued, lovingly but without remission, to urge more speed from the forty weathered survivors as their coracle-like autonomic toboggans edged the burden carefully into the marriage chamber, settling it into a rune-scarred transfer niche beneath the matrix nest of the storage Pharaoh of antique visage which contained the *da*, the *da-da*, the Lord Himself. The eyes of the great mask bulged with omens of sunrise.

The moment of the birth approached. Three senior mimes conferred by menu touch alone, ex-spider, recitativo. It was now time to awaken Him into the huge body with its long smooth dense muscle tissue, its toughened skin, its unprecedented size, the houseling furnace of its heat. The deft fingers of the mimes made short work of the task of connecting the great hot body to the purring Pharaoh above it, which began to hum one of the interminable songs of belatedness and of plummets fathoms, fathoms deep. Gingerly the eldest mime looked into the eyes of the keening Pharaoh and entered the releasing commands onto its tentacular protruding tongue. Joining began, the hieros gamos, as the Pharaoh extended itself from its matrix nest and sank over the head of the Model, the cortex maze within the mask settling placenta-like over the face of the new body. As He might awaken in a state of rage, in the terribilita of *sounding*, and of huger compass than even the oldest of the *Dene* mimes here present could remember experiencing, the mice now scattered into the icy wainscotting of the chamber, and their coracles followed, with umbilical gestures, tinkling with nanny urgency, for autumn was the breeding season; and each mated coracle was trailed by a numb singleton whose mouse had died outdoors, on the surface of the planet. Through gaps in the walls and ceiling, snow drifted softly onto coracles of the living and coracles dying, and onto the peaked caps of the mimes, who themselves paced with grave, burgher-like calm into hiding, for they bore the dignity of a more than facial likeness, after all, to the Model. Through the shattered roof, snow sifted downwards, muffling their silver bells. Snow fell upon the life-support of the Lord's body, and upon the moon-eyed Pharaoh, silvering its tongue. Snow fell onto the naked body and turned to steam. There was no sound at all in the great chamber as the Pharaoh finished its task of implantation. The gates of the dream snapped shut within it, and from the mazes of the heart of things the Lord, who could be called Nicholas Dene, was ousted into flesh, fell plumb into the shredding and abysm of the world, into the glamour of time. Already time began to pass, the thousandfold fletched arrow. *Da da*, *da-da-da*, he breathed. It was the diapason of being.

He began to preside. He opened his eyes within the mask, and commanded them to focus, and the Pharaoh gave him a range of sight. He asked for sensors, which registered the extreme cold, and the warmth of his life-support, and a chiming sound, as though the world-wood had awakened into its Noël, then a skittish chuntering echo, as of animal paws scrambling across ice into the rose garden.

'My pipe,' he whispered. 'My fiddlers three.'

He called down a systems display, and saw that he was fully fleshed, but that lacing the readout were strange indices of unmanacled hugeness, which he redflagged as an internal memo, ex spider. He then asked the Pharaoh for an external view from above, and through the eyes of the mask gazed suddenly downwards, as it seemed, at his huge human body lying in its opened life-support tank. An antique Pharaoh, displaying the helmeted brusque visage, the staring eyeholes and protruding tongue of long-term storage mode, sat over the head of the massive shape, snow gathering on its brow. From the heart of the matrix nest, umbilicals descended bearing heavy winter gear fit for Wenceslaus, and began to clothe the figure.

Something glittered in a newly gloved hand.

Dene shot his remote gaze upwards. As he did so, the

chitinous eyes of the mask also gazed heavenwards, in anguish and in joy.

Above the Nicholas Dene form something like a bubble roof was suspended in gaping straggles, and through these vacancies were visible, in the remote empyrean, shapes mottled and hurtling. It was the sky itself, and clouds whickering with albedo from the bright snow, which loosened downwards in tiny constant flakes, descended through the roof onto the Pharaoh in flutters of delft utterly silent applause. Snow. He could taste the amnesia welling up his throat. Shantih.

He commanded a gaze downwards, though away from the glittering hand. Dozens of small footprints and coracle marks and a strange elongated hollow slur surrounded the low platform on which his body lay, risen from the womb of Promerops. In the darkness through the drifting snow glittered broken vials, tubular ganglia and consoles, a Bison mask. Time flew. Snow softened the footprints and the other signs that his body had been transported to this marriage chamber by a great assemblage of mice. The floor was deep in snow. He cancelled the external view and returned to the real-time vision of his own eyes within the mask.

'Timor mortis,' he said aloud.

'It is not recommended at this stage,' rumbled the tank monitor, interrupting.

He ignored the tiny brain.

'Timor mortis, sirrah.'

Thus commanded, the Pharaoh had no option path but that of obedience, and slowly lifted therefore from the naked face of the man and into its nest. A silver umbilical extended a pair of goggles downwards, which Dene put over his eyes. In his hand glittered a warm oval tablet with a beard of snow and his own stony countenance. It was a live jester face-watch. The antic gape of its mouth read 3:15, 3:16, 3:17, his time on Earth. The gay eyes were open and very bright, numbers flickering within the pupils. When it saw that it had caught his eye, the face-watch began to chime softly a tune of urgent message. Dene turned the face-watch over, and saw that indeed the read-out at the base of the skull was alive. *Dene Dene Dene*, it flashed. He thumbed the softness of the skull to release it. The chiming stopped. The message began.

Nicholas Dene! Nicholas Dene! You awaken in Bath Home. Danger, O Kingpin! Is your Pharaoh spidered? Alack if so, Nick. Do not don a spidered Pharaoh. I offer the hospitality of Old England said Midwinter. Ciao.

He turned the tiny mouth of the tablet to his furred ear, and it repeated the message, between its utterance of the seconds, in a solitary feckless calm chordless voice, not human. Again and again the voice of his tiny face told him that he was in a snow-choked narthex of Bath Home in an unnamed year, that Dr Promerops was nigh and spidered, that he himself was Nicholas Dene and capable of bearing winter tidings. Snow continued to drift onto his body, Bath lay under ice and snow, a dark world. But there was no sound of crystal, nor of the youngling nomad pines. Snow coated his goggles as he lay. He was too far north to be eaten by his children, who were alive, or dying, or ten generations dead. He lay like a giant in a spell, and smiled. With great care, as though swimming through a falling of dense snow in the paperweight to make an angel, he began to move his arms and legs, like froggie going a wooing; so children had once done in his genuine youth. Amnesia never touched the fossil circuits.

With an air of dense canny thought, he very slowly sat upright. Snow drifted from his goggles. He moved the arms and legs of the body. The feet were encased in great black furry boots with autonomic directional icons. He began to realise that he had been born into something enormous, that he must be very nearly of human girth. And unmanacled.

Suddenly the face-watch put on a jesting guise, and its mouth gaped and fluttered, uttering a syllable, a dove's cry. His new heart began to pound, burring its chest. He closed his eyes for an instant. In a rasping whisper, he told the face-watch to shut up. Snow fell upon the living.

'Ciao then,' said the sly intolerable voice of the Fool.

His hand clamped over the tiny hot lips, which continued to fibrillate for a moment, then ceased. With one furry gloved fist, Dene touched his own salved, snow-whitened lips. He was alive.

But he was standing, somehow he was standing upright, his heart welled agerdows and tidal within the unmanacled corse, mothering, like frankincense. In a moment he would begin to *sound*.

He would be a world figure.

'Get down,' he whispered to himself. 'Get down. Hush now.'

He was too huge. He had been born to human size. He had almost *sounded*.

At this moment, surely, tiny analogue Dene mouths were opening to announce, clear as a bell in the corridors of the white webbed immortal world of Dr Promerops, his coming. Beings of every description that resided in the world or under it were dangling animalcule Denes in their crustacean claws to read the message of his birth, toying gravely at this moment with his salt-encrusted fabergé lips.

'Think,' murmured the face-watch with a gape, 'O Kingpin.'

Dene nodded, nodded, nodded.

'Sirrah,' he said, finally.

The Pharaoh glowed suddenly above him in its nest.

'Descend.'

The great mask obeyed, dropping in its chassis.

The human being swivelled the Pharaoh around so that the recessive mazes of the interior, from which he had been born, were exposed. A web of spider circuits coated the placenta as he had known they must. But they were blackened and charred. They had been eaten.

Mice?

The countenance of the man began to grin.

'Sirrah,' said Nicholas Dene. 'Timor mortis conturbat me.'

The Pharaoh closed obediently over his grinning face. They sank into the warmth of wedlock.

The chassis slipped upwards again, empty, to the nest, and the huge human figure stared through its Pharaoh at the ruined chamber. Its legs took a first step, and a second. The body of Nicholas Dene moved hauntingly like a body in a dream of Eden. It was like his own body.

He stepped slowly through the chamber, past a rack of bottles gorged with ice like tongues his boys might have stored in the home cellars against a dearth of Bison, who fled south in the colder seasons. He entered a corridor and saw many footprints, the long slur that marked the slow progress inwards of the life-support tank, a shepherd's crook and the horny tufts of the Dog set ceremonially into the wall, a shattered ornamental door.

He stepped under graven mistletoe into daylight. Snow fell into the genuine street from the frozen welkin, gauzing the broken windows of the shrine. Not a single youngling could be seen. Through the Pharaoh mouth filter, his breath glinted in the sharp silent air like snow haloes tossed by a zephyr of the north, presaging winter. He wore heavy luminous winter life-support furs, with glinting brass buckles and antennae glinting daedal. He gazed through his Pharaoh into the world as Father Christmas might, risen from eclipse. Crunching into the middle of the street, he stood in deep snow, which did not melt upon his gloves. The small bald sun muscled for an instant into view, and he glinted in the poison flare.

'Quiet,' he said aloud.

Overhead, with great speed, the sky cleared outright, and the rays of the sun flashed upon the Earth in splendour. Bath lay about him, magically extant, like a quilt of similes knotted ages past in his genuine youth by the dead wives and builders of the original spa, before the sun first began to strafe the shaking world, which was the death of them. His pupils dilated. The heart organ within his sleek heavy torso seemed to bulge. With a gesture so characteristic that it had long since become a standard

113

marker in the interminable potlatches staged between Summer *Denes* and the relentlessly adoring Bison, he quickly and brusquely shook his ornamented head, as though brushing off something physical, a web or trapezoid of memory bits, spider-spawn.

But he was far too late.

He caught sight of his glowing form in a jagged ice-coated window. He saw the Nicholas Dene mirrored there. He saw a figure of ivory and gold with a Pharaoh visage; comnet antennae grew like horns from the mask. The figure was clad in russet, in crepuscular winter furs, none of them of terrestrial origin; snow glittered and scumbled and danced epithalamion; the antlered Pharaoh helm shot snow round and about, shook aloft a gossamer veil of sunshot snow, chryselephantine whirlwinds. I am that I am. The figure was poised at the edge of violence, like a dwarf about to stamp through meerschaum snow in the paperweight, cracking the bowl forever, wodewose. The figure of the Dene was latticed like a mappemonde of gold, sewn through with golden leaf. The Dene was shining.

Exceedingly moist and warm upon the frozen surface of the planet, the huge figure of the Dene glowed like molten gold, so that from data relay modules in orbit his life-support webbing and his icons of command seemed radiant. Sunlight bounced off the duplex antennae sprouting from the horns of his ornate Pharaoh, giving the impression — had the comnet been properly monitored — that the potentially savage monad clone bore antlers. But there were no spider redflags to trigger a system alarm, and all data input on the heat anomaly was therefore scumbagged into a glitches file. As a consequence, Dr Promerops was not awoken for many hours from hibernal slumber under Crete.

This proved fatal.

The monad clone continued to burn upon the planet from the heart of Bath spa, and even through the primitive

Plug-in Faces allotted tourists the condition of the man was clearly visible. One tourist in particular, well into her real-time jaunt down the gravity well, queried the hearth glow of warmth there in the very bowels of the Earth, so close to winter.

'Holos,' she indited.

The Plug-in Face could only obey.

The figure of a full-grown Dene appeared on her monitors. The figure was clearly at the heart of its drama, and could be hunted for the anguish.

So it was well begun.

Given her fare options and the depth of her insurance worms and the proximity of her next taping, the Plug-in Face had no option but to piggyback her into a hunt scenario. A replica helipig was roused from its Irish kennel, along with one of the sharper Dene umbraculae, capable of human behaviours under some circumstances, and the tourist was soon sideslipping downwards and westerly towards rendezvous.

Suddenly, from the frozen river hidden somewhere beneath the streets of Bath, there came a noise, marrow cracking in the intense cold, the deep bones of the city edging closer to rock. Ice coated the shaggy twin windows of Bath, and the commissures of stone, making insect eyes and their cold thorax. Dene stiffened, his breath drifting like fleurs de lis on a ground of snow woven by nomad pines in greensleeves carolling of roots. Higher in pitch, like tiny bells, the noise came again, as though a bone of the city had begun to sing; but maybe it was only water shifting deep under the ice, or an entablature of salamanders loosed suddenly into a myoclonic can-can, before getting on with the maintenance work. Or umbraculae – mimes or mice – rehearsing saturnalia. Or escaping. The echoes faded into the thin deadly air.

Dene glanced upwards at the straitened winterish sky. The muscles of his body were flat, heavy, supple. The body was unmodified, unmanacled, unspidered, undeterrable.

He was younger in the flesh than he had been for an immense time. The small sun glittered bruise-like against the surviving shards of Bath spa, and shot a sting of bleached light through the orifices of a splintered building, like a sudden thigh thrusting into life, the world populous again at kindergarten. He breathed out sharply, as though belly-punched, memorious; but there were no longer any tourists close enough to burn out. Wherever he looked, icicles glistened in the wounds the sun shone through; there was a chiming sound of water dripping like distant birds squabbling in token trees. Nor could you really call them birds.

The lyre-like cheek runes of his Pharaoh glittered with rime.

He gazed down at the wizened umbraculum on his wrist.

'What now?'

The face-watch gaped back.

'Co co co,' it whispered like a dove, a flute of ice.

Dene raised his hands to his cheeks.

'Cochise,' he said.

His hands clawed at the cheeks of his Pharaoh.

'Cochise,' he said.

The voice was chordal.

The tourist was already out of range, and so was not burned out.

He was beginning to *sound*.

'Cochise,' he said.

'Hang about,' whispered the face-watch.

Tiny tears trickled from its eyes and froze.

'Hang about, hang about.'

Dene dropped his hands and there was silence.

'Where is she?' he said.

He stood like a rock in the snow. He was as still as a mouse.

'Follow your shoes, ninny,' said the Fool.

Snow began to fall again.

He found that he was walking through the streets of Bath toward a wall of roots and ice, where the world began. Like fine tendrils of handed gold enamelling, the roots of the world forest laced the perimeters of the spa, so that Bath was held in the cup of the world. The truce held. Something like a ladder of roots began to form.

There was a chiming sound.

Dene turned.

A mime in cap and bells stood, erect with the dignity of its calling, beneath a shattered stone arch. Unguents salved its small antique face, which shone like porcelain, gamboge and depthless.

'Have I you to thank?' said Dene.

The mime seemed to shiver, but opened its mouth into the sprechstimme of its clan:

'We were commanded, and we obeyed.'

'Well,' said Dene. 'Well, I'm here.'

'It is time.'

'Gorge then.'

The mouth of Dene's Pharaoh opened wide for him to utter the *da*, the *da-da* of blessing, but the mime quailed.

'Why do you flinch?' said Dene.

'You are burning,' sang the mime. 'Burning us to death.'

'Ah.'

The mouth closed, the runes folded into themselves.

'So how many are you, my little jackstraw?' tinkled the face-watch.

'Brothers only,' sang the mime. 'Brothers only. We are dying. She is – '

'Rataplan! Rataplan!' shrieked the face-watch.

The mime put a mittened hand to its mouth in horror.

'A close call, wee brother.'

'We thank you,' sang the mime.

'What is this?' said Dene.

'Never you mind,' whispered his watch. 'Not yet.'

'Lord,' sang the mime, 'help us out of Bath. We cannot climb alone. Command the roots to bear us. We are entreating.'

'Ah,' said Dene.

He turned to the ladder of roots.

'These are my brothers,' he said, 'who desire safe passage.'

He made a sign of truce.

'Leave me some snowshoes,' said Dene to the mime.

The ladder held still without clamouring.

Bells chimed, and the remaining mice sledded through the arch of stone on their dray snowshoes, herded by a handful of mimes. They had continued to age, but were generally fit. Coracles bound tightly over their backs, they clambered up the strands of the ladder of roots until they came to cavities that led to their distant demesne, and fled inside. Having extruded the necessary suckers, the snowshoes followed. On the snowy ground below, hollow bereaved coracles milled and scritched and convulsed, until finally they broached themselves and died at the foot of the woven ladder homeward. Snow soon began to drift over the minuscule lifeships. The last mime to climb the ladder made a stiff bow.

Dene bowed.

But his foot half-crushed a coracle buried in the snow, causing its circuits to bell one final carillon or gloss upon its dead mate. Then it became hollow. Snow filled it.

'Time flies,' murmured the Fool.

So Dene clambered up the intricate knots of the ladder, through funnels of glowing ice and capillary spindrifts of root, until the ancient city lay far below. It remained intact. The truce held. There were no 'birds' within the deep hollow, no cadres of nomad youngling pines to carol the diapason of the spheres, anthems no mortal might trace to a close: given our tiny span. The moment would come, though not yet, for Bath to wed the roots and younglings of the world forest, deep within the cloistered planet, and there chime endlessly the carillon of the cities of the human hegemony of long ago, antiphonies of mirrors within mirrors without surcease ringing the changes of desolate Terra and her faithless sun, glosses most artful. Symbionts and singletons, umwelt surfers and genome pacts, the tourists came in droves up the galactic arm, in their sage coffers, to hear the world round.

He climbed until he stood within a groin of packed snow and bole, very close to the surface of the planet. Snow sifted downwards through the veins and arteries of the upper reaches, settling festively though in silence on branches, on the amaranthine Pharaoh of the hieros gamos, on the comnet antlers. Wind from the open sky rang the ambages of ice and root. Like a masque of axons, the tunnels homeward through the heartwood of the world beckoned in the wind and snow. This close to the hollow that held Bath, no mother could be seen. Mare's-nests of capillary vines swung in slow fugues lazily through the chambered air above his head, but did not enfold the man wearing the Pharaoh with a bared tongue and eyes like the astonished Moon.

'*Da*,' murmured Dene through the mouth command of the Pharaoh, *da-da*, and in obedience to the code of truce the vines coiled haiku-like downward to darkness at his feet, in lingering curtseys, on extended wings. He brought up a data scan northwards of the shades of night. The sky was penumbral but polished, the wind having rubbed it to a higher gloss in the upper reaches, near vacuum. Bruises were forming along the edges of the north, and there would be more snow before morning. Something began to rhyme in the figured passages of the world before him, and he felt a deep throb of something like homesickness. But he would not say her name. He saw that a pair of drays had followed him as he had ordered, keyed them to his boots and to his Pharaoh, and turned his back on the north, and rode homewards. The forest enfolded him utterly, and all signs of his passing.

He was invisible from orbit.

The dray snowshoes bore him southwards through hillocks and moraines of snow. Ranks of stark sleep-drenched nomad pines loomed suddenly through eddies of fine drifting snow, mummers of the Great Noël. He gazed in silence. The snowshoes bore him. He dozed. The shoes slid to a halt. He opened his eyes. He was standing on a vast snow-decked branch which crossed an abyss too deep to plumb. At his back, a hundred yards in girth, the veined resin-choked luminous trunk of a mother pine stretched higher than Dene could see into the darkness above, under an immense canopy of snow, sounding her bass ritornello. Above him, phosphorescent cones wept pearly tears of nutrient upon the branch. Around the mother clustered nomad pines in ardent, slumbering ensembles. There were intermittent sounds of feeding; fragments of youngling melody from the depths descanted against the song of the mother. Couched in a snow-encrusted womb hollow of the mother, a winter bird began to carol softly from its polished drowsy throat, as though for Dene's own ears; the orbed glabrous feathers of the bird were mounded over with fresh snow, a violet halcyon eye flickered from its mask of snow. Drink sang the bird. Dene beckoned upwards and a crystal cone came loose in gift, a helical Pierrot orb of translucent *virtu*, eternally lachrymose; and fell into his gloved hand. The face-watch stirred from slumber and made the sound of a dove. In the beginning was the Word. He sucked the rich nectar until he was full. Honey stung his lips. The carol of the enamelled youngling soared with unremitting translunar clarity. It was not possible to go astray. Once empty, the cone began to sing.

He slept again.

The snowshoes carried their burden south.

A half-shattered dome gave off an obsidian glitter in the night, from within its hollow in the heart of the wood. The access coffer was alive, and began to purr. Dene awoke. He keyed himself through the armed portal, which snapped shut behind him. He thanked the drays, which released him with slow ox-like farts, and fastened themselves to niches in the wall to feed and sleep. The inner hatch of the coffer opened.

He stepped outside, into the ruined hollow.

Long ago, perhaps, something had shattered the roof and walls of the surface levels of the home. The snow-coated bony shafts and cavities of the upper chambers gaped into open air, like the relics of a ship gone onto the rocks of a dangerous tidal coast.

'Co Co Co,' carolled the face watch, barbershop, from within his clothing.

There was no other sound. Nothing survived of her. On his own feet he walked knee-deep through powdered snow into the shambles of the home. The read-outs were dead. In a sheltered coign, however, he came upon a desiccated human corpse, nothing but bones and ice now, though dressed in the remnants of a sober grey cloth, harshly woven. Bits of russet hair adhered to the skull. Ice glittered through the eyeholes, she stared fixedly through a narrow embrasure into the west. She could see the iced stalagmites of the shattered dome, the icy combe descending into the lower depths of the hollow. Ice banked her skull, her eyes were very wide. She achieved wonder without surmise. There was no mistaking her. He bent over to touch her remaining teeth, blocking her view of the black night.

'Sorry, Co.'

Within the Pharaoh, his salved lips were trembling. Something within him, probably the face-watch, continued to murmur her name.

She had been eaten.

Very deep is the well of the past for a clone.

Suddenly the sky spoke to him.

Over his head, through the black air, toppled a blotched broken whirlwind of debris and snow. Authentic plastic bullets spat and stank, as programmed in the hunt scenario, and the corpse of his wife scattered into a heap of shards. His protective clothing absorbed a second round of spattle. An archive Cochise holo ricocheted through the air, screaming her husband's name.

Holos of the children began to eat her.

Piggybacked within the helipig command centre as the replica copter veered into a descending spiral, the tourist opened her brindle eyes and her top mouth, the one with 'teeth'. The shadow pilot continued to pretend to monitor the controls. The Dene figure stood on splayed legs staring

121

upwards. Its anguish was visible in the contorted cruciform spread of its arms and legs. She prepared to feed.

Nicholas Dene stared upwards at the pig and its cargo. His mouth gaped into something like a boyish carol. His hands began to claw at the lyre runes of the blessed Pharaoh of the hieros gamos. He began to *sound*. Caught in an ornate rictus of glee, the tourist had no chance to shut her eyes. The pilot stared through its monitors at the rogue Dene. He could not shift his eyes away. His standard-issue Plug-in Face – its Warrior Mode icons almost entirely ornamental, for the benefit of tourists – attempted for an instant to damp the huge spike of naked *sound*, but the barbs of Dene's unmanacled anguish raked through the frail protective quilt-scum without noticeable impairment. A burst of intolerably hot *déjà vu* burned through the very tissues of the pilot's mottled doggy brain, and his face bellied like a sail.

He turned to stone.

The tourist continued to stare through her augments into the round anguished eyes of the Dene Pharaoh. Her brain began to bake.

She turned to stone.

The helipig attempted without success to medicate its charges. Taking a rough brain-scan of the female being, it stashed her rigid body in a life-support pod. The pilot was beyond repair, and was dumped. Mayday signals were sent.

Dr Promerops was finally awoken, barking ravenously, from kyphotic slumber in the command centre under Crete. He knit his brow and ate a snack of squirmers. He spoke aloud to his Warrior Pharaoh, in the decorous terms that had evolved over the centuries to govern interaction with the stored Self.

'Sirrah,' said Dr Promerops. 'Timor mortis conturbat me.'

The Pharaoh settled slowly over the eye sockets and muzzle of its commandant, and Dr Promerops sank into the recursive chiaroscuros of executive mode. He was now spidered. From high synchronous orbit, data relays displayed the oily shining dense anomaly on his protective screens. At the heart of the spasm stood the rogue Dene in a knot of veins and patches of chitinous heat, glaring upwards through its Pharaoh as though it could see into orbit; and turn the rulers of the world to stone. Dr Promerops looked away from his fail-safed readouts with a rancid cough. He ordered a trace on the sabotage worm that had blocked his arousal for so long. He suspected mice. He punched up a kill squad from the vats. Within the brailed carapace of his Pharaoh, Dene began to plummet pastwards into the world he had *sounded*, which was Eden. The Pharaoh kept him warm. He could not know how far he was to fall.

BRIAN ALDISS

Confluence Revisited

When an Earth ship discovered the Myrinian system, the planet Myrin's civilisation was already eleven million years old. The Myrinians traced their history back that far; they had erected a memorial of vertiginous beauty to the passing of the ages every million years, either in reverence or fun.

Most of that lengthy period was passed in what one Earth philosopher has termed 'fruitful stagnation'. Stagnant or not, the Myrinian cultural complex is to be envied for the general level of contentment in which its peoples live, referred to as *Bi Jo* (approximately, Stylised Submerged Individualism). The people eat moderately and sleep well at night.

Bringing back with it many records of the venerable Myrinian culture, the Tenth Research Fleet has just returned to Earth, android-manned, since the human crew in the main elected to remain on Myrin in the state referred to as First Lobby. Unfortunately it has not yet proved possible to receive a visitation here from representatives of the Myrinian system, despite many pressing invitations. Doubtless we may expect acceptances when levels of radiation decrease. Meanwhile, terrestrials must be grateful that Myrin does not ban all human visits. Even the unfortunate incident involving the Earth ship *Bombast* has been clemently overlooked.

The complexity of the chief Myrinian language, Confluence, has already been noted. That it is a language-cum-posture, or lingopost, was established by the Seventh Research Fleet, members of which were privileged to attend special lectures at the Oeldrid Stance Academy on Myrin Centre, in Sector Ten. Meanings in lingopost can be radically altered by the Stance assumed by the speaker (or *S'Ih Hin*, the Intoner, also a rather transparent curtain) or even by that of the listener. The positioning of a single finger can negate or reverse the meaning of several classes of lingopost words. It is clear that there is no possibility of compiling a dictionary within the ordinary meaning of the term.

The Tenth Research Fleet was confined to Sector Nine on the chief Myrinian planet. As is well known, the Myrinians have for convenience (or some say for amusement) divided their territories into squares, so that they resemble a gigantic checker-board. There the researchers spent considerable time investigating Confluence. Their special report on terms for wine will be published separately. They also compiled a holographic record of various Stances assumed in lingopost. Findings will be available shortly.

Meanwhile, the brief listing that follows displays something of the interest of a lingopost which far excels Solar English in its nuances. Definitions must be regarded as tentative.

The Romanised phonetic system employed here is that suggested by the leader of the Etymological Division of the Seventh Research Fleet, Dr Rohan Harbottle.

AH BLAK HOO	Oblong eyes; the inhabitants of Sector Nine say that persons with oblong eyes live longest
AH SHEN SHI	Having learnt any classical book by heart
AH IH WAN	Courtesy to an old lady in cognisance of her previous beauty; an over-cooked egg or fish

126

ANEY	A place much used by great-grandfathers
ARP RUH HIG LO TON	Being busy in an office after lunch; a dotard studying history; sounds of leaves falling in early autumn
ARTH	Conversation; a cave with echoes
AS DIN	A family holiday less than a complete success; a fever
BACH HOANG	A machine factory; a long worm in a tiger's intestine
BA YEF NA	One's recognisably second-rate thoughts
BAZ YEF HO	Striving to better one's thoughts; restocking a lake with fish of improved quality
BI	A reverie sustained for twenty years; crowing like a cockerel without making a sound
BI JOWA	Ninety per cent contentment; half of a chocolate egg
BOL I PEIU	Those who worship tigers; perhaps a ceiling with blood on it
CH'N DOGBA HAN	The kind of conversation one expects between two robots; singing for the sake of it
CHUK CHEE	Answering back to owls; laughing at one's own jokes; a concoction of raw egg and alcohol
CHU PAT	A learned person in a low tavern
CUR	Persistent attempts at flight; any hilarious suicide
DA EST KO	A hypothetical form of reason which will reach to the roots of unreason, at present being developed by sages in Sector Nine

DI CHI'FAN I	The laughter of women in the next room; restaurants with doubtful reputations
DOBGAT	An irresistible tendency to laugh at what is not funny
FAN	Beloved female
FANG TO	A rarity; cream on mare's milk
FAN N'M	A slightly less beloved female
FANOW	A surprisingly pleasant female cousin; a miniature painting
FAN SEE KIT MEE	An undiscovered continent; a well-cultivated female mind; cream
FEE MAABA	An obsolete weapon once used for beheading robots; the shinbone
FEET	A kind of hedgehog skilled at climbing trees; old hair brushes
FOH TAT	A dog singing; laughter towards nightfall
HA LIT	A special dish of jellyfish; jokes told to the wrong people
HANG TAK	A robot which thinks it thinks
HE'CHI YAY	Borrowing and not returning books; a certain smile
HE HANG TUK TI	A robot which thinks it can walk straight but deviates to the left consistently
HI HANG TUK TIN	A robot which thinks it can walk straight but deviates to the right consistently; a devious politician
H'KAI TURK	The malfunction of a semi-computer; a small child farting
HI IH HI	Listening to choirs and similar activities
HI IH HU YA	Making a habit of listening to choirs; conversation with a green bear
HO HOO'FAN	Dining on Farinese oysters and

	wine; having eyes only for the beloved
H'YA TO	An unintended gesture; a posture; a furry type of fish from the Clement Sea
ICT P'EEM SHA	To be pulled apart by four cart-horses; any similar punishment
I JOW N'A	Poor forms of contentment; on the Southern Continent, a game with fingers as counters, some say, cat's cradles
IMOO	A kind of pudding; a planet
IMSK IMOOT	A pudding with inedible parts; ineffectually riding a white horse
INA O YEF	Achieving perfection of thought
JA	A type of depraved underground mammal; mathematics; one's appearance on certain mornings
JA LULI	Any depravity, especially if practised in brothels.
JAL UM	Standing in such a way as to annoy a mother-in-law; a pimple not concealed by garments; the young pig or eagle
JALUM PI	A preoccupation with money; an elusive ache; diseases of middle age
JIN PAH T'HA	A waterwheel beginning to work again; kissing a lady on her private parts
JOW TSEE	The division where soft ends and hard begins; a tiger's tale
KA'RENI	Visiting a distant country; an assignation with a sister-in-law
KEY HANG	Annoying thoughts: robot with a conical head

KO HO LAM	Two people looking sideways at each other
KOISAL T'PEEM	The Four Realisations:
EEM AD AH	The realisation that one is eighteen and already a failure
EEM HA WAK	The realisation one is eighty and has achieved nothing
EEM YA AK	The realisation one is popular only in vulgar company
EE 'OH MOI	The realisation one is shunned by one's own family
LEONG M'BEE	Congested bowels; an over-populated city
LIEM TU'H	Highest form of art; in Sector Nine, also the stories one tells children in order to prepare them to conduct themselves wisely in adulthood
LI LIH JUH	Superconductivity; an orgy; illicit communication with a female prisoner
LUH PU SMAK TI	Constant dripping of water; conversation in which one cannot join; listening unwisely
MAK TI IH	Talking only slightly to impress
M'BEE GOH	General discourtesy to old ladies as a principle
M'BEE WA	An old city; ancient thing; article; or a certain desolation which descends when one sees a beloved house demolished
MEE KIT	A well-cultivated mind; fatness; like a little continent
MEN TATI YI	Discerning the differing qualities of each hour of darkness; 'parting the night breeze'

M'FEE BAH	An obsolete instrument used for giving exact measurements of genitalia; any kind of one-armed lobster
MIN RETSO	Thinking of someone dear but distant; a row of little houses, perhaps a village
M'KO HA BLIT	Avoiding a friend who has written a book one has not read; bad sunrises
NAH	Purity; blue sky before the eleventh hour
NA TAT MA DATO	Divorce while one's partner is not looking; having a chimney relined
NIK TRIT	A state between something and nothing; scarcity; abundance
NIN TU WOL	Any form of behaviour lacking inward control; a child's toy
NUT IMGI	Managing to die without causing inconvenience to others; cooling egg custard
NUTRED JOW	Achieving death in an amused daydream
N'JAH TUR	Mild depravity; a spring fair for children only
OI PAH SMA GEE	A young lady seen through a looking glass; a little cress growing between storms
OPI NIN	Any form of behaviour which improves on what has been before; a drink that wards off intoxication
ORAN BAL	The uneasy feeling that change is on its way; death of the Ruler
OTA TI HA	Gesturing circumspectly to the left; the picturesque
OTA TIN HI	Gesturing circumspectly to the right; a mystery

131

OUTA	Several feet washed under the same tap; a haul of squid; a parliament
PEET	Four people sitting companionably round a table
PUH TIH	Oh, hell!; also used for urine
QUAM	Delicate feelings towards older persons; poetry of an especially obscure kind
REEN	Getting in touch with a distant country; confessions made through a red mask
SHEN	Any fruitless task undertaken through embarrassment
SHIN HOI BAA	The toes; playing a musical instrument with strings, some say by blind musicians
SIN LIN H'KAY	A robot pretending to belch; anything above its station; also, some say, low comedy, such as a custard pie about to be delivered
SMAK T'HAH	A one-eyed fish, so that two have swim close to see the way forward; the place; any silly behaviour by twins
SNI TO'SI	Compulsory counting; 'he is adding up the stars'; any venerable astronomer
SZE PU LO LO	An icicle of urine; cryonic superconductivity
TEI FEET PU	Excessive hairiness; a great victory
THEE DO	Examining three or more graduate-level students; an owl's nest

TH'HOW	Boundless lapses of time since the universe began; what astronomers say
TIG TRAG	Creature most resembling mankind, said to smile in its sleep; a rival imitating one's best garment
TRIH H'YA	A gesture with the fingers where one wishes to speak but cannot
TRIH YA	Any dumbshow; 'he has more fingers than brains'
T'SMAK TH'HOW CHE	Rattling of reeds by a flooded lake; any northern breeze; useless thinking about boundless lapses of time
TU LA LAT	Holding a high note in opera; letting sunshine into the back of the mouth; speaking purely to please; a lizard
TURK TOH	A little child laughing; gutters; like firecrackers thrown into water
UK'WAN AS	To hasten towards one's death; in general, to enjoy oneself
UK'WAN TA	To hasten towards marriage
UK'WAN TAMA	To hasten towards an unwelcome marriage
ULI WAS	Fasting; going a year without food
UNIMGAG BA	A machine dream which takes some time to recall; a lethargic flea
URK AY	A custard pie after delivery; a deficiency of wit
USANO NUTO	A novel about love written by a computer; a vain thing
WAN	A type of tortoise used in races

133

WOON HA	Parking a chariot; the smell of over-heated horses
YAG ORN	Passing on knowledge; the honourableness of passing on knowledge; a president (archaic)
YEP YAY	Disillusion; an empty wine bottle; new legislation in an old town
YEEF	Any place more than a thousand miles from the ocean
YEEF N'YI	One day in adolescence; a pale lemon
YUK NA	Predicting the future; looking through a bamboo blind into the night; certain low autumn fogs
YU UZ'NIT	A very large person who fails to realise he resembles his father
ZEI TAI'	A short-haired dog with dignity

JOSEPHINE SAXTON

Getting Together

I first met Shivvi, whose full name was Siobhan de Sauveterre, when I visited Grindwal's Planet on a rare therapeutic vacation. I had often dreamed of emigrating to that twin-sunned Paradise, but there was no call for a Functional Symbolist such as myself. To study and teach my subject, a secure niche in the underground world of planet Earth is needed, safe from surface radiation, fed by imports from happier climates. Perhaps you need to live on a planet such as our ruined Earth to have an interest in this obscure branch of practical philosophy. At the time I was turning in upon myself, and twenty years of successful publications was seeming void and useless. This syndrome is not uncommon amongst academics.

Ms de Sauveterre, whom I quickly learned to call Shivvi, saved my life, in a sense – although in the doing we both almost died, several times in the course of a day.

I had almost recovered from the travel-shock when I received an invitation to lunch with her at the Adventure Club. I am quite well known in spite of the obscurity of my subject, and it transpired that the Club kept abreast of visitors who might be entertaining, especially 'intellectuals'. Feeling rather like a clown commanded to fool at court, I went along.

I had been looking forward to solitary sunbathing and swimming, and walking in the natural landscape, so it was with a certain concealed sourness that I waited indoors for

135

our meeting. But it was not for long, and when Shivvi hurtled in to greet me, my *ennui* evaporated. She was energetic, and her pace infectious.

Very quickly we were laughing together. Living underground in a studious atmosphere is not good for friendships or the personality. It felt wonderful to me, as we began to talk, that I had found someone oriented so differently who was such good company. I was a blighted plant beside her flourishing health, her fair hair shining, her skin glowing. She ordered local wine to be served outdoors, full of the goodness of two suns. My psychic leaves began to lift up then, with the fresh air and the view of lush vineyards and fields of crops. When I told Shivvi of my negative state with regard to my work, she leaned back and laughed in astonishment, and used my personal name for the first time.

'Shelley! You amaze me! Your work is deeply interesting. I've read all your stuff and always thought how marvellous it must be to have no distractions, to focus down on abstract matters and write such creative works.' She topped up my glass with the ruby light, the taste so fresh I was half drunk before our food arrived.

'No,' I told her, 'not true, or at least, I'm at an impasse. I envy your job.'

'Oh! My job — there is a lot of waiting about, I'm bored with it.'

She was a Preventer, a useful role in the Social Hygiene Corps. Using a Pre-event Timedrive which detected disaster and disharmony before it occurred, she visited potential victims throughout the galaxy, showing them their fate if they did not take avoidance measures.

'You've no idea of the hostility towards Preventers. We are accused of spying, inventing trouble, invading privacy — some people would rather commit murder or suicide than change their partner, their work, their habits or their diet. And I'm trained in self-defence because sometimes we get aggression. Even so, we have a high success rate. Most people, once you've shown them a likely future, actually respond positively to help and advice.'

I recall that as she spoke we were eating a delicious crustacean, which had been marinated in some sour fruit juice, roasted over a wood fire, and basted with thick green olive oil. On earth there had not been fresh food like that for many generations. Eating out of doors was such a heady novelty that I suppose I was quite high and a bit reckless – partly why I got into adventures I could not have dreamed up previously. Shivvi told me more about her work.

'Well, of course, we don't spy, because we only see what might happen, although that is what *will* happen if the drift is not altered. Sitting there on watch can be so tedious. I enjoy the dangerous aspects, to be honest, when we are out there and something happens. Not long ago I turned up to try to sort out some violent kids on a street on the dark side of – now where was that, a hell of a long way out – and the whole gang turned on me. I handled it, but only just. I never retro. We need to earn people's respect.'

'Retro?' I enquired, peeling a delicious fruit which had a scent which made me dizzy with lust. She explained to me then, in strict confidence, their mode of travel, still top secret. It involves the touch of a couple of acupuncture points connected to a miniaturised transmitter set into the brain. The thing had been inserted via the back of her eyeball, without pain or side-effects. It began to dawn on me what might be coming next. I had thought that she went to visit people in the present, but she often actually travelled into the future. I had always understood this to be outlawed, largely because so many people in the early days of time travel had returned with wrecked mental health. The stress had proved to be far greater than at first imagined – also, of course, there were the paradoxes of altering the present by being in the future. As a child I had dreamed of travelling around in time, and always having an interesting life, but had put away such dreams with my toys. She explained further.

137

'Just a few people in government departments have the use of time-travel, in carefully monitored situations. Use outside of that is strictly illegal because it is still thought to be dangerous and would cause chaos to society if everyone had access. People would be tripping off to other times and places and not returning, and we'd be flooded with people from elsewhere – the possibilities for disastrous muddle are endless. I think it will eventually be developed for safe general use, but not for decades. I can't wait for decades.' She swore me to secrecy then, and told me of her illegal hobby.

'Being born out here, I'm fascinated with the history of Earth. Especially the history of medical and social sciences, the way that sick and troubled people were helped in the past. I have an extensive collection of videos I've made of events in history, although most of them aren't very valuable: I'm not in total control of exactly where and when I journey to, yet. But some day I'm going to astonish the world and I might even go commercial, arrange educational trips for groups. Imagine a guided tour around the Temple at Pergamum, when the medical school was functioning. Or Ancient Egypt, or China!' Her eyes gleamed with excitement; it was good to be with a person so filled with enthusiasm. I had to question her though: I wasn't entirely happy about what she was doing.

'But Shivvi, what if you were back in time somewhere, and you accidentally killed somebody important in history – that would change everything.' I thought of going back to wipe out those fools who put Earth under a deep poisoned cloud forever, but of course, if I did that it would be unlikely that I would exist, all destiny being altered, so could not very well travel back to . . .

'Ah, *that* one,' she said. 'Well, you will have to forget any logical approach to this, Shelley, because it means nothing in this field. You travel through time, literally through it. You can interact, but not in the way of this reality here. With this method, you could kill someone – or, I suppose, even be killed – er, no. Because then you

138

could not retro. Well, I was going to say, the moment you retro, all events on the trip would be elided.'

'And if you get killed, then everything stays the way you reworked it.' She nodded. 'That's why it's illegal.'

'Tell me, how do you manage to get back with videos? Surely even the image on the tape is made up of molecules from the future.'

'No. A video is magnetic memory only, the way I do it. My memory isn't wiped clean, and fortunately neither is that of my recorder. I'm working my own technics, obviously, with a bit of help from a couple of sympathetic friends of course. It would appear that I am in the process of inventing new methods of direction-finding. Not yet totally reliable, but better than you could imagine. It is something to do with the acupuncture points, the magnetic body-energy in the acupuncture meridians, and the fact of it being connected into my brain module. Not sure just how, yet, it's all very pragmatic. Do you see?'

'Yes,' I lied, trying to take it all in.

'Pragmatic, and technical, a few problems here and there. I'm using cast-off parts from my department, there's nowhere else to get the stuff. But I'm using it all in a different way. I'll demonstrate when you visit.'

We went for a stroll in the lovely outdoor warmth, down to the side of a lake, the first I had ever seen. She took off her sandals and paddled, which I also did, hardly believing that some people were within reach of pleasures such as this all the time. That she would want to leave such a wonderful place and go journeying in the past of Earth! But, I thought, if I could do such a thing, it would be a marvellous escape from the claustrophobia and tedium of the present day. I watched the effect of sunlight playing in shallow water, and saw little fishes pollinating underwater flowers. The real thing, not a video. Very exciting.

As if reading my mind, she suggested that I needed something exciting in my life, the real thing instead of a video. She told me that she had almost completed a second set of equipment for a companion traveller. At first I did not connect the two ideas, my mind refused to contemplate the dangerous business of travelling with her on some uncertain jaunt. My holiday was enough for me!

'As I said, I've still got one or two bugs to iron out, such as, say I wanted to explore a certain time or place — for example an early chemistry lab. I might be lucky and get there spot on, or I might turn up in a television play about it instead. I don't know why, either. And once or twice it has shifted me around a bit madly without my wanting it to. That can be disconcerting.'

I would have used stronger words, but she was such a self-possessed person nothing daunted her. I also suspected that she was an adrenalin addict, slightly suicidal, a bit mad but very brilliant.

'With my method, a person could exist in any reality which has ever been dreamed up by the human mind, I think. I also think you should accompany me on a trip. I don't know why, but I'm certain that we shall work together, and that you have something I need, and vice versa. I've been tantalised by some of the stuff you've come up with, how symbols work upon reality. Say you will.'

When I tentatively agreed, she was overjoyed because she had already made an appointment for me to have the module fitted into my brain. Her final work was on the base module which remained in her apartment, set to return us home and also monitor and direct the journey. She began immediately showing me how to find the pattern of acupuncture points I would need to be adept at stimulating. This was not as easy as I had thought but eventually I began to feel the tiny hollows, and then to sense the point of energy within them. Applying the right kind of pressure needed skill, for it would need to be effected rapidly on some occasions. She warned me, once I had the module in place, not to mess about with those points or I could go shooting off on an unscheduled trip and have nothing to come back to. I wondered (as who would not?) what I was getting into. But I had caught the desire for adventure, and it was too late to back out. I had, after all, been half dead from boredom; had not fate brought me exactly what I needed?

A few days later, there we were, in her apartment together, ready to travel. It was a light and simply furnished place with a small roof-garden. I was horrified to notice a few flies buzzing around, and a beetle crawling about on the tiles, and tactfully pointed these out to Shivvi, who seemed not to care. On Earth there are no longer such creatures in domestic surroundings. Shivvi laughed, and explained that on Grindwal's planet, unlike Earth, the ecology is still balanced, and that her rooms had several spiders as well, there was no problem. I must have trembled visibly, I'd only ever seen pictures of spiders and they terrified me. She explained that disease only came to people whose energy was in bad shape, and that spiders were harmless.

We went into her lab, otherwise a spare bedroom, to look at her 'high-tech' base module. To me it looked like a muddle of flimsy circuits, and a tankful of pink gel containing suspended dots which, she said, were partly chromosomes cultured from my cells.

'All it needs now is for me to measure your exact cell-charge, activate the tank to exactly the same wavelength, and the programme I've entered into Maureen here (a computer with her name painted on the cover) and we are instantly where we want to be. More or less. And look at my video camera, isn't that clever?' She held up a small gold earring.

I was suddenly full of misgivings, but somehow the moment passed in which I could have backed out. Shivvi has a powerful personality, capable of carrying others along.

'You ready?' she asked, as if we were going out to dinner.

We were standing in a very bleak kind of room. Our dresses were white cotton and we wore paper masks. We held cardboard dishes full of − I almost fainted − stinking human shit.

'Act quietly,' whispered Shivvi. 'We seem to be student nurses, not quite what I'd programmed but near enough. We are to observe an early attempt at prosthetic surgery. Let's dump these, wash up and follow the others. I've done student nurse before, it can be quite good for gathering information.' She wasn't as disoriented as I was. She'd warned me I'd have to think quickly, copy her actions and say as little as possible. We dumped our foul parcels down a chute, merely washed our hands, removed our masks and walked along echoing corridors with a party of other young people, mostly girls. They chattered and giggled like children, perhaps to keep up their spirits in drab surroundings. It was towards the end of the twentieth century, if the programme was correct. At that time still, Shivvi said, the immune system was not understood properly at all and a lot of energy was wasted on sterile surroundings instead of protecting the patient from within, using their own energy. She had lost me there, but it was her field not mine. I was just coming round from the shock of my first time-trip, and my eyes must have shone like lamps with the adrenalin.

'Anyway, they still did marvellous things, just watch this.'

We sat at the back of a theatre behind a screen of glass, and down below lay a patient and a surgeon and his assistants. He was to replace an arm, completely crushed in an accident, with an arm taken from a corpse. This was very primitive; I thought that people had always had replacements grown *in situ*.

The patient lay as if dead, tubes everywhere. The surgeon had the air of a priest in one of those mad religions which arise from time to time, where deluded people think they have contact with some superior form of intelligence. Everyone in the place was paying attention to his every move, and Shivvi touched her earring.

A lot of the proceedings were too grisly for me to watch; I am somewhat squeamish, and I noticed that all but we two were making notes. I hoped we were not conspicuous.

142

When that patient finally had the new arm in place, and was sprayed with an anti-bacterial sealant (I thought, but that seals infection *in*, the surgeon is breathing on her constantly, through that mask), the whole audience applauded and then filed through into a small lecture room. A tired-looking man began to recap the operation and ask spot questions. I was picked on, and began stuttering some nonsense, and he asked my name. Shivvi nudged me and hissed: 'You're blundering, let's move.'

In the corridor outside, to the sounds of outrage at intruders, we activated our points and got out.

I will never forget the horror of the next phase of our adventure. Shivvi actually hooted with laughter, but stifled it as best she could. I realised that this was not on the itinerary at all.

We were enclosed in a frightful stench, blood was everywhere, and terrible noise. I could hear the appalling sound of animals in a state of extreme fear, and the clanking of primitive machinery. People were shouting, some-one was singing very loudly. I was naked and crouched on a moving belt about twice my own width, next to a skinned animal hanging upside-down, its eyeballs still rolling although its throat was cut. My own screams added to the cacophony. I saw the flash of steel cut through flesh, I saw deep tubs filled with shivering viscera, an impression of iridescence over still-throbbing tubes imprinted itself as clearly and permanently on my mind as upon Shivvi's camera. A man's face as shocked as mine must have been was staring at me nearby. People were running, and I heard somebody screaming in a strange accent something like: 'Bloodyell, Bert, two loonies wanting to turn themselves into sausages!'

For me, that was studying the subject much too closely, and quite frankly I could not see what any of that had to do with historic social and medical services. It hadn't, of course. Shivvi shouted out to shift again, and I needed no further prompting. I wondered if those people, in what was presumably a sausage factory, thought that they had suffered a group hallucination . . . I didn't care, really. I was so relieved to be out of there I burst into hysterial laughter. I can hear myself now, just thinking about it. I'm not that kind really; it was an exceptional situation.

'I told you it might be tricky,' Shivvi said. 'Stay calm, and remember, you are in no real danger.'

I wasn't totally convinced. 'It's all too real,' I told her. 'What if your module back home goes wrong, what if the capsule in my head . . .' and so on.

'True adventurers do not stop to think "what if" at times like this.' And then we noticed where we had landed. Shivvi was puzzled and disappointed, which was nothing to my concealed reaction. She told me she had been hoping to get some information on malnutrition in primitive societies. At one time people had swallowed tons of vitamin concentrates because the food was denatured, and she hoped to find out precisely what. She thought that it would be useful to geneticists, because it is now known that excessive amounts of concentrated foods cause some inherited diseases. She was not to get anything on that where we were; we were subjected to more shocks. The place stank horribly but differently somehow; I surmised, correctly, that the smell was rotting meat. But it was mixed with the delicious smells of roasting, a strange combination. We looked at one another with a mixture of interest and fear, and Shivvi shrugged. I remember that shrug, it seemed to summarise her whole attitude to life. It said 'What the hell, let's explore', a casual and genuinely brave attitude.

My heart was pounding under a check shirt worn with tight blue trousers, very uncomfortable, with hot rubber-soled shoes. It was obvious from this 'disguise' clothing which her equipment automatically provided for us that once more we were to do something not exactly academic. My instincts told me that something awful was happening and I broke out in a sweat, something which rarely happens in the controlled environment of Inner Earth. It was also very hot in that place, with large blue flies buzzing about. I looked around with concentrated attention.

144

Sunbeams were coming in through a dirty broken window, alighting on a loathsome scene. The floor was thick with feathers, animal dung, bones and bundles of clothes. In the next room, partly visible through an open door, someone started singing. A deep male voice, a happy sort of song.

Then we were suddenly terrified by a very loud mechanical noise, a dreadful roaring which made me cover my ears. I saw beads of sweat form between Shivvi's eyebrows and thought, she is human after all. Then silence, then the sound, on and off. We tiptoed towards the door and I peered cautiously around, to discover hell.

A very tall man stood over a large wooden table on which lay the naked body of a woman, her long hair catching the sunlight. With an old-fashioned power tool, a chain-saw, he was dismembering her. I stepped back and whispered to Shivvi that we must move on but she shook her head, no. This was too strange to miss. I felt it was too strange to see any more but I stayed, trembling and sweating. The man sang an old song about Little Jack Horner, while chucking pieces of the woman into a metal tub. He was huge and wore an apron with an advertisement for ketchup. When he turned his head I saw he was wearing a mask made of some wrinkled skin, a terrifying effect. He lifted up his filled tub effortlessly and took it out of the far side of the room. His singing receded.

'Shelley, what is this?' We stared at one another. To this day I do not know, except that we seemed to have stumbled into the lair of a homicidal maniac. Things could not have been much worse in that place; neither of us had ever heard of such human behaviour. Such murderous acts never happen either on Earth or on Grindwal's; we were stunned. Perhaps we were being shown a disease before the cure?

We began to explore further. The whole place was a bizarre house of horror, a big old dwelling-house built of wood and set amongst thick trees. Mostly it was very dirty, but we found a kitchen full of clean equipment, and outside the window a smouldering barbecue with chops and sausages cooking. There were tables and chairs out there in the sun, and a menu-board. A grisly cafe, with no customers at this moment. In the distance I could hear sounds of roaring, and Shivvi said this would be the traffic on the road.

'Where do you think we are?' I ventured to ask. I could see no connection with her studies at all.

'America, twentieth century. That last was in Europe, I think — I set the trip for comparable situations in different locations. But it isn't exactly what I had in mind.'

'I'm very relieved. I was beginning to wonder how the human race survived at all, if this is the social services.' And as far as I knew, America had been a highly civilised and hygienic culture. I said no more. Our nerves were stretched to snapping, the tension in that place was hideous. It smelled of fear and death, a nightmare house. Had such things taken place often, I wondered?

Next to the kitchen was a room filled with large white chests. We opened one to find a young girl asleep in ice, her curls exquisitely frosted. Shivvi touched her face and the eyes flew open. An expression of fear so great lay in those eyes that I almost fainted with the shock. But contingency moved us, we hauled her out and dragged her into the sunshine, away from the cafe into an overgrown garden. She began to jabber, breathing raucously. We chafed her arms and legs and thought that she might live. She had almost died of hypothermia, it seemed, not to mention shock. She told us that she had been driving with her friend and seen the sign for a roadside diner; as she had been waiting for her order she'd been hit over the head. Her friend had disappeared. No, it was not the girl we'd seen being hacked up. We found her later, hanging from a huge hook thrust under a shoulderblade. It was at that moment that the masked giant discovered us. He roared like a great animal.

'Stand your ground!' Shivvi shouted. But he held his power-saw, and he switched it on and the noise unnerved me and I screamed. He came at me with this weapon, close enough for me to smell blood and body odour on him. I was supporting the girl and could not get to my points to shift location. I knew we were really there, nothing could have convinced me that he could not hurt me, kill me forever, no tricks with time and space. A frightful death stared me down. But my foot came up and kicked him hard between the legs. The girl seemed to spring to life then, and she brought her clasped hands down on the back of his neck with all her force, and Shivvi kneed him up the backside and kicked his head as he fell. The three of us ran, then, out past the garden into rough woodland, haphazardly fleeing. As we ran I hardly noticed the thorns and stinging plants, but they were torture afterwards. We were soon on the road, but we could hear the power-saw behind us, roaring away. He was chasing after us with it, insane and as strong as a machine.

The young girl was trembling violently and seemed not to be able to speak any more, but a vehicle came along and she ran out in front of it so that it stopped. Shivvi and I hid in the bushes as it drove away. I heard the girl manage to say 'hospital', and feared for her life then.

'Let's move on,' said Shivvi, but I just had, leaving behind the crashing of branches and the roaring of the cannibal killer.

We arrived somewhere in the darkness and the cold, with a keen wind blowing. We were close together though, so we huddled to keep warm. It was an awful place, I knew, even though I could not see it. I would have known, I believe, if we had come to a safe place, it would have felt so different to our previous locations. I realised on that last short sojourn why people used to have religions. Those times were so barbaric and hostile to peaceful life that a belief in something more powerful than the human, which may be called upon for help, is at times the only thing which keeps the mind in place.

It was so cold that I could almost believe that the ghastly ogre had thrown us into his freezer, but we were dressed in smelly animal skins, rough and itchy wool, and were covered in grease with overtones of some strong flower-scent. My eyes began to get used to the darkness after a while, and also a faint wash of light began the dawn. Very slowly we saw where we were, making out dim shapes which we could hardly believe. If there was such a place as Hell, this must be it, I thought, hating and fearing the cold much more than eternal fires. There were patches of snow, rocks strewn about, a landscape all around unbelievable in its breadth and scope, and nothing else except one human being, seated not far from us.

I thought at first it was a statue, it sat so still, with its legs crossed. What was more strange was that the figure sat in the midst of human remains. Arms and legs and heads, scattered around, some new, some not. A skull leered at me and I thought it spoke, saying well, you wanted something different, and here it is! I knew I would go mad if I did not get back to 'normality' immediately, I had had enough. Not Shivvi – she stood there, looking about her with interest.

'There's a theme to these trips, isn't there? Not what I intended, but a theme.' The figure then moved. It had been staring into the distance, eyes slightly crossed, its tongue out and pointing up. I had registered as much but was no longer trying to make sense of anything. The eyes focused, it lifted its arms, and a most wonderful delighted smile appeared, a smile of welcome, suffused with sheer joy. My response, which I regret in a way, was to activate my points and land home, in Shivvi's apartment. I have never been more glad to be anywhere. She followed immediately, undaunted.

'That was Tibet, you know, but what he was doing in a graveyard I just don't know.' She went straight into the kitchen and called back, did I want a meat sandwich? I was not hungry, and haven't touched meat since, but Shivvi is made of sterner stuff. So I took a shower while she ate. When I emerged feeling slightly restored, she was checking over her equipment for errors.

'Everything seems to be okay. I can't understand why we got all that dismemberment stuff. Anyone would think that the whole of Earth's history is full of stuff like that.'

'It is — but there must be other things too.' And then, looking over her shoulder at the Base Module, I saw something which suddenly became full of meaning, which appeared to explain everything. In her tank of gel there floated a dead fly, one wing separated from the thorax. I pointed it out, certain that she too would understand.

'This may be the beginning of a pragmatic approach to showing that a symbol may exert influence over matter,' I said.

She did understand, but to her it meant greater opportunities for her travels.

'All I would have to do would be to find the correct symbol for a journey, put it into the gel and zoom!'

Well, perhaps. But catch me experimenting with it until it is more certain.

The rest of the vacation was a delight, and of course we had a great deal to discuss. Shivvi had this theory that I, with my work on functional symbolism, had turned up at the exact time in her experiments to make sense of this new possibility, she would never have seen it for herself. This is not impossible, synchronised events are often full of useful meaning. I want to work on it further, and I have to think of a reason to give to the authorities to emigrate to Grindwal's planet. But all that is in the future. Shivvi writes to tell me that she floated a flower and turned up in a fabulous garden. I don't know if this constitutes proof or not, we need numerous repeatable experiments. One thing is certain; no more research into early medicine for me.

M. JOHN HARRISON

The Gift

1: *The Rainbow Shuts Its Gate Against You*

If you probe in the ashes, they say, you will never learn anything about the fire; its meaning has passed on.

There are as many as seventeen good hotels in the city. On the 'entresol' floor of one of them, the Central, a woman lounges in the tropical heat of her single room, drinking rum. The TV is on, the sound turned down. It's eleven o'clock at night. Downstairs, the railway station from which the Central takes its name is almost deserted. When a train arrives the air is filled for a few minutes with shouts, laughter, people calling to one another in the crush, and the concourse sounds like a zoo or an asylum. As if to soothe the inmates the concourse muzak will suddenly play a schmalzy, faraway version of 'Rhapsody in Blue'. To this the woman in room 236 listens only briefly, tilting her head at an intent angle as though she is trying to catch some tune underneath the music, before she shrugs and turns away from the window.

' "Black Heart Rum",' she reads from the bottle in her hand, ' "the Heart of Darkness".' She laughs and adds, ' "All the sweet lacunae of the Caribbean Sea —" '

Now it is the television that captures her attention, and she turns up the sound just in time to hear ' — unease in the minds of ladies. Considerable unease in the minds of ladies.' But this sentence, read out in a bright yet concerned voice, is the end of the item, and the scene changes abruptly to some grainy night footage of lorries being manoeuvred in and out of a shed. 'Real unease in the minds of some ladies,' she thinks, sitting on the bed with her shoes off and allowing her arm to rest briefly along the padded headboard. In this position she is revealed as a tall woman whose clothes − a black two-piece suit with lightly padded shoulders, a striped grey and black blouse of some glazed material − scarcely hide a kind of untidy sexuality, a gawky and almost absent-minded sleepiness of the limbs.

Her eyes are blue, a little watery and indirect. Her age is hard to tell.

Wherever you are at night in the city you can always see, beyond the roof of the next building, the faint glow of the floodlights of some monument. This is less a light than a sort of luminescence of the air itself, soft and tremulous, as if it is full of mist or water. Out of it rises a Victorian minaret, which you cannot quite see; the crenellations of a castle, which you can; or a flagpole. The parks are full of statuary.

The woman in room 236 remembers how, at the end of a holiday in Europe, she flew back into the city on board a jet: first passing over the great cool neon signs hanging in the air at its outskirts − TEXACO, MOWLEM, ALFA-LAVAL, the Internationals signalling steady as beacons into the night − then entering that soft meniscus of light, that city of floodlighted movements as far as the eye can see. Her loneliness, she felt at the time, was complete.

Now, with the room darkened and the television turned off, she lies back on the bed and allows this faint illumination to fall on her from the open window. Turning restlessly one way and then the other, as if she were trying to sleep in her clothes, on the undisturbed counterpane in the trembling light, she stares up at the ceiling. At first her hands are quite still at her sides. Soon though they draw themselves up along her thighs, flat, palms down, pulling the hem of the skirt up with them. They are tender but nearly impersonal. With the skirt bundled awkwardly around her waist, and her silk knickers rolled down round her ankles, she seems to be offering her sex not so much to her own hands as to the room, the city, anything as long as it is beyond herself. 'Oh,' she says quietly after a minute or two, 'it's so beautiful!' But then a train clatters into Central Station, and the muzak plays 'Rhapsody in Blue', and she gets up from the bed in despair or rage and switches on the fluorescent lamp above the make-up mirror.

Her name is Sophia. She was disfigured at birth by a mark like a splash — as if, her parents said, someone threw red ink in her face the very day she was born — down the right side of the nose, all round the eye on that side, and across the right cheek. Splatters and dots radiate from the raw-looking central stain like the headlands and islands of some heavily fjorded coast.

2: *Narcissus Fires*

At this time of night Peter Ebert can usually be found at the Doric Restaurant, which is not far away across the city at the corner of Acol Street.

The Doric is often crowded with young men like himself. Hands thrust into the pockets of their baggy black trousers, they wait for a table, gazing at the bottles above the bar with the musing expression you give to art, while the pictures — gigantic loving pencil sketches of a link of dockyard chain, which looks pumped-up and organic and about to explode, like a black pudding or a huge turd — go unnoticed on the walls. Bottles are a feature of the decor: spirit bottles in optics over the bar, green ends of wine bottles goggling into the room from racks, empty bottles stuck with cheap white candles to light the long oilcloth-covered tables. At the height of the evening, waitresses are running in and out distractedly, the room becomes suffocatingly hot, the air stuffed to bursting with the smell of choux pastry with ham and cheese in a gooseberry sauce, the walls yellow with cigarette smoke.

'After all,' someone shouts across the racket, 'it's no good cutting the Speak Your Weight machine out of your will because you don't like everything it says about you!'

'I know.'

At Peter Ebert's table a girl passes her finger through the candle flame, an expression on her face of distant enquiry, as if objectivity were not so much an act as a very faint emotion: one so removed from humanity – or at least everyday humanity – as to be hardly detectable in oneself without special training; yet an emotion nonetheless. Ebert stares at her.

This morning someone gave him a book.

It was such a curious transaction – hermetic, contingent, having its own rules, like a bubble of meaning in the ordinary events of life – that even now he feels tempted to tell someone, 'I bet this has never happened to you. At the station this morning' – Ebert means not Central but the city's less important station, Eastern, popularly known as Regent's – 'a man I had never seen before came up and offered me a book.'

Between the end of Regent's platform 4 and the mouth of the tunnel which takes the line out of the city centre, there is a deep, walled cutting. On a wet day rain blows about in this space; as it circulates there, the light striking into it from the street above the station makes it seem distinct and photographic, as romantic as rain falling in a new Russian film. Watching from the dim, sheltered platform, you have the impression of an illuminated curtain, out of which noses every so often the yellow front of a train, streaked with oil, shiny with water, and bringing with it a cold stream of air. People waiting near the edge of the platform step back momentarily to let the carriage doors swing open; passengers alight and rush away.

Making room like this with all the others, Peter Ebert found himself staring someone's face. It was quite close to his: one of those old or ill-looking faces at whose salient points small tight lumps of muscle seem to have gathered, as if the flesh had retreated there to leave the bones

prominent and bare − or as if blobs of putty had been arranged on the jaw and cheekbones of a skull, then covered
with white pancake make-up. Later he was to say 'a man',
but in fact he was never sure whether it belonged to a man
or a woman. Of the body beneath it he caught only confused impressions − a pale brown raincoat, thin shoulders,
a leather case or bag. A hand, its knuckles reddened and
enlarged by years of work or illness, offered him the book. He
took it without thinking: imagined he heard someone say
in a contemptuous, dismissive voice, 'Narcissus' or 'Narcissus Fire': lost sight of the figure in the crowd pressing
towards the ticket barrier.

He stared at the book in his hand. He was suddenly convinced that there must be some other way to live. What he
meant by this he couldn't think; except that it wasn't what
you would normally mean. He had to catch the train, or
he would have dropped the book into the nearest waste
bin. When he got out at the other end it was in his pocket.

'All at once,' he now thinks of saying to the girl at his
table, 'you can't make head or tail of anything, can you?'

As he opens his mouth to speak she smiles at him and
pinches out the candle flame. He sees how the naked small
of her back would curve up out of the waistband of her
skirt, how astonishingly real and human its warmth would
make her seem to him. But the book is in his pocket −
though its cover has fallen off long since he thinks it was
a paperback, quite an old one from the thirties or forties
− and he knows he will be going home to read it. It is
Ebert's belief that understanding ought to come by
epiphany rather than by increments: it has never occurred
to him how completely this might limit his intellectual
reach. Behind him the waitress says,

'Whose was the plain chocolate mousse?'

3: *Sophia's Gift*

Every story is a cup so empty it can be drunk from again
and again.

Once or twice a week she brings a man home to room 236 at the Central Hotel. If men see too much of her face they sometimes become puzzled and unkind, so out of consideration she keeps it turned away when she can, and on the way home tries as often as possible to be looking at something on the other side of the road: an old bicycle propped against a wall, the brightly-lit shop window where a display of popular wedding stationery seems to merge indistinguishably with the cigarette ends and chip wrappers on the pavement outside. She always leaves the door of the room open a crack, so there will be no need for a light.

Tonight she is with a man called Dave.

When they got inside the room he wouldn't lie down. He had been drinking whisky and Coke, so she had to struggle with his clothes as well as her own. 'I love you, Dave,' she said, kissing his face. 'At least do something to help,' she said. 'Dave, I love you.' He kept trying to find the light switch. Eventually he managed to put one of the bedside lamps on. Please don't change your mind now, she thought, and looked away so quickly that the tendons stood out in her neck. But he only said, 'Women!' and switched the light out himself. Then he fell on to the bed, where — after trying to lever her legs apart, unaware that they had become fastened together at the knees by the muddle of tights and underwear she had not had time to push down any further — he made a few disconnected movements, came with a groan between her closed thighs, and fell asleep. 'No, wait,' she was still whispering, 'you're not — ' She held his head tenderly.

Dave's semen is drying in the warm hotel air, tautening a patch of her skin. A hotel is so comfortable, she thinks: if you had really wanted to do that I could have helped you, and now we could be having a bath together or anything. Sophia stares at the diffuse line of light round the open door. The last train has come in, and now the station concourse is so quiet you can hear someone's shoes squeaking across the polished floor. This faint dry sound

156

reminds her of her holiday in Norway: the sound of feet on the shiny museum floors of Oslo, which smell of care and polish and respect.

She loves pictures. At the Munchmuseet she was careful to see *Consolation*, *Madonna*, and *The Mountain Path*; at the Nasjonal Galleriet, *Den Sarede Engell*. A friend took her to the Vikingskipmuseet so she should have a chance to see the Oseberg Ship before she left. He showed her a runic inscription scratched on a piece of black wood one thousand years old. 'It means,' he told her, ' "Mankind knows so little".' He was a quiet man, a little younger than herself and determined to entertain her, who sold books in Scandinavia for a firm of English academic publishers, and lectured at the Universitet on the early film documentarists with their theories of 'camera eye' and 'redemption of reality'. He had made short films for a living, and still wrote scripts. 'I read everything about this once,' he said. 'I think that's what it means.' The old ships, their planks laid together in bunches of hurtling curves like diagrams of a slipstream, sailed round her through the dim light of the museum, ignoring her.

'It's hard to imagine them buried,' she said. 'How they must have flown across the sea!'

'A boat like this was built only for funerals, I'm afraid.'

Later she had to wait for him in the darkened cafeteria of one of the university buildings. There, a boy with long red hair played desultorily on an out-of-tune piano; after a moment he got up with an exclamation of impatience and went out into the corridor. Outside, the rain was falling into a courtyard, the high brick walls of which, though quite new, looked authentically old and tranquil. To foster this impression weeds had been allowed to grow between the unworn cobbles. The rain turned to hail, then after a moment of violence passed over; the fountain bubbled up. Yellow roses and dark earth. The red-haired boy came in again and said with Norwegian irony, 'I suppose we are all waiting for something!'

That was the last day of the holiday. When they drove

back to her friend's home along the coast it was late. On one side of the Drammensveien the moon hung diffused and dark orange, bloated like a bag; on the other, the morning light, clean and green. The moon, though, would not set; and the dawn, endlessly promised, was endlessly incomplete. She was so tired and happy. They had stayed on in the cafes of Tingvallakaia, which at half-past two every morning begin to empty themselves of couples so drunk they can only look straight ahead.

The next day, through the scratched and smeary window of the British Airways 757, she caught sight of the great granite rock of Kolsås. Because she had stared at it so often from the balcony of his flat, she was eager for it to be the last thing she saw in Norway. Touching her face gently at the airport, he had promised her: 'This is not a birthmark. It's a map.'

4: *The Precious Discoveries of the Senses*

At three in the morning Peter Ebert makes himself a cup of tea.

The hotel is quiet. At this time of night you might hear a door open then close, a muffled laugh from another room: but though the lights burn in the carpeted corridors, no one is walking along them. The central heating touches your skin gently and evenly. Ebert loves the sense of freedom this gives him; he loves nothing better than to be awake at night and let the hotel press round him its padded silence.

At six, grey light comes through the curtain, and he opens his window. Cold air spills over his feet; pigeons clatter away between the buildings, a sound unannounced and without issue; somewhere out of sight a pink and gold dawn is colouring the edges of the statues in the city's hilly little parks. Ebert rubs his hands over his eyes.

At nine o'clock he telephones his office.

'Another puzzle,' he thinks as he waits for his secretary to answer, 'is the *title*.'

What sort of book has he been given? Peter Ebert is unable to say. It lies open on the table in front of him amid a litter of crumpled hotel notepaper, empty cups, and torn sachets of non-dairy creamer: a hundred and thirty pages which end in the middle of a sentence — 'the precious discoveries of the senses —' Even the surviving text is incomplete. Some pages are missing, others have been torn in half longitudinally, to leave only curious groups of words: 'years of swill', 'the subsoil account' and 'comically little value'.

Everyone who has owned it has stained and defaced it with his humanity, thinks Ebert. They have annotated it in pencil too faint to read, spattered it with food, slashed it in straight careful lines with a razor blade on a wet Monday in a bus station. They've sweated into it and worse whilst reading listlessly, sick in bed in Mottingham or Manchester. They've rubbed tomato sauce into it in thumbprints, and left impacted in its central creases cigarette ash like the grey flock which bursts from padded bags. Its outer pages are a pissy-yellow colour, glazed with grease yet furry from being handled, their corners rounded off and thick as felt. Its spine is rotten. All that remains of its title pages is a blank leaf on which is printed centrally in bold letters EON HEART; and even there they have spilled bleach or semen on it, Ebert thinks, so that 'eon' is only part of a word which might as easily have read 'Simeon' as 'Pantheon'.

'I'm not coming in today,' he says suddenly into the telephone. Then: 'Tell him no.'

His eye has been caught by the words, '. . . the little Fennec with its beautiful ears!'

Last night, though he had no idea what they meant, he gave a shiver of delight every time he read these words.

'To make the little white Fennec, butterflies mated themselves to foxes, fluttering into their uplifted faces in the desert air at evening. The faces of the foxes were like flowers to them, they circled closer.'

Ebert's hotel room looks out on a deep, four-sided yard

built in Victorian Gothic, with pointed windows, peaked gables and brick finials. The lower part of the yard – where, less than thirty years ago, traffic still went in and out – has become choked with small buildings. Wires sag aimlessly from wall to wall above them, rotten ladders run over their roofs. Where hotel guests once stepped down from cars and taxis, moss thickens the rusting gutters. Where laughter once flew up like birds, everything is indescribably filthy. Every flat surface – even the collars which hold the drainpipes against the walls – is covered with a soft roll of pigeon shit, which hangs beneath each window ledge like a cream-coloured beard.

When he first got the book home, his excitement was so intense that he could feel the whole of his upper body rocking slightly and rhythmically to the beat of his heart. All the way home he had looked forward to the moment when he could open it. At every junction the familiar streets had seemed to lurch into new arrangements, as if he was seeing them after a long absence or from an unexpected angle.

5: 'As if by Moonlight'

'If my face was a map,' Sophia wonders, 'what kind of country would it reveal?'

An island, with other islands outlying, in a warm sea.

From its central highlands fissures and ridges radiate, napped with jungle: green velour sleeves which fall right down to the tide. Coral snakes curl up like strings of lacquered beads, water lizards bask in the sun, macaws thicken the noon sky in flocks. Up there in the highlands the light slants between the trees in distinct beams. At night you dream you are down in the island's fever-haunted valleys, where the aboriginals – painted ash-white with blackened eye-sockets – pursue you without mercy to the shore. 'While the currents are generally labyrinthine,' the guidebooks promise, 'the water unforgiving and wine-dark, you can sometimes find a shallow bay filled with water of an intense blue.'

160

She stares into the make-up mirror.

'I'm like a whitewashed wall,' she decides. 'Should I go to the zoo?'

On the way she thinks of Dave, who never got in touch.

The streets smell of burning rubber, and cold has made the air transparent. You can see every building in the city centre – every duct and aluminium window frame, the gilded iron on every old bridge – from miles away, and sense the river flowing grey and gelid to the sea. At the zoo a few Japanese and Italian tourists shiver from cage to cage, photographing one another while waste paper and empty peanut shells blow about their ankles. Wherever you go in the zoo you can hear the strange, carrying, bird-like cry of the lar gibbons.

These coffee-coloured animals huddle like lookouts among the metal struts in the ceiling of their tall cage. They hold their delicate hands curved in front of them as if the joints are painful. Their eyes look bruised. They face steadily into the cold wind and cry out as though there is some message in it they cannot understand, only celebrate. Sophia can't bear this. To escape them she takes the underpass to the Nocturnal Mammal House, thinking: 'If my face is a map, it must never show a wilderness – '

All down the west coast of the island at night glitter the lights of a modern city five miles long, its towers like black and gold cigarette packets standing on end. In its shopping malls fluorescent light catches the surfaces of hard and soft designer goods: matte plastics, foams of lace and oyster satin, the precise curves of cars and shoes and shoulder pads. This city is well known for the scent of Anaïs-Anaïs in the streets; stacked video screens in the cocktail lounges; and, down by the sea-front, where men push past you smelling of sweat and Chinese food, neon of green, red or frosty blue. Music pulses from its amusement arcades and night clubs. In the jazz bars they serve only Black Heart rum, and you can hear the intricate bass and saxophone lines twenty miles out to sea.

'It's none of these things,' she admits to herself. She laughs.

'My face is the map to an island off the coast of Norway. A few quiet people from Oslo live there at weekends, in coloured wooden houses. To get there you first catch a train to Sandvika, where a bank of wild flowers comes right down to the station platform.'

The further you go into the mammal house, with its walls of undressed brick, the darker it gets. The Moonlight World itself is illuminated only by the dim yellow lamps in each specimen compartment. Its air is full of the recorded blips and warbles of nocturnal insects or birds. Groups of people come and go preoccupiedly in front of the animals; pause silhouetted on the edge of vision; vanish murmuring round an unexpected corner. It is quite crowded: attracted immediately by the most beautiful miniature fox with creamy beige fur, soft thick tail and enormous ears, Sophia finds herself standing next to a young man.

'Isn't it lovely?' she exclaims, for something to say.

But he seems less interested in the fox than its compartment, in which has been reconstructed — with a bit of stone, brushwood, and the skull of a camel embedded in fine sand — a dreary little corner of some desert. The fox trots so intelligently about this lost or reduced territory! You can feel its warmth and liveliness even when it curls up and goes to sleep. At first Sophia is delighted like this by every animal she sees — lemurs, echidnae like soft toys, civet cats and desert mice. But soon the air feels too warm. It smells increasingly like sawdust and urine. The animals, she notices suddenly, often move in agitated, repetitive patterns behind the smeary, fingerprinted glass. A child, laughing shrilly, makes claws of its hands and runs up and down in front of a puzzled cat.

On her way out, Sophia has to pass the young man.

'Still looking?' she calls, but he doesn't seem to hear. In the feeble light from the compartment she can see how tight he grips the plastic rail; how drawn his face is, how wide and tired his eyes. He takes out a notebook and

162

begins to write intently in it. He is copying down the details of the animal, which are recorded on a small plaque.

6: *In Omber Grove*

Whatever else it may be, EON HEART is the record of a journey, made some time during the last fifty or sixty years, into one of the less-travelled countries of the world. And often a plain record, too:

'For four miles round the bay at Enchidoche,' the author tells his readers, 'where the deeper water runs inshore, will be found meat-packing plants and sheds which, until recently, were used for drying fish.' He includes specific sailing instructions – 'Half a mile from Tharasalla Point, sandbars and wrecks show themselves at half tide. We went in boldly and got ten feet of clearance at low water. Keep Mutton Rock in line with the derelict flensing factory on Auxilliadora Island and it will take you clear of the sand.' – though they are not for major ports; and clear sketches in pen and ink of items of special interest:

'A diadem of yellow and blue macaw feathers, with the Clan Sign.'

Yet this country is never referred to by name. And if, in its original condition, Peter Ebert's copy contained a map, it has been lost with the title pages. The surviving text, a description of the interior, speaks only of villages, minor towns and rivers too small for any atlas to record. The kinds of clues it might offer are obscured by the author's style:

Exploration, anthropology, natural history. Metaphysics, poetry and fear. A travel book should be about all these. But then it must whirl itself away beyond them; and, at once runaway boat and racing current, plunge between the dark walls of its own silence until it becomes only a spume of visions and metaphors – so that its reader, gripped by the vertigo of new experiences, is compelled to close it suddenly and walk away in an attempt to control his own excitement. In short, it must address our *desire*.

— or lost among the partly-torn pages, stains and defacings, of which Ebert has now compiled a list so exhaustive it defeats any use he might make of it. 'p43: two words of text heavily deleted in red ballpoint pen, and another word — perhaps "fugazi" — inserted above.' 'p53/9 missing.' 'p60 detached, folded in half, and reinserted between pp75/6. Scrawled across it in black marker pen the words, "Mary I cant believe this. See you at ten." This unsigned, and the ink has deeply penetrated the paper.'

Peter no longer eats out in the evenings. He has exchanged his room at the Midland Hotel for a cheaper one in a boarding house a short way out of the city centre. From his window he can now see: a short stretch of cracked, littered pavement (Omber Grove), curving away to a junction (with Quex Road); a unisex hairdressers called 'Nueva Swing'; and a newsagent owned by an old man with the acronym FUGA tattooed on the inside of his left wrist. Though Peter still wears the expensive, generously-cut suits and striped shirts you would expect to see at the Doric Restaurant, he no longer shaves every day and even forgets to wash. Obsessed by a puzzle his intelligence is unequal to, he has resigned from his job, and goes agitatedly from one lending library to another, from reference library to museum, looking for a complete copy of the book.

He has often wondered why it was given to him, speculating, 'It's not uncommon for a commuter to pass on, say, a newspaper he's finished with.' But when he reviews the circumstances of the gift — the crowd, the train, that white face with its shiny lumps of flesh — he understands that this is too simple an answer. His notebook describes a visit to the zoo, concluding disappointedly:

'After all, the Fennec is only a kind of fox.'

Every morning the pale light throws on to the wall of his room the shadow of a tree outside in Omber Grove. At first the image is so clear and sharp Ebert can make out the patches of condensation on the windowpane and construct the whole depth of the tree — its nearer branches sharp and black, the further ones less and less distinct. Later it fades until you have to work just to see it. Before it vanishes altogether it seems more like a product of the wall than of optics: as if, lighted by a very faint inner radiance, the wall has offered some memory of its own as a curio, as an almost random pattern. Someone pushes a pram down the street outside.

7: *The Truth Which Most Contradicts Itself*

Sophia often gets up late and walks about the city in her fur coat, watching the afternoon light die out of the residential streets. From the recreation grounds come the shouts and whistles, the tragic howls of some football game. At this time of year, with the sun setting at half-past three behind a frieze of bare sycamores, the big red-brick houses round the parks have a comfortable November style: yew, holly and privet make their gardens mysterious, their lighted front rooms warm and inviting, as if Christmas had already come.

On the pavement one woman says to another: 'He's had no proper dinner then?'

'No, he's like a whitewashed wall. Eating chocolate all the time, well it's no good, is it? Just no good at all. All he thinks about is that CD.'

This reminds Sophia of Oslo. The phrase 'en koppe caffe og en koppe sjokolade' comes back to her very clearly. 'The morning we went to Tøyen,' she thinks, 'to the Munchmuseet, we sat in an upstairs cafe. He looked into his cup and said in a lugubrious, Norwegian voice, "Nothing lasts forever!" and we laughed.'

Whenever she recalls something like this a shiver of

excitement runs through her, itself an echo of the excitement she felt every moment in those days. ' "Nothing lasts, especially a cup of chocolate!" He was so clever at mimicking himself.' Her own cup, she remembers, was decorated with three thin horizontal lines: pink, maroon, pastel blue. 'They seemed so precise and yet so fragile against the bluish-white depths of the china. I was afraid to move the saucer in case they rippled and broke.' She felt the tendency of all things to quiver without warning and fall away from perfection. But as long as she left her coffee untouched, and the sun continued to pour in so brightly across the marble table-top, the world would remain fixed. It would maintain its exact edges.

At Oslo airport, waiting for the flight back, she bought a box of matches. On its label an attractive little landscape − a tree, some low hills, a lake − was silhouetted in black against an ochre ground. 'Bruks-Eske', ran the legend. She had no idea what it meant. 'Hjelpestikker.' For a long time she kept it on the make-up table in 236. It was an impulse of love not so much for him, she recognised, as for Oslo itself: she never used the matches, but the box could make her think so suddenly of the view from Holmenkollen, or the seagulls in Pipervika harbour, that everything seemed to rush out of her and empty itself away like water.

'En koppe caffe og en koppe sjokolade: that's what we had.' Though which of them gave the order to the waitress she is no longer sure. Weakened and tranquillised by these memories, Sophia stands in the middle of the pavement, staring helplessly over some railings at a strip of grass strewn with fallen leaves where two dogs are running in opposite circles in the gathering dark. Then, wondering what people must think of her, she walks off quickly towards the city centre and goes into the first bar she finds.

'Black Heart rum, please.'

Leaving it two or three hours later, she wishes she could fly up into the trembling meniscus of light over the city. Some rain has fallen and the air is warmer. High up there

166

are a few clouds like ribs. From above, she imagines, they must look like something drawn on a transparency between the aeroplane and the earth.

'I did think it would last forever,' she admits. 'I did think it would.'

8: *Peter Ebert's Gift*

Meanwhile Ebert lurches about the city, the EON HEART clutched to his chest, now in one hand, now in the other. The streets are glassed with rain, the long cotton coat he often wore to the Doric is sodden and filthy, his route has become as habitual as any dosser's. By seven or eight a.m. he's on the pavement outside the Midland Hotel where he used to live. He spends much of the morning at Regent's, shuffling his feet in the cold draughts under the great Victorian vault. At lunchtime he takes himself off to one or another of the city's little parks. He has stopped pretending that by this means he can 'understand' the book. Neither is he driven any longer by the urge to revisit, venue by venue, the stages of his own descent – the platform where he was given it, the libraries in which he searched for it, the rooms in which he copied it out.

Instead he reads the book to himself for itself. Mid-afternoon finds him in the Natural History Museum, moving his lips over the words 'fly down mass' (p62) or returning to the most resistant passage of all:

After all why *should* our goal be the reinstatement of an illusory 'exact' relationship between events and words? If you probe in the ashes you will never learn anything about the fire: by the time the ashes can be handled the meaning has passed on. Every adventure is a cup so empty it can be drunk from again and again and again. Every adventure is so perfect it verges on silence. (p112)

His hair has gone grey.

167

Perhaps from all this reading, his eyes are inflamed, caked at the corners, deeper-set than he remembers. If he is ever frightened it is not when he smells his own breath in the morning. Or when in the mirror he sees a man twenty years older than the one who, in an unguarded moment a month or two ago, accepted a book just because it was offered him. These shocks soon pass. He slides them over his real fear, that he will begin to read the book aloud to passers-by. There are days when every park bench is a pulpit. He feels himself begin to speak. If he did, how could he bear their contempt?

Regent's Station, 4.30: commuters prowl uneasily beneath its scrolled iron girders in the bitter cold. The arrivals board makes a fluttering, disappointed noise and train is wiped off as they watch. In his turn, Ebert watches them, looking for the one he could talk to; makes off, limping, just in time. He has the intolerable sense of being at a locus, where something is struggling to be revealed.

'I – '

Every adventure verges on silence.

Trapped by the rhetoric of the EON HEART, he sees how impossible it will be to say anything ever again, and by nightfall finds himself standing on an obscure corner in the pool of light outside the New Venus dry cleaners. Across the road a few market stalls are closing down for the night. There is a smell of rain, leather, soapsuds, food; in a gust of wind the plastic over the stalls shifts uneasily; a tortoiseshell cat is staring intently down a drain. Inside the New Venus a woman in a fur coat is arguing with the proprietor.

'What colour were the trousers?'

'There weren't any trousers,' she repeats tiredly.

Ebert sees a tall untidy woman with brown hair and wide shoulders, whose age is hard to guess because her face is turned away from him. Beneath the bulky fur, which is itself in need of a clean, her body has heavy, relaxed qualities, as if she has always been comfortable with it. Her shoes are scuffed, black suede peeling off to reveal the plastic heel; and wet pavements have left little pale splashes of mud on her stockings. In one hand she holds a pair of gloves, in the other a carrier bag printed with the name of a well-known off-licence.

'Ah,' says the proprietor, an elderly Asian. '*No trousers.*'

He takes her ticket and stares at it for some moments.

'One white skirt. Two pullovers. A blue dress,' she reminds him. 'You said I could have them before six.' But the proprietor can find none of these garments on the rack behind the counter. Instead he keeps offering her quite different ones.

'This?'

'No.'

'This?'

Making a gesture of disgust she walks quickly to the door. Ebert, who has been following their exchange as if it represented some warm real world from which he is now endlessly separated by the existence of the book, turns guiltily away from the window. He hears the door of the New Venus swing open. In a gust of heated, solvent-laden air she crosses the road. Heels click, bottles clink. Before he can stop himself Ebert has pushed his way between the market stalls and is hurrying after her. Bare electric bulbs illuminate his face, her retreating back. Spoiled vegetables slither under their feet. He hears himself call out.

'Wait! I was given a book!' And then, managing at last to touch her arm shyly, 'Please let me read you this – '

Horrified by his fatal loss of self control, and hallucinating in his anxiety to escape before he can add anything more, a strong smell of rum, Ebert dodges away from her and runs blindly into a brick wall.

9: *The Hearts of Things*

'All at once you can't make head or tail of anything, can you?'

Tonight Sophia is with a man whose name she doesn't know. This has happened before, if not often. When they got back to the Central Hotel the bar was still open.

'Would you like a drink?'

'It's kind of you,' he said. 'No.'

He was so preoccupied she found it easy to keep her face turned away from him. While she collected her room key he sat on the edge of a chair in the foyer, staring down between his shoes at the design in the carpet as though he were trying to see past it. Every time the door opened, a cold draught came into the foyer and he looked up suddenly. He was thinner than she'd thought, and his coat was ruined.

'I hope you didn't hurt yourself too much,' she apologised. 'I thought you were the man from the dry cleaners. I was so angry with him!'

'It's a relief to talk to someone,' he said obscurely.

'Didn't I once see you at the zoo?'

He passed his hand puzzledly across his face.

Now they are up in 236, with the door a little open so that the room is filled with a brown light. She has helped him off with his coat. He doesn't say much, but sits there on the bed, leaning forward with his hands between his knees. She likes his face, which though young is so tired it seems all bone, stubble, grey eyes; which is incapable of taking shelter; which admits desire but never alleviation. She wants to touch it gently round the eyes and cheeks, and at the same time say, 'You can just sleep if that's what you'd like. I mean, we don't have to do anything at first.' She can imagine herself saying just those words: 'I mean.' Then a couple go past in the corridor outside, talking and laughing quietly. At this a shiver runs through him and he pulls away from her.

'All at once you can't make head or tail of anything – '

Out of the pocket of his coat comes an old book; and before she has time to realise what he is going to do, he has reached out and switched on the bedside light –

– To Peter Ebert the lamp seems brighter than it can possibly be, a kind of lightning flash that splits the air

170

diagonally between them to reveal the appalling rose-coloured *map* which obscures her face.

He recalls the words, 'Instants of self-awareness too confused to be of any use.'

The book has become agitated in his hands, leafing through its own pages with increasing hysteria until they flicker and blur like destinations on the 'departures' board at Regent's Station. In slow motion Sophia averts her face from the light, turning her head to the left and dropping it forward and down so that her chin will be tucked protectively into the hollow of the clavicle on that side. Before she can complete this characteristic passive gesture, it seems to Ebert that the EON HEART has left his hands and embedded itself in her face. As it is sucked away, a white arc hangs fluorescing in its wake, overlapping images of an open book fossilised in the very air of the room.

Sophia opens to it like a flower –

– Every story is so perfect it verges on silence: in this moment none of us can ever be sure whether the map receives the book or is received by it. The light flares up, room 236 is filled with the strange, carrying, bird-like cry of the lar gibbons, while a voice repeats endlessly:

'It's lovely. It's so lovely – '

– It isn't a dream. The book lies on the bed, its accumulated defacements glowing like stigmata. With the light dying out of the air between them, Peter and Sophia are flung apart. They will find one another again confidently enough. She will be surprised by the heat of his skin and whisper, 'I only felt the slightest touch.' The way the hollow of her back curves up out of the waistband of her slip will make her seem astonishingly real and human to him. Just before dawn there will steal over the 'entresol' floor of the Central Hotel that silence which enfolds lovers and lovers' cries and is only deepened by them.

Aware of it pressing upon them its padded warmth, they will go to the window of 236 and smile out at the city –

five miles of coloured neon where the jungle comes down to the sea, buildings like elegant black and gold cigarette packets standing on end, music from the amusement arcades trailing out like lights across the water: the smell of Black Heart rum and the scent of Anaïs-Anaïs in the streets.

Sophia will sit before the mirror in the morning, while Peter reads (already planning how to pass the book on, in some jazz bar or pizzeria) and then scribbles on the flyleaf, just under the title in that intense, endlessly expectant white space –

> Take me aside. Tell me a sign.
> Send me a neon heart. Seek me inside.

COLIN GREENLAND

The Wish

They were good to Steve, when he got over there. They fixed
him up with a car, and put him in an apartment, rent free,
for the first month. The apartment was very big; too big,
really, for one. He had left all his stuff in storage, and what
he had brought with him was lost in this open-plan cavern.
He hung his suits at one end of the louvred wardrobe. There
didn't seem to be very many of them. The other end was
completely empty, nothing in it but a little spiky twig, a bit of
a Christmas tree lying forlorn on the white melamine. Steve
closed the door again.

The kitchen looked more like a spaceship. Baffled by its
keypads and readouts, Steve went out, nodding vaguely at
the whiskery old man who was always in the lobby and so
must be, he supposed, some sort of concierge. The car was
some minutes away, in an underground car park. There was
a moment of panic while he searched for the strip of plastic
that would open the grille; then he ventured out into the unfamiliar city.

It had been raining. The roads and pavements were slick
with wet gold. High overhead in a glistening battery of
adverts and animated signs the foreign traffic signals flashed
inscrutably. Steve cruised cautiously for an hour. The radio
offered nothing but stupid polkas and jerky electronic
noises he thought were morse until he realised there was
someone singing.

He got lost trying to follow a railway line and had to

drive through mile after mile of shuttered factories and
boxy estates. At a dingy takeaway he tried to ask for directions. The woman spoke no English. She bellowed through
the kitchen hatch. A man's voice answered unintelligibly,
but no one emerged. The woman stood frowning and pulling at her lip.

Annoyed, Steve pointed to something in the hot cabinet,
some kind of sausage, and flung a couple of coins on the
counter. This had the effect of jogging her memory, or else
she was just trying to get rid of him. At any rate, when he
finally arrived back at the flats it was much later than he'd
meant to stay out, nearly midnight, and he was in a bad
temper. The sausage was cold. The grease had soaked
through the bread and the paper before it congealed. It was
unappetising, but there was nothing else. He put it in the
microwave and went off to have a shower. Later he sat in
the kitchen, a towel about him, eating sausage and drinking fizzy beer by the blue light of the control surfaces.
Below, the city gleamed and growled.

On the whole he was not lonely. One or two people at
the shop were friendly enough, in a non-committal sort of
way, though the man who had made all the arrangements,
who had met him with the car at the airport and driven him
into town, had never appeared again since. Paulus, in
whose charge he had been left, seemed to have no use for
him at all. He gave him a catalogue and sent him to the
stock room, to familiarise himself with the range. Steve
suspected Paulus was less than delighted to have a
superfluous foreigner dumped on him by head office.
Nobody said another word about the management training
course they'd promised. They were a shifty lot, he
reckoned.

The boy at the sandwich bar nearest the shop had an
English girlfriend. He would like very much one day to
visit London, Buckingham Palace, Piccadilly Circus. He
told Steve to call him Matt, and practised his English conversation on him, every lunchtime. Matt was a cheerful,
irritating sort of bloke Steve would probably not even have

174

noticed and would certainly have ignored if he had, back home. There were compensations, though: a free cup of coffee, once in a while; and Matt would let him boast about life in England, which none of the shop people wanted to know about. Supercilious and smelling faintly of good aftershave, they heard his anecdotes, then started chattering, nodding to each other and laughing. Steve knew they were sending him up.

One day Matt invited him to a party.

'My girlfriend and her friends. She would be so happy for you to come.'

'I'll think about it.'

Steve was imagining students and hippies, red light-bulbs everywhere, washing-up bowls full of coleslaw. It was on a Friday night, and he had to work the next day. But out of desperation, he went.

It was somewhere in the north. The area was more affluent than he had been expecting. The house was narrow and cramped, with old furniture they'd tarted up. All the lights were on and some sort of coloured music was playing very loudly. There were children running around shrieking and, in the front room, an elderly couple sitting very upright on a sofa, smiling politely at everyone.

Matt, when Steve found him in the crush, was depressed. He had had a row with his girlfriend. Now would not be a good moment to introduce Steve. Matt excused himself, and disappeared.

There didn't seem to be much in the way of alcohol. Determined to make the best of a bad job, and stuck for someone to talk to, Steve drank most of his own bottle of wine. He was already a bit smashed when he noticed the woman.

She was wearing a long embroidered skirt, old-fashioned, and her hair was a mess, frankly; but she had a nice face, long and rather pale, with huge eyes. She caught him staring across the room. He smiled, and she looked away at once. A few minutes later, he caught her looking at him.

175

Later Steve went upstairs, searching for the loo. He listened carefully at every door, dreading bursting in on some amorous couple. Then he found the bathroom and had a piss. There were weird pictures everywhere, pictures of little children, with snakes and all sorts. He wondered how the people had the nerve to put them up, in smart steel frames too, as if they were art or something. Hurrying out, he bumped into the woman, who was waiting to go in. He thought her smile warranted hanging around on the landing for her. He rehearsed the phrase, and when she emerged, greeted her awkwardly. She replied in English.

'Were you waiting for me?' she asked. Her voice was clear and low.

Steve winked.

'Very well,' she said, calm as anything. She did not smile.

Steve wondered if his intentions had been misunderstood, but then decided she was probably the cool sulky type. He would soon warm her up. He held up his glass in mute enquiry.

'Yes, please,' she said.

Steve lifted a hand. 'Wait here,' he told her, went downstairs, and struggled through the mob in the hall. When he came back she was still there, leaning against the wall. He leant beside her, his back to the stairs, shielding her from the constant flow of people in and out of the bathroom.

Much later he remembered what he was about, and offered to steer her into a vacant bedroom, where they would be more comfortable. But she said, 'I must go home.'

'Where do you live? I'll drive you,' said Steve at once.

'A long way. Right up in the mountains.'

'No, really, I'll drive you.'

'I should like that,' she said.

Steve hadn't felt so excited since he was a teenager. He found his coat; but she had come just as she was, apparently, in the white peasant blouse that hung so nicely over her little breasts. Steve put his hand on her breast as they

176

sat in the car, and kissed her. She did not resist, or respond, really, apart from smiling slightly, which was not in the least discouraging, but he felt a bit daft, and took his hand away. He was well in, anyway, obviously. He felt on top of the world.

'I live in the country,' she said. 'Many kilometres away.'

Steve reflected that he had been talking to her for an hour, and that her name was Linzl; but he knew nothing else about her, or what they *had* talked about. Yet he was not drunk any more. In fact he felt supremely clear.

'How did you get here, then?' he asked.

Linzl seemed to misunderstand him. 'I always come,' she said.

Steve noticed that she seemed to relax the minute they got out of the suburbs and onto the highway. Fields began to appear either side the road. The mountains were ahead, dark shapes shouldering towards them over the dark hills.

'Now you will see our country as she really is,' said Linzl.

He drove boldly with one hand, and put the other on her knee. Again, she did not require him to remove it. The women here were all right, Steve decided.

It was indeed kilometres away. The road began to climb. They passed through a little old village with a wooden church and a hump-backed bridge. Everyone was fast asleep. There was not a sign of life. It was the sort of place you see on Christmas cards, with a sleigh, and children in mufflers skating on the river. After that it was all thick pinewoods. For the last mile there wasn't even a road, just a steep, stony track that the first decent rain would wash away, probably.

'However do you get up and down without a car?' asked Steve, wrestling with the strange transmission.

'I don't go out often,' she said.

The cottage was wood and stone, quite small and low, with a mossy roof. Steve got out of the car and stood under the stars, enchanted. There was even a well. It had a stone wall and a little mossy roof of its own, just like in a kid's picture-book.

'A wishing-well!'

'It is for water,' said Linzl.

But Steve insisted, no, it was a wishing-well. 'It's got to grant me a wish,' he said.

'You must throw in a coin,' said Linzl. 'For a wish to come true, of course, you have to pay.'

So Steve threw in a coin, one of the small ones, and held his breath until he heard it hit the water, wishing he could stay there with her forever and not thinking himself foolish at all.

'Do you know what I wished?' he asked her, lasciviously.

'You must not speak it,' she warned him. 'It is not lucky.'

'I'm lucky, all right. Tonight I am. Aren't I?'

She opened the front door. It was not locked; nor was there any gate or fence.

'You go in,' said Steve. 'I've just got to – you know. Commune with nature, ha, ha.'

He went up behind the house, to the edge of the clearing, where there was a dead tree, an ugly great spike sticking up at the beautiful sky. The branches had mostly broken away, though the trunk seemed solid enough. He ought to carve his initials on it, he thought, so they would be here always, after he was back in England, after he was dead and gone, probably.

Steve zipped up his fly and went back indoors, through a tiny flagstoned kitchen to a room crammed with lumpy furniture and hung with thick rugs. Linzl was sitting at the table with a candle, reading a small book.

'Hello,' said Steve.

She looked up and saw him. She pushed her hair back with one hand, closed the book with the other. For a moment it was as though he'd disturbed her, as though she'd been reading for ages and had forgotten all about him. Then she said 'Sit down, please,' and pointed to an upright, uncomfortable-looking armchair.

Steve sat.

'You will want a drink.'

She reached to the top of the dresser and took a decanter and glass from among the clutter.

'Aren't you having one? Cheers, then.'

It seemed natural to knock it back in one.

Linzl got up then, abruptly, took the candle and went into the other room, leaving Steve in the dark. He sat fingering the tablecloth. It was thick material, red as blood. The brandy burned in his throat.

'Linzl? What are you doing?'

She said only: 'Be patient.'

The bloom of the candle came out through the half-open door and wavered among the hangings. Within, Steve could see small pictures in oval frames, and a brown frieze of dried flowers, leaves and feathers. He could not see Linzl, nor hear a sound.

'Linzl, don't leave me all alone!' he said. 'I'll get scared.' He laughed. 'I'm coming in,' he called, but did not move.

'Come in now.'

He went. She had taken off all her clothes and got into bed. She was half covered by a faded golden quilt. She lifted her arms to him. Stirred, the candle made the shadows of her arms swoop up to the roof.

As he pulled down his jeans Steve caught sight of himself in a long mirror with a veil half over it. He seemed to have a peculiar expression on his face. He looked back quickly at the bed, at Linzl, who was worth looking at, oh god, she was beautiful.

The mattress was horsehair, and worn to a cosy hollow. It was like making love in a nest, Steve thought. It felt strange — it felt *healthy*, sort of, which puzzled him and amused him hugely. And then he had neither time nor wit to feel puzzled or amused, only terrified and delighted.

In the morning he woke to Linzl's face leaning over his, her hair falling on his cheek. The sun was shining brightly.

'Good morning.'

'Good morning, Steve.'

He smiled with satisfaction, remembering. 'How about last night, then?'

She kissed him, and got out of bed.

'Come back . . .'

Linzl shook out her hair, then reached for her gown.

'Oh, don't put that on,' he pleaded. But she pulled it tight in front and belted it securely with the sash.

'Would you like tea?'

'Tea . . .'

Steve sat up. The room was just big enough for the bed, with narrow shelves and poky cupboards on every inch of the wall that wasn't covered with some sort of curtain or other. There were little birds carved on the edges of things, and heart-shaped holes. It was exactly like something from a fairy story. He heard Linzl outside, cranking at the well. It was incredible that people still lived like this. But then Linzl was incredible.

She came back with a tray, and a teapot wrapped in fur. Steve coaxed her back into bed. They sat cuddling while the tea brewed.

'You really like it, don't you, Linzl?'

'Yes,' she said.

'I've never had a woman who liked it the way you do.'

After a while he said, 'Was I good? What did you think?' and when he failed to get an answer to that, asked, 'Are they all like you, here?'

'I am ordinary, I think,' said Linzl. By day her eyes were a slightly distracting blue. Steve tugged at her gown.

'Take this off and I'll show you if you're ordinary.'

She demurred.

'Go on,' he said, kissing her. 'Just a quickie. You know: quick.' Something occurred to him. 'What time is it?''

It was already eight. The shop would be open in half an hour, half a world away.

Any other morning Steve would have been appalled, and angry with himself. But the world had been different then. He grinned and blew on his tea. 'I'll phone in sick. It's not as if they need me.' He took a mouthful and hopped out

180

of bed, rummaging for his underpants. 'Where's your phone, Linzl?'

'Telephone? There is no telephone here.' She spoke as if he had asked something stupid. Well, perhaps he had. After all, there was no mains water. She was pretty much cut off out here. It must be horrible in winter.

Linzl sat in her robe of midnight blue, her face and hair pale against the fat white pillows. She looked different, too, this morning, older somehow, but even more wonderful. He got dressed, gazing at her, grinning like an idiot, he didn't care.

'Stay right there. I'll drive into the village and phone, and I'll be right back.'

Outside the forest was soft and encroaching. The air was like dusty amber. The car would not start.

'It won't even turn over.' He sat on the bed and drank some more tea. 'What am I supposed to do? How long does it take to walk to the village? Do the buses run this far out?'

Linzl said, 'You came a long way last night, Steve. It will take you a long while to get back again.'

'To hell with it,' he said. He felt very frightened, and very bold. 'Linzl, I love you. I don't want to go home ever, not to the city, not to England either. I want to stay here with you. Please, please, please take that dressing gown off.'

She took it off.

They made love in the morning, and again in the afternoon. Steve wanted to go up the mountain, into the wood, to make love in the open air, but Linzl kept him to her bedroom, though it was cooler there. In her bedroom, with all the fur and wood and the sombre autumn colours, it was as if it were late September already, the summer over and done.

She put on a voluminous apron and went around with a besom; she cooked a soup with zucchini, which he had never liked before; she painted melancholy swirling patterns with Indian ink and sat staring at them for hours. He believed she was a fabric designer.

'Don't you need a phone, in your line of work?'

'It is not necessary to speak to anyone,' she told him.

She got out of bed, and took a large towel from a chair in the corner. He hadn't noticed it before, under the towel. It was vacuum-formed plywood, a bit modern for her. In fact he was pretty sure there was one exactly like it in his kitchen, in the apartment.

'Where did you get that chair?'

It was irritating, the way she would just not answer sometimes. It wasn't as if she didn't understand him. He would have to do something about that.

But what was he thinking? He had to get up soon, and start walking into the village, or that would be another day gone. It was getting ridiculous. He had to go back, and go to work. He couldn't just stay here forever. Nevertheless, though it didn't bear thinking about, he knew he could. An illegal immigrant. It happened all the time. Linzl's way of life didn't seem to require money, and anyway he had his chequebook. He could drop a line to Mum and Dad, to let them know he was all right, and then just − disappear. No, this was daft, he *had* to go back, he'd get up in a minute but now all he really wanted to do was sleep, just a bit longer.

He was woken by a shrill, hostile buzz from somewhere just above his head. His hand had found the button and turned it off before he realised it was a small square digital alarm: his own. Or one exactly the same. What a coincidence. It looked an unlikely thing for Linzl to own, but he couldn't believe he'd been so drunk he'd brought his own alarm clock with him and then forgotten all about it.

The light in the room was odd. By the clock it was only the middle of the afternoon, but Linzl was asleep beside him, warm and firm and very real. The alarm had not woken her. He wondered if perhaps it had not gone off at all, and he had only imagined it had. He wondered if she would be cross if he woke her.

Steve heard a siren go keening past. They could hear the traffic quite clearly up here. He'd not noticed that before.

He lay and watched the headlights sweep across the ceiling. *This is impossible*, he told himself, *we're half a mile up the mountain*. There was no traffic on that backroad, anyway.

That was the last time Steve felt any fear. The sound of cars was curiously comforting. He drew close to Linzl, shaped himself against her back, and fell fast asleep once more.

When he next woke, there were birds singing. It seemed to be a perfectly normal morning. What day was it, though? He wasn't sure. Linzl was gone from the bed. He called, but there was no reply.

Steve dressed, determined to pull himself together. There was sunlight in the clearing. His car was completely covered with a film of sticky dust. He turned the key and, when nothing happened, did not know whether he was pleased or not. He sat sideways in the driver's seat and ate some small wrinkled apples he had found in the kitchen, after a search through drawer after drawer of meticulous collections of dead things no one could possible eat, not even here. He knew he should start out at once on foot, but could not go until she came back. He ran inside more than once, thinking he heard the phone; but of course she had not got a phone.

He went for a piss, by the dead tree. If he was going to be here for a while, he'd have to find something to do, to make himself useful, to keep himself awake. Something like, like cutting down this tree. It was dead, wasn't it? And it wasn't that big.

He took an axe from the back of the door, and a log-saw, though it was very rusty. It felt great, hacking at that old tree with no one there to know whether he was doing it properly or not. He had it down and almost chopped in half when Linzl appeared suddenly. She was wearing a cape with a long pointed hood, and carrying a rush basket of ragged black mushrooms.

'Where did you spring from?' He wiped his forehead. 'Look – I've got your tree down for you.'

'Why?' she asked.

183

'Why? For firewood!'

'That is kind of you,' she said; but he could tell she didn't mean it. She was just being polite.

Later, in bed, Linzl said, 'I liked that old tree standing there. On clear nights in November it looked like a giant claw, gripping the moon.'

Before Steve could marshal a reply, she was asleep.

Next day he heard the sound of an engine and ran outside, thinking someone had arrived on a bike, or, absurdly, that Linzl was trying to start the car. She was dismembering the tree with a chain-saw he hadn't found. She worked all day, splitting the logs and nailing the slats to a frame. It became a sort of kennel, Steve supposed, looking out of the kitchen window. He wished she would come in soon and make a cup of tea.

At that moment she came, sunlight and sawdust in her hair.

'Are you thinking of getting a dog? You really should, you know, out here on your own, I mean, a girl like you.'

She stood in the doorway. 'Go and lie down,' she said.

He was confused for a minute, thinking about the kennel. 'What?'

'Go and lie down,' said Linzl. 'I'll come to you.'

He went into the bedroom and undressed. They always seemed to be going to bed, but he hadn't had a decent night's sleep since he got here, not just because she was insatiable, but because of the dreams: strange, shadowy dreams that felt like being awake, but couldn't have been, because of the things he thought she was doing to him, and he was doing to her.

In the middle of the night Steve got up and went outside for a piss, by the stump of the tree. It was quite light in the clearing. They had so many stars here, it was impossible to tell where you were. They glimmered among the trees, and on the roof of the kennel. Steve squatted down to look inside it. It looked all right: plenty of room, really.

KIM STANLEY ROBINSON

Remaking History

'The point is *not* to make an exact replica of the Teheran embassy compound.' Exasperated, Ivan Venutshenko grabbed his hair in one hand and pulled up, which gave him a faintly oriental look. 'It's the *spirit* of the place that we want to invoke here.'

'This has the spirit of our storage warehouse, if you ask me.'

'This is our storage warehouse, John. We make all our movies here.'

'But I thought you said we were going to correct all the lies of the first movie,' John Rand said to their director. 'I thought you said *Escape From Teheran* was a dumb TV docu-drama, only worth remembering because of De Niro's performance as Colonel Jackson. We're going to get the true story on film at last, you said.'

Ivan sighed. 'That's right, John. Admirable memory. But what you must understand is that when making a film, *true* doesn't mean an absolute fidelity to the real.'

'I'll bet that's just what the director of the docu-drama said.'

Ivan hissed, which he did often while directing their films, to show that he was letting off steam, and avoiding an explosion. 'Don't be obstructionist, John. We're not doing anything like that hack-work, and you know it. Lunar gravity alone makes it impossible for us to make a completely realist film. We are working in a world of

185

dream, in a surrealist intensification of what really happened. Besides, we're doing these movies for our own entertainment up here! Remake bad historical films! Have a good time!'

'Sure, Ivan. Sure. Except the ones *you've* directed have been getting some great reviews downside, they're saying you're the new Eisenstein and these little remakes are the best thing to hit the screen since *Kane*. So now the pressure is on and it's not just a game any more, right?'

'Wrong!' Ivan karate-chopped the air. 'I refuse to believe that. When we stop having fun doing this,' nearly shouting, 'I quit!'

'Sure, Sergei.'

'Don't call me that!'

'Okay, Orson.'

'JOHN!'

'But that's *my* name. If I call you that we'll all get confused.'

Melina Gourtsianis, their female lead, came to Ivan's rescue. 'Come on, John, you'll give him a heart-attack, and besides it's late. Let's get on with it.'

Ivan calmed down, ran his hands through his hair. He loved doing his maddened director routine, and John loved maddening him. As they disagreed about nearly everything, they made a perfect team. 'Fine,' Ivan said. 'Okay. We've got the set ready, and it may not be an *exact* replica of the compound − ' fierce glare at John, 'but it's good enough.'

'Now, let's go through it one more time. It's night in Teheran. This whole quarter of the city has been gassed with a paralysing nerve gas, but there's no way of telling when the Revolutionary Guards might come barrelling in from somewhere else with gas-masks or whatever, and you can't be sure some of them haven't been protected from the gas in sealed rooms. Any moment they might jump out firing. Your helicopters are hovering just overhead, so it's tremendously noisy. There's a blackout in the compound, but searchlights from other parts of the city are beginning to pin the choppers. They've been breaking like cheap toys all the way in, so now there are only five left, and you have no assurances that they will continue to work, especially since twice that number have already broken. You're all wearing gas-masks and moving through the rooms of the compound, trying to find and move all fifty-three of the hostages — it's dark and most of the hostages are knocked out like the guards, but some of the rooms were well sealed, and naturally these hostages are shouting for help. For a while — and this is the effect I want to emphasise more than any other — for a while, things inside are absolutely chaotic. No one can find Colonel Jackson, no one knows how many of the hostages are recovered and how many still in the embassy, it's dark, it's noisy, there are shots in the distance. I want an effect like the scene at the end of *The Lady From Shanghai*, when they're in the carnival's house of mirrors shooting at each other. Multiplied by ten. Total chaos.'

'Now hold on just a second here,' John said, exaggerating his Texas accent, which came and went according to his convenience. 'I like the chaos bit, and the allusion to Welles, but let's get back to this issue of the facts. Colonel Jackson was the hero of this whole thing! He was the one that decided to go on with all them helicopters busting out in the desert, and he was the one that found Annette Bellows in the embassy to lead them around, and all in all he was on top of every minute of it. That's why they gave him all them medals!'

Ivan glared. 'What part are you playing, John?'

'Why, Colonel Jackson.' John drew himself up. 'Natch.'

'However.' Ivan tapped the side of his head, to indicate thought. 'You don't just want to do a bad imitation of the De Niro performance, do you? You want to do a new interpretation, don't you? Besides, it seems to me a foolish idea to try an imitation of De Niro.'

'I like the idea, myself,' John said. 'Show him how.'

Ivan waved him away. 'You got all you know about this affair from that stupid TV movie, just like everyone else. I, however, have been reading the accounts of the hostages and the Marines on those helicopters, and the truth is that Colonel Jackson's best moment was out there in the desert, when he decided to go on with the mission even though only five helicopters were still functioning. That was his peak of glory, his moment of heroism. And you did a perfectly adequate job of conveying that when we filmed the scene. We could see every little gear in there, grinding away.' He tapped his skull.

'De Niro would have been proud,' Melina said.

John pursed his lips and nodded. 'We need great men like that. Without them history would be dead. It'd be nothing but a bunch of broken-down helicopters out in a desert somewhere.'

'A trenchant image of History,' Ivan said. 'Too bad Shelley got to it first. Meanwhile, the truth is that after making the decision to go on with the raid, Colonel Jackson appeared, in the words of his subordinates, somewhat stunned. When they landed on the embassy roof he led the first unit in, and when they got lost inside the whole force was effectively without leadership for most of the crucial first half-hour. All the accounts of this period describe it as the utmost chaos, saved only when Sergeant Payton – *not* Colonel Jackson – the TV movie lied about that – when Payton found Ms. Bellows, and she led them to all the hostage rooms they hadn't found.'

'All right, all right.' John frowned. 'So I'm supposed to be kind of spaced-out in this scene.'

'Don't go for too deep an analysis, John, you might strain something. But essentially you have it. Having committed the force to the raid, even though you're vastly undermanned because of the damned helicopters breaking down, you're a bit frozen by the risk of it. Got that?'

'Yeah. But I don't believe it. Jackson was a hero.'

'Fine, a hero, lots of medals. Roomfuls of medals. If he pinned them on he'd look like the bride after the dollar dance. He'd collapse under their weight. But now let's try showing what really happened.'

'All right.' John drew himself up. 'I'm ready.'

The shooting of the scene was the part they all enjoyed the most; this was the heart of the activity, the reason they kept making movies to occupy their free hours at Luna Three. Ivan and John and Melina and Pierre-Paul, the theoreticians who traded directing chores from project to project, always blocked the scenes very loosely, allowing a lot of room for improvisation. Thus scenes like this one, which were supposed to be chaotic, were played out with a manic gusto. They were good at chaos.

And so for nearly half an hour they rushed about the interior of their Teheran embassy compound — the base storage warehouse, with its immense rows of boxes arranged behind white panels of plywood to resemble the compound's buildings and their interiors. Their shouts were nearly drowned by the clatter of recorded helicopters, while intermittent lights flashed in the darkness. Cut-outs representing the helicopters were pasted to the clear dome overhead, silhouetted against the unearthly brilliance of the stars — these last had become a trademark of Luna Three Productions, as their frequent night scenes always had these unbelievably bright stars overhead, part of the films' dreamlike effect.

The actors playing Marines bounded about the compound in their gas-masks, looking like aliens descended to ravage a planet; the actors playing hostages and Revolutionary Guards lay scattered on the floor, except for a few in protected rooms, who fought or cried for help. John and Pierre-Paul and the rest hunted the compound for Melina, playing Annette Bellows, the woman who had been so crucial to finding all the hostages. For a while it looked as if John would get to her first, thus repeating the falsehood of the De Niro film. But eventually Pierre-Paul, playing Sergeant Payton, located her room, and he and his

189

small unit rushed about after the clear-headed Bellows, who, as she wrote later, had spent most of her months in captivity planning what she should do if this moment ever came. They located the remaining comatose hostages and lugged them quickly to the plywood helicopter on the compound roof. The sound of shots punctuated the helicopters' roar, and as they leaped through the helicopter's door shafts of white light stabbed the air like Islamic swords.

That was it; the flight away would be filmed in their little helicopter interior. Ivan turned off the helicopter noise, shouted 'Cut!' into a megaphone. Then he shut down all the strategically-placed minicams, which had been recording every minute of it.

'What bothers me about your movies, Ivan,' John said, 'is that you always take away the hero. Always!'

They were standing in the shallow end of the base pool, cooling off while they watched the day's rushes on a screen filling one wall of the natatorium. Many of the screens showed much the same result; darkness, flickering light, alien shapes moving in the elongated dancelike way that audiences on earth found so surreal, so mesmerising. There was little indication of the pulsing rhythms and wrenching suspense that Ivan's editing would create from this material. But the actors were happy, seeing arresting images of desperation, of risk, of heroism in the face of a numbingly loud confusion.

Ivan was not as pleased. 'Shit!' he said. 'We're going to have to do it again.'

'Looks okay to me,' John remarked. 'Son of Film Noire Returns From the Grave. But really, Ivan, you've got to do something about this prejudice against heroes. I saw *Escape From Teheran* when I was a kid, and it was an inspiration to me. It was one of the big reasons I got into engineering.'

Pierre-Paul objected: 'John, just how did seeing a commando film get you interested in engineering?'

'Well,' John replied, frowning. 'I thought I'd design a better helicopter, I guess.' He ignored his friends' laughter. 'I was pretty shocked at how unreliable they were. But the way old De Niro continued on to Teheran! The way he extricated all the hostages and got them back safely, even with the choppers dropping like flies. It was great! We need heroes, and history tells the story of the few people who had what it takes to be one. But you're always downplaying them.'

'The Great Man Theory of history,' Pierre-Paul said scornfully.

'Sure!' John admitted. 'Great Woman too of course,' nodding quickly at the frowning Melina. 'It's the great leaders who make the difference. They're special people, and there aren't many of them. But if you believe Ivan's films, there aren't any at all.'

With a snort of disgust Ivan took his attention from the rushes. 'Hell, we are going to have to do that scene again. As for my theory of history, John, you both have it and you don't. As far as I understand you.' He cocked his head and looked at his friend attentively. On the set they both played their parts to the teeth: Ivan the tormented, temperamental director, gnashing his teeth and ordering people about; John the stubborn, temperamental star, questioning everything and insisting on his pre-eminence. Mostly this was role-playing, part of the game, part of what made their hobby entertaining to them. Off the set the roles largely disappeared, except to make a point, or have some fun. Ivan was the base's head of computer operations, while John was an engineer involved in the Mars voyage; they were good friends, and their arguments had done much to shape Ivan's ideas for his revisionist historical films, which were certainly the ones from their little troupe making the biggest splash downside — though John claimed this was because of the suspenseful plots and the weird low-gee imagery, not because of what they were saying about history. '*Do* I understand you?' Ivan asked curiously.

191

'Well,' John said, 'take the one you did last time, about the woman who saved John Lennon's life. Now that was a perfect example of heroic action, as the 1982 docu-drama made clear. There she was standing right next to a man who had pulled out a damn big gun, and quicker than he could pull the trigger she put a foot in his crotch and a fist in his ear. But in your remake, all we concentrated on was how she had just started the karate class that taught her the moves, and how her husband encouraged her to take the class, and how that cabbie stopped for her even though she was going in the other direction, and how that other cabbie told her that Lennon had just walked into his apartment lobby, and all that. You made it seem like it was just a coincidence!'

Ivan took in a mouthful of pool water and spurted it at the spangled dome, looking like a fountain statue. 'It took a lot of coincidences to get Margaret Arvis into the Dakota lobby at the right time,' he told John.'But some of them weren't coincidences – they were little acts of generosity or kindness or consideration, that put her where she could do what she did. I didn't take the heroism away. I just spread it around to all the places it belonged.'

John grimaced, drew himself up into his star persona. 'I suppose this is some damn commie notion of mass social movements, sweeping history along in a consensus direction.'

'No, no,' Ivan said. 'I always concentrate on individuals. What I'm saying is that all our individual actions add up to history, to the big visible acts of our so-called leaders. You know what I mean; you hear people saying all the time that things are better now because John Lennon was such a moral force, travelling everywhere, Nobel Peace Prize, secular pope, the conscience of the world or whatnot.'

'Well, he was the conscience of the world!'

'Sure, sure, he wrote great songs. And he got a lot of antagonists to talk. But without Margaret Arvis he would have been killed at age forty. And without Margaret

Arvis's husband, and her karate instructor, and a couple of cabbies in New York, and so on, she wouldn't have been there to save his life. So we all become part of it, see? The people who say it was all because of Lennon, or Carter, or Gorbachev — they're putting on a few people what we all did.'

John shook his head, scattering water everywhere. 'Very sophisticated, I'm sure! But in fact it was precisely Lennon and Carter and Gorbachev who made huge differences, all by themselves. Carter started the big swing towards human rights. Palestine, the new Latin America, the American Indian nations — none of those would have existed without him.'

'In fact,' Melina added, glancing mischievously at Pierre-Paul, 'if I understand the Margaret Arvis movie correctly, if she hadn't been going to see Carter thank his New York campaign workers for the 1980 victory, she wouldn't have been in the neighbourhood of the Dakota, and so she wouldn't have had the chance to save Lennon's life.'

John rose up like a whale breaching. 'So it's Carter we have to thank for that too! As for Gorbachev, well, I don't have to tell you what all he did. That was a hundred-eighty degree turnaround for you Russkies, and no one can say it would have happened without him.'

'Well — he was an important leader, I agree.'

'Sure was! And Carter was just as crucial. Their years were the turning point, when the world started to crawl out from under the shadow of World War Two. And that was their doing. There just aren't many people who could've done it. Most of us don't have it in us.'

Ivan shook his head. 'Carter wouldn't have been able to do what he did unless Colonel Ernest Jackson had saved the rescue mission to Teheran, by deciding to go on when they didn't really have enough functioning helicopters.'

'So Jackson is a hero too!'

'But then Jackson wouldn't have been a hero if the officer back in the Pentagon hadn't decided at the last minute to send sixteen helicopters instead of eight.'

'And,' Melina pointed out quickly, 'if Annette Bellows hadn't spent most of a year day-dreaming about what she would do in a rescue attempt, so that she knew blindfolded where every other hostage was being kept. They would have left about half the hostages behind without her, and Carter wouldn't have looked so good.'

'Plus they needed Sergeant Payton to find Bellows and follow her around,' Ivan added.

'Well shit!' John yelled defensively, which was his retort in any tight spot. He changed tack. 'I ain't so sure that Carter's re-election hinged on those hostages anyway. He was running against a flake, I can't remember the guy's name, but he was some kind of idiot.'

'So?' Melina said. 'Since when has that made any difference?'

With a roar John dove at her, making a big splash. She was much faster than he was, however, and she evaded him easily as he chased her around the pool; it looked like a whale chasing a dolphin. He was reduced to splashing at her from a distance, and the debate quickly degenerated into a big splash fight, as it often did.

'Oh well,' John declared, giving up the attack and floating in the shallow end. 'I love watching Melina swim the butterfly. In this gravity it becomes a godlike act. Those muscular arms, that sinuous dolphin motion . . .'

Pierre-Paul snorted. 'You just like the way butterfly puts her bottom above water so often.'

'No way! Women are just more hydrodynamic than men, don't you think?'

'Not the way you like them.'

'Godlike. Gods and goddesses.'

'You look a bit godlike yourself,' Melina told him. 'Bacchus, for instance.'

'Hey.' John waved her off, jabbed a finger at the screens. 'I note that all this mucho sophisticated European theorising has been sunk. Took a bit of Texas logic is all.'

'Only Texas logic could do it,' Pierre-Paul said.

'Right. You admit my point. In the end it's the great

leaders who have to act, the rare ones, no matter if we ordinary folks help them into power.'

'When you revise your proposition like that,' Ivan said, 'you turn it into mine. Leaders are important, but they are leaders because we made them leaders. They are a collective phenomenon. They are expressions of us.'

'Now wait just a minute! You're going over the line again! You're talking like heroic leaders are a dime a dozen, but if that were true it wouldn't matter if Carter had lost in 1980, or if Lennon had been killed by that guy. But look at history, man! Look what happened when we did lose great leaders! Lincoln was shot, did they come up with another leader comparable to him? No way! Same with Gandhi, and the Kennedys, and King, and Sadat, and Olof Palme. When those folks were killed their countries suffered the lack of them, because they were special.'

'They were special,' Ivan agreed, 'and obviously it was a bad thing they were killed. And no doubt there was a short-term change for the worse. But they're not irreplaceable, because they're human beings just like us. None of them, except maybe Lincoln or Gandhi, was any kind of genius or saint. It's only afterwards we think of them that way, because we want heroes so much. But we're the heroes. All of us put them in place. And there are a lot of capable, brilliant people out there to replace the loss of them, so that in the long-run we recover.'

'The *real* long-run,' John said darkly. 'A hundred years or more, for the South without Lincoln. They just aren't that common. The long-run proves it.'

'Speaking of the long-run,' Pierre-Paul said, 'is anyone getting hungry?'

They all were; the rushes were over, and Ivan had dismissed them as unusable; they climbed out of the pool and walked towards the changing-room, discussing restaurants. There were a considerable number of them in the station, and new ones were opening every week. 'I just tried the new Hungarian restaurant,' Melina said. 'The food was good, but we had trouble when the meal was

195

over, finding someone to give us the bill!'

'I thought you said it was a Hungarian restaurant,' John said.

They threw him back in the pool.

The second time they ran through the rescue scene in the compound, Ivan had repositioned most of the minicams, and many of the lights; his instructions to the actors remained the same. But once inside the hallways of the set, John Rand couldn't help hurrying in the general direction of Annette Bellows' room.

All right, he thought. Maybe Colonel Jackson had been a bit hasty to rush into the compound in search of hostages, leaving the group without a commander. But his heart had been in the right place, and the truth was, he had found a lot of the hostages without any help from Bellows at all. It was easy; they were scattered in ones and twos on the floor of almost every room he and his commandos entered, and stretched out along with the guards in the rooms and in the halls, paralysed by the nerve gas. Damn good idea, that nerve gas. Guards and hostages, tough parts to play, no doubt, as they were getting kicked pretty frequently by commandos running by. He hustled his crew into room after room, then sent them off with hostages draped over their shoulders, pretending to stagger down the halls, banging into walls – *really* tough part to play, hostage – and clutching at gas-masks and such; great images for the minicams, no doubt about it.

When all his commandos had been sent back, he ran around a corner in what he believed to be the direction of Annette Bellows' room. Over the racket of the helicopters, and the occasional round of automatic fire, he thought he could make out Melina's voice, shouting hoarsely. So Pierre-Paul hadn't got to her yet. Good. Now he could find her and be the one to follow her around rescuing the more obscurely housed hostages, just as De Niro had in the docu-drama. It would give Ivan fits, but they could argue it out afterwards. No way of telling what had really happened in that compound twenty years before, after all; and it made a better *story* his way.

Their set was only one storey tall, which was one of the things that John had objected to; the compound in Teheran had been four storeys high, and getting up stairs had been part of the hassle. But Ivan was going to play with the images and shoot a few stair scenes later on, to achieve the effect of multiple floors. Fine, it meant he had only to struggle around a couple of narrow corners, jumping comatose Revolutionary Guards, looking fierce for the minicams wherever they were. It was really loud this time around; *really* loud.

Then one of the walls fell over on him, the plywood pinning him to the ground, the boxes behind it tumbling down and filling the hallway. 'Hey!' he cried out, shocked. This wasn't the way it had happened. What was going on? The noise of the helicopters cut off abruptly, replaced by a series of crashes, a whooshing sound. The sound put a fine electric thrill down his spine; he had heard it before, in training routines. Air leaving the chamber. The dome must have been breached.

He heaved up against the plywood. Stuck. Flattening himself as much as possible he slithered forward, under the plywood and out into a small space among fallen boxes. Hard to tell where the hallway had been, and it was pitch dark. There wouldn't be too much time left. He thought of his little gas-mask, then cursed; it wasn't connected to a real oxygen supply. That's what comes from using fake props! he thought angrily. A gas-mask with nothing attached to it. Open to the air, which was departing rapidly. Not much time.

He found room among the boxes to stand, and he was about to run over them to the door leading out of the warehouse – assuming the whole station hadn't been breached – when he remembered Melina. Stuck in her embassy room down the hall, wouldn't she still be there? Hell. He groped along in the dark, hearing shouts in the distance. Lights, too. Good. He was holding his breath, for what felt like minutes at a time, though it was probably less than thirty seconds. Every time he heaved in a new breath he expected it to be the freezing vacuum, but the supply of rushing, cold — very cold — air continued to fill him. Emergency supply pouring out into the breach, actually a technique he had helped develop himself. Seemed to be working, at least for the moment.

He heard a muffled cry to one side, began to pull at the boxes before him. Squeak in the gloom, ah ha, there she was. Not fully conscious. Legs wet, probably blood, uh oh. He pulled hard at boxes, lifted her up. Adrenalin and lunar gravity made him feel like Superman with that part of things, but there didn't seem to be anywhere near as much air as before, and what was left was damned cold. Hurt to breathe. And harder than hell to balance as he hopped over objects with Melina in his arms. Feeling faint, he climbed over a row of boxes and staggered towards a distant light. A sheet of plywood smacked his shin and he cried out, then fell over. 'Hey,' he said. The air was gone.

When he came to he was lying in a bed in the station hospital. 'Great,' he muttered. 'Whole station wasn't blown up.'

His friends laughed, relieved to hear him speak. The whole film-crew was in there, it seemed. Ivan, standing next to the bed, said: 'It's okay.'

'What the hell happened?'

'A small meteor, apparently. Hit out in our sector, in the shuttle landing chambers ironically. But it wrecked our storage space as well, as you no doubt noticed.'

John nodded painfully. 'So it finally happened.'

'Yes.' This was one of the great uncontrollable dangers of the lunar stations; meteors small and large were still crashing down onto the moon's airless surface, by the thousands every year. Odds were poor that any one would hit something as small as the surface parts of their station, but coming down in such numbers . . . In the long-run they were reduced to a safety status somewhat equivalent to that of mountain climbers: rockfall could always get you.

'Melina?' John said, jerking up in his bed.

'Over here,' Melina called. She was a few beds down, and had one leg in a cast. 'I'm fine, John.' She got out of bed to prove it, and came over to kiss his cheek. 'Thanks for the rescue!'

John snorted. 'What rescue?'

They laughed again at him. Pierre-Paul pointed a forefinger at him. 'There are heroes everywhere, even among the lowest of us. Now you have to admit Ivan's argument.'

'The hell I do.'

'You're a hero,' Ivan said to him, grinning. 'Just an ordinary man, so to speak. Not one of the great leaders at all. But by saving Melina, you've changed history.'

'Not unless she becomes President,' John said, and laughed. 'Hey, Melina! Go out and run for office! Or save some promising songwriter or something.'

Ivan just shook his head. 'Why are you so stubborn? It's not so bad if I'm right, John. Think about it − if I am right, then we aren't just sitting around waiting for leaders to guide us.' A big grin lit his face: 'We become the masters of our fate, we make our own decisions and act on them − we choose our leaders, and instruct them by consensus, so that we can take history any direction we please! Just as you did in the warehouse.'

John lay back in his bed and was silent. Around him his friends grinned; one of them was bringing up a big papier-maché medal, which vaguely resembled the one the Wizard of Oz pins to the Cowardly Lion. 'Ah hell,' John said.

'When the expedition reaches Mars, they'll have to name something after you,' Melina said.

John thought about it for a while. He took the big medal, held it limply. His friends watched him, waiting for him to speak.

'Well, I still say it's bullshit,' he told Ivan. 'But if there is any truth to what you say, it's just the good old spirit of the Alamo you're talking about anyway. We've been doing it like that in Texas for years.'

They laughed at him.

He rose up from the bed again, swung the medal at them furiously. 'I swear it's true! Besides it's all Robert De Niro's fault anyway! I was *imitating* the real heroes, don't you see? I was crawling around in there all dazed, and then I saw De Niro's face when he was playing Colonel Jackson in the Teheran embassy, and I said to myself, well hell, what would he have done in this here situation? And that's just what I did.'

IAN McDONALD

Approaching Perpendicular

A thorn in his flesh and an image driven like a wedge into his mind: these things bring Brendl the poet across the specula of High Space to the Glass Hotel.

The pain, the swift, gutting pain; that is an old familiar. Twenty doctors on twenty worlds have failed before Brendl's thorn; twenty philosophies of medicine proved only that there are places within a poet their art and science may not touch.

The image: that comes a stranger. Like a succubus it swims out of the bestiary of High Space into the exalted dreams of poets: gold upon black, cleaving his dreaming skull like a falling axe, a fine edge, a balance point upon which a great poem may be suspended.

A vision, and a pain. Drawn to the one, flying from the other. Prismatic colours melt and run, the air shivers with the surreal chiaroscuro of the Aesthetic Medium as the starcrosser slips into corporeality. Brendl the poet has come to the City.

The Glass Hotel stands on a rise, its back to Sothis the Ash Desert, its face turned to the City; an antique aquarium aswim with those colourful and curious exhibits the City draws to itself. Rare fish, they swim shy, never touching. Brushing softly, shyly past, they move, they glide within their bowl of chrome and glass, wary of each other, warier yet of the city without and the long shadow it casts over the gelid banalities and inconsequentialities that pass between these denizens of the Glass Hotel.

'They say that within its walls a dozen races may have lived and died,' says the rich, clever, frightened young man called Anneway. He pours a glass of water-clear wine for Brendl the poet. 'Indeed, it is mooted that the founder race, the so-called Architects, may still be living there, close to the spindle. It is mooted.'

And in the water-gardens, at tea with the woman called Moon-of-May upon a punt shaped like the petals of an open ash-flower: 'It is still growing, you know.' An intimate touch of conspiracy, complicity upon Brendl's knee. 'The distortion. They have found courses of earlier walls, long abandoned, within the current constructions. The discontinuity mirror is still running, drawing reality after it in its mad pursuit of infinitude.' Perfect hands, shapely as lilies, rest lightly upon his knee. 'Does that not frighten you? It does me.'

That evening, at dinner with the Venerable Dowager Duenna Chun-Yen-Yi:

'Do you know how long I have been here, young man? Twenty-two years. Twenty-two years this summer and I have seen it all. Everything. There is nothing new under the sun; this sun, any sun.' The twittering of a songbird in a mulberry tree. Brendl smiles graciously. In his head, the black and the gold, 'I have seen everything, and yet I have never seen the City, is that not strange, Mr Brendl? I have never seen the City; never wish to, never will. I shall probably die in this Glass Hotel without ever having set foot beyond the gate of Doubt-No-More. And I shall tell you why, young man. When I was a girl, my tutor, Dr Morpeno, once demonstrated the principle of electrostatic repulsion by suspending a pith ball between the charged plates of an electrostatic generator. An idle enough pastime, you might think, and I might agree, except that I am the ball of pith, Mr Brendl. I am suspended in perfect equilibrium between the fear and the fascination of that thing out there and that is why I will never leave this Glass Hotel.'

'Fear,' muses Fleyn the Consular Officer, astroll beneath the floribunda pergolas of the rose walks. Now and again he pauses, the perfect diplomat elegant in silk coat and plantation hat, to scent the blossoms. 'Ah, the roses. No other world can boast a bloom to rival the roses of Earth, do you not think, Brendl? You have, of course, been talking with that old coward, the Dowager Duenna Chun-Yen-Yi. The dear woman is correct, but only to a certain extent. While there are many who come to this world who never pass through the gate of Doubt-No-More because, quite frankly, this big, old, alien city terrifies them, the great majority find within its walls a richness, a splendour, a sweep of history and vision which transforms their lives. Surely you are not one of the fearful ones, Brendl? You are a poet; what could a poet fear that he has not already faced in his imagination?'

Brendl shrugs: a nothing. He is thinking of the people rubbing their fear onto each other like musk.

– Tomorrow, he says. Tomorrow I will go. Tomorrow I will run the image of the black and the gold to ground in the streets and closes of the City and I will not be afraid.

But tomorrow comes, and tomorrow and tomorrow and Brendl the poet is afraid. And because day after day he refuses to name that fear, Brendl the poet gradually, gently, becomes another creature of the Glass Hotel, a trivial thing of grace and air and perfect banality incapable of the meanest line, the meanest word of poetry. But on the twenty-fifth night he catches a vagrant glimpse of his face in a distant mirror. Too remote for the carefully composed expression he wears when purposefully regarding his reflection, Brendl regards his true face. And seeing himself thus, he knows that he must look upon the City and see his face mirrored in its monumental arrogance.

Alone in his suite, he crosses to the window and repeals the word which has rendered it opaque since his arrival in the Glass Hotel. A knife of fears turns slow in his gut, he shudders, fearing the onslaught on his personal demon (incredible that it has not yet come to smite him). Brendl steels himself and in time the spasm passes. And then he turns his eyes to look upon the City, the spindle of land heaved up by the alien discontinuity mirror, heaved up and shaped like clay on a wheel into that form called the 'conic hyperbola', a curving spire dotted and streaked with the lanterns of night reaching ever upwards, ever inwards, dwindling to the ultimate dimensionless thread at that infinite point of perfect perpendicularity which is its exact centre, the heart of impossibility where the discontinuity mirror lies.

The City lies open before him like an impatient lover, yet Brendl turns away from it, for no man can look long upon infinity. It pains his eyes. It sears his soul. It fires his imagination.

His pack is small and light; it is not intended that this be a major expedition to the hidden heartlands of the City, this adventure through the gate of Doubt-No-More is more a symbol of personal resolution. Yet that resolution falters a little, fails a little with each step he takes away from the butterfly world of the terminally fearful, each step he takes towards the hyperbolic mountain that is the City. Between Glass Hotel and City Gate lies a sordid kilometre of shameful tar-paper and packing-case shanties, the domain of those shameless creatures who take their living from the visitors, concealed from the soul-dwindling view of the hyperbola by the shadow of the soaring walls. Brendl moves among them a fool in paradise; fingers stroke his pockets, hands tug his sleeve: 'Mister, mister, a guide, mister, mister, you need a guide Man o' Earth? You need a guide show you the city, the wonderful, wonderful city?'

'No thank you!' he shouts. 'The heart of a poet is all the guide he requires!' Protected by his innocence and arrogance, like some holy angel, Brendl draws a train of indeterminately gendered urchins and street-arabs through the dung-strewn laneways beneath the city wall.

And now he stands before the gate of Doubt-No-More; thirty times higher than a man, a mouth wide enough to swallow a world, let alone a proud poet. He passes under the inscription from which this one of fifty city gates takes its name: Doubt-No-More.

But Brendl doubts.

And now he has entered the City.

People, people, people, pressing close on all sides, pressing their bodies, their smells, their lives, their fears against his, pressing their noise; the sheer clamour of the myriad voices calling, calling from windows, calling from terraces, calling from closes and tiled squares, calling from shops and cafes, calling their wares, their trades, their friends and their families, a babelogue of calling voices calling in that rough, vibrant dialect of human called Ternary. Brendl the poet walks slowly amongst this life, breathing slowly the breath of the City, absorbing slowly through his skin, his senses, his whole person, the boundless human energy of this bustling commercial district. Warrenways of small merchandisers and workshops spool off this main thoroughfare: drays, wagons, omnibuses, cycle-cabs hurry past Brendl as he stands, a solitary island of motionlessness in the surging sea of activity, looking, seeing, living the city.

And, looking about him, he is possessed by a vision.

In a dark alley piled high with red fruit is a doorway of intricately carved wood, a blue lantern and the hem of a black gown, trimmed with gold. It shines bright as a new sun and is gone.

Idle hands frozen in the air, Brendl stands paralysed in revelation. Then, without conscious volition, he is reaching towards the alley, the door, the blue lantern. And the pain smites him.

It does not permit him even one cry. From sternum to groin it slits him open, a burning, gutting blade tearing through stomach, bowels, bones, soul. Breath driven from his lungs, Brendl lies helpless beneath the knife looking up into the hyperbolic heart of impossibility. But he sees only the colours of pain. For three eternities he is crucified upon it, an eternity of agony, an eternity of helplessness, an

205

eternity of enduring; then hands lift him and place him on a litter to bear him away, through the markets, through great Doubt-No-More, through the sordid aisles of snatching hands and pleading voices to the Glass Hotel.

That evening the staff are ordered to deck the terraces with bunting and hang paper lanterns in every tree. Every lounge, salon and pavilion is opened with the announcement of universal euphoriants, and drawn like curious moths to the light, the guests gather in a flock of questions. What is the occasion of this unexpected jubilee? What is the identity of the mysterious host, whose the largesse? With such speculations the patrons of the Glass Hotel amuse themselves until at twenty minutes of twenty the onyx doors of the Peacock Pavilion are swung wide and the chattering, cackling gaggle of revellers draw back to give passage to a man, a short man, heavily bearded, clothes in an eclectic patchwork of clashing styles, yet brimming with a peculiar, radiant energy.

His name is Bulawayo.

He is back from the City.

A year before, to the day, to the hour, he departed the Glass Hotel and passed through Doubt-No-More. Since that hour his death has been many times mooted, his imminent return no fewer. An entire edifice of rumour has its foundation upon Bulawayo which even Fleyn the Consular Officer can neither substantiate nor deny. In short: he is legend.

Bulawayo's stories that night of the strange and marvellous draw murmurs of admiration from even the most world-weary of his guests. He has been deep within. He has climbed far up the asymptotic land. He has journeyed into the empty places where the human settlers, in their millennial migration into the vast reaches of the City, have yet to penetrate; that land where shadows flit on abandoned boulevards, the animate memories of older, nobler races who have moved onwards, inwards, upwards, drawn up the ever-lengthening, ever-narrowing spindle by the energies of the alien power mirror. With hands and eyes he spins his tales and binds the creatures of the Glass Hotel to him with cords of wonder and they offer him their praise and adulation for he has done that which they can never do.

Some. Not all. From his table in the shadowed recesses of the Peacock Pavilion, the shadow-man listens; the pale man, the man with the fear of the ghost of pain. Brendl is not a man given to vain adulation. He is a poet, and poets do not give adulation. They receive it. Vanity is the sin of the poet; vanity, and envy. Yet Brendl listens to the rough voice. He listens well.

It is four minutes of four and Brendl wakes with a cry in the deep darkness before the dawn. It is not the remembrance or anticipation of pain that has woken him, not this time. It is a vision, an image so potent that it follows him out of the dreamtime into the waking world.

Green eyes, slitted eyes, upturned to the sun.

Alone in the pre-dawn dark with the green eyes and the hem of black and gold, he feels the shadow of the City lying heavy across him, heavy as if all the unspeakable bulk of the great spire had fallen and crushed the Glass Hotel like a cage of crickets, and he knows that he must return to it, pass once more beneath the vault of Doubt-No-More. For he is well enough acquainted with the ways of poetic inspiration to know that until he does the images will give him no peace.

Thus it is with emotions mixed in equal measures of anticipation and dread that Brendl retraces his path through the jostling parasites, beneath the spirit-dwarfing arch of Doubt-No-More into the borough of markets. He nears the alley of his vision. Sweat beads his brow, a sudden hot panic mounts in him, the bright edge of the knife. It takes all his small courage to look into entry. He sees yellow melons piled against a wall under a yellow gaslamp. What he had taken to be a door is a wooden shutter carved in intricate arabesques. Of the hem of black-and-gold, there is not even the whisper of a memory.

Beyond the markets lies a prefecture of alien ceramic

architecture, a porcelain place where the straight line, the Euclidean plane, are despised, and houses, streets, roofs, walls and gardens meld into each other in sensuous terracotta curves. No line is level, no plumb true, and the streethousegardens glitter with liquid glazes, as if entire neighbourhoods had been left to soften and melt in the sun. The name of this district is Toltlethen, a soft breath of a name, a spoken spirit of a place which inspires Brendl as, aimless as a riddle, he meanders through the molten courtyards and soft glazed streets. Before him the land rises gently upwards, forever rising beneath Brendl's feet as ignorant, innocent, he climbs the lower slopes of the asymptotic curve. As he walks, imagery flocks to him; he tastes his metaphors, tests them, tries them on his lips for euphony, then sets them down in the black leather notebook which, when the muse is on him, is as inseparable from Brendl as the skin of his own writing hand. Free from the imagining of pain, his spirit is light within him and the images which gather about him like a congregation of ghosts waft him on through the porcelain streets of Toltlethen.

When he hears the sound, he cannot be certain whence it comes for it seems to surround him on every side. Running feet, voices raised in excitement, the rattle of a tambourine, the pounding of a drum, the bleating of a bag-pipe: the pottery houses reflect, refract the sound so that it is everywhere apparent but nowhere visible. Then in their ones and twos, their dribs and drabs, their threes and fours, the people quit their streethousegardens, filling the terracotta lanes with an ever-swelling throng and Brendl, curious, yielding, permits himself to be carried with the flow.

From what small glimpses he is afforded, Brendl gathers that he has been swept into some great civic festival. At the procession's head, eighty men in crimson perform upon a preposterous array of instruments from tiny clay okarinas shaped like the birds they mimic to the serpentine coils of massive ophicleides so ponderous they must be supported upon small wheeled trolleys. Behind these, the dancers;

some tottering upon stilts, some with wheels fitted to hands and feet, some earthbound but wondrously acrobatic, some concealed behind huge triangular fans which, from time to time, are thrown high into the air to open, catch the light upon their intricately worked interiors, and fall gently on the breezes to be caught unerringly by the hands which had cast them. Smaller replicas of those fans are carried by the jubilating citizens of Toltlethen as they wind through the streets, through echoing greens, past lofty glass towers, through vaulted arcades, across squares and piazzas dense with the suspended life of fountains and statues, over bridges hung over bridges hung over bridges hung over dark bottomless ravines. Brendl the poet breasts this tide of humanity until at last the ritual energy fails and the procession empties itself into a wide cobbled square flanked by grey brick tenements so tall, so many-windowed they seem like a host of monstrous faces.

Here the musicians take up station and the dancers, seemingly possessed of an inexhaustible energy, commence a complex ballet comprising of an astonishingly acrobatic trading of fans between stilt-dancers, four-wheelers, gymnasts and the central group all dressed in yellow so that every three exchanges the entire cycle of fans rotates once. Brendl asks a bystander what this spectacle is he is witnessing.

'This is the Exaltation of Charmed Quarks,' says the man. He clutches a coloured fan to his breast. 'The Third Cycle of the Tlantoon.'

And, as if the man's words had shone the light of revelation before him, Brendal sees them.

Green eyes, slitted eyes, upturned to the sun.

A dancing woman in a sleek tiger-striped costume and mask, a woman with the head of a cat.

Brendl bursts through the ring of festival-goers into the Exaltation of Charmed Quarks. Stilt-dancers loom and sway before him, acrobatic bodies twist and turn away, wheeled demons hurtle past, grazing him, scorching him with the speed of their passage. There are shouts, cries, a vast, vague, incoherent roaring. But Brendl the poet sees only green eyes, slitted eyes, upturned to the sun; the pale afternoon light silhouetting sleek, tiger-striped flanks. He reaches that place where, without doubt, he saw her. Nothing. He casts frantically about him, scattering alarmed celebrants but his only reward is a final taunting flick of tiger-striped sleekness, impossibly slim and supple. Slipping into the gloom of an inter-tenement alley; green eyes, slitted eyes luminous for an instant in the sun.

Alone after the Tlantoon has dispersed, Brendl searches the cobbled square for some clue to her being. He searches, he calls for her with the names his imagination has given to her but the cliffs of the greybrick tenements are as devoid of intelligence as the mottled face of the moon. And the rain begins, a thin drizzling rain spun down from the arrogant spindle at the centre of the world like a mockery of poets and their imaginings.

After the recitation, the acclamation.

'Wonderful, truly wonderful,' says Mr Anaxemides, the transplanetary merchant.

'A contemporary masterpiece.' This from young Anneway, no less fearful than on their last meeting.

'Truly magnificent. I stand in the presence of a truly great talent,' says Moon-of-May, flower hands open to bless.

'Mr Brendl, dear Mr Brendl, that was beautiful,' says the Venerable Dowager Duenna Chun-Yen-Yi, dewy-eyed and fluttering like a moth at a lantern. 'I feel that now, after twenty-two years, I have at last visited the City.'

'The Exaltation of Charmed Quarks,' muses Fleyn the Consular Officer. 'Excellent, my man, excellent. Your visit to our city has had a most invigorating effect upon your imagination.'

Brendl smiles, a mask of false modesty. The vanity of poets, like their fables' love, is a thing apart.

'The Tlantoon,' continues Fleyn, drawing Brendl aside

from his admirers to an intimate conversation booth. 'Ah, without doubt, one of the greatest of the City's Festival Cycles, if not the greatest, and, if not the greatest, certainly the most ancient. Ignatieff at the Mission has made a comprehensive study of the ethnology of the Tlantoon and he is certain, quite certain that the Central Liturgy of the Five Cycles predates human occupancy of the City. Do you see what this means? That in the ceremonies of the Tlantoon we have a living link with those alien races that have long since passed into the heartlands − Ignatieff's expression is "internal migration", I quite like that − indeed, it is Mr Ignatieff's opinion that through the Tlantoon we are in contact with the semi-mythical Architects, the creators of the City and the engineers of the discontinuity mirror, the effects of which you must by now be well familiar with, my dear Brendl. Personally, I believe that as a coherent racial group the Architects have been extinct for millions of years; if any remain, it must be as isolated individuals, grubbing a living from the fringes of human society, sadly fallen from their noble estate.'

Brendl does not much care to hear about elder alien races who may or may not be semi-mythical. He wishes for the praises of his admirers, for their fawning adulation of the icy cascades of his poetry. But he smiles politely, for politeness covers a multitude of sins of disposition. Fleyn continues.

'Yes, as Ignatieff says, the city is great, so great that some prefectures may celebrate Tlantoon only once in a generation. You were damnably lucky, Brendl, damnably lucky.'

'I would love to see more,' says Brendl looking over Fleyn's shoulder to the knot of coy admirers.

'Which of us would not? But you may have to be content with what you have seen, my dear fellow. In addition to moving to God-knows-where in the next cycle, each successive level of the Tlantoon is increasingly exclusive. You must remember, my dear Brendl, that though the Tlantoon may be un-matched as a spectacle for us Men o' Earth, it is a ritual of deep spiritual significance to the people of the City. In all the years travellers have been visiting the City, only the meanest handful have ever succeeded in being admitted to the Fourth Cycle, the Celebration of Distorted Reflections. As for the Fifth Cycle, all we know of it is its name, the Pious Descent of Infinite Gradient, so holy and secret is the ritual. We Men o' Earth maintain our presence in this City purely by suffrance. We must be respectful.'

'Well, I shall persist, and who knows? Precedents are set to be broken, and I have by no means exhausted the treasury of imagery contained within the Tlantoon.'

That night, as if inspired to renewed life by Brendl's arrogance, they caper through his dreams, mocking, taunting: the hem of gold braid, the cat-headed dancer, fleeing from his clumsy attempts to land hand on them.

Therefore, in pursuit of peace of heart, in pursuit of the terminal pin through their hearts to his pure white pages, Brendl embarks upon his greatest expedition into the City. Three days in the planning, amassing funds, equipment, comestibles, clothing, then one morning the denizens of the Glass Hotel rise, late as is their custom, to find him gone from their midst. Accustomed to such ventures into realms where clocks run askew and space is stretched into a carnival ribbon, the management maintain the poet's suite, the society clothes, his toiletries and personal sundries, his reams of black-scribbled paper; all preserved in readiness against his return, be that hours distant, or months.

And in his wild hunt, Brendl the poet wanders far across the City, living from his small nightpack and those necessities he can purchase from the arcades and gallerias, boarding overnight in whatever hotel, tavern or guesthouse will suit his purse and his pride, chasing the spirit of the Tlantoon. Time and again he thinks he has run it down, voices carried on the wind, the skirling of pipes and strings swirled out of a sullen sky but always when he bursts, breathless, expectant into that courtyard, square, green, piazza, he finds himself caught up in the hurly-burly of some local carnival or public flogging or bridal procession or street auction of repossessed furnishings. Time and again his disappointment sends him into the infantile rage of poets, yet his obsessions with the green eyes and the hem of gold-on-black drive him on through avenues of pleasingly-proportioned red-brick townhouses, through convoluted nests of animate architecture swarming with humanity, through floating markets and waterboroughs and garden villages and ponderous glass arcologies packed with transparent souls, kilometre after kilometre, the ground rising gently before him, rising gently to the perfection of pure verticality. Yet for all the kilometres he has put beneath his feet in the days? weeks? since he passed through Doubt-No-More, the central pinnacle is not a footstep nearer. Confusion, has he been meandering, time out of mind, has he wandered, trudging an idiot's Great Circle around the base of the hyperbola, a slow spiral of the lost? Has the Great Spire been mocking him, hiding itself from him, withholding its promise of fulfilment like some painted Jezebel?

Some subtle subjective phenomenon is at work, he decides. As space and gravity are bent into a preposterous upcurve, so the Brendl that occupies that space is similarly deformed, to his very sub-quarkal fundamental fractions. To that quasi-Brendl no change is perceptible, yet if he were able to regard himself from some remote vantage, as if upon the great city wall, he would see himself distorted out of all credibility into a dull brown thread of impossibility wriggling along a street stretched into a cobbled ribbon. The thought of himself deformed into something alien, repugnant, impossible, deeply disturbs Brendl. Appearance, perception, is all to him. Therefore he turns away from those few fellow travellers who have strayed this deep into the City. Turns away from their greetings without a word, for he sees reflected in their faces the blind wriggling worm of hyperbolic function. He flees from them, possessed, obsessed, and in time his flight brings him beneath the graceful almond trees of the Prefecture of Ranves and there he halts in his flight, for he can see the flurries of notes caught in the branches of the trees that line the boulevards. Brendl knows with sure certainty that he has arrived at the Fourth Cycle, the Celebration of Distorted Reflections. He has lived too long, too close with his obsession not to recognise its perfume, the scent of a stale lover. Rude, barging, shouting; elbowing nannies with perambulators, scattering skeins of kindergarten children, upsetting the carefully piled ziggurats of the sherbet sellers, the barging, shouting Man o' Earth presses his way through the crowds frequenting Ranves Park. But his efforts are not enough. The people are dispersing from that open area where the park walks converge, the musicians loading their cumbrous instruments into ox-drawn pantechnicons, the dancers pulling warm leggings over their sweat-streaked costumes, the players folding away their reflective umbrellas and mirror kites. Discarded plastic mirrors snap like the bones of small rodents beneath Brendl's feet. The unthinkable has come to pass: the Tlantoon is over, the Distorted Reflections celebrated without Brendl the poet.

He clenches his fists and roars his frustration, his betrayal, to the graceful trees, spinning round, round, round, round, howling like some fell creature that has put off all humanity. And the next moment he is on the gravel, knotted into a writhing fetus by the pain, the gutting, shattering, searing pain. He rolls upon his back, a struggling insect impaled upon a needle of agony and the people back away from the sick, mad man. His lips shade silent pleas for assistance, then out of the fire, hallucination: a cat-face bending over him, cat-eyes drawn into lines of puzzlement: green eyes, slitted eyes.

'So, Mr Brendl, you too are a seeker of the Tlantoon.' The man's name is Banaco. He is a man of gentle deception, that deception being that though his face is old, his eyes are young and his hands, the hands that lifted Brendl from his torment and brought him to the Three Lanterns

Hotel, those hands are strong with a strength no human hands should possess.

'Such a pity that you were not able to witness the Celebration . . . still, you are a fortunate man, in the short time you have been visiting the city you have been party, in a greater or lesser part, of two of the cycles; it has taken me four years, I think it is four years (clocks run askew in this City), to progress from the Exaltation to the Celebration.'

The small private room is lit by hissing gas-lanterns, beneath its soft yellow glow Banaco's old-young face seems carved from meerschaum.

'Like you, Mr Brendl, I am a connoisseur of the City and its life. So much that is paradoxical: where does the food come from, the water, the power, even the gas which lights this very room? A miracle of faith worked by this miraculous power mirror, transubstantiation of matter and energy? No less miraculous, Mr Brendl, than the wonderful impossibility of an infinite area existing within a finite boundary: do these things not provoke a deep fascination? They do in me: fascinate me.'

'Such things are beyond me,' says Brendl, ash-pale and trembling still despite remedies and potent liqueurs. 'My sole fascination is the Tlantoon.'

'But do you not see how central the Tlantoon is to the paradox of the City?' Evangel-light burns in Banaco's eyes. 'Why, each level of the festival, each cycle, enacts, or is in some fashion, symbolically representational, of the mystery of the discontinuity mirror. The Calculation of Hyperbolic Function, the Exploration of Potential Domains, the Exaltation of Charmed Quarks, the Celebration of Distorted Reflections, even the Pious Descent of Infinite Gradient; all are telling people of the City, and, at a greater remove, us Men o' Earth, of the heritage of the alien power-mirror, its inception, its function and, I believe, its inadvertent side-effect, that in drawing energy from free quark/sub-quark probability fields, it has caused an inversion of local space and as casually thrown up this monstrous pinnacle as it has turned gravity and distance inside out: all, I repeat, Mr Brendl, all contained within the liturgy of the Tlantoon.'

Again the visions conjure themselves in Brendl's spirit-vision: his black-and-gold, his green eyes, slit eyes, and regarding them thus he is appalled by their paucity, their poverty, whining in the shadow of this man's towering, asymptotic spire of symbolic cosmology. Resentment, envy, spread their bitter green roots through his soul. The old man continues.

'Of course, my ambition, my crowning achievement, would be to attend the Fifth Cycle, the Pious Descent of Infinite Gradient.'

'But that is closed to all outsiders, my friend. We know of it only by name.'

Banaco leans forward in the yellow gas-light, intimate, conspiratorial.

'But I know where the Fifth Cycle is to be held, Mr Brendl.'

Such a swell of dizziness breaks over Brendl that he fears even the excuse of the recency of his attack will not conceal the lust in his trembling hands, his pallid cheeks.

'Oh? Pray where?' Surprising, the suave control in his voice.

'On the edge of the Barrens, the uninhabited zone at the limit of human expansion. I have learned that this place has a special ritual significance and is therefore always the stage for the final Cycle. Two days hence, at Belerophon's Cross, the Pious Descent of Infinite Gradient will be celebrated.'

'And despite the restrictions, you intend to be there?'

'But certainly. And you?'

Brendl merely smiles and the conversation is ended. But later, when the old man's eyes are diverted by some glint of light, some gleam from a raised instrument or the thigh of some perfect whore, Brendl slips his purse and black book of poetry into Banaco's handsac. For like the old man, Brendl too is a creature of deception. But the deceit of poets is not so gentle.

His impersonation of rough, City Ternary pleases him; the whispered tip to the Prefecture Constabulary, handkerchief wrapped round fish-shaped telephone mouthpiece, an admirable performance.

'Hello, Commissioner, I'd like to report a theft . . . yes, I saw it happen, in the Three Lanterns Hotel . . . you must understand my need for anonymity . . .'

Presently the scream of ground-effect cars slewing to a halt fills the cobbled courtyard without. Doors slam, voices are raised, accusations made, defences dismissed, evidence produced, voices raised in heated exchange. Feet scuffle, doors slam once more, ground-effect fans power up and Brendl can go to his bed secure in his absolute possession of the Tlantoon.

In his sleep the third image comes to him.

It is less defined than the others, a sense, an impression: white light drawing a line of silver along a dull flat plane; glass, steel, water? A wall, a roof, a spade, an abstract of geometry? The very vagueness of the vision sends associations and allusions whirling within Brendl's imagination like speeding moons.

The next morning, upon settlement of his bill, he asks directions to Belerophon's Cross. The host supplies these with civil comprehensiveness and returns to Brendl his stolen purse and notebook.

'Terrible, sir, that such a fine gentleman as Mr Banaco should be at heart a common thief.'

'The finest gentlemen are often the greatest scoundrels,' says Brendl without the least taste of duplicity in his mouth. And, ever inwards, he goes forth, up the gently sloping land.

Towards mid-day he reaches a dome-shaped hill rising out of a busy district of tumbledown brick tenements, solitary and incongruous as a bald head at a wedding. At the summit of the grassy rise is a small belvedere from which the citizens of the tenements may contemplate the striking views. This noon hour the hilltop is deserted. Brendl's sole company and consolation is a small breeze stirring the windchimes which hang from the cupola, the spirit of place, a ghost of conscience. Brass telescopes have been provided by whatever philanthropic soul designed the hilltop preview; it is to the southward-looking of these that Brendl turns first. The telescope calls to his eye the vast traverse of urban landscape he has already crossed. But now Brendl sees that the land flares upwards, outwards like the bell of a colossal instrument poised on its edge. Barely perceptible at the limit of the telescope's range is a ludicrous crayon-scribble line of encirclement: the wall, Brendl realises with a start of surprise, Doubt-No-More a mean rat-hole nibbled in the perimeter. And what can that minute mote of light be but the sun shining from the blind reflecting face of the Glass Hotel? And, almost at the zenith of his craning vision, at the point on this world-stood-on-edge where the positive curve of hyperbolic city meets negative curve of round world; three globes, joined as if in some simple model of molecular theory, can that be any other than the starcrosser from Earth, hovering like smoke above Sothis the Ash Desert?

And now he turns to the northward telescope and looking through its eyepiece beholds the central spire of the world, reaching upwards, outwards, a preposterous mountain dwindling to an infinitesimal thread spun out into boundless space. Yet, that line of geometrical abstraction is as much a city as the dilated lands behind him, streets, houses, public buildings, markets, parks, alien lives.

Contemplation in the lonely belvedere; the land sloping up both behind and in front of him can only mean that Brendl has reached the Equipoise, the boundary between Outer and Inner Cities where the gradient of the land equals forty-five degrees, the place from which all paths are equal. Brendl stands upon the edge of the City of Men, before him the Barrens, empty alien boulevards, plague-haunted plazas of dereliction and decay, dead buildings painful as snapped teeth. Here, on the edge, the culminatory rites of the prehistoric Architects will be performed a day hence. Coming down from his hilltop like some prophet of obsession, he finds that the land beneath his feet is now sloping gently downhill.

He lodges that night in a shadowy hotel perched on a hillside like some bird of carrion presiding over the Barrens. This poor establishment is managed by a surly wife and husband who, whilst welcoming his custom, regard Brendl with the weightiest suspicion. Whether for being a Man o' Earth or for having read the blasphemous intent in his heart, he cannot tell. But that night, watched by the alien window-eyes of abandoned manors, Brendl writes. His Muse has him; in the possessed ecstasy of poetic inspiration Brendl writes and writes and writes, the words coming in such a spurt and rush that his always-perfect handwriting smears into distorted blots and scrawls, pulled out of true along the axis of an alien power-mirror. The Muse rides him hard, like a succubus, until with the slate-grey dawn she rolls from him to leave him lying in an incomprehension of reason, rhyme, nonsense and divine revelation, sheet after sheet after sheet of it. And it is the morning of the Pious Descent of Infinite Gradient.

The air is clear and cold here in the deadlands, crystal with a whisper of winter. Brendl's spirits are high. He glows with a creation-light that confounds his mistrustful host and hostess. To avoid undue attention he has dressed this day in the clothes of a city dweller. In the belt pouch of his leggings are the crumpled sheets of his frenzy. He walks with brisk good cheer along the great abandoned marble boulevard. Tufts of wiry grass sprout from between the uneven slabs of travatine and on each side range colonnades of statuary so eaten by time only pockmarked torsos remain; yet Brendl cannot rid himself of the sensation that they are watching his passage with senses other than vision. And in their ones and twos, their dribs and drabs, their threes and fours, the people come, out of everywhere, out of nowhere, out of the eroded statues and tilted paving slabs, a trickle, a stream, a river bearing Brendl towards the circus at the centre of the wheel of heartbroken avenues where Belerophon's Cross rises, ambiguous memorial to alien significance.

The heart-mystery is about to be enacted.

In the centre of the great open space the crimson orchestra has gathered around a remarkable pageant wagon, a man-made caricature of the familiar curving funnel of the City. Suspended upon its needle-point is a wooden armature to which four masked figures are roped. About the foot of the pageant wagon caper the stilt-dancers draped in comical costumes of straw. The orchestra strikes up, the tumultuous sound echoing and re-echoing from the girdling colonnades. The crowd stirs to the rhythm of the Tlantoon and Brendl finds himself pushed to the front of the mob. Suddenly exposed, he nervously examines the integrity of his disguise but the eyes of the people are rapt upon the astonishing acrobatics of the stilt-dancers. Upon their wooden crucifix at the apex of the City, the Pious Descenders raise their arms in readiness.

Suddenly there is a cry.

Suddenly, in mid-chord, the orchestra falls silent.

Suddenly, in mid-leap, the stilt-dancers are motionless.

Suddenly from across the circle of faces a finger is pointing. The finger of an old suspicious woman, the hostess of the crumbling hotel in the wastelands. She is screaming. Brendl cannot make out her screams. He has no need to, for he looks at the faces and sees that they are all about him, the faces of the Police Commissioner and the Manager of the Three Lanterns Hotel and the nannies he elbowed out of his way in Ranves Park, the faces of the City, turned upon him in accusation.

A tiny squeak of fear escapes Brendl the poet and that tiny animal cry releases him from the paralysis of exposure, for now he is running, running, running, down the shattered marble boulevard, running with the sound of an old woman's curses, of following feet, of angry voices, loud in his head. He cries, he sobs with fear: the quisling stitch in his side begs him stop, cease, give up. He runs, he knows not where, he runs lost to all but the sound of his pursuers.

And in the twinkling of an eye, she is there.

She beckons with her body. Escape: Brendl follows her into a warren of decomposing alleys and entries. Within seconds he is lost. His spirit-guide has vanished. He casts about him in desperation, first one blind alley, then another, then another, all the while imagining the beating footfalls of the hounds of the Tlantoon. A whisper of sound, he whirls, panic-stricken, sees a dark-robed figure in a mask beckon him forth. Lost in flight, Brendl follows. A hiss, a purr, his name? The half-glimpsed silhouette of the cat-dancer leads him deeper, running, running . . . 'Brrendllll . . .' black and gold skirts whisk round a cornerstone, cat-eyes flash in dark entrances. Any possible pursuers have long since been left perplexed in the archaic maze but still Brendl runs, runs, runs for there is nothing a poet fears more than his own imagination. The images have, at last, taken their due from him. He rounds a corner, enters another blind alley.

And there is a door, a carved wooden door, and there is a blue lantern, and there is a hem of black trimmed with gold sliding across the stone saddle into the doorway. Brendl approaches the wooden door. Everything is as he has hoped. Everything is as he has feared. Brendl passes under the blue lantern and enters the house. In a blue room lit by a painful blue light, the figure in black stands; masked, unspeaking. At its feet, the woman with the head of a cat crouches, coiled, potential.

'Thank you.'

The figures are motionless, suspended in time.

'The thanks of Brendl, poet of Earth, are yours.'

Silence, statis.

'Whoever you are, I am indebted to you . . .' Brendl's words, Brendl's smile, Brendl's hands, are frozen. The figure in black and the cat-headed woman are lifting their hands to remove their masks.

Brendl's cry rings and rings and rings from the four blue walls of the blue room: the wailing cry of pure dread.

Noseless, lipless, parchment-skinned and huge-eyed,

221

slit-eyed, whatever the people to which these triangular faces belong, they are not human.

Not human.

Never human.

But what makes that inhumanity unbearable is that there is nothing but friendship in those faces, the fellowship of the hunted, the hated. Brendl's lips work soundlessly, then, without conscious thought, he is running from the house of the blue lantern, blundering blindly along the staggering, crumbling lanes. The hands. The hands. The pale, thin beautifully alien hands had been reaching out to him, imploring him to put off his humanity and his self and join them down in the deadlands.

Within moments he is quite lost. Possessed of a malign sentience, the labyrinth of alleyways sends him hither, thither, this way, that way, crossing and recrossing his path time after time. Numb, heedless, Brendl is past rational thought and choice. The streets ring with cries, his own and those of his pursuers, for his drunkard's walk has led him away from the alien sanctuary at the heart of the warren where no man of that prefecture will dare go, outwards, away, close to the highways of men. Flailing at the air, striking at the invisible images which have betrayed him, Brendl stumbles on until at last, bursting around a corner, he delivers himself into the hands of his hunters.

Those hands seize him, those hands hold him: voices call, meaningless wrapped in their thick, alien-tainted dialects. Two persons press forwards through the mob; the mistrustful woman, the surly man; the managers of the brooding hotel. A brief nod of identification, a word of command and the knife is drawn.

A vagrant shaft of afternoon sunlight penetrating the darkness of the warrenway limns a line of pure, holy silver along the steel edge of the blade.

The trinity is complete; the trinity of betrayal.

Brendl shrieks, struggles, then in a stabbing, slashing flash the knife tears Brendl the poet open from crotch to sternum.

Through the fire, through the rushing, mobbing dark, Brendl casts his eyes to heaven, to the clouds spinning like fleece into threads twisted around the twisted hyperbolic world. And he knows.

He knows that as casually as a discontinuity mirror distorts space it can twist time back upon itself like a skein of wool, throwing echoes of future things into the past so that a man, if he has the vanity, the pride, the arrogance and naïveté of a poet, may ignorantly chase the presentiment of his own death in the name of inspiration, and art. And Brendl knows it all and he smiles, a warped, distorted smile, and the darkness closes in around him and draws him into itself.

Hands clasped behind back in the proper attitude of diplomatic mourning, Fleyn the Consular Officer walks slowly beside the catafalque as it is borne up the access ramp of the starcrosser. He finds himself caught incongruously between realities: the air shivers with the imaginings of the High Space drive-fields, yet a little soft grey ash has settled on the sleeve of his dress uniform, carried on the world-circling wind from Sothis the Ash Desert.

Sad, strange, terrible, a cruel dying in a lonely, alien place. On what might a poet's final thoughts linger? Home? Love? Mortality, perhaps, or a parting sneer at the cosmic comedian out of whose bad jokes life was shaped? Some answer must lie within the crumpled sheets of paper they brought with the body: the final work of Brendl the poet. Doubtless a masterpiece, can posterity consider it otherwise? But what of those odd creatures that bore the body, dragging it by the sweat of their limbs on that rude travois across the incredible reach of city between Belerophon's Cross and the Consular Offices? What of the cat-woman and the masked figure in black?

What relationship had found its expression there?

And now Fleyn stands upon the verandah of the Glass Hotel, a face among faces, the faces of the fearful and the vain who had not the small courage to accompany Brendl

223

on his last slow journey into High Space. The Starcrosser is readied for its journey now, the air stirs, gels, and suddenly is aswarm with the spiritual, inspirational creatures of the aesthetic medium. A bubble dissolving, a waft of grey ash and the vessel is gone. But the city remains, the infinite within its finite boundary, forever ascending, forever approaching perpendicular.

MICHAEL MOORCOCK

Mars

The wandering earth herself may be
Only a sudden flaming word,
In clanging space a moment heard,
Troubling the endless reverie.
      W. B. Yeats
      The Song of the Happy Shepherd

Hesitating at the edge of the beautiful ghost town Morgan watched red rust run like a river over a smashed Cerum screen. From below came the uncertain vibration of some abandoned atmosphere plant, its echo murmuring through endless catacombs where the majority of Martians preferred to survive. Only a few like Morgan chose to live beneath the pale wash of the planet's pastel skies and breathe dusty air smelling of licorice, lilac and the sweet old Earth of childhood.

Morgan was sixteen when the community congregated within pink brick Gothic arches to watch an accelerator picture bloom on the viewing wall. Earth, then Neptune, had quietly vanished from the solar system. 'A great experiment.' Gran had seemed regretful. Scientists who had issued warnings of just such dramatic results were vindicated, but since the colonies were self-sufficient it merely meant the end of innocence, not of civilisation. This was to be a period of forgetting.

Mars had already developed a consciously introspective

culture. To them the idea of Earth's departure was more interesting than the fact. Symbolism offered at once a larger and less involving reality.

Morgan reached through the thin, fast-flowing dust to pick up an old paperback lying on the fused clay beneath. It was obsolete and the expensive machines to play it belonged only to collectors, but the cover was interesting. Even after so much exposure the holograms were garish, crude, ungraduated. A figure in a red-and-purple smock threatened another with some sort of weapon and the calligraphy was so complicated it was almost impossible for Morgan, trained on the spare alphabets once fashionable in Morocco, to decipher. It was clearly from Earth. Had the whole planet been so loud? To Morgan's ears much of the music had the same unsubtle quality; it was brutal, almost alarming, though some Martians thought it vivid, possessed of a primitive vitality they had lost.

'We're too cultured for our own good,' Wren had said the other day. 'It's Mars. At this rate we'll go the way of the other civilisations.'

Mars has seen at least nine major cultures thrive and fade. The youngest had lived in the deepest caverns of all before dying out as peacefully and as mysteriously as all the rest. 'Mars was never meant to support life. Mars represents the tranquillity of death. Perhaps you should have gone to Venus while you had the chance?'

Once, aged eleven, Morgan had visited Venus and found the elegant landscaping, the elaborately geometrical gardens, the tastefully arranged forests, far too classical. Because her surface had hardly been worth altering, Mars remained much as she had been when the first Earth settlers arrived, her limitless deserts and worn mountains, her craters and her shallow valleys relieved only by occasional bands of low vegetation marking the existence of subterranean rivers and oceans serving those twilight countries whose original architecture had been so carefully adapted and utilised by the latest Martians. At least two previous civilisations had been humanoid and one of them had certainly been a colonising culture, either from another system or possibly even marooned here from another space-time. There was a theory that Mars herself had not originally been part of this system. Fragments of old machines suggested attempts to use the whole planet as a means of transportation. The remains of what were evidently spaceships could have brought visitors to Mars or had perhaps been built in a failed attempt to leave the planet. Only one culture – the huge four-armed tusked bipeds – had apparently succeeded in travelling on.

'They come to Mars to die,' Wren had said. 'Or they leave. We have no intention of leaving. Mars lets us grow old gracefully.'

Nothing in Morgan could easily resist the idea. Few babies had ever been born on Mars and in spite of all efforts fewer still had reached healthy adulthood. Regeneration maintained the race.

'Mars rejects children.' Wren's voice had contained a certain depth of satisfaction. 'She rejects everything which isn't already mature. She's a planet for people who've grown tired not of life but of exploration. You, Morgan, are in an uneasy position here, for you were almost an adult when you arrived and you never expected to stay. Do you miss your parents?'

Morgan's grandparents had always seemed much closer. They had settled on Mars as part of a scheme offered on Earth to encourage early retirement, but their parents had been born here, to the first real settlers who built the surface towns and the Cerum screens.

'Mars has no secrets from those who love her.' Wren had smiled and, in a gesture of sad regret, caressed Morgan's hand.

But Morgan loved Mars. Possibly Morgan's love contained too much passion for the planet to bear. Mars's mysteries were everywhere and were part of her fascination. Morgan enjoyed curiosity for its own sake and was rarely disappointed by unanswered questions.

The paperback replaced in the river bed, Morgan moved towards ochre walls; some old public buildings in the Second Arabian style. Adding water to Martian clay produced a cement as strong as stone. The cheapness of their materials had always allowed the Martians more fanciful and elaborate structures than the Venusians or Ganymedians. Dust could be moulded into baroque splendour and some mock-Versailles raised from the desert in days. It never rained on Mars so only the action of the winds affected these fantastical towns whose architecture recorded the history of Earth's finest periods. Impossible to combine with tints, the towns were the same pale oranges, yellows, browns, pinks and rusty reds as their surroundings, the subtle skies which never quite formed clouds. Attempts to vary the colours by raising holograms and even 2D billboards, by using the picture facilities of the Cerum screens whenever possible, had produced tones too bright for eyes grown accustomed to subtler shades and before their exodus to reinhabit the prehistoric cities few Martians had desired anything but the planet's familiar spectrum. On arriving, Morgan, at first unable to distinguish easily between colours, had thought the place sinister. Even the people had a faded quality, their voices like whisperings in a graveyard. Though they were robust enough, it had been easy to believe in grandparents over two hundred years old.

Morgan's grandparents' generation still tended to call the planet 'Pacifica', from the first colonial advertisements. While it bore a closer relationship to the landscapes, the name was hollow to Morgan. Mars had not been associated in anyone's mind with a Roman war god for centuries. What had been 'martial' to Morgan's ancestors meant almost its opposite now. To Morgan the word Mars had always been a synonym for peace.

Profoundly opposed to any return to the surface, for weeks Morgan's grandparents had spoken of nothing but the danger. Cheap generators and equipment from Earth factories were no longer available to maintain meteor beams or control dust-storms. Morgan and the others had tried to explain how these unpredictable elements were part of the reason for going back.

Familiar with defeat but not reconciled to it, Morgan had on that occasion persevered, eventually winning the agreement of the community. A year ago twenty-eight people, mostly of Morgan's generation, had set themselves up in Egg City, close to the Little Crack, a dust-river which coursed without interruption across half the planet before joining Main Run near the equator.

Used to solitary lives, the majority gradually went their separate ways until only Morgan and Wren were left in Egg. Faad was furthest away, on the Back Line, some three thousand kilometres from Egg. Faad had travelled on an ancient dust-coaster brought from underground. They were dangerous, inclined to capsize, but you could ride the dust-tides down the deep cracks and cover an enormous distance. Faad had the whole of Whistler to live in. This was the most elaborately fanciful of all Martian cities, with replicas of almost every monumental building Earth had ever raised, from the Taj Mahal to the Empire State to the Gibraltar Berber Mosque, though the location let the winds erode them into extraordinary versions of their originals.

Morgan had not lost any love for the underworld's beauty, the great plumes of atmosphere rising from the hydros in the morning, and shafts of sunlight cutting down from a mile above to strike water which glowed like copper; the pewter caverns, the carved gold-green stalactites whose disturbingly alien faces bore expressions of unguessable sorrow. Or was it sorrow at all? What did humanity really know of any alien entity? Once it was realised that dead aliens offered no threat they were forgotten by everyone save a few academics, as if people refused to consider the implications, the fact that not one race, no matter how perfectly adapted, had continued to exist on Mars for more than eleven or twelve millennia?

Along the banks of frozen rivers and lakes, wonderfully

symmetrical structures had been erected, side by side with crazily angular buildings, clearly the productions of two different races who at one time had shared the planet equably. One race had been humanoid, the other avarian but flightless.

An earlier species resembling fine-featured Oriental cats had left statues to themselves all over Mars and Morgan had become almost as familiar with their culture as with Earth's. Their celebrations had all seemed to concern enormous failures. They seemed a race addicted to defeat. Morgan believed in the power of habit, of rituals maintaining patterns of behaviour which had long since lost their psychic or practical usefulness. Humans were the same, especially around power or powerlessness. For millennia, when gender had been a class definition, half the race had seemed addicted to power and half to powerlessness, producing profound philosophies and art forms, religions and sciences out of their addictions.

To Morgan much of what those ancestors had valued seemed trivial or debased and it was only possible to hold faint distaste for so barbaric a past. With Earth's disappearance had gone the reminders of their shame, while the reminders of their glories lived on as magnificent Martian ghosts.

If Earth had contained the descendants of those addicted to power, then Mars sheltered a people who made a virtue of powerlessness; this remained the element in Martian culture which caused Morgan greatest unease. There was no nobility in surviving for the sake of surviving – unless a virus or an amoeba were instrinsically noble – but neither was there any particular moral purity in reconciling oneself to extinction.

Sometimes Wren said that every single piece of architecture on the planet was nothing more than an elaborate tombstone. Wren's ideas were easily understood when, alone, you looked out across red dunes towards eroded cliffs and a sky turned to smoky yellow streaked with orange; but they were too easy, Morgan had decided. Mars was not dead and her people were not dying. It would be a million years before anyone needed to consider the notion.

Morgan got back on the brog and hovered a few feet above the surface before moving forward. There was a good chance of reaching Egg before twilight, though there was no urgency. Any of the old cities were capable of giving temporary shelter. Morgan's vehicle offered electronic intimacies as it calculated distances and speeds, warming the cabin to compensate for Mars's slow, wonderful sunset. Wren waited in Egg and Morgan was nervous of returning, wary of a new relationship which, no matter how perfect, might interfere with this abiding love-affair with Mars, this sense of coming to know profoundly the identity of an entire planet, the nature of her history, the qualities which made her unique among the planets.

Already Wren had introduced a note of scepticism. 'You're not exploring Mars. You're exploring yourself, Morgan. That's surely all anyone does? That's what Mars makes you do. That's what Mars gives you. And in turn you learn how to explore and understand others. You're the youngest of us but I always trusted you, most of all, to realise that.'

'Mars isn't me,' Morgan had said. 'I'm not greatly interested in myself.'

This statement was so contrary to fundamental Martian belief that Wren's only possible response had been laughter. 'Your Mars is you!' Then Wren had dropped the subject. Wren was in love with Morgan, whose pale skin and black hair were strikingly similar to Wren's own. It was the epitome of the Martian ideal of beauty.

Morgan's fascination with Wren had something to do with narcissism but was also a wish to retain emotional contact with another human being, as if that in itself were some sort of safety-line. Aware of Wren's stronger infatuation, Morgan knew it did not matter if a day or two went by before returning to Egg. Wren would almost certainly be waiting. Martians were not encouraged to form intense relationships. Wren would probably expect no more of Morgan and it was not for Morgan to speculate about and respond to Wren's possible or unstated feelings.

Deliberately slowing the brog, Morgan rode beside a line of ridges that were probably an old crater rim. The sun continued its tranquil descent. Delighted by the almost imperceptible alternation of shades, Morgan next re-ordered the magnetics to let the vehicle drift off towards Rose de la Paix where once spaceships had come and gone in such numbers.

Just before dark, when the main constellations shone a greenish blue in the depths of the sky, Morgan reached the old port's outskirts, surprised to see that someone had changed its familiar silhouette. Morgan was sure a new building had been added since Faad had driven them here when Isutep and Katchga left for Venus.

Finding a cocoon-bay, Morgan prepared for the night, welcoming the positive security and comfort of the coffin-shaped survival box. In the morning it would be interesting to investigate the new addition to Rose, perhaps one of those random sculptures erected by the Caziz siblings, Mars's leading artists and a constant source of irritation to the underworlders.

An hour or so after dawn Morgan watched fragile sun-light fragment red and gold bands layering the horizon like geological strata. There was, indeed, an addition to the port, sitting half on a launch-disc which shone like polished lead, a massive thing of ornate brass curves, silver loops and sinuously interwoven tubes seemingly partly metallic and partly organic, its function impossible to guess. But it was clearly not by the Cazizes. There were no materials like it on Mars. Morgan decided it must surely be a vessel, its occupants recognising a spaceship port. Was this the vanguard of the next wave of colonists?

The vessel's colours had now become predominantly greens and dark rich blues, with some glittering reds and almost jarring metal pinks. Morgan could not look at it for any length of time without developing a mild headache.

Searching amongst the miscellaneous stuff in the back of the brog, Morgan found an antiglare mask and put this on. The ship now appeared to shift very slowly back and forth through the spectrum, an unexpected effect which gradually stabilised. After some minutes there was a kind of flickering passage across part of the lower latticework of the ship and two indistinct figures stood almost gingerly on the gleaming disc.

Morgan eventually realised they were moving. They were bipeds, chunky in outline but at the same time ethereal. A further flicker in the air and heads were revealed. To Morgan the creatures, almost without necks, with flat features and dramatically deepset eyes, were not immediately attractive. When one of them spoke, it was like a distantly heard harp, the notes drawn out and indistinct, yet Morgan understood a few words.

. . . *unpeace* . . . *targettable* . . . *apologisation* . . . *unfamiliarian* . . . *intraspaced* . . . *relationates* . . . *upsetforthuns* . . . *plastmaritum* . . .

Clearly the aliens had learned from Earth broadcasts, for this was spaceship patois and technonlex, which Morgan could speak a little. Replying in the same mixture, Morgan asked them if they had travelled far. They did not understand initially, but after several attempts, lasting almost until noon, they responded, each word drawn out so that it took them hours to deliver their information.

They had come intraspacially and picked up the megaflow which brought them most of the way. Believing themselves in danger, they needed, Morgan thought they said, to contact a ship-controller so they could be buried.

Were they pursued? Morgan asked, and it was almost dark before he began to understand their reply. Probably not. They were being cautious and wanted to hide their ship. There had been home planet 'beleaguerments'. Considerable 'unpeace'. The newcomers seemed chiefly concerned for the safety of their fellows. They seemed to be advance scouts or else were already the sole survivors of some catastrophe. They referred sometimes in technonlex and sometimes in English to a place called Erdorig or Three. When Morgan asked them the name of their planet they hesitated until just before dawn the next day and then said 'Earth', which Morgan thought a fairly useless piece of translation.

Morgan tried to explain the need to sleep and eventually simply returned to the cocoon for a few hours. On Morgan's coming back to the disc they reappeared before him, ready to continue. Morgan was bewildered by their mixture of terrible urgency and unreal tranquillity. The way the aliens spoke and moved perhaps reflected a radical difference in the texture of their home space. They would pause sometimes for quarter-of-an-hour between words, clearly from need and habit, not because they were seeking the appropriate phrase. Morgan wondered if in their language silences of a particular kind were in fact a form of communication. Their exchange could still take over an hour and still prove meaningless. Morgan maintained this intercourse for almost two more days with little sleep before deciding that Wren must be brought here. Wren was better qualified to continue the dialogue, having a background in semantics and anthropology.

Privately joking that the journey from Rose to Egg and back could probably be completed before the aliens finished their next observation, Morgan assured them they were welcome and that he went to seek others who might help them better. Morgan raced the brog back to Egg, the red dust shrieking and spiralling as it reacted to the vehicle's overtaxed magnetics.

As usual, only Wren was in Egg, sitting in the main square on the steps of a sandstone Los Angeles City Hall watching old newscasts. As Morgan drove in Wren folded the viewer and smiled. 'I knew you'd be late. It's all right.'

Before Wren spoke Morgan had been full of the event, but now felt a great reluctance to say anything at all, let alone the half-lie which emerged. 'I was delayed in Rose.'

'Something happening?' Clearly Wren was torn between

relief at seeing Morgan and irritation for having been made to speculate.

'Nothing really.' Climbing down from the brog, Morgan took a rag and began removing a layer of bronze-brown dust from the side. 'I'm glad you weren't disturbed.'

'I'm a Martian. We're never disturbed.'

Morgan failed to detect Wren's irony and instead looked back towards Rose. 'There's a new ship on one of the launch discs.'

'Going to Venus? From Venus?'

'Alien. From sideways I'd guess. They're not quite in focus, if you know what I mean. I've been with them most of the time. I can't find out what they're here for. They speak a form of technonlex, bits of other Earth languages, ship's patois.'

'Two days and they haven't told you why they're here?' Wren began to walk towards the slender triple towers where they always stayed when in Egg City. 'Not what I'd call communication, Morgan. What are they hiding?'

'They seem to fade out – physically, I mean. Then they'll become so solid and immovable I think they're turning into statues before my eyes. You'd have to see it, Wren.'

Wren paused, the anger and frustration dissipating. 'What?'

'It's the oddest thing I've ever experienced. It's as if they're fluctuating between maximum stability and maximum entropy. They probably have means of controlling the space they occupy. They're very nearly human. Superficially.'

'Remember Faad's joke?' Wren was sceptical.

'This isn't like Faad's joke. It's very easy to tell. These people are frightened. Or angry. I don't know.'

'Frightened of you?'

'Maybe. Perhaps of something they've left behind. You should come out to Rose, Wren. You know all those versions of technonlex. You're trained for this. It might be the only real chance you ever get to make use of that prolonged education.'

235

In a newly-relaxed face Wren's smile was beautiful. It was their running game. Wren came striding back to embrace Morgan who beamed with the pleasure of reconciliation. 'I can't be everything you'd like, Wren. But I love you.'

'Yes,' said Wren. 'That's what makes it painful. We're fools, we Martians. Is all of this imposed? Is it just the stupid, useless rationalisations of the early settlers? Shouldn't we be trying to change how we look at things? I was considering all that stuff we talked about the other day . . .'

Already Wren was moving the conversation towards abstraction. Morgan could see this typically Martian trait objectively, but Wren was almost entirely unaware of it.

'This is a real event, Wren. These people seem desperate. Do you want to help them?'

'Why not? Can the brog stand a return trip?'

'We'll take the spare. I got careless. Do you need anything?'

'Some food. Some reference stuff. You fetch the brog and I'll be ready.'

Suddenly enjoying Wren's companionship, Morgan drove them back directly towards Egg, sailing up over smaller obstacles, gracefully curving around cliffs.

'You seem happy,' said Wren. 'I mean happier. Is it the excitement?'

'I like doing things with you, Wren, better than I like having conversations. People talk too much for me.'

'That's Mars.' Wren again unconsciously refused any reason for action or change. 'Good old Mars. She does that.'

'Well, these people might need something than talk.' Morgan grinned at this. 'If there's time.'

'You're goony today.' Wren enjoyed Morgan's mood, sitting closer and offering an affectionate hug. 'You're like a kid. I suppose you are our kid, really. What can we offer the visitors? Or are you just being rhetorical?'

'Help.' Morgan shrugged, keeping an eye firmly on the

236

forward terrain, for the automatics were off in order to achieve greater speed. 'I think that's why they're here.'

'They're not would-be colonists, then? I thought everyone wanted to settle on Mars. Have you ever wondered why such a barren place is so attractive to so many different races?'

'You're sliding off the point again, Wren.'

Wren was amiably baffled. 'I didn't know there was one. They're emissaries? Are they?'

'That's why I need you, Wren.'

Clearly flattered by this, Wren settled more comfortably in the seat. 'I like a good problem.'

'We might have to start solving this one as rapidly as possible.'

'I'll try not to disappoint you, Morgan.' Head shaking in amusement, Wren studied the copper-coloured mossy South Dales in the distance. The light caught a sheen of tiny stems so that the entire landscape resembled a vast jewelled snake warming its body beneath the sun. 'Oh, this is so good, Morgan. Don't you love Mars?'

Soon Morgan saw Rose coming up on the horizon: fractured skyscrapers, rusted geometries of disused instruments and signals, eroded control towers, domes the colour of pale chocolate and bleached strawberries, ruined customs buildings, a silted quarantine enclosure and, beyond, the Art Hazardos splendours of the Mannaheim Apartments, raised in the days before the fashion for imitation became the ruling aesthetic and gave Martian cities their characteristic appearance of bizarre monuments to a lost planet.

'Awful,' said Wren without thinking. Like most Martians, Wren believed any style not previously seen on Earth was vulgar and simply lacking in any beauty. To Morgan the buildings were only hard to read, almost like the spaceship which now came into view and made Wren exclaim noisily about its oddness. 'This is stranger than anything we have already. They won't shoot me or anything, will they?'

The two aliens had not moved very far from their original spot. Currently they were so utterly solid, standing firmly on the faintly reflective disc, that almost everything surrounding them seemed a little unreal.

'Well, first things first,' said Wren, raising a hand in a sign which no real logic accepted as a universal gesture of peace. Yet the salute was eventually answered, awkwardly, as if the aliens were trying to recall forgotten briefings. Their stolid, ugly faces stared with considerable alertness from massive hairless heads wearing some kind of transparent, protective covering, possibly a membrane or thin bone. 'Could you tell me your names? I'm Wren. This is Morgan.'

Morgan felt foolish for not having considered this simple first step. Yet the aliens were bewildered until Wren, growing a little more sober, tried a whole series of technonlex versions. The process was as slow as it had been earlier, but at last Wren turned to Morgan with some information. 'They're Directed Beings from the Pastoral Choice, they say, and are called Sendes-endes-Ah and Luuk Shenpehr, as far as I can tell. Directed Beings, I think, are people who choose physical work and the Pastoral Choice is probably the nearest thing to a country — a province, maybe. What are they? Farm labourers? There'll be a long way to go before we have a true notion of how they live. But that's all we need for the moment.' Wren had become unusually engaged. 'Now I'll try to find out a bit more as to why they came here.'

A little disturbed by Wren's brusque, almost proprietorial tone, Morgan knew a protective pang. 'They must be exhausted. Should we offer them food?'

Wren shrugged, as if finding this question unnecessary, but nonetheless addressed the aliens and after less than twenty minutes discovered that they had taken nourishment while Morgan was away. 'I think I embarrassed them.' Wren grinned. There was, indeed, a great deal of fading in and out and both aliens had changed from pasty white to a kind of lime green. Now they resumed their solidity and original colouring.

Unhappy with the anthropologist's lighthearted attitude to the aliens, Morgan felt Wren should display more respect. But the aliens were almost certainly unaware of any nuances and Wren was making far greater progress with them. By the following morning the aliens retired to their spaceship while Wren and Morgan, occupying some old crew's quarters not far away, had pieced together a large part of the basic story.

'They were coming back.' Wren frowned. 'They're sure of that. They've said it every possible way. They were coming back, hoping to find help or escape. They seem to be saying they're Martians, Morgan. Yet there's nothing like them anywhere on Mars. Were they the original inhabitants, so long ago no trace remains?' Wren looked out at the ship. 'Their own planet, which either has no name or a name which sounds very much like Earth, is no longer inhabitable. A new species has attacked? Possibly a disease? Their knowledge of technonlex is excellent but it's a version I've never come across. There are gaps, in other words. They want to hide their ship. We should humour them in that, I think.'

'Humour them?' Again Morgan was unhappy with Wren's choice of phrase.

'Respect their wishes, then. Don't those pads lower into the ground? They'll have to make a more precise landing, though. They're funny-looking creatures. Old, old people would be my guess. I asked how many inhabitants of their race were left on the planet and they said twelve. But it might have been twelve hundred, twelve thousand — technonlex won't do it, so far. We'll have to consult with the community. I told them. They seem a worthy enough pair, if a bit boring and ugly.' Wren laughed. 'Sorry, Morgan. But have you considered this could be a clever trick on their part. What if they're the conquering bully-boys?'

They looked up and saw the air flush with a yellowish red, then the spaceship grew insubstantial for a few seconds. When it regained its solidity it stood dead-centre

239

on the disc. Emerging again, the two aliens settled themselves in front of Wren and Morgan, ready for the next day's conversation. The first thing they did was repeat, rapidly in their terms, that the ship must be hidden.

'We'll need permission from the rest.' Wren was clearly impressed. 'You'd better go and ask, Morgan. Find your grandparents. I'll carry on here.'

Though reluctant to leave and even more reluctant to confront the underworlders, Morgan responded to the urgency and took the brog over to Rose's nearest shaftgate, driving down into the cool half-light of the hollow world below.

When Morgan returned, having once again earned some subtle kind of disapproval for a failure, as the underworlders saw it, of courtesy, Wren was sitting on the ground with hands in the air and looking at one of the aliens who, perhaps aggressively, brandished what might have been a weapon.

Obviously afraid, Wren looked back at Morgan. 'I made a serious gaff, Morgan. I've asked them not to shoot me, but I'm not sure their technonlex has a word for mercy.' Wren's mouth was dry. 'We made some progress. Maybe too much. They're from Earth, Morgan. Old Earth which went off with Neptune, sideways through the multiverse – not deliberately, you'll recall – and now they're a million or two years in our future. Well, you know more about physics than I do.' Wren was talking from panic rather than enthusiasm. 'These are the descendants of our original ancestors. They *were* "coming back" – not to their home planet but to their home star-system. They knew about Mars. Morgan, they were coming home to die! I was right. Everyone comes to Mars to die! Even me, it seems.'

Frowning, Morgan stared uncertainly from what appeared to be the weapon in Luuk Shenpehr's hands to the seated, frightened Wren. 'To live,' said Morgan firmly. 'They're here because they're trying to find a way to survive. Surely that's more logical? How did you offend them, Wren?'

'Maybe I got a bit noisy when I realised the truth. Obviously their space-time is now radically different to this one and that explains their apparent slowness and the occasional insubstantiality – which incidentally they seem in the process of correcting . . .' Wren paused. 'Don't let them shoot me, Morgan. They like you.'

'They said that?'

'They're not pointing a gun at you.' This irritating tendency to trivialise even in such circumstances almost made Morgan want to abandon Wren to whatever fate was in store.

'But they were looking for help.' Morgan did not want to believe in any reverse.

'The interpretations are tricky. They say they're seeking transformation – resolution? – this is their technonlex, maybe hundreds of years ahead of ours, maybe more.'

Earth unpeace . . . Sendes-endes-Ah spoke again in a voice like the distant song of a harp, but stronger, less hesitant. Still Morgan could only understand the one phrase. Was it some kind of ultimatum?

'They won't respond to me.' Wren was shaking now. 'Please intercede.'

'They're not being attacked?' Morgan's voice was faint.

'They're being "pushed down", they said. Another force is simply occupying their planet as if they don't exist. Morgan!'

Morgan moved cautiously forward. Behind the alien ship the Martian sun had risen like an angel's armour, proclaiming some unspecific glory. The old, red hills began to pulse. The smell of orange blossom crystals sweetened the thin air and made it magical.

'But, Wren, you haven't explained how you angered them.'

'Perhaps I was facetious. I couldn't believe they hadn't resisted the invaders. They say they're fewer than twelve now.' Wren took deep breaths, trying to control panic. 'A civil war? Oh, Morgan.' The gun moved in Luuk Shenpehr's hand. The risen sun made it blossom with sudden colour. Then, in a second of inspiration, Morgan stepped foward and took it from the alien. There was no resistance.

Shaking with relief, Wren stood up, while Morgan held the thing to the light. Wren began to smile sheepishly, but Morgan's features had grown profoundly sad. Morgan understood the object's function.

'I think you saved my life.' Wren was anxious to fill in the silence.

Morgan's head moved in a tiny gesture of contradiction.

Stretching towards the blazing, complicated thing, Wren asked: 'How does it fire?'

'It doesn't,' said Morgan, sighting along it. 'It can't.' There were no moving parts.

'It's clearly a gun. I've seen stuff like it in paperbacks.'

Morgan turned the object this way and that to let the sun's rays play on its awkward curves and peculiar angles, this icon, perhaps created in desperation from insubstantial data on a race's long dead past. 'It's not a gun, Wren.'

The dust blew for a moment around their legs while from the Northern Shafts the Martians, masked against the light, were emerging, moving hesitantly towards their Earthling cousins. At last Morgan handed the object to a still baffled Wren.

'It's only the memory of a gun.'

TANITH LEE

A Madonna of the Machine

> Industrial canticles
> Sing the steel.
> A secret language,
> Pain.
>
> John Kaiine

Touch touch touch the dial, and the dial turns. Now to the left, and now to the right. Grey light flickers down the coil: half a mile below the platform, where the spiral ends, a lever raises its leviathan head. *Ting* says a bell. And the process is accomplished.

peter sits on his bench. He watches the figures moving noiselessly along the panel. After one seventy second unit, a soft flare glows in the panel. peter reaches out again and touch touch touches the dial, and the dial turns, left and right, and the grey light flickers away down the snake-bowel coil, down down into the dusk below, and there the leviathan raises its head, and *ting* says the bell.

And the process is accomplished.

And peter sits on his bench, watching the figures move until another seventy second unit passes and the flare glows, and he reaches out and touch and turn and left and right and flicker and down and raise and *ting*.

Sometimes, as he sits, or periodically stands for a unit

or two, when the passing mechanical overseer reminds him, peter thinks. He thinks about whether he is hungry now or not, and if he is, he takes a fibre bar from his overall and eats it. Or if he is thirsty he presses a tube in the grey-silver wall beside the bench, and the tube issues him a vitamin drink. Or he thinks of the talkto in his home, which tells him things or answers questions, if he has any, or murmurs him to sleep. Or he notices the other persons who sit or stand before their own sections on the platform; lines of people six or seven metres apart. He has been among them all his adult life. They are the same people he has always been with, here. And in the start of the diurnal, after the mechanical lark trills him awake, he has heard, for twenty-five years, the other mechanical larks in main building of d district going off one by one, to wake these others. Then they, like him, enter their hygiene cubicles, rid themselves of waste matter, are cleansed and dried, go to their food counters and are fed, expel themselves into the two thousand metre long corridor, for the twice-daily walk necessary for their health. And in the cage-lift they go down into the street, where the pale grey verticals and horizontals stretch away and away, and the air-bus comes and sucks them in and bears them off and sets them down here, together, in the heart of the Machine.

peter knows the names of some of his neighbours. But they have never really spoken. There is no point. What is there to discuss? Each has a talkto in his or her home. The talkto adapts entirely to each individual personality. It knows, by mechanical instinct, what to say, and even when to speak and when to keep silent. It knows the proper sounds and encouragements to aid occasional vague masturbations, or to soothe the aftermath of some unremembered yet disquieting dream.

There is no need for human conversation, awkward and effortful.

The flare glows, and peter touches touches touches, and the dial turns. The harmony of the activity and its result are satisfying. It is a dim yet pleasing thought that

244

throughout the Machine, hour by hour, unceasing for its duration, so many millions of men and women carry out, endlessly and faultlessly, similar or complementary actions. The Machine serves and is served. The empathy is perfect.

The light reaches the lever which raises itself. *Ting* goes the bell.

There is a meal-break, and peter leaves his section for the moving ramp which goes down under the platform. On the ramp with him, peter recognises yori and marion, ted and malwe and jane. They reach the lower level and step off, into the canteen. Everything has a mild gloss of cleanness. The clean walls, in reply to the pressure of his fingers, give peter a slice of protein and some vegetable cubes, and a caffeine drink.

peter sits at a table to eat. The table is shared by yori, jane and ted. They do not speak to each other. Everyone thinks their own thoughts and slowly consumes the food.

It is as peter is finishing his drink that there comes to him the first Intimation.

He does not know it for an Intimation.

It is a feeling he has never felt before; it has no name.

It startles him, and wondering if he has not chewed his food properly and so has caused some gastric imbalance, he half-rises to approach the canteen health dispenser. But then the feeling without a name ebbs away. It goes so softly (not as it came, sheer and hard, like a glass sliver), that peter is reassured. He does not, however, finish his drink, subconsciously blaming it.

On the ramp back to the platform, ted speaks.

He says: 'There was a pinkness over my screen, before meal-break.'

No one answers. jane glances at him, then politely averts her eyes.

ted says nothing else.

They return to their positions.

peter touches. The dial turns.

Just before the next meal-break, peter feels the second Intimation. It is unlike the first, coming insidiously, sweetly, like the gentle libido which sometimes wakes him in the twilight of sleep prior to the trilling of the mechanical lark. This is not a bodily feeling, nevertheless, even though it invades his body. What is wrong with him?

peter is struck by a sort of paralysis. He stares inward at the feeling, trying to determine its shape.

It is a type of wave, with an upcurling head, pliant, mutable, yet formed. Running in.

It strikes him, somewhere in the region of the heart.

He is ill. There is something medically wrong. His heart is beating strongly and very fast. peter looks up from his panel to the emergency button in the wall. And there, above his section, he sees a gleam of light that is pink, the colour of a rose, a special colour that perhaps his genes recall, although he has never seen a flower of any type. peter looks at the rose light and, gradually, it unfolds itself, and it too, like the wave-shape within him beating on his beating heart, takes on a form.

He thinks it is like a woman. Yes, it is like a woman. She is clothed in a flowing, pleated garment, all the rose-colour, and on her head is a drift of scarf, the palest yellow, also rose-like. Her flesh is pale, luminous and white, not like skin. She has eyes, although the rest of her features seem to him blurred. The eyes of the woman fix on peter. He tries to look away. It is not possible. Something terrible is in her eyes, something he has never, in all his twenty-five years, seen in a human face and expression.

peter opens his mouth and makes a sound, and something happens to him. His chest is heaving, and the air is coming out of him in gasps and liquid is rushing down his cheeks, as if he bled, but it is only water pouring out of his eyes.

And then, the rose light fades from the wall above the panel.

peter comprehends, as he struggles helplessly with the paroxysm of the body once known as weeping, and which he does not understand, that the figures have reached the seventy unit interval and the soft flare has gone off and he has not touched −

Then he sees that the dial is turning left and right. The flickering energy is running down the coil to the lever below which lifts, and the bell goes *ting*.

peter has not touched the dial, the three immaculate touches. Absorbed by the dreadful vision above the panel, peter has failed the Machine. But despite this lapse, the dial had turned, the coil has been activated. The process has been accomplished.

peter stops crying. His chest and throat are raw, and his eyes sting. He wipes his nose on the sleeve of his overall without thinking, and as the light flares again, he touch touch touches −

He does not know what else to do.

He hopes what has happened will fade, as the first Intimation faded.

In a way, it does.

The talkto comes on as peter enters his home.

'peter,' says the talkto. peter smiles. The smile is involuntary, not precisely automatic. When he hears the low mechanical voice, he is always pleased. A kind of happiness envelopes him. It is hour seventeen, and now he is here in the room that is his home, to relax and to sleep, for ten hours.

Home is rather bare, like every home (with variations) in main building, and in d district, and in all districts and buildings about the heart of the Machine. The walls of home are concave and dust-resistant, although every diurnal they are mechanically wiped. The cushioned floor supports a low sleeping-couch. On one wall is the food counter, and through a sliding door the box of the hygiene cubicle, with its water-tap, lavatory bowl, and shower.

There are no windows in peter's home. Air is constantly breathed in and out via hidden orifices. It is the clean, dry, odourless air, common throughout the Machine.

In one corner, near the convex ceiling, the talkto perches, a small grey bulb that faintly shines when peter is at home. Nearby, the mechanical lark waits above the bed. The light, like the air, is constant, never-changing, muted yet clarified.

There is, too, a languid, unmodulated hum, which is the eternal music of the Machine.

The Machine is outside, and all about, and home is merely a tiny microcosm of the Machine. Home needs no textures and no patterns, as peter himself needs no decoration or individual markers. He, all humanity, are the pattern within the Machine, the jewellery of its vistas that stretch in every pale grey direction upwards, downwards, and in parallels towards an infinity which Is.

peter knows this and is consoled by this. He speaks to the talkto. He speaks a sort of meaningless, friendly jargon, which the talkto answers in the same vein.

Going to the counter, peter is given a light supper, and a mineral drink. He and the talkto exchange banter throughout the meal. When peter falls silent, the talkto falls silent, only continuing to shine.

peter takes off his overall and drops it into the chute. Tomorrow a fresh garment will be ready for him, complete with a fibre bar snack in the pocket. He goes into the hygiene cubicle, where his teeth are cleaned, and his body sluiced with warm water. He urinates at the lavatory bowl, and finally comes back into the room.

'Today,' he says, 'today.'

The talkto waits, ready to take up his phrase.

'Today,' says peter, 'I saw a woman above the panel. How can that be?'

The talkto pauses, then it says, 'A woman. Yes, peter.'

'How could she be there? She was in the wall of the Machine.'

'Machine, peter,' says the talkto.

'And I missed touching the dial. But the dial turned. As if I touched the dial. As if —' peter fumbles for his own meaning. He says: 'As if I needn't touch the dial.'

The talkto says, 'Bedtime, peter.' And it begins a sort of song it murmurs before he sleeps.

Normally, he finds the song very soothing. Now, an unaccountable tension runs through him, and sensing it, infallibly, the talkto becomes utterly silent, only shining there above him as he lies down.

Presently, he loses consciousness.

peter dreams he is walking up the pure surfaceless wall of the Machine above his section. A woman in a pink garment and silver-yellow veil is walking before him. Her feet are white as roses, and they leave, in the steel endurance of the wall, delicate indentations that vanish in a few moments, as if she walked over the film of a lake — the memory of which his genes recall, although he has never seen water save from a faucet or in a lavatory bowl.

As peter follows the woman, he is aware of a powerful brimming bursting within himself. This is like the feeling he has experienced in his penis, sometimes, in the seconds before his hands and the murmurs of the talkto have caused him to climax. But the feeling is not sexual, actually, although it is orgasmic, far more so than the jetting irritation of random lust.

The woman walks up the never-altering face of the Machine.

peter comes to wonder what he is doing, following her.

Then his feet slip. There is no purchase. He falls.

'Hush, you're here,' says the talkto. 'Here you are. You're safe.'

peter realises he has cried out.

He listens to the talkto as it comforts him, then sinks back into sleep.

anna arrives at the heart of the Machine, as she always

does, in the one-seater air-car. It sets her down before d top two, and she enters the round office where, with three others, she overlooks the d levels of the Machine. As usual vaslav and rita are already at their panels. anna crosses to her seat and allows it to form itself about her before giving it her weight. This diurnal she is wearing a pale grey one-piece suit. In her two-room home, she is always offered a choice of clothing in off-white, pale or dark grey. rita is clad in dark grey, anna notes. Sometimes at meal-breaks anna and rita exchange a little conversation. They talk about the Machine, the abstract comeliness of its lines in some new area they have, on a free walk, discovered. Or they speak contemptuously of the workers who man the d levels. These do not seem as efficient as workers of other levels, q, for example, or y. But since all workers are efficient in deed if not in essence, nothing can be done. It is the aesthetic of the workforce that troubles anna, rita. Both anna and rita have, at prescribed times, met with vaslav for sexual union. However, they do not speak very much to him, nor he to them. At meal-breaks he tends to sit with han or olif from d top three.

As anna sits into the chair, her panel shows her a portion of the d levels. After a minute, it shows her another portion. The panel continually shows anna portions of the d levels, as the panels of rita and vaslav show them, also, portions of the d levels.

The coils and pipes are flickering with energies, the wheels turn, the levers lift and engage.

anna is rested by these images. Only now and then, she has a wish to move the human figures a little, put their bodies into slightly more effective angles, or simply to make them stand when they are sitting, sit when standing up.

Sometimes she thinks of what she will order from the tops canteen at the meal-break, or sometimes of the poetry which her talkto has made for her. Although she discusses the Machine and the workers with rita, and intermittently meets with vaslav, for sex, anna prefers — as rita and vaslav do themselves — reticence, and the solitude of a home.

At the end of the diurnal, anna's talkto had recited:

> grey is the line for ever
> for ever is as the grey line

and this fragment has become locked into the memory of anna, and as the panel shows her the parts of the levels where the workers touch and touch, the coils sparkle and the wheels turn, the poem weaves together with every view, contenting her in a deep and tender fashion.

So that when an alarm goes off, like a tiny white firework somewhere in the screen, anna is horribly jolted.

In the thirty years during which anna has watched the d levels, no incident has ever occurred. Nothing has occurred at all.

Now she feels personally slighted. Threatened.

She stands on the bridgeway, and looks down to where a mechanical medical is attending to one of the workers. Because something has happened to him while working, she will have to speak to him. anna knows this is the procedure, although such an event is unprecedented.

anna waits until the medical is finished. Then the worker is taken by an overseer to the ramp which connects with the bridge. He gets onto the ramp reluctantly. As he rises towards her, anna looks away. She sees that none of the other workers has paid any attention. They regard their sections, and at the proper intervals their hands go out to touch the transmitters of the Machine.

Despite the fact anna has sometimes walked three levels on a free walk, when the Machinery is quiescent and the workers in their homes, to be so near the manned levels makes her uneasy.

The male worker is deposited ten metres away. He stares at his hands, which he holds out slightly in front of him.

251

All workers resemble one another. anna accepts that her own class of watchers is not exempt from familial resemblance — but the worker is alien. He is a worker.

The overseer approaches anna and she is glad to have it between her and the worker. The overseer says: 'The worker peter climbed up onto the panel-housing of his section. He then attempted to climb up the wall-surface above the panel. He then fell. Injuries are superficial and have been corrected.'

anna is forced to look at the worker, peter.

She speaks clearly. 'Why did you do this?'

The worker peter opens his mouth. Then he closes it.

'You must tell me why you climbed up onto the housing,' says anna. 'Such a thing is unheard of.'

'There was a light over the panel,' says the worker peter. Abruptly water pours out of his eyes. He drops on his knees and anna beholds a man weeping, which she has never been shown before. She knows the idea of weeping. She knows what tears are, although she has never grasped the notion, and does not really grasp it now. She sees the man is shaking from head to foot. She is amazed. She can think of nothing to say. And so she says, 'This must never happen again. Do you understand? Now go back to your section.'

The overseer takes hold of the man and helps him up and the man says distinctly, 'A woman walks over the Machine. Her eyes — her eyes — ' Then he stops and the overseer puts him on the ramp and he is carried back down into the levels.

anna watches from the bridge and sees peter return to his section where, standing before the dial, after a moment, and at the correct instant, he touches, once, twice, three times.

She lets out her breath and finds her ribcage is aching from holding the sigh pent within herself. Her nails have dug into her palms.

She peers down at the housing over peter's section, where the shimmering grey wall runs up and up and up and away and away.

252

The wall of course is empty.

'anna,' says the talkto in her two room home. 'Grey is grey. The Machine is the Machine is the Machine is the Machine . . .'

The concave walls are done in grey and off-white. The bed has a pillow in a dark grey case. There is a window, that reveals the horizontals, verticals, parallels of the streets of the limitless complex that is the Machine.

'. . . is the Machine is the Machine . . .'

anna summons a soporific from her dispenser.

She drinks it, lies down with her head on her pillow, and closes her eyes.

'The Machine.'

anna sleeps. She dreams. The worker peter is walking up the wall above his section. His face is full of a wild joy. anna approximates the look to that of successful sexual climax, which she has seen on the face of vaslav. anna herself finds coitus debilitating. When she experiences pleasure, for several diurnals after she cannot bear the sight of vaslav.

No, the look of rapture on the face of peter is more profound than anything she has ever seen. anna stares beyond peter, and there is a glimmering incoherent pinkish light wavering on the surface of the wall. anna thinks of roses, of which somehow she has been informed, which she has never been shown. A ghost of a rose glides over the Machine.

anna wakes up. Her face is wet and this frightens her. She has been crying in her sleep.

At six hours, the levels of d are empty, and as she walks along them absently, anna can hear only the faint tympanic hum of the Machine. The walls slide up, and the coils descend down and down. When she looks from the bridges, anna sees eternity stretching away below and

253

above, and on all sides. Caught in this web, she searches after the accustomed peace such vistas have always brought her. But there is a slight vertigo, too. Perhaps there always was.

She is drawn towards the section of the worker peter. She reaches it, and stands there, where peter habitually stands or sits. anna can see nothing unusual. She finds she is straining her eyes. To see — something. What? A woman. But what kind of woman? A worker? A watcher? Intuitively anna knows that she will never see, or learn, by looking.

At twenty-one hours that evening, anna arrives for her quarterly meeting with vaslav, at a cell in tops building. She had almost forgotten the appointment, and her talkto had had to remind her twice. anna is always perturbed when she goes to have sex, although sometimes she is also uncomfortably eager. She has come to dislike such eagerness. It generally means she will be disappointed, but that in turn ensures more cordial after-relations with vaslav.

In the cell, beside the couch which can be adjusted to complement a number of positions outlined in diagrams on the walls, a beaker of alcohol is served to anna. She drinks it as vaslav, tonight rather impatient, begins to touch her in the ordained manner.

anna tries to respond, and succeeds to a certain extent. vaslav wishes her to mount him, a position she finds awkward and in which, never, has she been able to climax. As she moves obediently to vaslav's rhythm, she feels a warm contempt for him, quite friendly and acceptable. He climaxes and she pretends to be satisfied.

As they are putting on their clothes, anna says, 'Do you know the word *vision*?'

'That is a sight; to *see*,' says vaslav. He too, after pleasure, is morose, not wanting further bodily contact.

'No, I mean in the sense of an image conjured or witnessed. An hallucination, possibly.'

vaslav orders a second glass of alcohol.

'Workers in d have seen – ' anna breaks off.

'The worker peter,' says vaslav. 'Probably there's something wrong with the brain. He will have to have a medical check.'

This reassures anna. She feels a bright flash of gratitude, and turns to vaslav impulsively.

'You're awkward in that position, anna,' says vaslav. 'rita is better.'

anna does not know what she is doing. She reaches out and pushes vaslav's glass so that the alcohol spills over him.

In the air-car on the way home, anna begins to cry again. She runs into her two rooms and the talkto shines and says to her: 'Here you are, anna. You're safe.' But for several terrible moments, anna does not feel safe in the least.

With its trilling the mechanical lark signals peter. He gets up from the sleeping place before he is quite awake. He has responded to a mechanical lark since his first year. His body knows exactly what to do. It walks him to the hygiene cubicle. It relieves itself of waste matter and is cleansed. As it stands beneath the shower, peter, carried by this body, wakens in fact.

peter leaves the shower, before it can dry him. He goes to his bed and lies down, on his back. He looks at the ceiling, and presently the talkto says, 'peter, get up, peter.' peter takes no notice. He blinks sometimes but makes no other movement. 'peter,' says the talkto, 'you will be late, peter.'

After an hour, the talkto falls silent. It continues to shine, but peter does not notice.

On the platform, at his section in d level, ted looks round, quite suddenly. He has become aware that peter is not working near him. ted has not defined the absence until now because, as ever, the dial at peter's section has turned regularly and the energy has gone flickering down the coil to the lever below.

ted gazes at peter's empty place. He assumes at last that peter is ill, which is uncommon among the workers.

ted looks back at his own section, in proper time to touch touch touch the button under his panel.

There is a pink light over the panel. ted has a jumbled notion he has seen it before. The colour, however, is so novel. He stares at it. The pink unfolds like paper, or a flower. ted sees a woman walking up the wall of the Machine. Involuntarily, he exclaims.

In the cage-lift to upper top two, anna avoids glancing at the levels of d. The vista makes her dizzy, the long, pure lines slipping effortlessly down, like the striations in an ancient rock she has never seen, perhaps never been told of, perhaps does not even genetically recall.

anna vacillates mentally between annoyance and nervousness. What she is about to do it seems no one can ever have done. The choice has always been open to her, but has gone unconsidered. Now, sometimes, in a rush of strength, anger braces her. But it fails to last out the long smooth journey in the lift.

What will she say? How phrase it, to throw the maximum of blame upon the other? Simple. Her very request will see to that.

The lift reaches upper top and anna gets out.

Before her is office corridor p nine. anna walks along the corridor briskly, ignoring the side ramp. Watchers like exercise. She begins to feel virtuous, strong again.

A door opens. The robot assistant speaks, inquiring who she is and whom she wishes to contact.

'Co-ordinator shashir.'

The assistant assures her her request is being delivered, and she will soon know whether or not co-ordinator shashir is available to attend to her.

256

anna stands biting her lip. She becomes aware she has been gnawing it since leaving her home early today. Should she not have come here? Will the co-ordinator be able to give her an appointment? Will he question her thoroughly? What will he say?

anna has an uncomfortable burned feeling in her stomach. She swallows and finds she needs to swallow again.

On the wall of the office cubicle she supposes there is something pink . . . it must be a trick of the eyes – she did not sleep very well. The murmurs of her talkto, and the soporifics her dispenser offered her, have rendered her up to the diurnal cloudy but not rested.

A screen in the wall comes on and shines, putting out the pinkness which she had imagined was there a moment before.

With tension and relief, anna beholds the face of co-ordinator shashir.

'anna. What is it that you wish to discuss?'

'I – ' anna swallows again. She drags in a breath and says tightly, 'I want to discontinue my sexual meetings with watcher vaslav.'

The face of shashir does not alter. Perfect and whole, he hangs there. What is this like? The word *icon* enters anna's mind. She is not sure what an *icon* is. With slight difficulty she realigns her brain with the image of the co-ordinator. He has started to speak.

'. . . to your liking?'

anna guesses. She does not desire an interrogation. She says swiftly, 'My pleasure in sex isn't great, and vaslav has told me he's unhappy with my performance. Watcher rita suits him better. He won't be sorry, I'm sure, if we don't meet again.'

'But for yourself, anna? You understand that you are highly sexed, and that these meetings are, for you, preferable to other more solitary methods?'

anna does not know what reply to give. She feels her face grow very hot.

Finally co-ordinator shashir says, 'Your view has been filed, anna. I suggest that now you return to top two. At the next period for sex, if you still decline to meet with watcher vaslav, you may omit the visit.'

anna turns. She is cold and sluggish now.

She takes the ramp back to the lift.

Along the platform, marion turns to see why ted has cried out. She glimpses a female figure which seems to float about ted's panel, but glancing quickly away, marion finds the figure is actually poised directly before her, looking down into marion's face. marion tries to avoid contact with the eyes of the figure, for they seem to contain a dreadful depth, or electric fire . . .

marion is not able to avoid the contact of these eyes.

She falls to her knees.

ted has done the same.

All along the line of the platform, the workers of the d levels are sinking down, as if it is some new procedure of their service to the Machine.

As anna reaches the round office, she discovers an event is in progress. Both rita and vaslav are on their feet, and vaslav is busily pressing the emergency button in the wall.

On the levels, small mechanics of maintenance and overseeing and medicine are whirling to and fro.

The workers have adopted strange attitudes.

The Machine contrives to function flawlessly, although no one, any more, appears to be engaged with or upon it.

The mechanical lark has fallen from the ceiling and landed on an area of floor, where it made a weird noise, hinting damage, and then became silent.

peter has no notion why this should have happened, but then he does not really care. He is not even disturbed that the light has gone out of his talkto, as if, indeed, he were not presently at home.

He lies on his back, on the bed, his half-closed eyes fixed without focus on the convex ceiling.

He has been lying here, in this way, for hours. He does not analyse how many. Time has ceased to matter. His body, which once or twice had itched, or disconnectedly wished to urinate, he ignores. All feeling seems to have left it now.

On the ceiling, she comes and goes. Whenever she comes back, at each appearance, she is more clear, better defined.

Day young, in her robe of roses, and dawn-veiled in yellow, under which fair fountains of hair flow out. On her feet are painted little silver flowers, and there is a golden flower between her brows. Her eyes are summer blue, or green, it is difficult to be sure which, but the colour is less urgent than the intensity of the eyes. This terrible wild emotion that is in them − peter does not recognise it, even now, but it no longer frightens him. He has surrendered. He has drowned himself in her eyes.

All bodily needs, all thought, all senses − these are unimportant. Only the vision, the icon, adrift there as if in the pale space of sleep or death, has power. And silver and golden flowers sift from her hands, and he believes they brush his face, and there is a perfume in the room he has never smelled until these moments.

And then at eighteen hours a wall opens and a tube comes snouting through, with a mechanical eye gleaming at its tip. peter shifts, not intending to, and his body returns about him with a pang of nauseating heaviness. He is very stiff, cannot roll away from the pursuing serpent, which probes him with its chill eye and with a poreless tasting tongue.

'No − ' cries peter.

'Everything will be quite all right,' whispers the tube from somewhere in its unessential being, 'lie still, peter. Let me examine you, peter.'

peter lets out a scream. As he plunges to his feet (like

259

a crashing upward fall), the icon of the woman breaks into stars upon the ceiling and scatters like soft snow which — even as he runs from home — he tries to catch with hands and mouth and eyes.

shashir partly sits and partly reclines in his globe in upper top, and permits his mind to wander through the labyrinth of its own self, after the shade of anna, whose recording he has just replayed.

Once before in the seven decades of his service to the Machine, one of the watchers came to shashir with a request to end sexual meetings with a woman of his class. The request was naturally granted, but a year later, the watcher, a man shashir dimly believes was called millo, developed health problems. He was reassociated with the woman, and their meetings were resumed. millo's health improved, but for some while, from time to time, he would still try to terminate the sexual meetings. His later requests were listened to but otherwise ignored.

By this juncture, millo has ceased petitioning.

It is as if anna has come to fill the gap.

shashir loses interest in the fundamentals of the problem. He allows himself to sink down through two or three of the upper sleep layers into the half-trance he mostly cultivates, and in which he is most comfortable. Some of shashir's most profound insights are achieved in this state. It is now he feels closest to the Machine.

The supportive globe cushioning shashir's body carries out for him all necessary bodily functions, by means of a series of concealed pipes and synapses. shashir, who has grown, over the thirty years of his englobement, into a sort of balloon, itself resembling a globe, has only to meditate and to think.

shashir thinks.

He thinks of anna, but anna has ceased to be either watcher or woman. She has become a rosy feather that floats across the inner screen of shashir's eyes.

The image is very peaceful. Shashir swims through the serenity of the trance. A beautiful yellow thought surfaces like a fish of crystal and he has just the time to see and wonder at it, before the thought submerges and he forgets —

The music of the Machine plays, and shashir hears it in rapt quietude. He senses filaments of himself which stretch out along the hollows of the Machine, which coil and combine with the Machine's intricacies. He makes medullary love with the Machine, and sleeps, wrapped in the cushion of his brain.

Robot overseers have herded away all the workers from the d levels. There has never before been such an emergency. Gradually, once the levels had been emptied, and the tops vacated by the alarmed watchers, the Machine has concluded its function in this area, closing down with muted sighs and pale flickerings of milky energy.

There is never darkness in the Machine, never any night as there is never any day, only the diurnal, and the obsolete words left behind — *today*, *tomorrow*.

At twenty-four hours, forgotten midnight, anna steals along the walkways, creeping from transparent shadow to opalescent illumination, avoiding generally looking down or up. Reaching the platform, she comes to peter's section, and peter is standing there.

anna stops, twelve metres away from peter. She says: 'Tell me what you saw. What you *see*.'

peter turns and stares at her. His eyes are large and dark, of a dense blue colour she has never noticed before, or perhaps which, before, they have not been. He says nothing.

anna tries to be impatient. 'You must tell me,' she says, officiously.

Then peter laughs.

'The lark broke on the floor,' he says, 'the talkto doesn't function. A tube came after me. I got away. What will happen next?'

261

'You must go to a medical cubicle,' says anna.

'Why? It isn't necessary. I want to see her again. I want to see her − beauty,' he says. He stares into anna's eyes and out the back of them at infinity. And all of anna's blood, which she knows she has though she has never seen a drop of it, spins inside her. 'I'm going away now,' says peter.

'Where? Where is there to go?'

'Everywhere. Nowhere. Out of − ' he struggles for a phrase and manages, at last, 'this. *Here.*'

anna trembles. She leans on a bank of dials and buttons which, quiescent, makes no response to erroneous pressures.

'There is no other place.'

'Yes,' he says. Suddenly he points at his own skull. 'In there.' And then he points away into the endlessness of the Machine. 'In *there*, too.'

anna stands and suitably watches as peter trots along the platform, metre after metre, and off the bridge and onto a ramp, loping ahead of its rhythm, springing off onto another bridge, along a walkway, growing smaller and smaller, vanishing into the horizon of the Machine.

anna sits down on the platform and rests her head on some part of the section. She has an abrupt sensation that everything is trembling, as she is, coming unjoined, disunited, that all of the entity about her may unravel, and float away, leaving behind something else, which it had hidden, naked there, burning bright, with colours that do not exist.

Inside the walls of steel and sound, the sheer total silence, inside the deepest wall of used and percolated time, the Machine ticks soundlessly, a pulse current solely with, known only to, itself. And the Machine Is. And the Machine Thinks. In one form the Machine is Thought. Composed of Thought, a cerebral capability made flesh in metal, fissions, clockworks, and therefore in endless powers, as if in archangels.

The Machine, if it can be said to have any purpose left, has become the purpose of Thought. Once, the purpose may have been different. Once the Machine was a mighty servant, which in turn was served. (But service also has become a mere capability, made flesh in flesh.) All service is now redundant. Anything that was ever essential to the service and servitude of, or to, the Machine, continues through a math of infallible mechanical habit. For centuries the Machine has been free to do nothing, and indeed the human infestation of the Machine (like ants in a hollow mound) has been freed. To this freedom humanity, but not the Machine, is blind.

So the Machine Thinks. It has been thinking almost but not quite for ever. The Thought Process is very slow, but extremely deliberate. (It is unlike the thinking dream of such as shashir, the co-ordinator.) Nothing is squandered. Every strand and fibre, artery and node of the Machine is involved.

Thinking.

Thought drips. Like water, and like mercury.

Like rain upon the face of a flower.

The rose lies in the heart of the Machine's heart, as the rain of mercurial thought drips upon it, curving its petals wide, its radar-bowls of sugar-tint receptors, pulled on tines of lustre, a rose that spills into sentience, wider than the core of the Machine, that softly explodes, passing by a savage osmosis, and leaking like wet fire, getting out by every link, interstice, and microscopic vent.

The levels of d are a desert. Nothing moves there save, now and then, a slender worm of some galvanic passing up or down, or there is the faintest rustle, a vibration, some piece of the whole engaging accurately with another.

A pink bead, part of the overspill of the inner rose, hangs like a butterfly on a panel.

anna has left the platform. She is not there to see the butterfly spread wings, become the angel of the rose, the goddess in a veiling of forgotten dawns.

In the levels, however, of b and k and l and s, the rose-angel-goddess poises like a young summer of the world ill-lost. She is waiting, for the workers and the watchers to return and find her. (And peter, as he lopes beneath the arching bridgeways of l, not glancing, does not see her there.) (And shashir, in his globe, his sleep-mind wandering accidentally to the levels of k, moves aside, finding a horned rose in the labyrinth. He is not ready yet for roses.)

So it is after all anna, lying on her grey pillow, who sees her insomnia take on, like stained glass in the wall, the madonna which the Machine has obliquely created.

anna knows at once what there is to fear.

The terrible eyes of the madonna are full of love.

The terrible eyes of the madonna are full of *life*.

peter has come to a wall which does not appear to have any aperture in it, or ending. He moves along it, sometimes climbing up the bridgeways that in parts run beside it, or descending again into the lower levels. There is no apparatus issuing from this piece of wall. It is a blank.

After a long while, several hours, peter stops moving along beside the wall. He sits down on a walkway, his back against a girder, and looks about. There is a great sameness. He has absorbed the idea of it, as he ran. Now he examines the blank wall. This is surely cessation. It is a barrier of the Machine. Presumably, the wall is impassable.

peter is conscious of hunger and thirst, but nowhere that he can see are there any dispensers or recognisable buttons.

Eventually, with a foul emotion which is shame, he is forced to urinate behind the girder.

He is tired out, and elation and terror have left him together.

He sits down again and dozes on the walkway, missing the talkto, missing the shape of his home. The way back is lost to him, and although the Machine hums here, as everywhere, no mechanical activity of any sort appears to go on. He has achieved an outer boundary before he is prepared for it.

He wonders if he will see her again, the madonna he has not put a name to. But there is nothing, no motion, no colour, no image but the wall, and behind and about, grey horizontals contracting away.

Detecting the disturbances of a life-reading, a rubber snake breaks into anna's home and locates her trying to drown herself in the hygiene cubicle. Somewhere she has grasped the notions of suicide, and drowning, but she has found the act difficult, forcing her head to remain beneath the spout of the shower, choking and swallowing, sightless through the water, half-conscious, but nowhere near dead.

The medical snake eases her into the outer room and resuscitates her.

No one dies. Dying is long over. Workers finally become watchers, after a supine interval during which the brain is modified. At length watchers become co-ordinators, after a period during which both the brain and the complete psychical ecology are reorganised and adapted. In the normal course, marions and teds and peters change to annas, vaslavs and ritas; annas, vaslavs and ritas to shashirs. shashirs endure neverendingly, until, conceivably, amalgamated into the very nature of the Machine, its very Soul, becoming flawlessly integrated fragments of the godhead itself . . .

(anna, maybe not in any form aware of this, screams and gags, fighting off life like a tiger her genes may recall.)

Later, lying in a medical cubicle, wired up to life, its claws deeply embedded, unble to escape, anna dreams poetry, and is a blonde goddess rising on a shell from a pink dawn sea.

But if it is certain that humanity is itself at last compounded with the Machine, *becomes* the machine, they are the ancientmost dreams of humanity, too, not merely the great Thought of the Machine, which are now causing an upheaval in the levels of b, k, l and s.

anna dreams only vaslav lies over her on the shell, in the

water. They are drowning, their hands sliding over each others' bodies in a frenzy of panic and joy.

peter sits before the blank wall for nine diurnals of tearing hunger, sickness, bemusement, calm, until a small mechanical apparatus approaches him, fluttering out of the parallel miles of the Machine, homing unerringly in on him.

When he turns to see, he beholds the small machine is a white bird, with pleated glimmering wings, and in its beak it bears a fibre bar to feed him, and a sealed container of drink.

As the dove settles on his shoulder, peter realises that, in a space of time, long or short, interminable or simply futile, the impassable wall will melt, metamorphose, give way, and he will see the vision, whatever it is to be, the truth (or the secondary dream) which lies beyond it.

There is no barrier which is ultimately infinite. There is nothing anywhere that cannot change.

Contributions

GARRY KILWORTH was runner-up for the BSFA short story award with 'Triptych' from *Other Edens I*. He has published seven novels and over fifty short stories, some of the latter being collected in *The Songbirds of Pain*. His latest novel is *Cloudrock*, to be followed by *Abandonati* and *Hunter's Moon*.

GRAHAM CHARNOCK's stories appeared in *New Worlds*, *Orbit* and *New Writings in SF* before he took a long break from writing. He works for a bookseller in London and has a novel in progress.

SCOTT BRADFIELD received a Ph.D. in American literature from the University of California in 1988. His first collection of stories, *The Secret Life of Houses*, is due for publication in autumn 1988. He reviews regularly for various publications, including *City Limits*, the *Evening Standard* and the *Times Literary Supplement*. He has just completed a novel, *The History of Luminous Motion*.

MICHAEL COBLEY was born in Leicester in 1959 and has lived in or around Glasgow since 1967. He briefly read engineering at university, then tried his hand as a DJ, a roadie and a freelance menial in the entertainments department of a students union. He wrote a column of eclectic polemic for a student newspaper for three years. 'Waltz in Flexitime' is his first published story.

IAN WATSON has lived in Tanzania and Tokyo but now resides in Moreton Pinkney. His latest books include

Queenmagic, Kingmagic, and *Evil Water*. He writes that
' "The Resurrection Man" is a slipstream story to my
novel of buggery and alchemy, *The Fire Worm*, to be
published by Gollancz in summer '88. I just couldn't waste
this material I unearthed when researching the Tyneside
background.'

GWYNETH JONES was born and raised in Manchester,
but she later lived in Singapore and travelled extensively in
South-East Asia before settling in Brighton. Her novels are
Divine Endurance, *Escape Plans* and *Kairos*. She also
writes for younger readers as Ann Hallam.

ANNE GAY lives in the West Midlands and works as a
teacher of Spanish, French and German. She has had three
sf short stories published, including 'Wishbone' in the
Gollancz/*Sunday Times* Competition anthology, and
'Howie Dreams' in Alex Stewart's *Demon Lovers* anthology. She has recently completed her first novel,
Mindsail.

JOHN CLUTE, a Canadian long resident in London, was
Associate Editor of *The Encyclopaedia of Science Fiction*.
His reviews and articles have appeared widely, and he is
the author of a non-sf novel, *The Disinheriting Party*. He
describes 'Eden Sounding', the first chapter of a novel-in-
progress (*The Widow Gloss*), as 'an sf treatment of both
the Orpheus and Christmas legends'.

BRIAN ALDISS's latest book is *The Best SF Stories of
Brian W. Aldiss*, a selection from a career spanning over
thirty years. A new novel, *Forgotten Life*, will appear from
Gollancz in autumn 1988.

JOSEPHINE SAXTON's novels include *The Hieros
Gamos of Sam and An Smith*, *Vector for Seven*, *Group
Feast* and *The Travails of Jane Saint*. She has published
stories in numerous anthologies and magazines, and a

collection of her short fiction, *The Power of Time*, was published by Chatto in 1985. She lives in Leamington Spa.

M. JOHN HARRISON's latest books are *The Ice Monkey*, a collection of stories, and *Viriconium*, a combined volume of *Viriconium Nights* and *In Viriconium*. Two new novels are in progress.

COLIN GREENLAND lives in Essex and reviews sf and fantasy for the *TLS*, *New Statesman*, and *Foundation*. He also spends time on a mountainside in Colorado, where he wrote his latest novels, *The Hour of the Thin Ox* and *Other Voices*.

KIM STANLEY ROBINSON until recently lived in Switzerland but has now returned to the USA. His novels include *The Wild Shore*, *Icehenge* and *A Memory of Whiteness*, while his short stories, including the award-winning 'Black Air', have been collected recently in *The Planet on the Table*. 'Remaking History' will also appear in an anthology of alternative histories, edited by Gregory Benford.

IAN McDONALD lives in Belfast. A novel, *Desolation Road*, and a collection of stories, *Empire Dreams*, have recently appeared in the USA.

MICHAEL MOORCOCK's latest books include *Wizardry and Wild Romance* and *Mother London*.

TANITH LEE lives in London and is a prolific author of both short stories and novels. Her latest work is *The Secret Books of Paradys*, comprising *The Book of the Damned* and *The Book of the Beast*.

OTHER EDENS 1
Edited by Christopher Evans and Robert Holdstock

This anthology represents the very first publication of seventeen stories by the brightest stars of British science fiction and fantasy working today.

It includes stories by:

BRIAN ALDISS
M. JOHN HARRISON
GARRY KILWORTH
TANITH LEE
MICHAEL MOORCOCK
KEITH ROBERTS
LISA TUTTLE
IAN WATSON

and many others

Take a flight of the imagination to distant planets, future worlds, other Edens: through mysteries ancient and modern, dark rituals, spine-chilling hauntings and creatures made from human flesh, and travel beyond the stars to the enigmas of science and time, and man's eternal battle for survival and for power.

VIRICONIUM
M. John Harrison

The light in Viriconium is the light you see only on record covers and in the colour supplements.

You can't just fly there; neither can you avoid Viriconium. It is all around us: one city, it is all cities, from the Plaza of Unrealised Time to the shopping arcades of Huddersfield.

Political apathy has engulfed the Low City. Its streets are full of illness and poverty. The High City cares nothing for the plague, but continues to indulge its taste for trivia. The Barley Brothers (gods of the city) roll drunkenly in gutters, inventing wellington boots and Egg Foo Yung.

M. John Harrison presents to us a two-way mirror in which we must recognise our dream and its failure, a grotesque comedy and a tragic reality.

THE PASTEL CITY
M. John Harrison

In his melancholy sea-tower, moody reclusive tegeus-Cromis, hero of the Methven, puts away his nameless sword, thinking that he had finished with soldiering forever. Then, on the road from Viriconium, came the massive mercenary, Birkin Grif, roaring out a filthy brothel song, bringing news of the war between two queens. In the great Brown Waste lives Tomb the Dwarf, as nasty a midget as ever hacked the hands off a priest. They must join forces to fight for Queen Jane and Viriconium, for Canna Moidart and the Wolves of the North have awoken the *geteit chemosit*, alien automata from an ancient science, which will destroy everything in their path, and now they march upon the Pastel City ...

'If you like elegantly crafted, elegantly written sword-and-sorcery, this book is all you could ask for.'
    Michael Bishop – *Fantasy & Science Fiction Review*

A STORM OF WINGS
M. John Harrison

Eighty years have passed since Lord tegeus-Cromis broke the yoke of Canna Moidart, since the horror of the *geteit chemosit*. The Reborn Men, awoken from their long sleep, have inherited the Evening Cultures. In the wastelands, to the north and west of Viriconium, a city is being built – but not by men.

In the time of the Locust a paralysing menace threatens to turn the inhabitants of the Pastel City into hideous, mindless insects ...

'the best writer of heroic fantasy working today ... Through the spoiled wastelands of our ancient planet travel a resurrected man, an assassin, a magician, a madwoman, a dwarf ... A superior read.'
    Daily Express

THE SONGBIRDS OF PAIN
Garry Kilworth

Set in vivid, exotic locations all over the world, from the Arabian deserts to eastern England, this powerful anthology offers the reader entrance into a place in which pain and torture become welcome nightmares, obsession a way of life, and death.

The Songbirds of Pain confirms Garry Kilworth in the front rank of British writers.

THE SECRET LIFE OF HOUSES
Scott Bradfield

In California nobody is simply who they appear to be:

Larry Chambers dreams of the wolf, stalking its prey across the white ice, beneath the cold sun . . .

Lured by promises of wealth and self-fulfilment, Sandra Mitchelson joins the Worldwide Church of Prosperity to learn that happiness never just comes knocking, rather one must reach out with both hands and buy it . . .

Every day Edward Thomas comes home from work convinced that in his absence another man has entered his house, his wife, and his refrigerator . . .

Margaret Detweiler discovers in the house of her imagination vast chambers and open corridors, the restless and secret lives of both herself and her broken family . . .

In this outstanding collection of short stories Scott Bradfield bears witness to the alien and desperate dreams we create and inhabit in the wasteland of our transient, acquisitive society. Funny and disturbing, *The Secret Life of Houses* marks the emergence of a major new voice in contemporary fiction.

THE UNCONQUERED COUNTRY
Geoff Ryman

When Third was a little girl, the Unconquered Country was tranquil, ordered and happy, its traditions proud and strong.

But one day the Neighbours came, armed with weapons given to them by the Big People. And with them came the Sharks.

They invaded and occupied the Unconquered Country and brought pain, terror, and great change in their wake . . .

Geoff Ryman's extraordinarily powerful story won the World Fantasy Award 1985 for the Best Novella.

'Geoff Ryman's THE UNCONQUERED COUNTRY is . . . a clear-eyed, sensitive account of a life that is almost destroyed by incomprehensible political events, while it remains a kind of wary, tender autonomy.'
Times Literary Supplement

THE WARRIOR WHO CARRIED LIFE
Geoff Ryman

'a densely crafted re-write of the Gilgamesh Epic with a brilliantly horrid start.'
The Guardian

'crackles like an unshielded power line with dangerous energy and originality . . . New ideas keep coming: strange warriors like the Men who have been Baked or Men who Advance like Spiders; the atrocious fate of Cara's family . . . Ryman is truly an author to watch.'
White Dwarf

interzone

SCIENCE FICTION AND FANTASY

Quarterly   £1.95

- *Interzone* is the only British magazine specializing in SF and new fantastic writing. We have published:

BRIAN ALDISS	GARRY KILWORTH
J.G. BALLARD	DAVID LANGFORD
BARRINGTON BAYLEY	MICHAEL MOORCOCK
GREGORY BENFORD	RACHEL POLLACK
MICHAEL BISHOP	KEITH ROBERTS
RAMSEY CAMPBELL	GEOFF RYMAN
ANGELA CARTER	JOSEPHINE SAXTON
RICHARD COWPER	JOHN SHIRLEY
JOHN CROWLEY	JOHN SLADEK
PHILIP K. DICK	BRIAN STABLEFORD
THOMAS M. DISCH	BRUCE STERLING
MARY GENTLE	IAN WATSON
WILLIAM GIBSON	CHERRY WILDER
M. JOHN HARRISON	GENE WOLFE

- *Interzone* has also published many excellent new writers; graphics by **JIM BURNS, ROGER DEAN, IAN MILLER** and others; book reviews, news, etc.

- *Interzone* is available from specialist SF shops, or by subscription. For four issues, send £7.50 (outside UK, £8.50) to : **124 Osborne Road, Brighton BN1 6LU, UK.** Single copies: £1.95 inc p&p.

- American subscribers may send $13 ($16 if you want delivery by air mail) to our British address, above. All cheques should be made payable to *Interzone*.

- "No other magazine in Britain is publishing science fiction at all, let alone fiction of this quality." *Times Literary Supplement*

- -

To: **interzone** 124 Osborne Road, Brighton, BN1 6LU, UK.

Please send me four issues of *Interzone,* beginning with the current issue. I enclose a cheque/p.o. for £7.50 (outside UK, £8.50; US subscribers, $13 or $16 air), made payable to *Interzone*.

Name _____

Address _____

_____